2/95

THE COMPLIMENTS OF THE CONNOISEUR

It was an accident that Alys had fallen with Davenport into the hay, but what happened then could not be called one.

Alys struggled to catch her breath, knowing that she should scramble up. But before she could make any progress toward that virtuous goal, Davenport said, "What a splendid idea."

Putting a hand behind her head, he pulled her face down for a kiss. Alys had been kissed before by a man, but with gentlemanly restraint. Now Davenport was filling in the gaps in her education.

His kiss was deep, intense, and enthralling. Transferring his attention to her ear and neck, he sent waves of warmth into her most secret depths. One hand moved down to caress her breast, and immediately Alys gasped with pleasure.

"You've a rare talent for this, Allie," Davenport whispered. . . .

MARY JO PUTNEY was graduated from Syracuse University with degrees in eighteenth-century British literature and industrial design. She lived in California and England before settling in Baltimore, Maryland, where she is a freelance graphic designer.

SIGNET REGENCY ROMANCE
COMING IN APRIL 1992

Patricia Rice
Mad Maria's Daughter

Irene Saunders
The Contentious Countess

April Kihlstrom
Dangerous Masquerade

Georgette Heyer
Devil's Club

AT YOUR LOCAL BOOKSTORE
OR ORDER DIRECTLY
FROM THE PUBLISHER
WITH VISA OR MASTERCARD
1-800-253-6476

The Rake and the Reformer

Mary Jo Putney

A SIGNET BOOK

SIGNET
Published by the Penguin Group
Penguin Books USA Inc., 375 Hudson Street,
New York, New York 10014, U.S.A.
Penguin Books Ltd, 27 Wrights Lane,
London W8 5TZ, England
Penguin Books Australia Ltd, Ringwood,
Victoria, Australia
Penguin Books Canada Ltd, 10 Alcorn Avenue,
Toronto, Ontario, Canada M4V 3B2
Penguin Books (N.Z.) Ltd, 182–190 Wairau Road,
Auckland 10, New Zealand

Penguin Books Ltd, Registered Offices:
Harmondsworth, Middlesex, England

Published by Signet, an imprint of New American Library,
a division of Penguin Books USA Inc.

First Printing, September, 1989

12 11 10 9 8 7 6 5 4

 REGISTERED TRADEMARK—MARCA REGISTRADA

Printed in the United States of America

BOOKS ARE AVAILABLE AT QUANTITY DISCOUNTS WHEN USED TO PROMOTE PRODUCTS OR SERVICES.
FOR INFORMATION PLEASE WRITE TO PREMIUM MARKETING DIVISION, PENGUIN BOOKS USA INC., 375
HUDSON STREET, NEW YORK, NEW YORK 10014.

To Bill,
my favorite friend of Bill W.

1

When two gentlemen are closely related by blood, they do not usually address each other with formality. However, the gentlemen in question were first cousins once removed, the younger had come from nowhere to inherit a title and fortune that the older had assumed would be his, and their relationship had been formally announced moments after they had come within ames' ace of killing each other.

Given those circumstances, it was not surprising that relations between the two were somewhat strained. Which is why Reginald Davenport, notorious rake, gambler, and womanizer, known in some circles as "The Despair of the Davenports," greeted his noble cousin with a terse, "Good day, Wargrave."

The Earl of Wargrave rose to his feet behind the massive walnut desk and offered his hand. "Good day. I'm glad you were able to come by."

After a brief, hard handshake, Reggie took the indicated chair and stretched out his long legs, crossing them at the ankle as he drawled, "I make it a point to obey summonses from the head of the family, particularly when that person pays my allowance."

Richard Davenport's mouth tightened slightly as he sat again, a fact which pleased Reggie. Among the earl's many irritating virtues was his calm good nature. Equally irritating was his politeness; rather than issue a command, he had left the time and place of meeting to his cousin, implying a willingness to transact family business in a tavern if that was the older man's choice.

While giving the earl grudging credit for that willingness, Reggie had no objection to calling at the Wargrave mansion in Half Moon Street to see what changes the new earl and countess had wrought. Reluctantly Reggie conceded that the changes had all been for the better; in the late earl's day, this study had been a dark, poky room designed to intimidate callers. Now it was bright, airy, and quietly masculine, with leather chairs and an air of settled comfort. The new owners had undeniable taste.

Since he could find nothing to criticize in his surroundings, Reggie turned his observant gaze to his host. Whenever they chanced to meet, he looked hopefully for signs that the new earl was running to fat, or decked out in green stripes and gold watch fobs, or showing other signs of vulgarity, decadence, or arrogance. Alas, he was always disappointed; Richard Davenport continued to be well-dressed in a discreet and gentlemanly way, he retained his trim soldier's figure, and he treated everyone he met, from prince to scullery maid, with the same well-bred courtesy.

Faced with such unflagging virtue, Reggie was unable to resist the temptation to probe for weak spots, to see if he could in some way discomfit his noble relation. However, with the spectacular exception of the time he had goaded Richard into a sword fight, he had never been able to provoke more than infinitesimal signs of irritation. Reggie sighed inwardly. In spite of irrefutable documentary proof, sometimes it was hard to believe that Richard was really a Davenport. Reggie himself was the epitome of the breed, very tall, very dark, with cool blue eyes and a long face that seemed more designed for sneers than smiles. In contrast, Richard was of only average height with medium brown hair, hazel eyes, and an open, pleasant countenance marked by smile lines. The young earl was also the best swordsman his cousin had ever seen, and Reggie had never liked him better than on the occasion Richard had lost his temper and demonstrated that fact.

Ignoring his cousin's scrutiny, Richard said in a level voice, "Actually, your allowance was one of the reasons I wanted to talk to you."

So Wargrave was going to cut his scapegrace cousin off with a shilling. Well, it was not really unexpected. Feeling tension in his shoulders, Reggie forced himself to relax as he wondered what kind of position he might find to support himself if gambling proved too unreliable a source of income. Many connections of the nobility held government posts such as Warden of the Port of Rye or Postmaster of Newcastle, but nobody in his right mind would give such a post to Reggie Davenport; even government officials had some standards, low though they might be. Perhaps he could open a shooting gallery like Manton's. Or, he thought with an inward smile, he could start charging women for his services, rather than giving them away for free. With creditable calm he asked,

"And the other reason?"

"Caroline and I are expecting a child in November."

The earl's hazel eyes were watchful.

"Congratulations." Reggie kept his face carefully expressionless. It was typical of Richard to personally transmit the news that his cousin was being superseded rather than let his heir find out through casual gossip. Well, it hardly came as a shock; to heir was human. Technically Reggie was heir presumptive to Wargrave, but the odds were high that a healthy, happily married man eight years his junior would soon have a hopeful family. Even if the first child was a daughter, doubtless there would be sons later. He asked politely, "I trust that Lady Wargrave is well?"

"Oh, very much so." Richard's face lit up with a smile that his cousin uncharitably described as fatuous. "She feels wonderful and is playing the piano so much that the child will probably be born with a music score in its hand."

"With proper training, perhaps you can be playing family trios by the child's third birthday," Reggie suggested.

"Perhaps," the earl said with amusement. "But that is not relevant just now."

"Ah, yes, you were about to cut off my allowance before we got sidetracked on the subject of your progeny," Reggie said, his voice even more drawling than before. He shoved his right hand into the pocket of his buff pantaloons in a pantomime of unconcern; he'd be damned if he'd grovel for money to the head of the family.

"Ending your quarterly allowance is only part of what I had in mind," Richard said, opening a drawer and removing a sheaf of papers. The hazel eyes lifted to meet Reggie's steadily, giving away none of his thoughts. "I decided it was time to make different provisions for you. As an interim measure I had continued the allowance, but it strikes me as"—he hesitated, searching for the right word—"as inappropriate that one adult male should be dependent on the goodwill of another."

"It's not that uncommon in our world." Reggie's voice was indifferent. He had guessed something like this might happen; it had been a surprise that Richard had continued the allowance after the two men had so nearly killed each other, but perhaps the earl thought he had a responsibility to support his heir. Another heir in prospect removed that obligation.

"I wasn't raised in the tight little world of the *ton*," Richard said dryly, "and I daresay I shall never understand all of the underlying assumptions. In the unelevated circles in which I was raised, most men preferred to have something that was truly their own."

Before Reggie could evaluate that odd comment, the earl tapped the sheaf of legal papers and continued. "Therefore I am signing over to you one of the unentailed Wargrave properties. It is the best run of all the estates, not excepting Wargrave Park itself. Since I have cleared the mortgage, the property should produce at least twice as much income as the allowance you have been receiving."

Reggie straightened in his chair, as startled as if the earl had hit him over the head with the brass candlestick. Having his allowance cut off would have been no surprise; this was.

Tactfully ignoring his cousin's reaction, Richard continued. "The estate's prosperity is due largely to the land steward, a man called Weston, who has been there for several years. I've never met him—the one time I visited, he had been called away by illness in the family—but he has done an excellent job. His records were impeccable and he has increased the productivity enormously. Since Weston seems both honest and competent, you can live in London off the rents if you don't want to get involved with the management yourself."

His expression hardening slightly, the earl said, "Or you can sell the property, or gamble it away. Whatever you decide to do, this is all you will ever get from the Wargrave estate. If you have serious debts now, I will help you clear them so that you can start with a clean slate, but after this, you are entirely on your own. Is that clear?"

"Perfectly clear. You have such a gift for expression, Wargrave." The touch of insolence in Reggie's tone was automatic rather than intentional; his mind still jangled with confusion. "As it happens, Lady Luck has been favoring me and I am rather beforehand with the world just now, so your assistance will not be required." After a moment of thought, he asked, "Which estate is it?"

"Strickland, in Dorset."

Bloody hell, Strickland! Since Wargrave owned only two or three unentailed estates, the news was not quite a surprise, but Reggie still felt as if he had been kicked in the stomach. It was an effort to keep his voice calm when he asked, "Why that particular property?"

Richard bridged a quill pen between his fingers as he leaned back in his chair, a slight frown on his face. "Several reasons. First, as I said, it is the most profitable of the unentailed properties and should support you very comfortably. Second, I understand that you lived there as a boy, and I thought you might be attached to the place. Judging by your expression, perhaps I was wrong."

Reggie could feel his face darkening with discomfiture. One of the many ways in which he failed to fit the ideal of a gentleman was in his too-visible emotions. A true gentleman would never show chagrin, or anger, or even amusement, as Reggie was all too prone to do when he wasn't concentrating. He was capable of maintaining a properly impassive face, but too often his countenance mirrored his every feeling, as it did now, when he would much rather have concealed the complex emotions that Strickland raised in him.

Ignoring the thundercloud on his cousin's face, Wargrave continued, "There is another, far more compelling reason why I chose Strickland. It should have been yours in the first place."

His eyes narrowed, and Reggie took a deep breath. Too many surprises were being dropped on him, and he didn't like it one damned bit. Gruffly he asked, "Why do you say it should have been mine?"

"I understand you left Strickland when you were only eight, so you probably never knew this, but the house and core of the estate came from your mother's family, not the Davenports."

Startled by the statement, Reggie sharpened his gaze as his cousin continued. "According to Chelmsford, the family lawyer, your parents met when your maternal grandfather approached the late Lord Wargrave about buying some land adjacent to Strickland. Your father went to Dorset to discuss the matter on his older brother's behalf, met your mother, and ended up staying. The Davenport property was added to Strickland and your parents lived there and managed it as one estate. As your mother's sole heir, legally you already own the bulk of Strickland. You knew none of this?"

Reggie's soft, vivid profanity rendered the question superfluous. So the old bastard had deliberately and illegally withheld Strickland from his nephew, one more tactic in their long-running war with each other. "I had no idea, or you can be sure I would never have let the old screw get away it," Reggie said with barely controlled violence, so furious he could scarcely speak. So during all the years his uncle had condescended to give him an allowance, the money should have been his in the first place. If the old man had been here and alive, Reggie would have wrung his scrawny neck. A pity the earl was now beyond justice.

Richard said in a neutral tone, "The most charitable interpretation I can put on my grandfather's behavior is that he never separated Strickland from the rest of the properties because he assumed the title and entire estate would come to you eventually. After all, you were his heir for many years."

Mastering his feelings somewhat, Reggie said icily, "Your generous interpretation of his actions stems from the fact that you never met him. I can assure you that he withheld Strickland from the basest of motives. The income would have made me independent of him, and he would have hated that."

For the same reason, perhaps the old earl had hated his younger brother, who had married a modest heiress and found happiness living with her in Dorset. That would go some way to explaining the old man's later treatment of his orphaned nephew; perhaps it had been a kind of revenge on his dead brother, who had escaped the Wargrave net. Reggie had never met the earl prior to his father's death, but he remembered adult comments implying that relations between the brothers had been difficult.

Sensitive to his cousin's mood, Richard busied himself with sharpening a quill and checking the ink in the standish. Without looking up he said conversationally, "The more I hear of my predecessor, the more I can understand why my father refused to live in the same country with him."

"Leaving England was the most intelligent thing Julius ever did," Reggie agreed. Though he didn't voice the thought aloud, more than once he had wondered if he should have done the same. Perhaps it would have been wiser to escape his uncle's heavy, controlling hand rather than to stay nearby and fight the old man's tyranny with inadequate weapons. Well, the earl had won the game by dying, and Reggie had no desire to bare any more of his feelings before the young man who had come on the scene only after the final curtain had come down.

Glancing up, Richard said, "Would you prefer a different property? Strickland is the best individual estate, but other arrangements could be made . . ."

Reggie made an abrupt gesture. "No need. Strickland will do well enough." He knew he should thank Richard for his generosity—not all men in the earl's position would have had the honesty to compensate for the sins of their predecessors—but Reggie still felt far too much anger over the revelation of his uncle's duplicity to be gracious.

Apparently Richard did not expect grace from his cousin.

Scribbling his name on the bottom of several documents, he sprinkled sand on the wet ink, then pushed the papers across the desk. "Just sign these and Strickland is yours."

Even furious, Reggie took the time to scan the papers, but all was in order and he scrawled his own name across the deeds. As he signed the last one, the sound of a light footstep caused him to look up and see a delicate, fairy-like young woman entering the study. Caroline, Lady Wargrave, was small and blond, with a dreamy counte-nance and an extraordinary talent for musical composi-tion, though the latter fact was not one she chose to advertise.

Both men rose as she entered, and the earl and count-ess exchanged a glance that gave Reggie a pang of sharp longing. While he envied Richard the inheritance of Wargrave, even more did he envy the intimate warmth that pulsed between the earl and his wife like a living entity. No woman had ever looked at the Despair of the Davenports like that, nor ever would.

After that brief, silent interchange with her husband, Lady Wargrave turned and offered Reggie her hand. She had always been a very pretty girl, but now, wearing a deep blue dress that matched her eyes, she was breath-takingly lovely. The last time they had met, Reggie had been very drunk and behaved very badly and Richard had damned near killed him for it. In spite of his lurid reputation, terrifying shy virgins was not something Reggie made a practice of, and he felt some awkwardness as he bowed over the countess's hand.

Mustering his best charm, he straightened and said, "My felicitations on your happy news, Lady Wargrave."

She smiled, lifting the deep blue eyes to his. The shy girl had grown more confident during her eight months of marriage; no one now would think her unfit to be a countess. "Thank you. We are very pleased." Releasing Reggie's hand, she said, "I never properly thanked you for the wedding gift you sent. Of all the things we re-ceived, it was the most special."

Cocking her glossy blond head slightly, Caroline said, "Where on earth did you find one of Handel's original music scores? Every time I look at it, I feel awe that he himself actually drew those notes and wrote those words."

For the first time in this unsettling visit, Reggie gave a genuine smile. Her ladyship had written him a formal thank-you for the wedding gift, but her desire to greet him in person must mean she had forgiven his boorish behavior; perhaps that was one less sin that he would fry for. "I came across the score years ago in a bookshop and bought it. I knew that someday I would know whom it was intended for."

Lady Wargrave laughed, a sound like silver bells. "That was remarkably long-sighted of you. You could have chosen nothing that would please me more." She started to turn away. "I'm sorry to have interrupted. I will leave you to your business."

Reggie said, "I was just leaving. Unless you had something else you wished to discuss, Wargrave?"

Richard shook his head. "No, there was nothing more."

Reggie hesitated, knowing he should express appreciation for what his cousin had done, but his emotions were still too turbulent to deal with the proprieties. Or perhaps he had gotten so used to fighting with Lord Wargrave that the habit was ingrained even though the holder of the title had changed. Picking up his curly-brimmed beaver hat, he settled for an abrupt nod of farewell, then exited the room, barely aware of the butler who opened the outside door.

Tossing a coin to the Wargrave footman who had been walking his horses, Reggie vaulted into the phaeton, but after settling in the seat he simply held the reins in his strong hands for a moment as the horses tossed their heads, impatient to be off. *Strickland. Bloody, bloody hell.* He now owned the place that had been the site of his greatest happiness and most profound grief, and he had no idea whether he felt pleasure or dismay.

Shaking his head in exasperation, he snapped the reins over the horses and turned the carriage neatly in the street. He needed a drink. Better yet, he needed a dozen.

Upstairs in the earl's study Caroline watched her husband's cousin depart, seeing the abstracted pause and the tension in the whipcord-lean figure before he drove away. Glancing up, she asked, "How did he react to the news?"

Richard crossed to the window with the limp that was his legacy of Waterloo. Life had been simpler in the army, when he had been plain Captain Dalton and had had no idea that he was heir to the trials and responsibilities of an earldom. Among those trials, his recalcitrant cousin loomed prominently.

"Fortunately I didn't expect gratitude, because I received none. My cousin was not best pleased to hear that I wanted to give him Strickland. More than that, he was understandably furious to learn that my late, unlamented grandfather had illegally withheld the estate from him." Putting an arm around his wife, Richard smiled wryly. "Reggie was surprised by the transaction, and he is not a man who likes surprises. If I had simply cut off his allowance, it would have been easier for him to understand."

Slipping his other arm around his wife, Richard pulled her close, resting his cheek against her silky blond hair. Settling herself against her husband, Caroline asked softly, "Do you think owning Strickland will make any difference to him?"

"I doubt it. My grandfather must bear much of the blame for ruining him; Reggie once told me that he had wanted to go into the army, but the earl would not allow it. Instead, my cousin was kept on a short leash, his debts paid, but his allowance insufficient to give him much real freedom." Richard sighed. "Still, Reggie must take some of the blame himself. He's highly intelligent and almost uncannily perceptive about people. Becoming a rake and drunkard was not his only choice."

Caroline could feel the sadness in her husband. She knew how seriously he took his responsibilities, and the part of him that had made an exceptional army officer was grieved at the waste of Reginald Davenport's potential. More than that, Reggie was the nearest relation on the Davenport side of the family and Richard would have liked to be on friendly terms with him. Regrettably, that seemed an ambition unlikely to be fulfilled.

Slipping her arms around her husband's waist, Caroline asked, "You think he is too old to change his way of life?"

"Probably." Caroline felt Richard shrug. "Reggie is thirty-seven years old now and very well-practiced in vice and outrageousness. Rakes sometimes reform, but drunkards almost never do. Lord knows I commanded enough of them in the army, and most drank until they died of either bullets or whiskey. I expect my cousin will do the same."

Caroline rested her head against her husband's shoulder. Reginald Davenport had once terrified her, but today she had seen him sober and polite, and for just a moment he had revealed a quite devastating amount of charm. There was good human material there, and now she better understood her husband's desire to help his difficult cousin. It was an effort likely to fail. Still . . .

Caroline raised her head and said with determined optimism, "Miracles do happen. Perhaps one will this time."

Putting aside his doubts, Richard said, "True. If Reggie really wants to change, I'm sure he is capable of it. But enough talk of my scapegrace cousin. Didn't you say at breakfast that the duet you've been working on was ready for us to play?"

Making her eyes huge and innocent, Caroline snuggled against her husband and said in a distinctly uninnocent voice, "There are more kinds of duet than can be played on a pianoforte."

The tanned skin around the hazel eyes crinkled as the earl gave the slow, intimate smile that she loved. "You always know exactly what to say, Caro, my love." Bending over, he gave her a long, thorough kiss that left them both breathless. "Shall we find a more private spot for our duet?"

As he followed his wife from the study, the earl wasted no more thoughts on his cousin. He had done what he could; Richard Davenport knew from hard experience that there was only so much that one man could do for another.

2

It was a bad day even before she awoke; whenever Alys had the nightmare, she was out of sorts for hours. Thank God it came only two or three times a year. In the nightmare she was always just outside the window, hearing the drawling voice ask with bored malice, "Why on earth are you going to marry a bossy Long Meg like her? Ten feet tall and all bones. Not exactly the sort to warm a man at night, and with her managing ways she'll keep you under the cat's paw for sure."

After a pause her beloved replied, not defending her, not mentioning the love he had eagerly proclaimed in her ears, "Why, for money, what else? She'll do well enough. Once I'm in control of her fortune you'll see who rules the roost."

Even in her dream Alys could feel the familiar constriction in her midriff, the disbelieving pain that had driven her to fly from the only life she had ever known. But this morning she was in luck. Before the dream could continue to her nadir of degradation, something tickled her nose and she sneezed, a sure way of waking up when one is near the surface of sleep.

Alys opened her heavy lids to see a golden nymph of morning. The shining vision perched on the bed had guinea-gold curls, a flawless heart-shaped face, and eyes of a guileless cerulean blue. The sight of Miss Meredith Spenser, Merry to her intimates, was enough to gladden the hardest of hearts. While Alys's heart was by no means hard, it took a great deal to gladden her at this hour of the morning; the sight of a young lady looking so cheerful, so early, was not enough.

Before she could do more than glare balefully at her ward, a soft furry object brushed her face and Alys sneezed again. "What the *devil* . . ." she exclaimed, batting her face free of extraneous objects and heaving herself up in the bed. "Oh, it's you, Attila. I warn you, cat, the next time you wake me up with a tail in my face, I'm going to find a dog to feed you to."

Dividing her scowls impersonally between Merry and the cat, Alys pushed her heavy hair from her face. The thick braid she kept it in at night had come untied as she tossed in the nightmare, and now her hair was down around her shoulders and would require an extra five minutes to brush out.

"Heaven help any dog that encounters Attila." Merry chuckled. Eyeing her guardian with the ruthless cheer of the natural early riser, she handed over a thick mug of steaming coffee. "Here, Lady Alys, just the way you like it, with lots of cream and sugar."

Wrapping one hand around the mug, Alys shoved the pillows up behind her and subsided against them as she took a grateful swig of the coffee. "Ahhh . . ." she sighed as the hot liquid began to restore life to her component body parts. Her brain clearing, she glanced at Merry. "Why did I want to get up at this hour?"

Merry grinned, looking much less like a porcelain doll and more like the lively minx she was. "The planting begins today and you charged me to be sure that you rose early."

"So I did." Alys sighed gustily, then gulped more coffee. "Thank you for waking me. Maybe I'll keep you after all."

Unabashed, Merry retorted, "You have to keep me, remember? You voluntarily agreed to take responsibility for me and the boys, and now you're stuck with us, at least until you find some demented male who will take me off your hands."

Alys laughed, a sure sign that the coffee was restoring her natural good temper. "All the males who cluster around you are surely demented, but it's always from unrequited love. My only problem is keeping them at a safe distance."

She gazed fondly at Merry. The girl had the kind of diminutive blond beauty that Alys would have killed for

when she was a girl; it would be easy to hate Merry if she
wasn't such a thoroughly nice person. Her ward was also
intelligent and had a worldly wisdom that was downright
frightening in a young lady of a mere nineteen summers.
She occupied a niche in Alys's life that partook equally of
daughter and best friend, though sometimes it was hard
to tell who was raising whom.

Seeing that her guardian was showing signs of life,
Merry said, "One of the farm lads left a note for you. It
was addressed to Lady Alice—A-l-i-c-e, of course."

"It's too early in the day to apologize for how my
name is spelled." Alys yawned again. "Besides, if they
did know how to spell it correctly, they would probably
pronounce it wrong. What did the note say?"

"Something about chickens."

The older woman nodded. "That would be Barlow. I'll
stop by later today." Finishing the coffee, Alys swung
her long legs onto the cold floor, fumbling for her sheep-
skin slippers. "It's safe to leave now—I won't fall asleep
again. Take that imbecile feline with you and feed him."

Merry chuckled but said nothing, leaning over the bed
to scoop the giant long-haired cat into her arms. Attila
was a substantial armful, a crazy quilt of stripes and
white splotches. His regal expression made it hard to
remember that Alys had pulled him drowning from a
stream when he was no more than a straggly kitten.
These days he assumed that rulership was his natural
due, and peasants who didn't provide his breakfast were
beneath contempt. He was yowling accusingly as Merry
carried him from the bedroom.

For a moment Alys's head sank onto her hands as she
sat on the edge of the bed, her good humor vanishing
under the lingering depression of the nightmare. After a
moment she sighed, then stood and pulled on her worn
red robe and went to sit at the dressing table. As she
combed her fingers through her hair to loosen snarls, she
stared at her reflection, dispassionately cataloging her
appearance in the way that she had learned was the best
antidote to the dream.

While she wasn't the sort of woman a man would
desire, it wasn't as if she was really ugly. Though her skin

was too tan for fashion, her features were regular and might have been called handsome if she were a man; it was just that her face, like the rest of her, was too large. She stood five feet, nine and a half inches in her stockings and was as tall as or taller than most of the men at Strickland.

Having undone the snarls, she picked up her wooden-backed brush and went to work on her hair. Back in the days when a fortune had endowed her with spurious desirability, her hair had been called chestnut; now that she worked for a living it was merely brown, a color of no particular distinction. Still, Alys secretly thought that her hair was her best feature. It had grown back even longer and thicker after the time she had furiously chopped it off, and it gleamed with auburn and gold highlights. Nonetheless, it was basically just straight brown hair. Parting it down the center of her head, she started on the first of two braids.

Rapidly finishing the second braid, she wound both about her head in a prim coronet. In the early-morning sun her most freakish feature was clearly visible, her right eye being gray-green while her left was a distinct brown. Alys had never met anyone else with this particular trait; it seemed unfair to be both odd-eyed and freakishly tall.

The thought produced a smile, thereby displaying her other regrettable feature. Usually she forgot the idiotic dimples that appeared when she smiled or laughed, but seeing herself in the mirror reminded her how utterly incongruous they looked on an over-sized creature like her. Doll-like, golden Merry was the one who should have had dimples, but perversely, she didn't. Life was definitely *not* fair. If Alys could have given her dimples to her ward, she would have done so with great delight.

Scowling eliminated the dimples, so Alys scowled. Her dark, slashing eyebrows were fearsome even when she was smiling, and made her scowl truly intimidating. She stood and turned from the mirror, having gone through the ritual of assuring herself that she didn't look as repellent as the nightmare always made her feel. A pity that today she must supervise the planting and would wear

pantaloons, linen shirt, and a man's coat. In her usual
dark dresses it was easier to restrain the excesses of
her figure, but the men's clothes she was putting on
today made it all too obvious that she had the normal
female curves. Given her ridiculous size, the effect was
somewhat overpowering. Not that all men thought so;
she had seen enough sidelong glances to guess that
some were curious about what it would be like to bed
a Long Meg. Well, they would never find out from
her.

Jamming her shapeless black hat onto her head, Alys
Weston, called Lady Alys to her face and other things
behind her back, thirty-year-old spinster of the parish
and highly successful steward of the estate known as
Strickland in the county of Dorset, stamped down the
steps to begin supervising a long day of work in the
fields.

The day turned out to be even more tiring than anticipated. The new seed drill Alys had bought was tempera-
mental, to the unconcealed delight of the laborers, who
were only too willing to say that the fool contraption
would never work. Having considerable aptitude for me-
chanical things, Alys got it to perform after an hour of
crawling around underneath on the damp earth. She
spent the rest of the day covered with dirt, too busy even
to stop for lunch. Merry, bless her, had sent Dorset blue
vinny cheese, ale, and the local hard rolls called knobs,
which Alys ate while riding to the sheep pasture to check
on the health of some lambs that had been sickly.

By the end of the day the scoffers were reluctantly
conceding that the seed drill was effective, though they
liked it even less now that it worked. Alys was hard-
pressed to keep her tongue between her teeth. It had
been a continuing battle to get these taciturn males to
accept her orders, and even after four years of proof that
her modern methods worked, every new idea had to be
fought over. Damn them all anyhow! she swore as she
rode home, the spring sun setting and a sharp chill in the
air. There wasn't another estate in Dorset as productive,
nor another landowner or steward that provided for dis-

placed workers the way she did. Sometimes she wondered why she bothered.

When she returned to the steward's house, Rose Hall, Merry was embroidering demurely in the parlor and the boys had not yet returned from school. After a quick, warming bath in her room, Alys changed to a dark blue wool dress and joined her ward for a glass of sherry and a quick glance through the post. As Merry laughed at the misadventures with the seed drill, Alys came across a letter franked by her employer, the Earl of Wargrave.

Frowning, she looked at the letter for a moment before slitting it open. Most of her communications were with the estate lawyer, Chelmsford, rather than with the earl. She had never met either of them, of course; if one of those respectable gentlemen learned she was female, she would undoubtedly lose her situation. The old earl had never left his principal seat in Gloucestershire, but the new one was young, active, and conscientious, and she worried that someday he might turn up unexpectedly. Luckily the one time he had visited Strickland he had given her enough warning to decamp with the children, leaving a message that illness in the family had called her away, and a stern warning to everyone at Strickland not to reveal her sex.

After a week by the sea in Lyme Regis, Alys had returned to find that no one had betrayed her secret, the books had been carefully inspected and approved, and Wargrave had left a complimentary letter that included several intelligent suggestions for her consideration. The man may have spent most of his life as a soldier, but he was clearly no fool. Apart from that one visit, Wargrave had left her alone to run the estate as she saw fit. It had been an ideal arrangement and she had hoped that matters would continue unchanged indefinitely.

It was an unlucky thought. Alys must have made some sound when she read the letter, because Merry looked up from her embroidery questioningly. "Is something wrong, Alys?"

With a brittle smile Alys said, "I knew I should have stayed in bed this morning."

Setting the hanks of silk thread in her workbox, Merry crossed to Alys's side. "What is it?"

Silently Alys handed the letter over. Lord Wargrave wished to inform Mr. Weston that Strickland had been transferred to his cousin, Reginald Davenport. He had no idea what his cousin's plans for the property were, but the earl had been most impressed by Mr. Weston's work, and should matters not work out with the new owner, Wargrave would be delighted to find him another steward's position, perhaps running Wargrave Park itself. Apologies for the inconvenience, etc., etc.

"Oh, dear," Merry said softly, "this could complicate matters somewhat."

"That is one of the greatest examples of ladylike understatement I have ever heard," Alys said bitterly, too upset to sit quietly. Jumping to her feet, she crossed the room in long, angry strides, stopping in front of the fireplace to pick up the poker and stab at the blameless hot coals.

"Perhaps it will make no difference," Merry said. "I believe I've read of Mr. Davenport. Isn't he some kind of sportsman? Perhaps he'll live in London and collect the rents and never come down here."

Returning the poker to its brass stand, Alys turned dispiritedly to face her ward. "It's one thing for Lord Wargrave never to visit when Strickland is just one of a dozen estates, but if this is the only property Reginald Davenport has, he's bound to come down here occasionally. He may even want to live here part of the year." She sighed, absently brushing a wisp of glossy brown hair that had escaped the coronet. "There is a limit to how many ailing relatives I can invent to escape from him."

Merry frowned. "You do have a contract."

Shrugging, Alys said, "A contract isn't much better than the will to uphold it. Davenport could make my life so miserable that I won't want to stay."

"Isn't it possible that he might want to keep you on? You've done wonders with the property. Everyone says so."

"Much of the hard work has been done," Alys pointed

out. "Any reasonably competent steward could run it profitably now."

"Mr. Davenport won't find anyone more competent than you, or more honest either!" Merry said loyally.

"Probably not," was the dry reply, "but that doesn't mean he won't discharge me just the same." Alys had heard of Reginald Davenport, though most of the tales were not fit for Merry's young ears. A rake was hardly likely to have advanced ideas of a woman's abilities. It was so unfair! Feeling her hands curling into fists, she forced herself to relax.

Determinedly seeking a silver lining, Merry said, "If Mr. Davenport doesn't want you, you can go to work for Lord Wargrave elsewhere. Wargrave Park would be quite a plum."

"Just how long do you think his lordship's offer would stand after he found that I was a woman?" Alys demanded, her hands beginning to clench again.

"Perhaps you could disguise yourself as a man?" Merry said with a twinkle. "You're certainly tall enough."

Alys glared, momentarily tempted to box her ward's ears before the girl's attempt at humor penetrated her mood. Chuckling, she said, "Just how long do you think I could get away with a masquerade like that?"

"Well . . ." Merry said thoughtfully, "perhaps ninety seconds? If the light was bad."

Alys laughed in earnest. "The light would have to be very bad indeed. Men and women just aren't shaped the same way—at least not after the age of twelve."

"True, and you have a very nice shape, no matter how hard you try to disguise it."

Alys snorted. Merry stoutly maintained that her guardian was attractive, a campaign that was more a tribute to her kind nature than her good judgment. Her comment now was intended as a distraction, but Alys refused the bait.

Her voice resigned, she said, "Even assuming that Lord Wargrave is radical enough to hire me, my supervision is still needed at the pottery works, and we can hardly move that to Gloucestershire. And it would be a pity to take the boys from the grammar school when they are both so happy there.''

Even Merry's golden curls drooped a bit before she said firmly, ''I think you are making a great many bricks out of precious little straw. Mr. Davenport may not come down here for a long time, and when he does, he might be delighted to keep you on to spare himself the work. All we can do is wait and see.''

Alys wished she could share the girl's optimism. As she glanced at her ward, she remembered what was said about her new employer and his womanizing habits, and she felt a stirring of apprehension. What rake could resist a delectable golden sylph like Meredith? The chit had good sense and morals, but she was still an innocent, and a cynical, amoral man of the world might easily turn her head.

Alys turned and crossed her arms on the mantel, staring unseeingly at the wall. As a young woman alone, she had spent the last dozen years fighting convention and prejudice to build a comfortable, productive life for herself. Now, through no fault of her own, all that she had worked for was threatened.

Sight unseen, she already hated Reginald Davenport.

3

The Despair of the Davenports groaned and shifted. After the previous night's debauchery, the shattering jolt of nausea and wretchedness that swept through him at the slight movement was not unexpected. He stilled, keeping his eyes tightly closed, since experience had taught him that mornings like this were best approached as slowly as possible. That is, if it was morning. His last memories were too fragmentary for him to be sure how much time had passed.

After a suitable interval while his head stabilized, Reggie opened his eyes a fraction. The ceiling looked familiar, so he must be home. A little more concentration established that he was in the bedroom rather than the sitting room, and on his bed, which was softer and wider than the sofa. The next question was how he had gotten here. Gradually he became aware of the sound of resonant breathing and he turned his head by infinitesimal degrees until the Honorable Julian Markham came into view. His young friend slept blissfully on the sofa, sprawled in a position that by rights should give him a sore back and neck but probably wouldn't.

Moving with great deliberation, Reggie pushed aside the quilt that had been laid over him and levered himself upright, then gasped and fell back on the mattress. He had been prepared for the aftereffects of drinking but not for the sharp pain that stabbed through his ribs. As his abused body ached and protested, he lay still for a few moments and tried to remember what the devil had happened last night that might have caused an injury, but was unsuccessful.

Deciding that it was time to face the consequences, he cautiously sat up again, swinging his legs over the edge of the bed. The vibration of his boots hitting the floor sent a palpable shock wave through his system, so he stopped moving until his brain recovered. After a swift inventory of damages, he decided that nothing was broken, though his ribs and right arm felt badly bruised and the knuckles of both hands were raw, as if he had been in a fight. He was fully dressed, his dark blue coat and buff pantaloons crumpled in a way that would make a really fastidious valet turn in his notice. Fortunately Mac Cooper was made of sterner stuff, or he wouldn't have stayed with Reggie for so many years.

Mac proved his competence once again by choosing this moment to enter the bedroom, a tall tumbler of orange-colored liquid in one hand and a steaming towel in the other. Wordlessly he handed the towel to Reggie, who opened it and buried his face in the hot folds. The heat and moisture were invigorating, and by the time he had wiped down his face, neck, and hands, Reggie was

able to take the tumbler and down half the contents at
one swallow.

Mac's morning-after remedy was one of the man's
major talents, combining fresh fruit juice with a shot of
whiskey and a few other ingredients that Reggie preferred not to think about. He turned his head carefully a
few times, relieved that it could be moved without making him sick, then sipped more slowly at his drink. Only
when the glass was empty did he look at Mac directly,
asking, "What time is it?"

"About two in the afternoon, sir." Though Mac's natural accent was an incomprehensible cockney and he had
the wiry physique and scars of a street fighter, it pleased
him to mimic the manners and style of the most snobbish
kind of valet. Actually, valeting was only part of his job;
he was equally groom, butler, and footman.

Yawning, Reggie asked, "Any idea what time we got
in?"

"Around five in the morning, sir."

"I trust we didn't disturb your slumbers too much."

"Mr. Markham did require my assistance to get you
upstairs," Mac admitted.

Dragging one hand through his dark tangled hair, Reggie
muttered, "That explains why I made it as far as the
bedroom." Glancing at his friend, he saw signs of returning consciousness and added, "Better get some more of
your elixir. I imagine Julian will need some, and I could
use another round myself."

"Very good, sir. Will you be interested in a light
luncheon as well?"

"No!" Reggie shuddered at the thought. "Just coffee."

As Mac left the room, Reggie stood and removed his
cravat, thinking that someday he was going to be stran-
gled in his sleep by one of the blasted things. He washed
his face with the hot water Mac brought, then sank into
the wing chair that stood at right angles to the sofa, his
legs stretched out before him. In spite of his ablutions
and the change from horizontal to vertical, he still felt
like death walking, and he eyed Julian's cherubic smile
with disfavor when that young man's eyes finally opened
and he sat up.

"Good morning, Reg," Julian said brightly as he reached for a glass of Mac's drink. "Wasn't that a great evening?"

"I don't know," Reggie said tersely. "What happened?"

Julian smiled, undeterred by his companion's gruffness. He was a handsome brown-haired young man with a charm and future fortune that made him much sought after by society hostesses with marriageable daughters. "You won five hundred pounds off Blakeford. Don't you remember?"

The coffee arrived, and after pouring a large, scalding mug and heavily sugaring it, Reggie crossed his legs and regarded his friend's clear eyes and cheerful mien morosely. It was his own fault for going about with a man a dozen years his junior, who could bounce back from a night's debauchery with such speed. Reggie used to be able to do the same, but not anymore. He gulped a mouthful of coffee, then swore as it burned his tongue. "I remember going to Watier's. Then what happened?"

"Blakeford invited a dozen of us back to his place for supper and whist. Wanted to show off his new mistress, a flashy piece named Stella. She took quite a fancy to you." Julian finished his juice, then poured himself some coffee. "Does any of this sound familiar?"

Reggie closed his eyes. It was coming back slowly. He'd gone directly from the Earl of Wargrave's to a tavern. After drinking alone for a couple of hours, he had met Julian, and after that, events were hazy. "This Stella—a little tart with red hair and a roving eye?"

"That's the one. Kept rubbing against you like a bitch in heat. Blakeford was angry enough about losing the money, but when you disappeared for half an hour and he realized that Stella was gone too, I thought he'd explode. Did she waylay you for a little dalliance?"

Reggie closed his eyes, letting his head fall back against the chair as he groaned, "More or less."

Ordinarily he would have avoided Stella, whose sensational figure was surpassed only by her stunning vulgarity, but she had chosen her moment carefully and accosted him when he had drunk too much for good judgment but too little to be incapacitated.

His eyes still closed, he drank more coffee, remembering what had happened. The trollop had been waiting in the hall when he returned to the card game, her hot, demanding mouth and eager little hands making it clear what she wanted. His body, which had no standards to speak of, responded immediately, and they had had a feverish, clawing exchange, only a closed door separating them from the rest of the party. Inflamed by the proximity of the protector she was cheating on, Stella had made little whimpering cries as her sharp nails gouged his back through his shirt. Thank God the card party was noisy enough to drown her out. He must have been insane.

No, not insane: drunk. Nothing remarkable about that.

Hesitation in his voice, Julian broke through Reggie's reverie with the words, "I probably shouldn't mention this, but you might want to be careful. Blakeford is insanely jealous of the wench. Between Stella and the money he lost, he looked ready to call you out when we left."

"You're right, you shouldn't mention it," Reggie said tiredly, his eyelids at half-mast and the invisible band across his temples aching acutely. Why did it have to be Blakeford, of all people? He was an odd, unstable fellow, and Reggie had always avoided him when possible. "If Blakeford is going to issue a challenge every time that slut waves her muff at someone, he'll have to fight every man in London."

Julian gave a nod of acknowledgment. "After Blakeford's, we went to that new gaming hell off Piccadilly."

"We did?" Reggie's eyes came fully open as he tried to remember that part of the evening, but he drew a complete blank. "Did anything noteworthy happen?"

"I lost a hundred pounds, and you got into a fight."

"Wonderful. With whom, why, and who won?"

"Albert Hanley. Said you were cheating. You won, of course," Julian said succinctly.

"Hanley said *what*?" Reggie jerked up in the chair too abruptly and his head went spinning. Swallowing bile, he leaned back. "No wonder we fought." In most ways he had a terrible reputation, much of it richly deserved, but in sporting circles his honesty was never questioned. Of course, Hanley ran with a different group.

"You did such a good job of putting him in his place that a challenge was unnecessary," Julian said, adding enthusiastically, "It was quite a mill. Hanley outweighs you by two stone and he has good science, but he never laid a fist on you. You broke his jaw, and everyone said that he should pay for the wrecked furniture, since his accusation was quite unfounded."

"Did Hanley agree?" Reggie asked with idle curiosity.

"Don't know. With his broken jaw, we couldn't understand a word he said."

"If I defeated him so thoroughly, why do I feel as if a horse kicked me in the ribs?"

"Oh, that was because you fell halfway down the steps when Mac and I were hauling you upstairs," Julian explained cheerfully. "You ended up crashed against the newel post. I was worried, but Mac said you weren't permanently damaged."

"Is there anything else I should know?" Reggie asked in a dangerously gentle tone.

"Well . . ." Julian's reply was embarrassed. "We saw m'father at Watier's and he gave you the cut direct."

"Nothing new about that, he always gives me the cut direct." Lord Markham was convinced that Reggie was leading his heir down the road to perdition. In fact, Reggie had taught the lad how to safely navigate London's more dangerous amusements, not to mention rescuing him from the Wanton Widow, who had decided that Julian was the perfect answer to her financial problems. Reggie gave a mental shrug. He had used his influence for Julian's own sake, not because he expected gratitude from his father.

Julian returned to the safer topic of the fight, but Reggie stopped listening. He leaned forward, his elbows resting on his knees, and buried his face in his hands, engulfed by profound depression. The worst things that he had done in a disgraceful life had always been when he was drinking, but in the past he had always been aware of what happened.

Then about a year ago the memory losses had begun, and they were getting both longer and more frequent. When he was very young, he had deliberately chosen to live in defiance of normal social strictures, and he had accepted the probable consequences. Now he could no longer be sure what he had done or why, and that lack of control terrified him. He knew that he should drink less, and had resolved to moderate his habits, but his resolution always disappeared once he started.

This way of life is killing you. The words were very clear and distinct in his head, spoken in a calm male voice. It was not the first time he had heard such a warning. Once the voice had told him to beware just before two footpads attacked, and he had dodged barely in time to avoid a knife in the back. Another time, the voice said not to board a friend's yacht and Reggie had made some excuse, incurring much taunting from his companions. A squall had blown up and the boat sank with no survivors.

This way of life is killing you. His fingers tightened, digging into his skull, trying to erase the sick aching, the memories—and the lack of memories. He had always lived hard, courting danger and skirting the edge of acceptable behavior, and in the months since the earldom of Wargrave had vanished from his grasp he had gone wild, taking insane chances gambling and riding, drinking more than ever.

Ironically, his luck had been phenomenal; he hadn't much cared what happened, and he had won, and won, and won. He was completely free of debt, had more money in the bank than he'd had in years, and what was the bloody point of it?

This way of life is killing you. It was like a litany, the voice repeating the words as if expecting some response from him, but Reggie was too drained to know the answer. He was weary unto death of his whole life; of the endless gaming and drinking, of coarse tarts like Blakeford's mistress, of pointless fights and ghastly mornings after like this one.

At the age of twenty-five, Julian was on the verge of outgrowing his wild-oats phase, while Reggie was doing the same things he'd done when he came down from university. He felt like he had been running for sixteen years, yet was still in the same place. The depression was black and bitter and he wished with sudden violence that someone like Blakeford or Hanley would get so furious that he would put a bullet in Reggie and end the whole exhausting business.

Why wait for someone else to do the job? He had pistols of his own. The idea flickered seductively for a moment before he recoiled mentally. Bloody hell, was he really at a standstill? His mind hung there, suspended in dark space as Julian's words sounded at a great distance. Then the inner voice spoke once more, saying only *Strickland.*

Strickland, the one place in the world where he had ever belonged. He had thought it lost forever, and then his damned honorable cousin had given it back to him. Strickland, where he had been born, and where everyone he loved had died. It wouldn't be home anymore—but, by God, now it was his, demons and all.

There was no conscious decision; he just opened his eyes and broke into Julian's dissertation, saying, "I've changed my mind about going to Bedford for that mill. Have to go to Dorset to look over my estate."

"Your what?" Julian blinked in confusion.

"My estate, Strickland. I've become a man of property." Reggie stood, not bothering to explain away the bafflement on his friend's face. He had always taken pride in his strength and physical fitness, but today he felt brittle and old. Wandering over to the window, he gazed down into Molton Street. He'd had these rooms on the edge of Mayfair for all the years he'd lived in London. The rooms were comfortable enough, quite suitable for a bachelor, but he had never thought of them as a home.

Behind him Julian asked, "When will you come back to town?"

"I have no idea. Maybe I'll stay in Dorset and become a country squire, complete with red face and a pack of hounds."

Julian laughed, treating the statement as a joke, but Reggie half-meant his words. The opinionated Dr. Johnson had said that a man who was tired of London was tired of life. Well, maybe Johnson was right; Reggie was

tired of London and life both. Perhaps there would be
something at Strickland that would make life worth living—
but he doubted it.

The high country of Dorset was bleak heath, but
Strickland included some of the richest agricultural land
in Britain. The rolling pastures and woodlands were
hauntingly familiar, though Reggie had not seen them
since he was eight years old.

After deciding to leave London, he had packed and
gone while Julian Markham was still asking puzzled
questions from the sofa. Mac would follow later with the
curricle and enough clothes for an indefinite stay, but
Reggie preferred to ride, and to ride alone. He slept at
Winchester and it was early afternoon when he approached
Strickland, his once and future home.

Though he had ridden hard most of the distance, he
found himself slowing his horse to a walk on the long
drive that led to the house. The road was lined with three
hundred sixty-six beech trees, one for every day of the
year, including the extra needed for leap year. At one
point there was a gap in the row, and he saw blackened
fragments of a lightning-struck stump. Next to the stump,
a brave young beech sapling grew. He studied it, wondering who had cared enough for tradition to plant that
tree. The exemplary Mr. Weston, perhaps? More likely
one of the local people. The Davenports had come and
gone, but the tenants who had worked this land for
generations remained.

The drive curved at the end and the house came into
view all at once, without warning. He reined in involuntarily, his eyes hungrily scanning the facade. Strickland
was a manor house, midway in size between the humble
cottage and the great lordly mansion. Built of the mellow
Ham Hill stone that was quarried locally, it was similar
to a thousand other seats of the English squirearchy.

When he was a child, the summit of his ambition had
been to become master of Strickland. As the eldest son
he would someday inherit, and his goal had been to
make himself worthy of wearing his father's mantle. He,
too, would care for the land, would know every tenant's

name, and have a sweet for every child he met during the day. He, too, would be a man greeted everywhere with respect, not fear. And, like his father, he would have a wife who glowed when her husband came into the room.

Then, in a few short, horrifying days, everything had changed. When his uncle's secretary had come to take the orphan to Wargrave Park, Reggie had gone without question, dazed but obedient to adult authority. He had dreamed that someday he would return to Strickland, until his uncle had told him in harsh, unfeeling words that the estate was not his, nor ever would be.

After that, he no longer thought of Strickland as his home; he tried not to think of Strickland at all. During the years he had assumed that he would become the next Earl of Wargrave, he had known that his boyhood home would be a minor part of his inheritance, but he never intended to live there again.

Now, in the end as in the beginning, there was only Strickland. His great expectations had vanished, and he was merely a man of good family and bad reputation, no longer young. But now, for the first time in his life, he was a landowner, and in England land was the source of power and consequence. If he ever hoped to find a meaning for his existence, it must be found here. If only he weren't so weary . . .

His thoughts were dangerously close to self-pity, and his mouth tightened into a hard line. Urging his horse forward again, he tried to recall what he knew about his mother's family. Her maiden name had been Stanton, but apart from that and his personal memories of her, he remembered nothing. Strange how children accept their surroundings without question; he had never guessed that Strickland was hers. Her family must have been solid, prosperous country squires, but since the aristocratic Davenports had taken charge of him when he had been orphaned, he had half-forgotten that the Stantons existed.

Strickland had been built in Tudor times, a sprawling two-story house with gables, mullioned bay windows, and bold octagonal chimneys. It faced south so that the sun fell across it all day long, while the back commanded a view of gardens, lake, and rolling countryside. It was typical; that didn't mean that it was not beautiful.

The really shocking realization was how little things had changed. The grounds were well-kept, the house in good repair. Only the faint air of emptiness said that his parents or young brother and sister would not walk through the door and down the front steps.

He shivered and his hand tightened so hard that his horse whickered and tossed its head. Forcing himself to relax, he dismounted and tethered the stallion at the bottom of the stairs, then went up lightly, two steps at a time, driven by an uneasy mixture of anticipation and apprehension. His hand paused for a moment over the heavy knocker, a brass ring in the mouth of a lion. He had admired it greatly as a child, longing for the day when he would be tall enough to reach it. He set the memory aside and rapped sharply, then experimentally turned the knob. After all, he owned the place, didn't he? He would begin as he intended to go on, and that was as master of Strickland.

The knob turned under his hand and the massive door swung inward, admitting him to a large entry hall with carved oak wainscoting. He passed through to the main drawing room, then stopped, the hair on the back of his neck prickling. He had not known quite what to expect; he had anticipated many things, but not that there would be virtually no changes at all.

Everything was neat, with only a slight suggestion of mustiness, the hearth beneath the elaborate mantelpiece cold and clean. The colors, the furniture dimly visible under holland covers, the hangings, were unchanged—faded certainly, and shabbier, but the very same pieces that had defined his world when he was a boy. Ghost memories of his parents sat at the mahogany card table, laughing over a game. He turned sharply away, stalking across the room to the passage beyond, wondering if there was anyone here. There had better be, or someone had better have a damned good explanation for why the front door was unlocked.

He circled around to the right, toward the morning room. There he found a plump woman removing covers from the furniture. She looked up in surprise as he entered, wiping her hands quickly on her apron and bobbing a curtsy. "Mr. Davenport! You gave me a start. You made good time. We only just heard the news, and there hasn't been time to set everything to rights."

Reggie wondered how she had known he was coming, then decided that it was logical that a new owner would want to inspect his property. "You have the advantage of me. You are . . . ?"

She was in her forties, a rosy-cheeked countrywoman who was polite but hardly obsequious. "I'm Mrs. Herald. You wouldn't remember, but I was a housemaid here when you were a lad. I was May Barlow then." Looking him up and down, she added with approval, "You've grown tall, like your father."

He narrowed his eyes thoughtfully. "Two of the tenant farms were worked by Heralds."

"Aye, I married Robbie Herald. We're at Hill Farm."

"The house is in excellent condition." Reggie spoke absently as his eyes scanned the morning room. Large mullioned windows on two walls admitted whatever sunshine was available; his mother had always particularly liked it here.

"Aye. It was leased to an old gent for a good few years. He maintained the place well enough, but never bothered making changes. It's been vacant since about the time the old earl died, and I've kept an eye on things, watching for leaks and dry rot so the estate carpenters could make repairs as they were needed."

"You've done a good job." Over the years, Reggie had learned the value of an appreciative word, and Mrs. Herald beamed at the compliment.

"I'm glad you think so, sir. We've done our best." She hesitated a moment, then blurted out, "We're all ever so glad to have a Stanton here again. It's not right, the way Wargrave ignored this place for so many years. The old earl never once set foot here, just took money out and put naught back in."

She blushed then, remembering that the old earl had been her new master's uncle and guardian, but Reggie just said mildly, "I'm a Davenport, not a Stanton."

"Your mother was a Stanton, that's what counts in Dorset," she said with a firm nod. "There have always been Stantons at Strickland."

Her words reminded Reggie of the way a judge pronounced a sentence. After a moment's reflection he asked, "You'll think this a foolish question, but do I have any Stanton relations?"

"The closest would be Mr. Jeremy Stanton at Fenton Hall. He was your mother's cousin, and he and your father were good friends. He's getting along in years now, but a fine gentleman."

Mrs. Herald shook her head. "Your mother, Miss Anne, was an only child. Pity that her branch of the family had dwindled down to just her. If there had been any nearer relations, they never would have let the earl take you away after . . ." She hesitated, then decided not to continue the sentence. Firmly she finished with, "The Stantons always took care of their own."

Perhaps that's why they died out, Reggie thought cynically, but he kept the words unsaid in the face of Mrs. Herald's vicarious family pride. Aloud he said, "My man will be along tomorrow with my baggage, but I came by myself."

"Shall I be putting your things in the master bedchamber?"

Reggie hesitated as a vivid image of the room flashed in front of him. His parents had unfashionably shared it, sleeping together in the carved oak four-poster. It seemed wrong to sleep in their bed. "No, I'll take the room above this one. The blue room it was called, I think."

"Very well, sir. Would you like something to eat? The house is all at sixes and sevens but my sister-in-law Molly Barlow is down in the kitchen, cleaning and stocking the pantry. She could do a light nuncheon."

"No, thank you, I'd rather see Mr. Weston. Do you know if he would be at the estate office now, or is he out on the property somewhere?"

Mrs. Herald stopped, her normal garrulity temporarily deserting her. "It's hard to say, sir. The steward is very active and could be 'most anywhere."

"I'm told Weston is very good."

"Oh, yes, Mr. Davenport. There isn't a better steward anywhere," she said with an odd, guilty expression.

Reggie eyed her curiously, wondering why mentioning Weston had such an effect. Maybe the housekeeper was having an affair with the steward? Or didn't country folk have such vices? If they didn't, Dorset could prove dull indeed.

He caught sight of two girls polishing wood and scrubbing floors as he made his way through the house. They stared with open curiosity, giggling bashfully and bobbing their heads when he nodded at them. An odd feeling, being lord of the manor.

The side door led to a wide cobbled yard surrounded by buildings of the same golden-gray stone as the manor house. The estate office was on the opposite side of the yard, adjacent to the stables. It was all so familiar. He remembered the time he had climbed a ladder behind the man repairing the roof and had happily skittered around on the slates, not understanding why his mother had come out and ordered him to come down immediately when he was having such a good time. Having no conception of what a fall to the cobbles would do to his life expectancy, he had been surprised that she was upset, but had come down readily enough. He had been obedient in those days; that was one of many things that had changed when he left Strickland.

His steps led him unerringly to the estate office, and the door opened silently under his hand. The light had been bright outside and it took a moment for his eyes to adjust enough to see that the office was occupied. His first impression was of a thin man standing in front of a rack of books, searching the shelves for a particular volume. The man's attention was engaged and Reggie had time to study the booted, mud-splashed figure.

Abruptly he realized that it was not a man, but a slim woman dressed in men's clothing, her brown hair wrapped in severe braids around her head. He studied the beautiful long legs appreciatively even as he wondered who the devil she was. Another of the numerous Heralds, perhaps? Hard to imagine one of that conservative clan dressed so outrageously. "Do you know where Mr. Weston is?"

She jumped and whirled around. Facing him was the tallest woman he'd ever seen. Her wide eyes and regular features were attractive, but wore an expression that was forceful to a point just short of belligerence, and she had a regal air that shone through her surprise. It was hard to imagine that he'd thought her male even in dim light; in spite of her rigorously masculine clothes, she was admirably curved in all the right places. Or perhaps it was the male garb itself that made her look so provocative.

His mouth quirked into a smile; perhaps Dorset would prove more interesting than he had anticipated. The woman appeared to be in her mid-twenties and was obviously no shy virgin. On the other hand, she gave every evidence of being mute, and her expression was definitely a glare. Amused, he repeated, "Do you have any idea where the steward, Mr. Weston, is?"

She drew in a deep breath, which did interesting things to her linen shirt, then said militantly, "*I'm* Weston."

4

Alys stared at the man, frozen with shock. Of all the ill luck! She hadn't expected that Davenport could be here so soon, and was not prepared to meet her new employer. She had no doubt whatsoever about the man's identity—he walked in with the confidence of ownership, not with the tentativeness of a stranger. As eyes the light clear blue of aquamarine met hers, she saw that he was half a head taller than she, a fact she did not appreciate. She was used to staring men in the eye, or even looking down; having to look up was disconcerting.

As a way of monitoring the world she had fled, she read the London papers regularly, and Reginald Davenport's name was one that turned up often. He was a Corinthian, one of a sporting set known for racing, roistering, and raking. Now the man in front of her confirmed her worst fears. He must be around forty, his dark hair untouched with gray but the long face marked by years of dissipation. He might have been handsome if his aristocratic nose hadn't been broken and reset somewhat less than straight. In spite of his athletic build and movement, there was a sallow, unhealthy tint to the dark skin. The wages of sin, no doubt. Her only satisfaction was that Davenport was as shocked as she was. He said incredulously, "A. E. Weston, the land steward of Strickland?"

"Yes." Her one syllable was unencouraging.

A look of unholy amusement in his eyes, he sauntered into the room, his insolent glance scouring her, lingering on her breasts and hips. He moved beautifully, with an intensely masculine swagger that reminded her of a stallion. Her back to the wall, Alys could feel herself flushing, and it took all of her control not to grab for the coat she had tossed over the chair. She felt like she was being stripped naked, a pursuit Davenport must be highly practiced in. Standing no more than three feet away, he drawled, "I do believe you are a female."

Suddenly furious, Alys subjected him to the same kind of scrutiny he had given her, her eyes slowly scanning his lean body, from powerful shoulders to expensive riding boots, with special attention for the buckskin riding breeches that clung to his muscular thighs. Her voice as pointed as her gaze, she said, "Gender is not difficult to determine."

He grinned wickedly. "Not usually, and there are surer tests available if vision is insufficient."

His implication was as obvious as it was insulting, and if looks could kill, Reginald Davenport would have been a dead man. Alys knew that she was not the kind of woman men desired or flirted with, and only an arrogant rooster who pursued anything female would speak so to her. She opened her mouth for a furious reply; she had not supervised recalcitrant workers for years without learning how to wield her tongue like a lash.

Just in time she remembered that she was supposed to placate this man, not alienate him, and her mouth snapped shut. The yearning to reply in kind was so great that her jaw ached as she struggled for control. Finally she was able to say in a level voice, "I presume you wish to see the books. Or would you rather tour the property first?"

He stared at her measuringly, his eyes narrowed. "What I would really like," he said at length, "is a discussion and a drink. Do you have anything here?"

Wordlessly she pulled open the door of the cabinet and removed a bottle of whiskey and two low tumblers, pouring two fingers' worth for each of them. She seldom drank herself, but sometimes she had visitors who appreciated a wee dram. Maybe it would help soften Davenport.

Taking the glass from her stiff fingers, he sat down in one of the wooden chairs and extended his legs to prop his feet on another chair, his body as relaxed as hers was rigid. After sipping the whiskey, he said, "I assume the late earl didn't know you were a woman; he would have never permitted it. Does the present earl know?"

Alys sat down behind the desk, the familiarity of it helping her to relax. Shaking her head, she said, "No, when he came to look Strickland over, I made an excuse to be away." She drank some of her own whiskey, needing its warmth.

"How nice to know that Richard didn't arrange this as an insult," he murmured, his pale blue eyes distant for a moment.

Wanting to know the worst, Alys asked abruptly, "Are you going to discharge me because I'm a woman?"

The cool eyes flicked over to her again. "Don't put ideas in my head—discharging you is a tempting prospect."

"Do you think a woman can't do the job?" Alys was too tense to be tactful; she was afraid that she had lost this battle before it had started.

Davenport shrugged. "You are demonstrably doing it. Though I've never heard of a woman being hired as a steward, it's hardly unknown for a woman to manage property that she has inherited."

"Then why would you want to get rid of me?"

He finished his whiskey and leaned forward to pour

some more. Instead of answering directly, he asked, "Are you single, married, widowed, or what?"

"Single, and why should it matter?" Alys was having trouble keeping her belligerence under control.

"First of all, you're rather young for the job, even if you were male. The fact that you are also single and apparently of good birth is a source of potential gossip when the owner of the estate is a bachelor."

Alys stared at him aghast. Of all the things that Davenport might have said, this surprised her the most. "A rake is concerned about *propriety*?"

He laughed out loud at the shock in her voice, humor softening his hard face. "I have the feeling that my reputation has preceded me. Is it so unthinkable that a rake should have some concept of decorous behavior?"

Alys had the grace to blush. Calling him a rake to his face was an unforgivable impertinence on her part; thank God he was amused. She said tentatively, "I can't imagine that my being a female would cause any eyebrows to raise. I'm thirty, hardly a girl, and I've been here for four years. Everyone in this part of Dorset is used to me."

"*I'm* not used to you," he said bluntly. "It's obvious from the way you talk that you're the respectable sort of female, a breed I'm almost completely unacquainted with. In the nature of things, you will be working with me regularly, and I don't relish having to watch my tongue around you."

She shrugged. "After four years of working with every kind of laborer, I'm very hard to shock. Treat me like a man." She couldn't resist adding, "It will probably be safer for me that way anyhow."

His face hardened. "Do you expect me to pounce on every female on the property?"

She gave him a challenging look. "Will you?"

"Not when I'm sober," he answered shortly.

Alys wished that she had never let the conversation go in this direction. She hoped that Reginald Davenport wasn't the sort to leave a trail of bastards across the county, but if that's what he wanted to do, there wasn't a thing she could do to stop him. Uncomfortable under his hard stare, she was grateful when he changed the subject. "Care to explain how you came to be a steward, Miss Weston?"

Alys stared down at the tumbler clasped in her hands on the desktop. "It was a series of accidents. I was governess at a neighboring estate. The owner, Mrs. Spenser, was having problems with her steward. I had . . . grown up on a farm, and was able to advise her. Eventually she discharged her steward and had me take over his duties."

"I see." His eyes watched her expressionlessly over the tumbler as he drank more whiskey. "How did you come to Strickland itself?"

Alys hesitated, not sure how much to say. Finally she answered, "Mrs. Spenser knew she was dying and that the heir to her property wouldn't keep me on, so when the Strickland steward was discharged, she suggested I apply for the situation. She gave me excellent references, and persuaded several of the local gentry to do the same. They all thought it a great joke to play on the Earl of Wargrave—absentee landowners are not much liked around here. Based on the references and some correspondence, the Wargrave business manager hired me sight unseen. Since the property has done very well under my management, there was no reason to question my credentials later."

Mrs. Spenser had exacted a price for her aid: that Alys would become guardian to the older woman's niece and nephews after her death. Alys had been quite willing to take charge of her former students; at the moment, she preferred not to mention them to her new employer. She glanced at Davenport, but his thoughts were impossible to divine. He was frowning at the toes of his boots, weighing her future in the balance.

The silence was broken by the entrance of the groom. Alys looked up and said, "Yes, Bates?"

"Excuse me, Lady Alys, but I think one of the plow horses has a splint forming." His words were for her, but his frankly curious gaze was for the new owner.

Alys said impatiently, "Apply a cold-water bandage and I'll take a look at it later. Is there anything else?"

Bates considered for a moment, then shook his head, "No, ma'am," and took his leave.

"Are you consulted about everything that happens at Strickland?" Davenport asked, his eyebrows rising.

"Of course not, that was just an excuse for him to get a closer look at you. Everyone is curious. After all, you have the power to make or break anyone on the estate."

Alys was pleased to see that her words took him slightly aback. Good; the more he thought about his new responsibilities, the better. He didn't look like a man who had had more than a nodding acquaintance with responsibility in the past.

With a sardonic glint in his eye, he said, "Lady Alys? What noble family do you spring from to merit the title?"

Flushing, she replied, "It's just a nickname. Someone called me Lady Alys, and it stuck." Under his probing gaze, she felt compelled to add, "Because of my dictatorial tendencies, I imagine."

He smiled faintly at her explanation. "Lady Alys . . ." he murmured. "It does suit you. Shall I call you that, or do you prefer to be Miss Weston?"

"Whatever you wish, Mr. Davenport," she answered, doing her level best to sound like an obedient employee. Inside, her stomach was churning and she sipped some whiskey, hoping it would have a soothing effect.

They drank in silence, Davenport frowning to himself, until Alys could stand the suspense no longer and asked, "Well?"

He glanced up. "Well, what?"

She could feel her chin lifting at his deliberate obtuseness. "Are you going to discharge me?"

His eyes were shuttered as he studied her. "I decided before I arrived here to make no changes until I was more familiar with the situation." He frowned again. "It will be a confounded nuisance to have a female steward, but everyone seems to hold you in high regard. Since you can do the work, it would be foolish to release you for a reason that is not your fault and which apparently doesn't hinder your performance."

Alys felt almost giddy with relief; she really hadn't expected such an enlightened attitude from a libertine.

Reading her expression, he went on, his heavy brows drawn together, "I will keep you on for the time being, but I want to make two things clear. First, I intend to take you at your word and treat you like a man, so I don't want to hear any spinsterish outrage about my crude language and behavior."

He waited until she gave a nod of acknowledgment, then continued, "Second, for the last four years you have been running Strickland, with authority for everyone and everything on the estate, answerable only to a London lawyer who never visited. For all practical purposes, you might have been the owner."

He set his tumbler on the desk and leaned forward for emphasis, his deep voice very deliberate. "Now, however, Strickland is *mine*. If I tell you that I want to plant orange trees in the water meadow, you will do it. If I want the laborers to cut a Saxon horse into the chalk of the hillside, you will give the orders. If I want to color the sheep pink, you will order the dye.

"I am quite willing to take advice on estate matters; after all, your experience is greater than mine. However, once I make a decision, I will expect you to implement it without further questions." His dark face was stern and implacable. "Your will is no longer supreme; what authority you have is derived from me. For you, it will be a change for the worse. I don't expect you to like it, but I do expect you to accept it and behave in a civil and cooperative manner. If you can't, you had better leave right now."

Alys stared into his cold aquamarine eyes and realized that it would be very easy to hate Reginald Davenport. Before today, she hadn't had time to worry beyond the question of whether he would discharge her out of hand. Now she had survived the first fence and it appeared that the rest of the course would be much harder. Her new employer had gone to the heart of her dilemma with uncanny perception; for four years she had run Strickland like a private fiefdom. Because of her position and the fact that she was an enlightened despot, her orders had been accepted, and she was proud of what she had achieved here.

Now he was saying in unmistakable terms that her reign was over; she was as much an employee as the youngest field hand. Authority came very naturally to Alys; subservience did not. Unfortunately, she had no real freedom to leave; she would never be able to find an equivalent situation anywhere else.

At her silence, he prompted, "Well?"

Swallowing hard to force down her resentment, she replied with creditable calm, "I can accept that, Mr. Davenport."

He smiled with a lazy charm that was a startling contrast to his prior manner. "You can accept it, but you would really rather have my guts for garters." He stood and looked down at her. "I don't care what you think of me as long as you do your work and don't sulk. Agreed?"

Alys stood and, after a moment's hesitation, offered her hand with grudging respect. "Agreed."

His hand was firm and hard, not soft like many London gentlemen's. After arranging to meet her early the next morning for a tour of the estate, he took the last six years of account books to the main house to study. After he left, Alys sank back into her chair and sighed wearily. Now she would consider the serious question of whether she could work for Reginald Davenport without murdering him.

Having survived ordeal by owner, that night Alys faced interrogation by her wards. She waited until dinner was over before announcing, "Mr. Davenport arrived from London today."

A chorus of responses overlay each other. Meredith looked up so quickly from the table that her golden ringlets danced. "Lady Alys," she said accusingly, "you didn't tell us!"

Her fifteen-year-old brother, Peter, asked eagerly, "How long is he going to stay?"

William, at seven the baby of the family, swallowed his pudding in haste and demanded, "Tell me about his horses!"

Alys grinned at her charges. All three of the Spensers were staring at her, bright-eyed with curiosity. Even Attila watched avidly, though in his case the cause might be hope for a handout rather than feline curiosity. "I wanted to eat before I told you, because I knew there would be no peace afterward.

"To answer your questions, I don't know how long he is going to stay, but it looks like he'll be here for a while. He rode down on a really magnificent black stallion. He has a carriage and some hunters coming, and if the rest of his cattle are half as fine as the stallion, William will be in horse heaven."

William, who had his older sister's golden hair and sunny disposition, sighed rapturously. Merry, mindful of Alys's concern, asked, "He didn't mind that you're a woman?"

Alys hesitated, remembering that dark, sardonic face. "He minded, but he's willing to overlook my failings in that area, at least for the moment."

Peter said wistfully, "I wonder if I'll be able to meet him. It's hard to imagine a real out-and-outer in Dorsetshire."

Alys regarded him thoughtfully. Unlike his blond and pragmatic siblings, Peter had brown hair and a dreamy, scholarly nature. While his ambition was the church, he tempered that with a lively interest in the doings of the London fashionable world. Like his brother and sister, Peter was remarkably happy and stable considering that he had been orphaned so young, but now he was at an age when he needed a father's guidance, and Alys couldn't give that to him. It would be all too easy for the boy to hero-worship a man like Strickland's new owner.

Hoping to reduce Davenport's glamour, she said dampeningly, "He may be an out-and-outer in London, but he looks like any other country gentleman here."

Undeterred, Peter said, "He's a member of the Four-in-Hand Club, and they say he's one of the best boxers in England, that he could have been a professional champion if he wanted to."

Alys sighed. Her four years as a foster parent had taught her that sometimes it was impossible to derail the direction of youthful thought. Peter was determined to be impressed.

"Is he handsome?" That was from Merry, of course. Alys eyed the girl with misgivings. Meredith handled her young suitors with innate skill, but she was no match for a man of the world like Davenport. Alys wished she could keep the two of them apart, but Strickland was too small for that. "No, he's not especially good-looking, besides being old enough to be your father."

She was uncomfortably aware that her words were less than the truth. Davenport was certainly no Adonis, but he had a sexual magnetism that would fascinate as many women as it terrified. Merry was not the sort to be easily terrified. Leaning her elbow on the table, the girl rested her chin on her hand and mused, "He's going to be lonely in that big house by himself. Perhaps we could invite him to dinner."

"He'll be getting plenty of invitations when the local gentry know he's in residence. He's a considerable property owner now, and there are enough unmarried daughters in the area to ensure instant social acceptance as long as he doesn't do anything too outrageous," Alys said cynically. "Besides, you know perfectly well that it would be inappropriate to invite my employer to dinner."

Merry smiled mischievously. "This is not the normal steward's household."

"No," Alys admitted, "but that doesn't mean that there should be any social relationship between Davenport and us. That would be both improper and uncomfortable."

Ignoring her guardian as thoroughly as Peter had, Merry said dreamily, "I've always wondered what a rake is like."

"Meredith, such talk is quite unbecoming," her guardian said with exasperation. "I don't want Mr. Davenport pestered by any of you, about his horses, his sporting activities, or his social life. Do you understand?"

She might as well have saved her breath. In a quiet neighborhood like this one, a dashing stranger was bound to be a focus of speculation and interest. Alys imagined that Davenport was too impatient and self-absorbed to waste time corrupting the boys. However, Meredith was quite a different story; her beauty attracted men like bees to a jam pot. The local swains were respectful

enough, but Davenport came from a very different world.
Merry handled her local admirers so deftly that she might
not realize that she was playing with fire until she was
burned. Which meant that Alys was going to have to
keep Davenport away from the girl, at the same time
satisfying the man with her stewardship.

It didn't take a prophet to foresee storms on the horizon.

Reggie had account books spread all over the library
table and it was nearly midnight when he set the last of
them aside. He stretched, then picked up his brandy
glass and wandered over to the French doors. In the
middle distance the gardens were lovely in the pale, cool
light of a waxing moon, though by day they looked
rather unkempt. The house and grounds were eerily familiar; the old man who had rented the house had made
so few changes that Reggie suspected that he could go to
his old bedroom and find it just the same, with books
and rocks and other childish treasures.

However, it was a proposition that he didn't intend to
test; he felt twitchy enough already. The house was wel-
coming but haunted, and he couldn't turn a corner without half-expecting to run into a member of his family.
Presumably that feeling would pass; it had better, or he
would be unable to endure living here. He drank deeply
of the brandy. Strickland might prove unendurable anyhow; what on earth did country people do in the evenings? He would perish of boredom at this rate.

In spite of his misgivings, he had the obscure feeling
that he couldn't go back to his old life. Mentally he had
burned his bridges when he came down here. His life was
hollow at the core; the only question was, what would fill
that space? Apart from brandy, that was.

Taking a branch of candles in hand, he prowled through
the ground floor. The music room opened off the drawing
room and the old pianoforte still stood there in lonely
grandeur. Placing the candelabrum on the shining mahogany lid, he sat down on the bench and ran his hands
across the keys experimentally. Wincing, he made a mental note to have the instrument tuned, but even though

the tone was off, he continued playing for half an hour or so.

His mother had taught him music on this very instrument, and if he had continued he might have become an excellent pianist. That possibility was one of many that had vanished when he left Strickland, but over the years he had always played when he was in the vicinity of a piano, doing it only for his own pleasure, preferably when there was no one around to hear. Polishing his musical skills would be one way of filling empty time.

Picking up the candelabrum, he continued on his midnight tour until he came to the morning room, where he halted on the threshold. This sunny chamber was one of the pleasantest spots in the house and had been his mother's special retreat, but even so he had never liked it. At night and devoid of his mother's presence, it made the hair on his nape prickle. The rest of Strickland's ghosts were amiable, but not whatever lingered here.

Scoffing at his imagination, he returned to the library and settled into the wing chair that had been his father's favorite. He was much the height and build of his father, and the chair seemed tailored to his shape. Picking up the brandy he had left, he ran his thoughts over what he had accomplished today.

Based on her efficiency at making the house habitable, he had offered the position of full-time housekeeper to Mrs. Herald. She wouldn't live in, but since her children were almost grown and she liked keeping busy, she had been pleased to accept. Mrs. Herald had also recommended several local girls as house and kitchen maids. Reggie assumed that they were all related to her, but as long as they were competent, there was nothing wrong with nepotism.

Molly Barlow, Mrs. Herald's sister-in-law, had proved to be a good plain cook and he had asked her to take that position. A plump, comely widow in her forties, she had accepted with alacrity, and in a few days she and her youngest child would move into the servants' quarters. Reggie eyed her with some interest but had already decided that it would be poor policy to make a mistress of one of his own servants. He'd have to make different arrangements, perhaps in Dorchester.

Or he could invite Chessie down for a visit. She would be a good short-term solution. He chuckled at the thought of what the county would think; it was likely that some of the men would recognize her, since Chessie ran one of London's best brothels. Having her at Strickland would certainly eliminate any risk that he would be acceptable to the women folk of the local gentry.

Amusement faded and he ran his hand tiredly through his dark hair as his thoughts circled around to his improbable steward, the imperious Lady Alys. He wasn't really worried about burning her tender ears with his language; the real danger was that he would be unable to keep his hands off the blasted woman. While Reggie found a very broad range of females attractive, tall slim women with long legs and richly feminine figures could turn him into a soft-headed imbecile. Garbed as she was this afternoon, the legs had been immediately obvious. If she had been dressed like a lady, he would have had to know her a good deal better for her attributes to have the same impact.

Under other circumstances, she might have been a real find, but as he had talked with her he had revised his initial impression: while she was not shy, she was undoubtedly a virgin. Beneath her unconventional dress and occupation there lurked the rigid soul of a governess, and she had been quite unable to repress her furious disapproval of having to work for him. Not that Reggie blamed her; if he had been ruler of the roost here for years, he would be equally furious at being displaced. In her case, anger would be supplemented by contempt for the kind of man the new owner was.

It would be much simpler to get rid of the woman, but he was reluctant to turn her out. She had reached her present position only through a lucky chance, and she was unlikely to find another such post. Which would be both unfair and unfortunate, because his review of the accounts had showed that the woman had a talent for her work that bordered on genius.

Reggie had always had a knack for figures, and had

deciphered a fascinating story from the account books. The previous steward had been fired by the Wargrave business manager for embezzlement, and when Miss Weston took over there had been an immediate jump in income just through honest record-keeping.

Then the story became really interesting. For the first two years under Lady Alys the income had increased but the profits had been canceled by heavy capital investment; in the last two years the improvements had paid off with a sharp increase in income. Many of the expenditures were clear from the books, but there were some unusual notations that he hadn't understood, things he intended to ask his steward about.

Refilling his brandy glass, he made a mental note to send an order to a Dorchester wine merchant the next day, then eyed the account books. Maybe Lady Alys would be unable to accept his authority and he could fire her for insolence or disobedience. As the brandy glowed through him, he thought of that splendid body and shook his head at how it was wasted on a professional spinster. If she had been as young as she looked, there might have been some hope of convincing her of what she was missing, but since she had reached the advanced age of thirty in a state of militant virginity, her attitude was unlikely to change.

Reggie sighed and slouched down in his chair, resting his head against the back. He didn't doubt his ability to control his base instincts when he was sober, but if she paraded that beautiful body in front of him when he was half-foxed, he might behave very badly indeed. And really, he didn't need any more reasons to despise himself.

Well, he was generally sober during the day and he was unlikely to be socializing with his steward, so her virtue should be safe. However, he had had just enough brandy that if Lady Alys was present, he would have forgotten that he was a nominal gentleman and made a most improper suggestion. Then she would have boxed his ears and he would have needed a new steward.

He chuckled and picked up the brandy decanter to carry to his bedchamber. In his present mood, it was much more amusing to imagine what might happen if she didn't box his ears.

5

Reggie awoke to the familiar temple-pounding aftermath of too much brandy. He had been able to put himself to bed, so he wasn't as badly off as two mornings ago in London, but this was quite bad enough. Groping for his watch on the bedside table, he discovered that it was seven-thirty, which gave him just enough time to get presentable and meet Lady Alys for the tour of the estate. Groaning, he rolled to the edge of the bed and sat there, his head in his hands, and prayed that Mac Cooper would arrive from London today. It was much harder to face the morning without Mac's skilled ministrations.

As he stood, he noticed that the brandy decanter was empty, which explained his head. He'd better make sure that new supplies of drink were arranged before the day was over.

The morning was damp and overcast, and by the time Reggie had saddled his horse, Bucephalus, he was wishing that he hadn't arranged this tour. It had been a deliberate choice to ride over the estate for the first time with someone else; alone he would run the risk of becoming maudlin. Still, it was a little early to face Lady Alys's censorious eye.

His mood was not improved when his steward entered the stables, bandbox-neat in a dark brown riding habit. The severe cut didn't quite disguise her excellent figure, though it did conceal the distracting legs. Idly he wondered how she would look if she ever let those thick braids down; her hair must be nearly waist-length. Like her body, her hair was another splendid asset wasted; the expression on her handsome face rivaled Medusa in paralyzing effect.

"Good morning, Mr. Davenport. Is there any particular part of the estate you would like to see first?" Alys knew that her nervousness was coming out as waspishness, but couldn't manage to sweeten her tone. She knew that she had a very difficult day ahead of her. Davenport's tentative willingness to keep her on could evaporate at any time, and there were things on the estate which were odd, to say the least. It didn't help that her new master looked like a bear with a sore ear; like her, he must not be a morning person.

Davenport grunted a greeting as she went for her side-saddle. To her surprise, he took it away from her and saddled her mare himself. "I thought you were going to treat me like a man," she remarked as he efficiently tightened the girth.

Giving her a slanting glance, he said, "It's more difficult to do when you're dressed like a woman."

Unsure how to respond, she nodded, then said hesitantly, "Mr. Davenport, you will see some . . . unusual things at Strickland. There is a reason for everything I have done, and I ask that you let me explain rather than condemning me out of hand."

He turned from the horse to face her, and Alys was once more uncomfortably aware of how tall he was. After a moment of detached study, he nodded. "Very well. I'll just add any oddities to the list of questions I have already."

The comment did not bode well, but Alys's spirits lifted as they went out into the open air. Davenport assisted her into the saddle, complimenting her on her horse as he mounted himself. "A beautiful mare."

As they trotted out of the stableyard Alys said defensively, "She belongs to me, not the estate. I have the bill of sale if you don't believe me."

Without turning in her direction, Davenport said, "Did I show any sign of doubting you?"

She felt like biting her tongue. "No." She continued hurriedly, "As you probably noticed, most of the horses in the stables are just for wagon and plow use. The estate owns two riding hacks, but nothing of great quality. I keep my mare there because the steward's house doesn't have its own stable."

He didn't dignify her inane comment with an answer, and they traveled together in silence until they reached the grain fields, some already planted, others only plowed. As she expected, he rode with the effortless grace and skill of a centaur, and it was a pleasure to watch him, though she did it discreetly.

As they reined in and surveyed the fields quilted by neat hedges, Davenport said, "As I recall, Strickland is just over three thousand acres, about half of it let to tenants and the other half run as the home farm. From the amount of seed you've been buying, I assume that you've improved a good deal of what was wasteland. What is the total acreage in crops now?"

"Almost two thousand acres, with most of the rest being used as pasture."

He nodded and moved on. "You recently bought a shorthorn ram and a score of ewes to improve the stock. What breed did you buy?"

"Southdowns from Ellman in Sussex."

He nodded again. "An excellent choice. Some of the best stock in England." Without a pause he immediately continued, "I gather that you use a four-crop rotation."

"Yes, usually with wheat rather than rye, then turnips, clover, and sainfoin. It has worked so well that we've been able to increase the size of the livestock herds."

Alys suspected that he was trying to impress her, and he was succeeding magnificently. For someone who had spent his life in taverns and gaming hells, he was incredibly well-informed about modern agriculture. His questions continued throughout the morning, with Davenport asking about the seed drill, about the efficiency of the threshing machine she had bought, about the oil cake she was feeding to the beef cattle to improve the quality, about the breeding stock used for the dairy herd, about what experiments she was trying on the home farm before recommending them to the tenants.

He made no comment about her answers, merely nodding or occasionally asking for clarification. By the time noon arrived, Alys had acquired a mild tension headache and a considerable respect for her new employer's understanding. They had covered most of the outer reaches of

Strickland, and Alys had introduced him to several of the tenants. Davenport was reserved but affable, and she could see that he was being surprisingly well-received by the farmers.

As they rode side by side down a lane toward the home farm, she commented on her employer's knowledge of farming.

Davenport shrugged. "I was the heir presumptive for the Earl of Wargrave for many years. The old earl wouldn't let me set foot on any of his properties, but since I was likely to inherit someday, I kept an eye on what was going on in agriculture."

Alys glanced at him speculatively. He had done more than "keep an eye" on what was going on; he had clearly made a serious study of farming and land management, fitting it in between orgies or whatever it was that he did to give him such a terrible reputation. She felt a surge of sympathy for him; Davenport had spent his life preparing for a position he would never fill, since another heir had appeared and claimed the title and fortune. How did Davenport feel about that? His hard profile gave no clues, but it would take a saint not to be resentful, and Alys saw no signs of a halo.

They were coming up on the irregularly shaped ornamental lake that lay near the manor house when Davenport pulled his horse to a halt and dismounted. "Excuse me, there's something I want to see." After tethering his mount, he disappeared into a thicket of trees next to the lake.

Curious, Alys dismounted and tied her own horse, then lifted the long skirt of her riding habit and followed him. The ground slanted down to the lake and her dress put her at a disadvantage in the thick undergrowth. Swearing under her breath as she unsnagged her habit for the third time, she was surprised to emerge from the shrubbery into a small clearing at the water's edge. Short lush grass carpeted the ground, violet-hued bluebells clustered beneath the trees, and a drift of pale yellow primroses lay to one side. The clearing was a private and magical place, the only sound the fluting song of a thrush and the whisper of wind in the trees. This part of the lake was a quiet cove that would be invisible from the manor, though they must be within ten minutes' walk of the house.

Davenport stood by the edge of the lake, looking over its surface as he idly twirled a bluebell in his hands, and Alys studied the picture he made. He didn't have the dandy's perfection of figure that she had so admired in Randolph when she was eighteen and besotted; Davenport was taller and leaner, with a whipcord grace that hinted at power even when he was standing still. He was disturbingly masculine, and Alys realized that was part of the reason she found him so unnerving.

It was easier to break the silence than to let her thoughts continue in that direction. "How did you know about this clearing? I've lived here for four years and never found it."

Without turning to look at her, he said, "I was born at Strickland, Miss Weston. Didn't you know that?"

"No, I didn't," she said with surprise. It was an interesting new fact, and explained why the tenants were so receptive of him. "I know that Strickland has been in the Davenport family for the last forty years or so, but not that it was your particular branch."

"I'm surprised that the local gossips weren't more efficient," he said, still gazing over the lake.

She stepped up beside him and said with amusement, "You caught them unaware. I only heard that the estate was being transferred two days ago, and you appeared yesterday. The gossip didn't have a chance to catch up."

"It will. Gossip always catches up with me." His tone was very wry.

Ignoring his statement, she asked, "How old were you when you left here?"

"Eight."

His terseness didn't encourage further questions, but Alys's curiosity overcame her manners. "What happened?"

"My family died."

Not just parents; family. A brother or sister, perhaps several? Alys felt a tightness in her throat as the ghost of old tragedy brushed her with chill fingers. Eight was very young to be orphaned and removed from the only home a child had known. She said softly, "I'm sorry."

"So am I, Miss Weston, so am I." There was infinite bleakness in Davenport's low voice.

Silence hung heavy between them; then he tossed the bluebell into the lake and turned to face her, the moment's vulnerability gone. "I didn't know until my cousin signed Strickland over to me three days ago, but the bulk of the estate belonged to my mother and should have come to me. Ironic, isn't it? My dear guardian told me that Strickland was one of the Wargrave properties, and it never occurred to me to think otherwise."

"Good Lord, that was the old earl's doing?" Alys asked with astonishment. It was no surprise that the man had been a wretched guardian, but she was appalled by such blatant dishonesty.

"Yes."

"How despicable!"

" 'Despicable' is an excellent word for my uncle," he agreed. "Wargrave is in much better hands now."

"And your cousin gave you Strickland?"

"What a quantity of questions you ask, Lady Alys." There was a sardonic note in his voice as he used her nickname, and she bit her lip.

"I'm sorry, curiosity is my besetting sin," she apologized.

He smiled faintly. "How nice to have only one sin, singular. Mine come in scores."

"I'm sure that I can come up with more than one," she said a trifle indignantly.

He chuckled. "And what might the others be? Sleeping during the Sunday sermon? Coveting a neighbor's horse?"

Well and truly irritated, Alys snapped, "I assure you that I can do better than that."

He laughed outright. "Perhaps someday you will tell me the full list of your vices, Miss Weston. I should enjoy learning what they are."

With a horrid sense of discovery Alys realized how charming Davenport could be with a sparkle in his light blue eyes and a wide smile that invited her to smile with him. She reminded herself sternly that a successful rake

would have to be charming, or he could never beguile
away a lady's virtue. How alarming that she, a woman of
great experience and no illusions, found herself wanting
to respond to that charm with a smile of her own. Hastily
she wiped the expression off her face before her dimples
could emerge. She felt obscurely that dimples would un-
dermine the progress she was making toward convincing
him that she was a competent professional.

Still smiling, Davenport lightly took her arm to guide
her across the clearing. It was a casual gesture, but Alys
was acutely aware of his touch, of the feel of his strong
fingers through the heavy fabric of her riding habit as he
led the way through the woods, holding branches aside
so they wouldn't lash into her. He was about to help her
onto her mount when he halted and stared down at her,
his eyes a bare foot from her own.

"Good Lord, Lady Alys, your eyes don't match," he
said with surprise.

"Really?" she said with asperity. "I never noticed."

Ignoring her sarcasm, Davenport studied her face with
interest. "Indoors you appear to have brown eyes, but in
daylight the difference is striking. I knew a boy in school
who had mismatched eyes." After a moment he added,
"A most unusual feature, but then, you are a most unusual woman."

"Is that a compliment or an insult?" she asked suspiciously.

"Neither." He bent over and linked his hands, effort-
lessly assisting her into her saddle. "A mere statement of
fact."

He mounted himself, then added, "You've done a
remarkable job with Strickland. Even though farm prices
have plummeted since Waterloo, you've increased the
profits, and the land and tenants are in very good heart."

She was absurdly pleased at the compliment; she worked
very hard, and it was good to be appreciated. Perhaps
she would have some security after all. Circling around
the manor house, they rode toward the village of Strickland,
but before they reached their destination Davenport reined
in his horse, his eyes narrowed in concentration as he

stared at the tall brick chimney that rose above a hilltop.
"What on earth . . . ?"

He signaled his mount forward to investigate more
thoroughly while Alys trailed unhappily behind him. The
new owner was about to discover one of the odder features of Strickland. He stopped again on the top of the
hill, where he could see the whole manufactory. The
round bottle oven with its high, circular chimney was an
unmistakable sign of a pottery, and in a voice devoid of
inflection he asked, "What the devil is a potbank doing
on Strickland land? Wasn't that one of the tenant farms?"

Alys said defensively, "The land is leased from Strickland,
and at a very profitable rate."

He glanced at her impatiently. "That isn't what I asked.
What is it doing there, and who owns it?"

Choosing her words carefully, Alys said, "It's held in
trust for three minors."

"Oh?" His cold syllable invited her to continue.

"This was the smallest of the tenant farms, with the
least desirable tenants. It was a relief when they sold off
their equipment and stock and skipped off without paying
the Lady Day rent three years ago. I combined the land
with Hill Farm, because Robbie Herald was best able to
work it, and leased the buildings to the pottery."

The cold blue eyes were piercing, as if he knew that
she was telling less than the whole story, and Alys's
defensiveness flared to anger. "The pottery has been an
excellent venture in a number of ways. It provides jobs,
pays a fair rent to Strickland, and is a good long-term
investment for the owners."

As her mare edged nervously away from Davenport,
she continued in a burst of words, "I know most landowners loathe anything that resembles industry on their
land, but you can't shut it down even if you want to—the
lease runs for twenty-two more years."

Her mouth was open to continue arguments when Davenport's hand shot out to catch her mare's bridle. The
horse tried to throw her head upward, but his powerful
grip held it steady. He was less than a yard away when he
turned in his saddle to face her, anger evident in his
clipped words. "Yesterday I said that I would give you a

chance to prove yourself. Will you extend me the same
courtesy?''

A fierce wave of embarrassment burned Alys's face
and spread down her neck, and it was an effort not to
drop her gaze before his. He was being entirely reasonable, and she was acting like a rabid hedgehog. For the
first time she really looked at him, not as Reginald Davenport, notorious rake and disastrous employer, but as an
individual. With jarring insight she realized that the man
in front of her was a good deal more—or less—than his
reputation. Under the world-weary air he had shown an
intelligence and tolerance that would be a credit to anyone. And he had the tiredest eyes she had ever seen.

She drew a deep breath and managed to keep her
voice level as she said, "I'm sorry." It wasn't enough, so
she added doggedly, "I am often unfairly judged and
condemned by others. It is unpardonable that I commit
the same injustice toward you.''

He smiled faintly and released the mare's bridle. "Considering how many years I have spent cultivating an evil
reputation, Miss Weston, I should be disappointed if you
didn't assume the worst about me."

Vowing to be less biased, she said, "I am beginning
to believe that you are a fraud, Mr. Davenport."

"Oh?" His dark brows rose in the sardonic expression
she was coming to recognize. "In what way?"

"I am beginning to believe that you are not at all the
wicked care-for-nobody that your reputation claims."

"You had best withhold judgment on that point, Miss
Weston," he said dryly as he gathered his reins. "I think
it's time we broke for lunch and you started answering
questions. As I recall, there used to be a tavern on the
Shaftesbury road that had good food."

"It's still there, and it still has good food," Alys said.
She wondered for a moment that he would invite her to a
common tavern, but the Silent Woman was a respectable
place, and it was less compromising to take her there
than have her share a private lunch at the manor house.
In spite of his stated intention of treating her like a man,
he was being careful of the proprieties.

Half an hour later they were facing each other across a

wooden table polished by years of sliding crockery and hard scrubbing. A good number of customers shared the beamed taproom and curious glances came their way. All of the men were local and knew the eccentric Miss Weston, and they could surely guess who her companion was. They kept a respectful distance from the new master of Strickland.

Having polished off the last crumbs of an excellent beef-and-onion pie, Davenport refilled his tankard with ale from the pewter pitcher. "Will you tell me the whole story of the pottery, or will I have to drag the information out of you a piece at a time?"

Alys finished the last bite of her own meat pie, chewing slowly as she thought. She had no doubt that he meant his words, and if he had to dig for the facts, it might ruin his expansive mood. "I'm sure you've heard about the problems there have been with so many soldiers being discharged after the war. There wasn't enough work to begin with, and to make matters worse, the new machinery reduces the need for farm laborers."

He nodded and she went on, "For example, the estate could never have managed without the threshing machine, there just weren't enough men during the later war years." Raising her hands expressively, she said, "Now that the machinery is working and paid for, it makes no sense to go back to slower, more cumbersome methods just to create a few marginal jobs."

She stared at him earnestly, trying to state her case as persuasively as possible. "Besides the fact that idle men make trouble, it would be wrong to let the soldiers who defeated Napoleon starve. Wrong, and dangerous for Strickland as well."

He took a draft of ale and prompted, "So . . . ?"

"I've . . . encouraged the creation of various businesses to provide work. The pottery is the largest, about twenty people work there, but there's a wood shop in Strickland village that employs nine men, and a brick and tile yard that has six workers. There's a good clay deposit nearby, though we import some ball clay from Devon as well. The pottery specializes in moderately priced ware that the average person can afford. There's quite a market for it."

"Who actually runs the pottery?" he asked next.

She hesitated before reluctantly admitting, "I do."

The dark brows shot up. "In addition to managing Strickland? Where on earth do you find the time?"

"I make all the decisions and keep the accounts, but a foreman supervises the actual daily work," she explained. "As you can see from the estate books, I haven't neglected Strickland. I—"

He held up one hand to stop her words. "Before we go too far afield, who are the three minors that are the actual owners of the pottery? Are they local children?"

Alys poured more ale for both of them before answering. "They are the niece and nephews of Mrs. Spenser, my former employer."

"More and more interesting. Where do they live now?"

With an inward sigh, Alys decided to confess, after all, he would surely find out soon. "They live with me."

"Are you their guardian?" he asked with surprise.

She nodded and took another swig from the tankard, her eyes cast down. "Yes, there were no close relatives that Mrs. Spenser trusted. One reason she helped me get the Strickland position was so I could keep the children with me."

"I now see why they call you Lady Alys," he said with a hint of mocking humor. "Managing an estate, several businesses, and children as well. You are an extraordinary woman."

"Most women are extraordinary," she snapped. "It compensates for the fact that most men aren't." Then Alys sucked her breath in. With his talent for getting under her skin, Davenport was making her forget how dependent she was on his goodwill. She, who had always prided herself on her control, found herself continually skirting explosion with him.

He laughed, his extraordinary charm visible again. "I suppose your next project is to advance beyond needing the male half of the species? As a stock breeder, you must know that that will be difficult, at least if there is to be a next generation."

Alys had no doubt that his supply of suggestive remarks could easily outlast her belligerence. "I have never denied that men have their uses, Mr. Davenport," she said with as much dignity as she could muster, reaching for the pitcher.

"Oh? And what might they be?" he asked softly. As the cool, amused eyes watched from his dark face, his hand came down on hers over the handle of the ale pitcher. She could feel her nerves jump, and she glanced down. She hadn't noticed earlier, but his hands were quite beautiful, long-fingered and elegant, the only refined thing about him.

She knew she should pull her hand away, but she couldn't. There was a current flowing from him that made her want to yield, to melt and mold herself, to discover the other ways he could touch, to touch him back . . . In a voice that seemed to come from someone else, she said, "We're out of ale. Shall we order another pitcher, or are you ready to see more of the estate?"

"More ale," he said, apparently quite unaffected by the contact between them. "I still have a number of questions to ask you. For example, the sixty pounds a year for schoolmasters, books, and other teaching supplies."

As he spoke, he signaled for another pitcher of ale, refilling his tankard when it arrived. Alys was four rounds behind him, and knew better than to try keeping up. She didn't doubt that in a drinking contest he could put her under the table. *And what would he do with you there?* a mocking little voice asked. Nothing, of course. More's the pity.

While her lower mind was busy with lewd asides, Alys was saying, "The teachers are a married couple—he teaches the boys, she teaches the girls. I require all the children on the estate to go to school until at least the age of twelve."

"Don't the parents resent the fact that their children can't start earning wages earlier?" he asked.

"Yes, but I have insisted," she replied. "In the short run, it's better for the children; in the long run, the estate will have better workers."

"Miss Weston, did some Quaker or reforming Evangelical get ahold of your tender mind when you were growing up?" Davenport was gazing at her narrowly.

"As a matter of fact, yes."

"Wonderful," he muttered into his ale, his dark brows arched ironically. "A fanatic."

Grabbing hold of her temper with an effort, Alys said with hard-won composure, "Not a fanatic, a practical reformer. You have seen the results at Strickland over the last four years. I would be hard pressed to say which reforms have produced what results, but the total effect has been more than satisfactory. The estate is prospering, and so are the people who work on it. The evidence speaks for itself."

"I keep reminding myself of that, Miss Weston," he said dourly. "I trust you appreciate that you are being treated to an example of open-mindedness and tolerance that none of my friends would believe of me." He shook his head in disbelief. "A female steward, and a reformer to boot."

"It's your income, Mr. Davenport," Alys pointed out in an icy voice. "If you make sweeping changes, there might be a drop in the profits."

"I keep reminding myself of that too," he agreed, pouring the last of the ale into his tankard. He had drunk most of two pitchers by himself. "What about the money given to help emigration?"

She sighed and traced circles on the table in a few drops of spilled ale. It had been a vain hope that he would miss her cryptic notes in the account books; the blasted man appeared to miss nothing. "Three of the men who returned from Wellington's army wanted to take their families to America. All of them had some savings, but not enough to pay their way and start over."

"So you just gave them the money?" He was slouched casually against the back of the oak settle, relaxed but watchful.

"Theoretically, the money was a loan, but it was understood that they might never be able to repay," Alys admitted.

"And the chances of collecting from another country

are nil. So you just gave it to them," he mused. "Are you running a business or a charity here?"

Defensive again, she said, "If you saw the books, you know that less than two hundred pounds were involved. Besides, the families had all worked very hard and loyally for Strickland. One man's wife worked on the harvest crew until an hour before her first baby was born."

Under his sardonic eye, she realized how foolish that must sound to a man of the world, so she added more practically, "Helping them leave also reduced the strain on Strickland's resources—that many fewer jobs to find and mouths to feed."

"If every worker on the estate wanted to emigrate, would you have given money to them all?" he inquired with interest.

She turned one palm up dismissively. "There are very few people who want to leave their homes for a strange country. Most of the people at Strickland were born here, and they can imagine no other end than to die here."

She thought, with piercing sorrow, of where she herself had been born, the home she could never return to. Alys had exiled herself as surely as the three families who had gone to America. She wondered if any of her feelings showed on her face; Davenport was watching her keenly, his light eyes dispassionately curious, but he said only, "Somehow I doubt that the old earl knew about your odd little charities."

Fortunately, he was amused by the thought that his uncle had been ignorant of what went on. "He never had any idea," Alys agreed. "His man of business must have known at least some of what I was doing, but he didn't interfere, since the overall profits were up."

"In other words, you gave away less than your predecessor stole," he summarized.

She blinked in surprise, then nodded. "I never thought of it that way, but I suppose you're right." After hesitating for a moment, curiosity drove her to ask, "Now that you know how Strickland has been run, do you have any comments?"

Davenport thought for a moment, his hands loosely

laced around his tankard. "As you have pointed out, your results are a justification for your methods. Also, everything you described belongs to the past, when I had no say in what went on, so I have no right to criticize your decisions.

"The future, now . . ." He drank his remaining ale in one gulp, then clinked the tankard onto the table. "That will be a different story. I expect I'll want to make some changes, but," he added, watching her face, "I shan't rush into them."

As an endorsement, it didn't go as far as Alys would have liked, but it was the best she was likely to get. At least he intended to move slowly. She started to rise, but her employer wasn't finished yet. He lifted his hand to halt her. "I have only one more question at the moment. As an eager reformer, have you had everyone on the estate vaccinated against smallpox?"

Alys was startled. "No, I've encouraged vaccination, but some of the workers are very suspicious about 'new-fangled ideas.' Only about half the people would allow it, and I don't really have the authority to insist on something like that." In fact, she had railed, begged, and pleaded with the tenants, and been furious at their pig-headed stubbornness.

"In that case, I will issue my first order." His eyes were cold and unwavering as they met hers. "Everyone who is not vaccinated within the next month will be dismissed and evicted. There will be no exceptions."

"But . . ." Alys gasped, torn between approval of the result and fury at his high-handedness, "you can't—"

"No buts, Miss Weston, or arguments about whether I have the authority." He stood and looked down at her, dark and implacable. "The cost will be carried by the estate, and there will be *no exceptions*."

Alys saw very clearly how he had earned the reputation for being dangerous. If she were younger or more timid, she would be diving under the table to avoid that stare.

He added with a hint of scorn, "If you are afraid to tell them, I'll do it myself."

Those were fighting words, and she stood also, since

glaring from a sitting position lacked impact. "I am not afraid to tell them, Mr. Davenport. It will be done." Meeting his stare with her own, she said, "Are you ready to continue your inspection?"

"Quite ready." He dropped a handful of coins on the table, then crossed the taproom with long, lazy strides. As she followed, Alys remembered that tonight she would face a barrage of questions about what kind of man the new master was. Shaking her head, she realized that she had no idea what the answer was.

6

Just as the morning had been spent visiting the fields and pastures, the afternoon was spent in touring the village, barns, granaries, and other farm buildings. They also called on the workshops and small businesses, including the pottery, the carpentry shop, and the brick and tile yard.

Davenport asked questions, keeping his own counsel about what he thought of the answers. Now that Alys knew he was a native of the area, she could see the subtle signs of recognition in the locals. They were watchful, but they looked ready to give him a kind of acceptance that Alys had not received in all her years in Dorset. Of course, it helped that he was male, she commented to herself acidly. No number of years in Dorset would change the fact that she was the wrong sex to be a steward. Even many of the people who had benefited by her management could not quite approve of the fact that she was a woman.

Just beyond the half-dozen acres of orchard that produced apples and cider for estate use, they came on a large patchwork area of vegetable gardens. Davenport reined in his horse curiously. "What are these?"

"Most of the laborers' cottages have only small gardens, so I have provided extra land for those who want to cultivate it," Alys replied. "Besides providing for their families, some of the more ambitious workers grow enough to sell produce in the Shaftesbury market as well."

There was a pause as a woman working in her allotment came over and proudly displayed her baby's first tooth to Alys, bobbing a nervous curtsy to Davenport when he was introduced. Alys chucked the baby's chin and admired the tooth, then handed the infant back to its mother and they continued on their way.

"It looks like everyone at Strickland eats well," her employer remarked.

"They do indeed," Alys agreed. "Eating well is probably the prerequisite for contentment. In addition to the allotments, I started raising rabbits on a large scale. Most are sold to people on the estate at a subsidized price so everyone can afford fresh meat. That reduces the amount of poaching, and we have enough rabbits left over to sell in the market, so the whole operation pays for itself."

They had arrived at the potbank, and as they dismounted, the supervisor, Jamie Palmer, came out to greet them. Jamie was a gentle giant of a man, Alys's oldest friend and ally, and he took his time surveying the visitor, looking for signs of how the new owner would treat Miss Weston. Davenport was aware that he was being judged, and Alys could see his hackles rising, so she quickly performed the introductions, then asked, "Would you give us a tour, Jamie? Mr. Davenport is interested in how pottery is made."

"Of course, Lady Alys." As Jamie led them inside, Davenport gave her a slightly pained look, but followed obediently through the works, observing clay preparation, throwing wheels, slip casting, the bottle kiln, and willow crates that were used to ship the fragile pottery to market. Meredith worked at the pottery several mornings a week, using her considerable artistic talent to develop designs for better-quality china services that could be made in the future. Alys was glad that this was not one of her ward's work days; the longer it was until Davenport met the girl, the better.

The last stop of the tour was the office, where there was a display of some of the pottery's finished products. Taking over from Jamie, Alys handed Davenport a richly glazed round brown teapot. "This is our most successful item," she said. "We can't compete with the large manufacturers, so I decided to aim our products at people of moderate income who like having something nice but who can't afford the fine china from places like Wedgwood and Spode."

Davenport absorbed everything, but didn't comment until they left to ride back to the estate office. "You continue to impress me, Lady Alys. If you hadn't been born a female, you could have succeeded at anything you chose. Strickland is very lucky to have you."

Alys glowed at the compliment; it was good to be considered talented rather than merely eccentric. Back at the office, Alys settled into her usual chair behind the desk and waited for the next round of questions. As he chose a comfortable Windsor chair, her employer surprised her by asking, "Has the sheep washing been done yet this year?"

"Why, no," she replied, raising her brows. "As a matter of fact, the washing is scheduled for the day after tomorrow."

An amused gleam came into Davenport's eyes. "Splendid. When I was a boy, I always wanted to participate in a sheep washing, but I was too small. Time has cured that."

"You actually want to wash sheep?" Alys was startled. It was a messy, time-consuming chore; hard to imagine anyone doing it voluntarily.

"Why, yes," he answered, the gleam deepening. "Would you deny me one of my boyhood ambitions?"

"It's your choice, of course, but an amateur could slow the process down," she said stiffly. "Besides . . ."

"Yes?" he prompted as her voice trailed off.

"Well, wrestling sheep in the water is not exactly conducive to dignity," she finished.

He gave her a sardonic look. "While I will listen to your opinions on matters agricultural, I'm not interested in your ideas about my nonexistent dignity."

She flushed, knowing that she had stepped over the line permitted for an employee, but was saved from answering by the arrival of Meredith, golden hair gleaming in the late-afternoon sun and a look of misleading innocence on her angelic face.

"Lady Alys," she said as she tripped into the room, "I wanted to ask you . . ." She stopped, looking at Davenport with a pretty expression of hesitation. "Oh, I'm so sorry, I didn't realize you had company."

Alys snorted in disbelief, but Merry's bit of playacting was not aimed at her guardian. The girl had probably been watching the estate office all afternoon, waiting for an opportune moment to bounce in and meet the new master of Strickland.

Davenport reacted as any normal male would, rising politely with a look of patent admiration on his long face. Judging by the twinkle in his eye, he undoubtedly realized that Meredith's entrance was no accident, but that didn't prevent him from enjoying the sight of the visitor. Merry was delightful in blue-sprigged white muslin, her golden curls tumbling around her shoulders with just the right touch of modest abandon.

Regarding the tableau sourly, Alys made the introductions. "Mr. Davenport, this is my ward, Miss Meredith Spenser. Merry, I'm sure that you know who this is."

Her acid tone was not lost on Merry, who tossed her guardian a roguish glance before turning to Davenport. "What a pleasant surprise!" she said with a flutter of eyelashes.

Eyelashes that had been carefully darkened, Alys noted. Part of her was amused at watching the girl's budding talent for flirtatiousness, but underneath, she worried about Davenport's reaction. Most gentlemen could be counted on to see Merry for the innocent she really was, but Davenport's reputation was enough to put fear in the heart of any guardian. *Damn* Meredith for flitting in like a houri! Even though Alys had a great deal of respect for her ward's underlying good sense, there could be trouble ahead. At times like this, she regretted taking on the responsibilities of a parent.

As Alys thought her dark thoughts, Davenport and

Merry were furthering their acquaintance. After a few
moments of badinage, Meredith turned to Alys as if
struck by a new thought. "Lady Alys, do you think Mr.
Davenport might be persuaded to take his potluck with
us tonight? Mrs. Haver is roasting a nice joint, more than
enough for company."

So that was Merry's main purpose in this little charade!
Not just to meet Davenport, but to inveigle him over for
dinner.

In the face of Alys's glower, Davenport hesitated.
"I'm sorry, Miss Spenser, but your guardian has been in
my company all day, and it hardly seems fair to inflict me
on her this evening as well."

Meredith said, "Oh, she won't mind, will you, Alys?"
accompanying her statement with a speaking look.

Cornered, Alys said, "We dine *en famille,* Mr. Davenport. A bachelor might find it rather hectic."

Merry turned to him and said coaxingly, "I shall endeavor to keep my younger brothers quiet. *Do* say you
will come."

In the face of such persuasion, he finally nodded and
said, "It will be my pleasure, Miss Spenser."

After suitable expressions of delight, Merry took her
leave. As he sat down again, Davenport grinned companionably at Alys. "Have you ever considered buying
her a chastity belt?"

"I certainly have!" Alys said with heartfelt agreement
before she had time to censor her words. At Davenport's
laughter, she said in a doomed attempt at dignity, "That
is a most improper thing to say."

Unrepentant, her employer said, "I warned you, no
missishness. I may help you into a side-saddle, but I have
every intention of being my normal vulgar self the rest of
the time." With a half-smile he continued, "She's a taking little minx, and she looks a good deal less 'minor'
than your words had led me to expect."

"She's nineteen, Mr. Davenport, and has seen little of
the world." Alys toyed with a Venetian glass paper-
weight, then decided to add, "Please remember that."

His humor evaporating, he slouched back into his chair

and crossed his legs. "I shall endeavor not to debauch her this evening. If it's any comfort, I find virgins boring."

Alys tensed, wondering if the words were intended as an indirect insult toward her. His observant gaze must have noted her expression, because he continued smoothly, "If you want an experienced rake's advice, find her a husband, and soon."

Alys glanced down at her hands, tensely linked on the desk. He had a talent for getting to underlying issues; over the last year, she had invested considerable thought in the question of a husband for Merry. "I'd like to, but the choice around here is not wide, and there has been no one she fancies. All of the eligible men in the neighborhood are mad for her, but they are either callow lads or widowers looking for mothers for their children."

She paused, then said haltingly, "Merry is a bright, lively girl, and very sensible except for her flirtatiousness. She was only practicing her wiles on you because she meets so few new people. She deserves better than provincial assemblies and the local lads." With a slight sigh she added, "Actually, I think she would make quite a splash in London if she could make her come-out there."

"Oh, the girl is definitely a diamond of the first water," Davenport agreed, "but does she have the birth and fortune to match her face?"

"That's the rub," Alys admitted. "She'll have a respectable portion, but it's not a great fortune, and her father was a London merchant. There are no family connections that could introduce her to the *ton*."

"She may be better off doing her husband hunting here," he said. "London can be a dangerous place for the innocent." Then, dismissing the topic, he asked curiously, "Whatever inspired you to take charge of three young people? The girl represents one set of problems, but the boys will probably be just as much trouble in different ways. It would be a heavy burden for anyone, and you aren't even related."

It was none of his business, of course, but Alys found Davenport's directness refreshing. His question seemed to come from genuine interest rather than idle curiosity, so she leaned one elbow on the desk and rested her chin on her hand as she considered her reply. "The obvious answer is that there was no one else Mrs. Spenser trusted. She had no children of her own; in fact, she was only their aunt by marriage, no blood relation at all, but she loved them, and wanted to make sure they were properly cared for."

"If that is the obvious answer, what is the unobvious one?" Davenport's voice was soft and encouraging as he probed toward what she wasn't saying.

"I'm very fond of them. They were my students—I've known William, the youngest, since he was in leading strings. Besides"—Alys gave a brittle laugh—"it's the closest I'm likely to come to having children, and I'd have been a fool to pass up the opportunity."

She stopped suddenly, wondering what had made her blurt out a deep and painful truth like that. Davenport was watching her thoughtfully, and he showed no disposition to probe into sensitive territory. "I hope they realize how fortunate they are to have you, Miss Weston."

After thinking about that a moment, she shook her head and said with a grin, "Merry might, but the boys look on me in the light of a necessary evil, always nagging them to do their studying, mind their manners, and make at least a token gesture to the proprieties."

At the sight of her uninhibited smile, Davenport sat up and leaned forward in his chair as he scrutinized her face. "Lady Alys, you have dimples," he said accusingly.

Caught, Alys blushed. "I'm sorry, I can't help them. I think God made a mistake and gave me someone else's dimples."

Davenport stood and closed the narrow distance to her desk. "Don't apologize, they are quite delightful. Dimples are called the mark of Venus, you know."

He was smiling that lazy, intimate smile, the one designed to make proper ladies forget their virtue, and Alys found herself smiling back. He raised one hand and lightly brushed her cheek, right where a dimple lurked. It was a casual gesture that some women would hate, and others find utterly entrancing. Alys was of the latter persuasion. His touch was warm, and her hypersensitive skin recorded the faint roughness of the whorls on his fingertips. It was as erotic as a kiss, and she felt a reaction clear down to her toes, which curled involuntarily.

Lord only knew what showed on her face, because he dropped his hand and stepped back, his expression growing cool and detached. "If you would prefer not doing the pretty through dinner, I can send my regrets to your ward. You really should not have your employer forced on you after normal work hours."

She swallowed hard, bringing her attention back to the mundane. "If you can bear it, it would be better if you came tonight. If you don't, I'm afraid of what Merry might do to get you there tomorrow."

He chuckled. "I'm sure the conversation at your house will be more enlivening than at mine. If you're sure you don't object, I'll be over at half-past six."

Alys sat behind her desk and watched him exit, his head nearly brushing the lintel of the door. With a dazed mixture of alarm and amusement, she realized that it was not Meredith's virtue she should be worried about; it was her own.

After she spent half an hour clearing her correspondence, Alys had just enough time to return home, bathe, change for dinner, and go to Meredith's chamber for a stern chat. Merry was sitting at her dressing table trying different coiffures, and she glanced up at her guardian with a mischievous smile. "That worked very well today, didn't it? The boys will be delighted to meet Mr. Davenport."

Alys sat down on the bed with an inward sigh. Clearly she had her work cut out for her. How fortunate that she had always believed in speaking plainly to her ward, avoiding missishness; it would make this discussion easier. "Merry, I'm very upset about your forward behavior today. It passed the line of what is pleasing. More than that, it is potentially dangerous."

Merry laughed, pulling a handful of blond hair to the crown of her head and studying the effect. "How could it be dangerous?"

"Meredith, stop fussing with your hair and look at me.

This is serious." When she used that tone, Alys was always obeyed, and her ward obligingly turned and faced her. "Reginald Davenport is a very different proposition from your shy young local admirers. If you issue him a blatant invitation, he may well take you up on it."

"But I didn't issue him an invitation, we were just flirting," Merry said, her wide blue eyes guileless. "He's very skilled at that, so it seemed a good chance to practice. He's hardly likely to ravish me, is he?"

Snapping with exasperation, Alys said, "Being ravished is not the danger. Davenport's dealings with women are notorious: just associating with him could damage your reputation. Falling victim to his charm could damage you a good deal more. Falling in love with him would be a guarantee of breaking your heart. Can I spell it out any more plainly than that?"

Merry gave a peal of laughter. "Good heavens, Alys, I'm hardly likely to fall in love with a man old enough to be my father. He's not even good-looking."

Remembering her employer's mesmerizing aura of virility, Alys had trouble believing that Meredith was unaffected by it. Then she cast her mind back to what had attracted her when she was Merry's age; certainly Alys had been susceptible to a handsome face, but she would never have been indifferent to a man like Reggie Davenport. Of course, even at nineteen she would have known better than to succumb to that kind of low appeal; perhaps Merry was just showing her common sense by refusing to find him attractive. Pray God she continued as wise.

Fixing her charge with a no-nonsense gaze, Alys said, "Will you take my word that it is better to be careful where Davenport is concerned? I've seen a good deal more of the world than you, and I promise you, the man is trouble."

Merry stood and crossed to give her guardian a quick, affectionate hug. "Poor Lady Alys. We do lead you a miserable life, don't we? If it isn't William sneaking into the stables, it's Peter trying to learn to drive to an inch, or hordes of my silly suitors underfoot. You must be sorry you ever took us on."

Her tone had the teasing confidence of a girl who knew she was wanted, and Alys found her lips curving into a smile of response. "I'll admit that with the three of you, life is sometimes too full. But without you, it would be very empty."

Meredith smiled, a wise, enchanting smile that made her seem more the parent than the child, then went back to the dressing table. "I promise I won't do anything rash that will ruin me forever, but I won't be able to resist the temptation to flirt. Mr. Davenport is not at all the sort of man I could fall in love with, but I did think he was rather sweet."

Fascinated, Alys tried to imagine how Davenport would react to the knowledge that a young diamond of the first water considered him "rather sweet." Suppressing a smile, she decided to take the opening Merry was providing to learn more about what the girl wanted from marriage; it was a topic they had never properly discussed. "Well, what *is* the sort of man you could fall in love with?"

Merry frowned at her reflection as she deftly pinned her ringlets into place. "I'm not absolutely sure because I haven't met him yet, but I would want him to be a man of grace and charm. Reasonably intelligent, but not a great scholar or wit, or he would find me sadly frivolous."

With a smile of satisfaction, she twisted the last lock of hair into place. "Of course, I must find his appearance pleasing, but it will be better if he isn't staggeringly handsome—I wouldn't want a man who is very vain."

Alys leaned back against one of the bedposts and stretched her long legs out before her in a most unlady-like fashion. "Need the gentleman be rich and titled?"

"Well, certainly comfortably well-off—I don't think I would find poverty very amusing. A title would be nice, but hardly essential. I'm unlikely to meet a man who has one, so why yearn after the impossible?"

She turned to face her guardian, her heavenly blue eyes lit with humor. "Even if I met a nobleman, a peer would imagine that he was conferring an enormous favor by marrying a girl of no great fortune or birth. I would prefer the gentleman be so smitten that he thinks I am doing *him* a favor by accepting."

"You're a cold-blooded wench," Alys said with some awe. Now their relationship had slipped from guardianward to a more sisterly mode, and as usual she was amazed at the way Merry's mind worked. The older woman wasn't sure if the girl was brilliantly clear-sighted or merely endowed with more than her share of feminine wiles.

Wiles had been left out of Alys's makeup, more was the pity; perhaps her unwanted dimples were what she had been given instead. "I gather that you want this future husband to keep you on a pedestal?"

"Well, I shouldn't mind a low one." Merry chuckled. then she looked down at her hands, flexing the fingers as if inspecting her carefully groomed nails. "When I find the right man, I'll make sure he doesn't regret his choice." In a voice that for once was entirely serious, she added softly, "I do intend to be a very good wife, you know."

The words were like the last piece of a puzzle, and as she studied her ward's lovely heart-shaped face, Alys realized that what the girl really wanted was comfort and security. Having lost both parents and her adoptive mother by the time she was fifteen, it was hardly surprising that her ambitions were modest, practical ones rather than dreams of mad passion or social grandeur. Merry was a very sensible young lady who wanted to be cherished both physically and emotionally; surely she was unlikely to fall victim to the fleeting pleasures of a rake's casual, lethal charm.

Relieved by the insight, Alys stood. "Our guest should arrive soon. I presume you will wait here so you can make a grand entrance?"

"But of course." Merry laughed. "A new man in the neighborhood is an opportunity not to be wasted, even if he is rather stricken in years."

Even though she knew Meredith was teasing, Alys shook her head in disbelief as she went down to the drawing room to await her guest. *Stricken in years!* Davenport looked like he could outride, outfight, and outwench any man of any age in Dorsetshire. She hoped he didn't feel compelled to prove it.

7

Reggie hesitated for a moment with his hand on the knocker of Rose Hall, the steward's residence. He had accepted the dinner invitation because he thought that anything would be better than another evening alone in the big house, but now he wasn't quite so sure. Two young boys, an aspiring femme fatale, and a magnificent Amazon who wished him at Jericho were odd company for a man who usually socialized with hard-drinking sportsmen like himself. Well, too late to retreat now. He grasped the knocker and rapped firmly.

The little housemaid that answered had a round face that Reggie was beginning to recognize as typical Herald physiognomy. Her eyes widened at his height and she bobbed a quick curtsy, then wordlessly led him to the drawing room. It was a pleasant old house, having no more than half a dozen bedrooms, but it was comfortable and well-maintained. Reggie had regularly visited the kitchen as a child; his father's steward had had a cook gifted at making tarts, and Reggie had ingratiated himself in the manner of all small boys.

Miss Weston was waiting for him, and she rose at his arrival. With her height and natural dignity she looked like a queen, even in her extremely conservative dark brown dress. Reggie spent a moment wondering how she would look in Gypsy red, with her hair tumbling around her shoulders rather than in a no-nonsense coronet. He rather thought she would be splendid.

Smiling, she said, "I thought you might like a few minutes of peace before the boys join us. Would you like a sherry?"

Sherry was hardly his favorite drink, but since it was better than nothing, he accepted. As she went to pour two glasses, Reggie felt an insistent pressure on his shin and looked down to see a very large, very shaggy cat twining suggestively around his ankles. With a small sound of distaste, he stepped back, pursued by the cat, which seemed determined to be his best friend. Turning, his hostess saw his predicament immediately. "I'm sorry, I thought Attila was safely out of the way. He must have been lurking under one of the chairs."

She handed Reggie a goblet, then bent to scoop up her pet. Even for a woman as tall as Alys Weston, the beast was a very substantial armful, a patchwork of striped and white fur with great curving whiskers that framed an expression of supreme disdain. "I take it you don't like cats?"

"Not much," Reggie admitted. "They're sneaky, unreliable, and selfish."

"That's true," Alys said gravely, "and they have many other fine qualities as well."

For a moment he wasn't sure he had heard correctly; nothing earlier in the day had led him to believe that his steward numbered a sense of humor among her formidable virtues. But a suspicion of dimple showed in her right cheek; he had noticed earlier that it came out before the left one. Grinning, he said, "Perhaps I don't like cats because they're too much like me."

Laughing, she turned and took the cat to a side door and dumped him, protesting, on the other side. "Go on down to the kitchen, Attila. There must be something there to interest you." Closing the door before her pet could whisk back in, she turned to her guest. "So you're sneaky, unreliable, and selfish?"

"Oh, indubitably," he said, sipping at his sherry. "And I have many other fine qualities as well."

This time both dimples showed as she laughed and sat gracefully in one of the brocade-covered chairs. "What *are* your other fine qualities?" Then she paused, a stricken look on her face. "I'm sorry, I shouldn't have asked that."

"Because it's too personal a question, or because you're afraid of what I might consider a fine quality?" Reggie asked with interest, choosing a seat opposite his steward.

"The latter reason, of course," she said sweetly, then looked even more stricken at her unruly tongue.

Taking pity on her embarrassment, Reggie said, "Since you are not on duty, nothing you say can be held against you. Although I must say I prefer your insults to having you frown me down."

"Oh, Lord," she said with a guilty start. "Is that what I was doing all day?"

"Yes," he replied succinctly.

"Part of it is the eyebrows, you know," she said earnestly. "Even when I'm in a good mood, people often think I'm about to bite them."

"And when you're in a bad mood?"

"Oh, then they fly in all directions."

He said thoughtfully, "I suppose that looking fearsome is a useful trait, given the work you do. It can't have been easy to get the Strickland tenants and workers to accept your authority."

It was becoming clear to Alys that her new master was a very keen observer of humanity. "There have been problems," she acknowledged, "and it is not a simple matter in which one victory wins the war. They would take orders more easily if I owned the estate, but they don't quite approve of a female steward. Still, after four years the tenants and workers and I understand each other tolerably well."

His heavy-lidded eyes surveyed her. "I can understand their feelings. I don't approve of you myself." As she bridled, he raised one hand. "Oh, nothing personal, but it's a confounded nuisance that the A in A. E. Weston doesn't stand for Albert or Angus. Actually," he said, his voice serious, "if you value your reputation, you would be wise to look for another position."

Alys froze, the hand holding her sherry glass poised in midair halfway to her mouth. After drawing a deep breath to ensure that her voice would be steady, she asked flatly, "Are you discharging me?"

"No," he said, his long face grave, "just giving you some good advice."

Relaxing fractionally, she said in a freezing tone, "In

that case, just as you prefer to worry about your own dignity, leave me to worry about my own reputation."

"As long as you work for me, your reputation will be affected by mine, no matter how blameless your behavior," he pointed out. "When people hear that I have a female steward, they will chuckle knowingly and assume you're my mistress, especially when it is discovered that you are young and attractive."

Alys's face colored with embarrassment and she stared down into her glass at the amber liquid. She was unsure whether it was the bold assertion that she might be taken for his mistress, or the totally unlooked-for compliment. Glancing up, she eyed him suspiciously, wondering if he was mocking her, but Davenport seemed perfectly serious. "I am no green girl who must always be above the merest hint of suspicion," she said stiffly, "and I am well known in the neighborhood. It's unlikely the local people will assume I have suddenly become lost to all propriety."

"Well, you might not be concerned about your reputation, but I am about mine," he retorted. "Believe it or not, I have every intention of behaving circumspectly. Strickland is my home now. It always has been, really."

He studied his nearly empty glass as if fascinated by the remaining sherry. "I have no desire to offend everyone in Dorsetshire."

"So you'll save your outrageousness for London?"

"Perhaps," he said. "Or perhaps I will give it up entirely. Being outrageous all the time is a confounded amount of work." His words were light, but as he spoke, Reggie realized that his vague thoughts of the last few days had crystallized into a decision. It was time to put down the roots he had always yearned for; to stop filling his idle hours with gambling and drinking and wenching. In short, it was time to grow up—before it was too late.

He glanced up to see that his steward was scrutinizing him closely, as if she sensed that his words were not casual, and was wondering what they implied for her. Both the brown and the gray eye were bright and individually attractive; though the contrast between them was startling, it exactly suited her. As a bonus, she had the longest eyelashes he had ever seen. Whoever had nick-named her Lady Alys was perceptive; Miss Weston was not at all like the common run of females. While honor compelled him to warn her off, he was glad that she showed no desire to leave Strickland. It was true that her sex was a complication, but he admired her competence and integrity, and enjoyed her occasional flashes of barbed wit.

Besides, she was the best-looking steward he had ever seen.

The silence had drawn on, and now she broke it to say with an air of innocence, "I suppose that outrageousness is boring once it has been mastered. Trying to be respect-able should present all kinds of interesting new challenges."

"It will certainly have the charm of novelty," he agreed. Then his mouth quirked into a half-smile. "It does seem a pity to deprive high-sticklers of the pleasure of con-demning me, but there are always new young rascals coming along to create scandal-broth."

She tilted her head to one side consideringly. "You mean that you became a rake as a sort of public service?"

"Exactly so. Virtue needs vice for contrast." He smiled wickedly, wondering if he could ruffle her feathers. She was very attractive when she forgot her dignity. "Good and evil are completely dependent on each other—even God himself needs Lucifer more than he needs his bands of well-behaved angels who never put one wing astray."

She gazed wide-eyed into space, considering his words, but her expression was arrested rather than shocked. "I'm not sure whether that is heresy or philosophy."

"What's the difference? Heresy is just philosophy that society doesn't approve of," he said lazily. Really, Miss Weston was showing a much more flexible mind than his first impression of her had led him to expect.

Before the theological waters could grow any murkier, the door opened and Meredith floated into the room. Reggie rose at her entrance. The girl really was very lovely; what made her even more attractive was the impression she conveyed that she didn't take herself too seriously. As he bowed over her hand, he wondered what Julian Markham would think of her; he'd have to invite his young friend down for a visit.

Lady Alys gave Meredith a glass of sherry and refilled Reggie's and they exchanged commonplaces for a few minutes until the two Spenser boys entered, dressed in company best and bursting with curiosity. Reggie rose to meet them. The degree of excitement on their well-scrubbed faces was a reminder of how quiet life in the country was, and how seldom new people arrived to provide diversion. If he really intended to make his primary residence at Strickland, it would be an enormous change from the ceaseless variety of London. But then, it had been a long time since mere variety had afforded much pleasure.

Peter was an attractive stripling, his brown hair and blue-gray eyes a contrast to his blond siblings. The height and starch of his shirt points and the complicated folds of his cravat showed aspirations to dandyism, but for the moment he contented himself with a handshake and a polite, "It's a pleasure to meet you, Mr. Davenport. I've heard a great deal about you."

Before Reggie had time to consider the implications of that, William, seven and effervescent, skipped the preliminaries to say enthusiastically, "That stallion of yours is a prime 'un, sir."

Reggie shook the small hand, which was not quite as well-scrubbed as the round face. "Yes, I think Bucephalus is the finest horse I've ever had," he agreed. "He has speed, style, and endless bottom." After a moment's thought he added, "He also has a chancy disposition; keep your distance unless I'm around. He broke the arm of one admirer who got too close, and he won't let anyone but me ride him."

If he had been better versed in the ways of small boys, Reggie would have been suspicious of the gleam in William's eye. However, the little housemaid entered to announce that dinner was served and the exchange slipped his mind as the party adjourned to the dining room.

While it was quite unlike any other dinner party Reggie had ever attended, it was not without amusement. Conversation was general around the table, and everyone, even young William, was accorded the courtesy of a hearing. Topics included local events, literature, and the boys' progress in their lessons, and it was clear that the young Spensers were all intelligent and well-educated.

Reggie concentrated on the plain but well-cooked meal, and observed the family dynamics. And it was a family, even though the relationship was not one of blood. Alys was the center around which the three young people circled, gently and humorously guiding the conversation, monitoring William's table manners, listening with total attention when one of them spoke. The Spensers were indeed very lucky, and Reggie's respect for his steward increased again.

The meal had progressed to the sweet course when Peter, who had been covertly glancing at Reggie, finally overcame his diffidence to ask, "Is it really true that you once wagered a thousand guineas that you could ride a hundred and sixty miles in fifteen hours, and shoot forty brace of grouse at the midpoint of the trip?"

Considerably startled, Reggie said, "Good Lord, has that story made its way this far south? That happened in Scotland, years ago."

"You mean you actually did it?" Peter asked again, a look of delighted awe on his face.

"Yes, I did," Reggie acknowledged. "One of my odder wagers, but not quite as foolish as it sounds. The actual terms of the bet allowed twenty-four hours, which gave me some leeway in case the grouse were elusive."

Not content with this episode, Peter said eagerly, "And you won a midnight coach race to Brighton?"

"Well, it was midnight when we left. I reached Brighton about four in the morning," Reggie said in a bemused voice.

There was worse to come. His eyes round with incipient hero worship, Peter said, "And you actually backed your mistress in a race against the champion jockey, and won?"

His eyes flicking to the other members of the party, Reggie said dampeningly, "This is not the time or place to discuss my misspent youth."

Peter was mildly chastened by the reproof, but ecstatic

at Reggie's implication that they were two men together, protecting the tender sensibilities of the women and children. Amused by the lad's blissful expression, Alys raised her eyebrows slightly. Remembering how fragile a young man's pride was, Reggie frowned at her, forbidding any comments. With a suggestion of a smile, she rose and said that it was time for William to retire to the nursery. After a brief battle of wills, which she won, William withdrew and the older members of the party adjourned to the drawing room. While Reggie thought wistfully of the joys of a bottle of port, staying at table to drink with a fifteen-year-old boy seemed inappropriate.

He had intended to return home soon after dining, but found himself lingering. It had been a very long time since he had observed the interplay of a happy family, and he found that he enjoyed it. With her combination of beauty, wit, and blithe good nature, Meredith would be a sensation in London. A pity that her birth was so mundane; if she were properly launched, she would have all the eligible young men in London clustered at her feet.

Peter must be more of a concern for his guardian; he was on the verge of adulthood, unsure of himself, and ripe for hero worship. Clearly he was fascinated with their guest's checkered past and asked eagerly about several episodes Reggie himself had half-forgotten. Heaven only knew where the boy got his information. His admiring inquisition was damned uncomfortable, but Reggie, whose ability to wither pretensions was legendary, found himself unwilling to snub the boy; he remembered too clearly what it was like to be fatherless.

Merry had just been persuaded to sit down at the pianoforte when the housemaid entered the drawing room with a clerical gentleman at her heels. Alys glanced up, stifling an oath. She should have realized that Junius Harper might pay a call; he was at Rose Hall almost as many evenings as at the vicarage. Junius was a very worthy man, she reminded herself, high-minded and well-educated, with a genuine interest in the welfare of his flock. He had been an invaluable ally to Alys in most of her reformist projects. He was also, alas, sometimes a self-righteous prig.

Rising, Alys said, "Good evening, Junius. I imagine you have not yet met Reginald Davenport, the new owner of Strickland. Mr. Davenport, Junius Harper has been rector of All Souls for almost four years now."

The vicar was a tall, full-bodied man of undistinguished features and thinning brown hair. Though still in his early thirties, he moved with a studied dignity which made him appear older than his years, but which would suit him very well if he ever became a bishop. After sketching a bow to Alys and Meredith and nodding at Peter, he turned to the newcomer. Davenport had risen from his chair and was offering his hand. Refusing to take it, Junius said in accents of deep foreboding, "Surely you are not *the* Reginald Davenport?"

"I suppose I am. At least, I don't know of any others," her employer said pleasantly, his hand still out.

A look of revulsion on his moonlike face, the vicar said in freezing accents, "I have heard of you, sir, and Strickland has no need of such as you."

Davenport dropped his hand, and his expression changed and hardened. Gone was the quiet, amiable gentleman who had watched the young Spensers with an indulgent eye; as Alys watched, his face fell into the practiced lines of a sneer and his weight shifted, so that he was lightly poised on the balls of his feet. It was a fighter's stance, and she saw that he was prepared for whatever might come. His voice harsh, he said, "Oh, do you propose to ban me from my own property?"

"Would that I could!" Junius drew in his breath, his hazel eyes glittering as his black-clad form expanded like a pouter pigeon's. "Unfortunately, English law does not go anywhere near far enough in the regulation of morals. However, I can say with confidence that the right-thinking people of Dorset will not tolerate your duels, raking, and debauchery. There is no place for you here, sir—you will be an outcast. Better that you return to London at once and leave the good souls of Strickland to Miss Weston and myself."

"Good Lord, Junius, leave me out of this," Alys said with exasperation. She was just beginning to relax around her new employer, and was loath to have him think she shared the vicar's intolerant views.

Ignoring the interjection, Davenport kept his attention on his antagonist, saying with a cynical gleam in his light blue eyes, "If you think the good souls of the neighborhood will cut a man who has property, money, and influence, you know precious little of the world, Mr. Harper."

"When the full story of your licentious ways is known, even money and property will not suffice to buy your way into favor," the vicar said flatly, his eyes narrowing into angry slits.

"Oh? You are well-informed about my licentious ways?" was the drawled reply. "You must spend a good deal of time reading the scandal sheets. Hardly the most elevating material for a man of God."

Davenport's tone was deliberately provocative, and his opponent took the challenge. The two men were face-to-face, no more than four feet apart, and Alys wondered with clinical detachment if they would come to blows in her drawing room. When Junius spoke again, there was a hint of a snarl in his mellifluous voice. "I have influential relatives, sir, among the highest levels of society. Your name is a byword among them for every kind of low behavior. Your mistresses, your gambling—"

Davenport interrupted, saying in shocked accents, "You forget yourself, Vicar. Remember, there are ladies present."

Indeed, Meredith and Peter were watching in fascination from their respective seats. While Junius flushed at having been caught in unseemly behavior, Alys glanced at her wards and said in a voice that brooked no opposition, "Both of you, out, *now*."

Casting regretful looks over their shoulders, her wards departed, probably to paste their ears against the door. Still, Alys felt she had done her duty by them. She could hardly leave her guests herself, could she? If she were present, there was less likelihood of violence being done.

Beside, she didn't want to miss the end of the confrontation; seeing a saint and a sinner square off together had all the morbid fascination of a carriage wreck.

Raising her voice, she said, "May I offer you gentlemen a glass of port?" Without waiting for a reply, she
went and poured three generous glasses, thrusting two
into the hands of the combatants. She briefly considered
intervening between the two men, but decided that it
would be the better part of valor to let them settle
matters on their own; she might end up like a bone
between two mongrels if she interfered. Resigned to
letting the altercation take its course, she subsided into a
chair and took a rueful swig from her own goblet.

Casually sipping his port, Davenport seemed to be
getting more relaxed as his opponent became more agitated. In a conversational tone the rake asked, "Perhaps
you should list the varieties of low behavior for me, in
case I have missed any. I should hate to ruin my record
for vice through ignorance or lack of imagination."

Furious, Junius spat out, "You mock me, but God will
not be mocked. Do not the faces of the three men you
have killed in duels haunt your dreams?"

Cocking his head to one side, Davenport said thoughtfully, "Surely it is more than three. Let me think a
moment . . ." He pondered, then said with an air of
discovery, "Ah, you must not have heard about the one
in Paris last year. You really must try harder to keep up,
Mr. Harper. We rakes don't rest on our laurels, you
know. Wickedness requires constant effort."

Alys almost choked with suppressed laughter. Her employer was the picture of calm reason, while the self-
appointed guardian of public morality appeared on the
verge of an apoplexy. His teeth audibly grinding, Junius
Harper said, "Would that you had been prosecuted for
dueling, as you deserve!"

"When even cabinet ministers duel, it's hard to get a
conviction," Davenport said sympathetically. "Besides,
while I've lost count of how many duels I've been in, I've
never actually killed someone who didn't deserve it."

Unable to find a suitable riposte in the face of such
effrontery, the vicar abandoned dueling for a topic nearer
to his heart. "They say that you own a brothel in London."

Arching his dark brows in surprise, Davenport said,
"You *are* well-informed. However, it's only a partial

ownership. I'm a . . ."—he grinned maliciously—"sleeping partner, you might say."

Junius gasped at the double entendre, then said furiously, "Don't think you can kidnap our innocent country girls to supply the vile needs of your whorehouse, or ravish them so they must flee their homes from shame."

"My, you do have a lurid opinion of me." Davenport drank half of his port off. His voice was still casual, but the tight grip of his fingers on the goblet stem showed the strain of controlling himself in the face of this attack. "I don't recall ever ravishing anyone, though. I'm sure I'd remember, unless I was too drunk, and then I'd be incapable of ravishing."

His fury barely leashed, the vicar barked, "You'll burn in hell, Davenport, for eternity. Does that mean nothing to you?"

"Well, I've always had my doubts about heaven and hell," Davenport said genially. "Still, if they exist, I'll be better off in the fire, since all my friends will be there. It might even be a pleasant change after a lifetime of English weather."

"Bah, you are beneath contempt!" Junius shook with rage. "I despise you and your whoring, your lying, cheating ways. I—"

The rest of the diatribe was lost forever. Davenport's right hand shot out and wrapped around Junius's neck, the strong fingers tight against the nape and his long, hard thumb pressing the windpipe with carefully calculated strength. As the vicar gasped for breath, too shocked to fight back, Davenport's gaze locked with his opponent's, his eyes as cold and hard as his sharply enunciated words. "I do not cheat. Neither do I lie. So far, I have never killed a vicar in my blood-drenched career, but if you persist in slandering me, I will be tempted to make an exception. Do I make myself clear?"

Junius's horrified reaction must have been satisfactory, because Davenport dropped his hand. Draining off the last of his port, he turned to Alys and said courteously, as if he hadn't just been involved in a near-brawl, "It is time I took my leave. Thank you for a most pleasant evening. If it's not inconvenient I would like to meet you in your office at nine in the morning."

At her nod, he set his empty goblet down and bowed twice, first with a distinctly mocking air to the vicar, and then more deeply to Alys. As he straightened up, his light eyes caught hers for a moment, but she couldn't interpret his remote expression. Was he blaming her for this unpleasant scene? Impossible to tell. Then he turned on his heel and left.

Junius was left staring at the closed door, stupefaction on his face. Ever practical, Alys rose and poured another pair of drinks, this time of brandy, and took one to her guest, pressing him lightly into a chair. A sip of brandy brought healthier color to his face, and he raised his eyes incredulously to his hostess. "the audacity of the man! That he should speak so to a man of God, that he actually threatened physical violence . . ." He shook his head in disbelief, then drank more brandy.

After a critical examination of her guest, Alys decided that he would survive the experience and chose a nearby chair for herself. "Well, you did provoke him, Junius," she said candidly. "He behaved in a perfectly gentlemanlike fashion until you started insulting him."

"Bah, that rakehell is no gentleman! that is the whole point. That you should permit such a man under the same roof as Miss Spenser . . ." After a moment's thought he said more temperately, "Forgive me I shouldn't blame you. It is not to be expected that a respectable, godly woman like you would be aware of his evil reputation."

"I'm no cloistered innocent, Junius," she said crisply. "I have a fair idea of what rumor says about Mr. Davenport. However, he's my employer and I must work with him. More than that"—inspiration struck and a pious note entered her voice—"remember that the Bible says, 'Judge not, lest ye be judged.' Who among us is qualified to cast the first stone? *I* certainly am not."

Even though she was mixing her quotes, the words were very effective. The vicar paused, his face stricken, before he finally said in a halting voice, "How noble is your spirit, Alys, how great your charity. Once more you are right and I am most grievously wrong. We are all sinners in the eyes of the Lord."

Junius brooded for a moment on his sins, but his moment of humility ebbed rapidly and he continued with a touch of acid, "Even the Lord would admit that some are greater sinners than others, and Davenport must be one of the worst."

"Perhaps he intends to reform his way of life," Alys suggested. Some of Davenport's statements today had hinted as much. "If so, it is our duty as Christians to encourage him."

A snort of disbelief greeted her statement, and Junius stared dourly into his brandy. If William had behaved that way, Alys would have reprimanded him for sulking, but she could hardly scold the vicar. Denied that outlet, she reminded herself how helpful he had been in organizing the school, how he had used the church poor money for those who truly needed it rather than lining his own pockets, and the numerous other ways he had helped make Strickland the thriving community it was. When the vicar had first come to All Souls, he had been shocked to learn that a woman was the most important person in his new parish, and it was to his credit that he had overcome his initial disapproval and accepted her as a near-equal.

In spite of his occasional self-righteousness, they had worked well together over the years; so well, in fact, that he sometimes hinted at the possibility of a closer partnership. Alys ignored his hints; quite apart from the fact that she could not imagine a lifetime spent with a man of blameless rectitude, she knew that Junius had a very inaccurate picture of her true character, and that he would not approve of the real Alys.

Besides, while Junius's lofty mind said that she would be a suitable God-fearing partner for a man of the cloth, it was young, golden, frivolous Meredith that his eyes followed hungrily when he called at Rose Hall. Like many a man before him, the vicar's higher and lower selves were not in agreement; Alys had once given him a copy of the writings of Saint Augustine for Christmas, but of course he hadn't seen the joke.

Junius broke the lengthening silence to say abruptly, "One of the men he killed in a duel was the husband of a woman who had run away to Davenport. He killed the man, then refused to marry his mistress, even though she was pregnant."

Alys inhaled, shocked in spite of herself. "She was carrying his child, he shot her husband, and he wouldn't marry her?" she repeated in disbelief.

The vicar nodded with satisfaction, pleased to have pierced Alys's tolerance. "That is an example of the 'gentleman' you are defending. The woman involved was ruined, of course. Davenport was cut in polite society, but suffered no real retribution for his wickedness."

Alys had long since learned that every story had at least two sides, but it was hard to imagine anything that would justify her employer's callousness in this case. Wondering why it was so important to her to think well of him, she said, "I think Mr. Davenport is here to stay, Junius. Wouldn't it be better to hope for the best about him, rather than assume the worst?"

He glanced up, then nodded glumly. "Once more, you are wise. We owe it to the good souls of the parish to do what we can to ameliorate that libertine's influence."

Intent on conflict rather than reconciliation, he missed the sense of her words. She also wished irritably that Junius would stop talking about "good souls," since the individuals in question were very much alive, opinionated, and capable of drawing their own conclusions. A vicar might have a flock, but that didn't make the inhabitants of Strickland sheep. However, it seemed a poor moment to take him to task, so Alys bent her efforts to mollifying his hurt dignity.

Her private hope was that her new employer wouldn't reform too much; no matter how disgraceful his past, she rather liked him the way he was. And while his behavior to the vicar had been quite reprehensible, there was no denying that it was also very, very amusing. No doubt if Alys was as good a person as Junius thought, she would have found no humor in the confrontation.

Her guest took his leave a few minutes later, and after securing the house and checking that Peter and Meredith had retired to their rooms, Alys decided to make an early night of it herself. Spring was her busiest time of the year, and tomorrow the laborers would begin setting potatoes, one of the estate's most important crops.

But sleep eluded her as she lay alone in her wide bed, a shaft of moonlight lying across her, her blankets twisted from her restless tossing. It was one of the great ironies of Alys Weston's life that she, who was too tall and alarming to attract any serious suitors, adored men. She liked talking to them, and seeing how their minds and personalities differed from women's. She enjoyed watching them, and took great, if surreptitious, pleasure in the powerful male bodies of the laborers who worked for her.

And sometimes, like now, her rest was troubled by hot, fierce dreams of what it would be like to lie in a man's arms, to give herself as freely as the wildest creature in the forest. If Junius Harper could see into her mind to her secret yearnings, he would be shocked to the core that a respectable female could be so shameless. But then, she was not really respectable, though she pretended to be. As foolish and undignified as lust was, she was unable to deny its existence in her. If she had been born with half of Meredith's beauty, she might have become a great wanton.

No, not a wanton; with a romanticism even more foolish than her inappropriate desires, her deepest, most carefully hidden wish was to have one true love, a man who would love and cherish only her. In return, she would give heart, mind, soul, and body; oh, yes, most definitely her body. It was humiliating to admit that she was as idiotic as any sixteen-year-old girl who read the kind of novels Junius deplored, but Alys refused to be less than honest with herself. Had she not been such a hopeless romantic, Randolph's casual rejection could never have devastated her as it had, and she would never have turned her back on her heritage.

Instead, she buried her passions behind a facade of rigid propriety. It was bad enough to be a wanton at heart, but she'd be damned if she would let herself appear ludicrous as well. She had no doubt that most people would find it deliciously amusing that a great horse like her pined for male attention as much as any accredited beauty.

Of course her fantasies currently revolved around Reginald Davenport; on a purely animal level, he was the most attractive man she had ever met, his lean athletic body radiating sexual authority. His dark coloring gave him a faintly exotic air, like a gypsy or a pirate, and she was intrigued by the expressive way his light blue eyes could range from warm teasing to icy mockery.

Blast it, she must stop doing this, Alys thought with disgust, trying to banish Davenport's too-vivid image. As she became more accustomed to his intense masculinity, her reaction would surely moderate; she hoped so, because even fantasizing about him held an element of danger. She might feel that she and her employer shared some kindred feeling, but in truth he was a stranger, a man who had killed other men, one who was unpredictable and dissolute. She should be grateful that to Davenport she was just an employee, scarcely more than a servant; he seemed hardly aware that she was a woman.

Alys rolled over on her stomach, feeling the faint roughness of the sheets against her bare legs as her nightgown twisted up around her thighs. In a burst of frustration she balled one hand into a fist and pounded it into her pillow. It wasn't fair. *It bloody wasn't fair!*

She wasn't even sure what she cursed, and after a few moments her anger ebbed away, leaving her depressed and resigned. She was luckier than most people; having walked away from position and fortune, she had now achieved comfort and the satisfaction of work well done. She had the respect of those close to her, and the love of the three young people she had taken in. Indeed, they gave her much more than she gave them. Given those blessings, it was hardly seemly to curse the fact that the Creator had deemed her unworthy of a mate.

Rolling onto her side, Alys pulled a pillow tight and wrapped her arms around it, as if it could ease the empty ache inside of her. The pillow was a poor substitute for a hard male body, but it was the best she would ever have.

8

Reggie was in a vile humor when he left the steward's house; he gave himself credit for not disassembling the bombastic cleric and leaving him in pieces on Miss Weston's carpet. Considering the pleasure he had always taken in setting people's backs up, it was surprising how irritated he was by what had happened. For all his wicked reputation, he himself would never have created an embarrassing scene on a social occasion, in front of women and young people. It took a respectable person like Junius Harper to behave so badly.

His mood was not improved when the only drink he could find in the Strickland pantry was a bottle of sherry. Quite apart from the fact that he was not partial to sherry, the quantity was nowhere near enough to drown the effects of the vicar. Swearing, he made a mental note to ask Mrs. Herald why she had not placed the large order for spirits that he had given her.

It didn't take long to finish the bottle, and he briefly weighed going out to a tavern, but the hour was late and country alehouses wouldn't keep London hours. Besides, much as he wanted a decent drink, he didn't fancy the picture of himself storming around rural Dorset looking for one.

By three in the morning, as he tossed sleepless and still angry, he was wishing he had forsaken dignity and found a tavern. The house seemed enormous in its emptiness, the creaks of floorboards and windows echoing through the hollow rooms and halls. Mac Cooper should arrive tomorrow, thank God, and servants would be moving in over the next few days. That should make a difference.

His temper didn't improve until the next morning, when he met his steward in her office and found her

standing in front of her desk, staring at a list of tasks with
a small, distracted frown. She was wearing a pair of very
well-fitted buff pantaloons, and the sight of her glorious
legs cheered him immensely. Instead of the usual coronet, this morning her shining hair fell down her back in a
single thick braid.

Miss Weston glanced up at his entrance, and after a
brief exchange of greetings he said, "Sorry to keep you
from your work, but this will take only a few minutes."

She perched on the front edge of her desk and pulled
the braid over her shoulder, toying with the end nervously. Before he could speak, she said hesitantly, not
meeting his eyes, "I'm sorry about what happened last
night. Mr. Harper is a very worthy and honorable man,
but . . ." Her voice trailed off as she searched for the
right word.

Reggie had been prowling around the office, but now
he turned toward her and suggested, "But he's a pomp-
ous ass?"

Her mismatched eyes gleamed with amusement before
she said repressively, "I was going to say that his high
ideals and blameless conduct lead him to be somewhat
less than tolerant."

"Tactfully put, my dear." The endearment slipped out
without his conscious thought. Wondering what it would
take to persuade the dimples to appear, he continued,
"Is his blameless conduct a result of his high ideals, or
the fact that he has never been tempted?"

This time a smile almost escaped her. She lifted her
head and tossed the braid back over her shoulder, saying,
"Junius is not entirely free of temptation—when Meredith is around, he gets a . . . a hungry expression. But I
think most normal human vices don't interest him."

"Sounds like a dashed dull dog to me." As he stood in
front of the bookcase, he pulled out a copy of *Every Man
His Own Farrier*, the horseman's bible, and idly leafed
through it.

"Well, he is rather," she admitted in a burst of candor,
"but he has done a great deal of good in the parish. He
takes his clerical responsibilities far more seriously than
most men in his position."

"And of course that responsibility includes condemning the ungodly, of which I am a preeminent example." He turned and leaned his powerful shoulders casually against the bookcase, his voice wry.

His steward gave him a long, level look. "From what I've seen, the wickedest thing about you is your sense of humor, which is quite reprehensible."

He chuckled. "I won't deny it. Officious idiots certainly bring out the worst in me, and your Mr. Harper is a superb example of the breed." With an edge of malicious satisfaction he added, "I wonder if he has yet realized that I now control the living of All Souls. Politeness on his part would have been a good deal more politic."

Her eyes widened. "Good Lord, I never thought of that, and I don't suppose Junius has either. He received the benefice because his grandfather had some connection with the late Lord Wargrave, when the earl was the apparent owner." Fearing the answer, she hesitated before asking, "Will you dismiss him?"

Her employer's smile became downright diabolical. "There's an old adage along the lines that forgiveness is the ultimate revenge, and indifference the ultimate insult. Ignoring Harper will provoke him far more than ousting him from the living. Besides, he seems like the sort who would thrive on martyrdom."

Alys stared at him for a moment, not quite believing what she heard, then gave way to the laughter she had been trying to suppress ever since Davenport had come in. Shaking her head in appreciation, she finally regained enough sobriety to gasp, "You are the most impossible man! And you're quite right, you know. His influential relations would soon find him another living, and it would afford Junius no end of satisfaction to be persecuted for his righteousness."

She stopped and straightened up, saying guiltily, "I shouldn't have said either of those things. I'm sorry."

"Never apologize for telling the truth, my dear. I undoubtedly *am* impossible," he said with a sardonic glint. After shelving the farriery book, he crossed to a chair and sat down in front of the desk, stretching out his long legs and crossing one beautiful boot over the other in a negligent manner that would have made a valet shudder.

Alys watched him, momentarily mesmerized by the fluent, athletic grace of his movements, remembering her fantasies of the night before. Devoutly hoping that Davenport was not as good at reading her as he seemed to be at understanding other people, she circled the desk to sit in her own chair. "I don't think stewards are usually addressed as 'my dear.' "

"But 'Miss Weston' is too formal, and 'Lady Alys' is downright intimidating," he said, raising his dark brows in mock question. "What should I call you?"

"Well, not 'my dear.' That will give rise to exactly the kind of gossip you said you wanted to avoid. I suppose 'Alys' would be all right." It would be unusual to have her employer call her by her Christian name, but it was difficult to be formal with Reginald Davenport.

"How about 'Allie'?" he suggested.

"Short for 'Alys'?"

He grinned. "Actually, I was thinking of it as short for 'alley cat.' You scratch like one."

"Mr. Davenport," she said frostily, while trying to repress a smile, "you are incorrigible."

"I hope so—I work very hard at it." His smile invited her to join him. "By the way, try calling me 'Reggie.' It may cure you of being respectful. It is quite impossible to take a Reggie seriously—the name implies either villainy or fatuousness."

"And of the two, you prefer villainy?"

"Of course," he said, brows raised. "Wouldn't you?"

"I daresay I would." Giving up the struggle to keep a straight face, she laughed. "In my blameless and well-organized existence, I have never run into anyone like you before. Forgive me if I don't know quite how to react."

"It's simple enough. Always tell me the truth, no matter how appalling." In spite of the lightness of his tone, she sensed that he was speaking in dead earnest. "And remember that a life without laughter is hardly worth living."

His words were surprisingly jarring. She had a sense of

humor; what person would ever admit to *not* having one? She enjoyed a good joke, she laughed with the children— but it was true that over the years, laughter had always been something that came after serious work was done. It was the reward, not an integral part of life. As a child, she had been constantly drilled about her future respon- sibilities; as an adult, sheer survival demanded that duty always come before pleasure. He must find her as dull as the vicar. Her mouth dry, Alys said, "You must think I am quite a sobersides."

"Yes—but not hopelessly so," The light blue eyes had a warmer glow before he said abruptly, "I want you to think about what improvements you'd like to see at Strickland—equipment, buildings, stock, whatever. I've some ideas of my own, but I want to hear your suggestions."

"You want to reinvest the income in the estate?" she asked, her surprise all too obvious.

"Did you think that I was going to take the income and gamble it all away?" His deep voice was cool now.

Well, he'd said to tell the truth, no matter how appall- ing. "It was a logical assumption," she admitted. "A good part of your cherished reputation concerns gambling."

"I always gambled to make money, Allie." He shrugged. "Now that I *have* a good income, I don't need to play deeply."

She tilted her head and considered that before saying reflectively, "I usually think of gamesters as losing for- tunes. But if there are losers, there must also be winners."

"Exactly, and I have usually been one of the winners." His half-smile was rueful. "I'll admit there have been times when I've been badly dipped because of a long run of bad luck, or because I was too drunk or pigheaded to quit, but over the last twenty years of gaming, I've won thousands of pounds more than I've lost. That's what has bridged the gap between my allowance and my style of living. Vice isn't cheap, you know."

Ignoring his last sentence, she propped her chin on her hand and studied him. "How did you manage to win so often?"

"Honestly, if that's what you're wondering."

Responding to the hard edge in his voice, she said, "I didn't doubt it, Reggie."

"Sorry," he said with a trace of apology. "I've won so consistently that my honesty has been questioned more than once. In fact, the trick to winning is to avoid games that are purely chance. A man who restricts himself to forms of gambling that require skill should be able to win more than he loses. At least, he will if he develops the skill."

She leaned forward and crossed her arms on the desk. "Could you elaborate? This sounds interesting."

"Well, take hazard as an example. It's a dice game and the object is to throw certain number combinations. Since some combinations are easier to achieve than others, a knowledge of the mathematical odds makes it possible for an astute player to do very well, especially if he hedges his bets." He grinned. "Am I losing you? You may take my word for it that most gamesters have neither the ability nor the desire to calculate odds, particularly not in the heat of play.

"And then there are the games where remembering the cards that have been played greatly improves your chances." He shrugged. "I have a good memory."

And also, she would guess, excellent judgment and nerves of steel. Intrigued by this glimpse into a masculine world, she asked, "What about the turf?"

He shook his head. "Very chancy. No matter how well a man knows horseflesh, there are too many variables, both in horses and in riders. I generally don't bet heavily on racing unless I'm riding or driving myself. Then if I lose, at least I know whom to blame."

"And you don't lose often." It was a statement, not a question.

"Losing is a bore, Allie. And I dislike boredom above all things." He stood now, looking down at her from his great height. "I'll leave you to your labors. Do they still do the sheep washing at the same pool in the stream, by the clump of beeches?"

She nodded. "As far as I know, the sheep have been washed there for centuries. Things don't change very fast in Dorset, you know."

"The land might not, but the people do," he said cryptically. Putting his hat on, he touched his fingers to the brim in a brief salute. "As I recall, the sheep have usually been gathered in by noon. I'll be there then."

Alys nodded again, then watched him leave. Shaking her head in bemusement, she looked at her list of tasks for the day without seeing it. She supposed it wasn't surprising that a rake would be physically attractive, nor that he would have charm. But who would have guessed that a rake would be so amusing?

Back at the manor house, Reggie sought out his housekeeper and in a few short, sharp words ensured that in the future there would always be an adequate supply of alcohol in the house, no matter what else was neglected. Then he went to his study and started to make plans. For years he had wanted to breed horses, mostly hunters, with the best trained for steeplechase racing. He had repressed the desire, since it was beyond his resources, but now his dream was within reach. Bucephalus would be the foundation; the stallion had superb bloodlines, incredible stamina and jumping ability, and speed that would do credit to a racehorse. Reggie had won the stallion at hazard, playing a nobleman who had no talent for calculating odds.

In the short term, the existing stables would be adequate, but new paddocks and training rings would be required, and as many good mares as he could afford. In the long run . . . His pen flew across the page, estimating costs, jotting questions to himself, laying out the outlines of what needed to be done.

He became totally absorbed, and hours passed unnoticed, so it was late morning when his concentration was broken by the entrance of one of the housemaids, a rosy young creature called Gillie. "Excuse me, sir, you have a visitor," she said nervously. Like all of the maids, she looked at him as if half-hoping, half-fearing that he would pounce on her. As one hand twisted the edge of her apron, she handed over a calling card.

Jeremy Stanton, Fenton Hall, Dorsetshire. It took only a moment to place the man who Mrs. Herald had said was his nearest maternal relation. Reggie stood and went to the hallway, where he found a slightly built distinguished gentleman with silver hair and shrewd gray eyes. Stanton smiled at him. "You may not remember me, Mr. Davenport, but I knew you when you were a child. I want to welcome you back to the neighborhood."

Reggie's brows furrowed for a moment in concentration; then an image clicked into place, followed by others. "Good God, Uncle Jerry! I'd forgotten your existence until now. How do you do, sir?" He offered his hand.

Stanton shook it heartily, his face pleased. "So you do remember. Of course, I'm not your uncle, but"—he paused and thought a moment—"cousin once removed. And your godfather."

"Whatever." Reggie waved his visitor into the drawing room. "It's good to see you again. May I offer you something?"

"Some tea would do nicely." Stanton glanced around the faded drawing room, his face reminiscent, then chose a chair. "I haven't been here in near thirty years now. The man who rented the house, Rogers, was a recluse and never received visitors."

After ringing for tea, Reggie paused a moment in the act of pouring himself some brandy from the new stock, another vivid image flashing across his mind—this very room, full of adults, dressed in black or wearing mourning bands. It must have been the funeral. Reggie had staggered down in his nightshirt, knees weak and head whirling. The coffins had been in a row by the windows. He had been near collapse when Stanton scooped him up and carried him upstairs, talking softly, then keeping him company while he cried himself to sleep.

He shoved the stopper into the decanter with unnecessary violence, then joined his visitor for a casual exchange of pleasantries. Jeremy Stanton had a sharp and well-informed mind, and it was a pleasure talking with him, but Reggie sensed that he was being weighed and judged. Measured against his father, perhaps? Or as a Stanton? Oddly, he realized that the old man's opinion mattered to him.

He must have passed inspection, because after half an hour Stanton asked, "Do you intend to stay in the district?"

"It's too soon to tell." Reggie shrugged. "I'm inclined that way, but I've only just arrived."

"We could use another magistrate," Stanton said tentatively.

Reggie stared at him. "Good God, are you suggesting I should be a justice of the peace? I'm not qualified in the least. In fact, there are those who would say you would be setting a fox to watch the hens."

The older man laughed. "In spite of your colorful past, you are amply qualified to be a magistrate. You're a principal landowner in the county and you come of a fine old local family. Most of what a justice does is common sense and simple fairness. I'm sure you could manage that."

Reggie found himself at a rare loss for words, not sure whether to be touched or amused at his cousin's vote of confidence. Yet as he thought, the idea of being a justice was not without appeal. Magistrates were the true local authorities, as involved with administering the Poor Law and fixing the roads as with judging lawbreakers. It might be interesting. Not yet willing to commit himself, he said, "The Lord Lieutenant of Dorsetshire might not agree to me."

"He'll agree to whomever I suggest," Stanton said peaceably. "He's been after me to find another justice for this age—we've been shorthanded at this end of the shire." Not giving Reggie a chance to object, he added, "I'll forward your name to him. Official confirmation should come back in two or three weeks."

Arching his brows sardonically, Reggie said, "Aren't you rushing your fences?"

Most men found that expression quelling, but Stanton was undeterred. With a quirked smile he said merely, "Am I?"

Reggie opened his mouth to say something caustic, then stopped. Hadn't he been thinking it was time to make some changes in his life? Becoming a part of the established order would certainly be a change. And he was arrogant enough to believe that he would make a capable magistrate. "No, I suppose you aren't," he admitted.

'Good.'' Stanton gave a satisfied nod. He frowned a little, then said slowly, "I'm surprised that you didn't return to Dorset earlier. I'd almost given up hope that you would.''

"You had that much interest in me?" Reggie was surprised, and moved. It had never occurred to him that anyone had cared about the departure of an eight-year-old boy.

"Of course. You are my cousin Anne's boy, your father was my friend." Stanton's voice was full of conviction. "This is where you belong."

Reggie was silent, thinking of that. Perhaps he did belong here; certainly he had belonged nowhere else since. He shook his head. "I really don't remember much about my childhood. Nothing at all before I was . . . oh, four or so. Only bits and pieces after." Which was odd, when he thought of it; in general, his memory was outstanding. But much of his early childhood seemed swathed in mists.

"Nothing before you were four? Interesting."

Stanton's eyes narrowed thoughtfully, and Reggie wondered about the significance of his words. "Is there anything I should remember?" he asked with an edge to his voice.

Stanton seemed about to answer, then changed his mind. "If there is, doubtless it will come back to you." Deliberately changing the subject, he said, "I was sorry you never wrote back to me, but not surprised. You were just a lad, and there were so many changes in your life. My own boys were never good correspondents. Still aren't," he added with a chuckle.

"Write back to you? I never received any letters from anyone," Reggie said, frowning.

Stanton looked surprised. "I sent you a letter every month for a year or so, then stopped when you never replied. I wrote to Wargrave Park, care of the Earl of Wargrave. Do you mean you never received any of them?"

Reggie swore, his language furiously fluent. When he had regained some measure of control, he said grimly,

"That's another mark to my guardian's account," then went on to explain how his uncle had withheld Strickland from him.

Stanton was shocked, and as furious as Reggie himself. "Good Lord, if I had had any idea that Wargrave was deliberately separating you from your mother's family, from your whole background, I'd have gone to Gloucestershire and brought you home. I was your godfather, but Wargrave was much more nearly related than I, so I didn't argue when he sent for you."

He made a sharp, angry gesture with one hand. "Your father had asked once if I would become guardian to his children if something happened to him and Anne, but he never got around to writing his will. Unfortunately."

Reggie said in surprise, "You would have challenged the Earl of Wargrave over me?"

"If I had known what was going on, of course," Stanton said, surprised in his turn. "You're family."

"The idea of family as helpful is new to me," Reggie said with desert dryness.

"With Wargrave as your guardian, I'm not surprised that you have a low opinion of relatives." Stanton shook his head sorrowfully. "I should have known there was a reason why you didn't write. You were always a considerate lad—your father was proud of how responsible you were. I should have tried harder to keep in touch, to find out how you were."

"Don't blame yourself too much. Who could have expected my uncle to be so determined to isolate me?" Reggie stood and offered Stanton his hand. "For what it's worth, I appreciate that you did try to keep in touch with me. You were a busy man, with your own responsibilities and family. There's a limit to what you could be expected to do for a distant relative."

Stanton stood also, taking his hand with a firmness that belied his silver hair. "I should have done more," he said simply. "But it's past mending. My wife asked if you could come to dinner Friday night. Will you be free?"

Another image clicked into place. A round, smiling face, placid in the midst of family chaos. "I'd be happy to come. I trust that Aunt Beth is well?"

"Elizabeth has some trouble getting around, but she's well enough otherwise. She'll be delighted to see you again. You were always a favorite of hers." Then, with a grin, "Don't be surprised if there is a single lady or two at the dinner table."

Reggie groaned. "Tell Aunt Beth that if that's the case, I may have a sudden attack of some disease that will require me to return home instantly."

"Well, perhaps I can keep her in check this time," Stanton offered, "but in the future, you're on your own."

The old man left Strickland with a sense of satisfaction. Over the years, he had kept a very close watch on Reginald Davenport's doings; even assuming that half of what was said about him was false, there had still been ample reason to worry. Stanton had called today fearing that there would be no trace of the bright, good-natured lad he remembered, that vice and dissipation had corrupted what had been so promising.

But now that they had talked, Stanton was sure that somewhere inside, in spite of outrageous fortune and a malicious guardian, Anne's son still existed. Oh, doubtless the boy had done things he shouldn't have, and it was likely that he suffered from his father's near-disastrous weakness, but there was still honor there, and humor. Get him involved in the community, encourage him to find a wife . . .

Full of plans, Stanton cracked the whip over his placid horse. He couldn't wait to get home and tell Elizabeth the conclusions he had formed.

After his guest left, Reggie found it impossible to concentrate on his future plans. Stanton's visit had released a whole whirl of memories, most of them happy ones. The Stantons and Davenports had been in and out of each other's homes all the time in the old days. The youngest Stanton boy had been a particular playmate of Reggie's; James was in India now, doing very well, according to his father.

When he thought about it, Reggie had realized one reason why he had suppressed so much of his childhood; as soon as his uncle had taken him in charge, Reggie had been packed off to school. In the fierce jungle of Eton, remembering a happy past that he could never return to would have weakened him, so he had tried not to think of what he had lost. He had been all too successful. But still, it was surprising that he remembered absolutely nothing from when he was very small.

His musings were interrupted by the arrival of Mac Cooper, looking dignified in spite of being covered with dust. Reggie looked up. "Am I glad to see you! Did you have any trouble?"

"Broken axle," Mac said laconically, accepting the glass of brandy his employer offered him. In general, servants and employers did not drink together, but the relationship between these two men was unusual in a number of ways.

Mac settled his wiry frame into a chair, sighing with satisfaction as he swallowed some brandy. "Quite a place you have here. Will we be staying awhile?"

"Permanently."

Mac's eyebrows shot up. "Not live in London?" he asked incredulously.

"Oh, I'd want to go up to town sometimes, but at the moment, I'm inclined to make my headquarters here." Reggie cleared his throat, then added gruffly, "I know you're city-bred. If you can't stand the country, I'll understand."

Mac gave him a look of intense disgust. "Did I say anything about leaving?"

"No," Reggie admitted, "but you've been here only ten minutes."

"If they have women and whiskey here, I'll manage."

"Don't worry, there's no shortage of either. Including," Reggie felt compelled to add, "the most extraordinary female I've ever met."

"In what way?" Mac asked with interest.

"Any number of ways. Her name is Alys Weston, and she happens to be my land steward."

"What!"

It was rare to see the imperturbable Mac startled; Reggie enjoyed giving a brief explanation of how his steward had reached her present position.

Mac shook his head in amazement, asking as an after-thought, "Besides being good at her work, is she pretty?"

Reggie thought of the strong, sculptured features, the tall, graceful body, the dimples he was learning to coax out, then shook his head. "Not pretty. Something a good deal more interesting than that."

9

Sheep washing was a communal affair, and neighboring flocks were included with Strickland's. As Reggie rode up into the heathlands at midday, even two hills away he heard the bleats of complaining sheep, punctuated by the occasional bark of a dog. A dammed stream formed the washing pool, and several thousand sheep were crowded together in the large fold as well-trained herd dogs paced restlessly around the stone walls. Close up, the baaing was cacophonous. A dozen or so men were clustered by the pool, as well as the unmistakable willowy form of Alys Weston in her work clothes. Reggie swung off his mount and tethered it, then joined the group by the stream bank.

Alys was in earnest conversation with a burly shepherd, but she glanced up at her employer's approach. "Mr. Davenport, this is Gabriel Mitford, Strickland's chief shepherd."

Reggie stared for a moment at the broad, muscular figure, then offered his hand with a slow smile. "We're acquainted."

Mitford nodded as they shook hands. "Aye." The shepherd's grip was powerful. "I'll be bound I can still best you at wrestling, two falls out of three."

Laughing, Reggie clapped him on the shoulder. "Don't count on it, Gabe. But if we have the energy after washing a couple of thousand sheep, we can give it a try."

"Only a damn fool would want to wash sheep," the shepherd said, his dour voice belied by the amused gleam in his eyes.

"It's not the first time I've been called a damned fool," Reggie agreed pleasantly.

A small chuckle escaped Alys Weston. Hastily arranging her face to sobriety, she was about to signal the workers to their places when one of the sheep dogs came galloping up with a stick and laid it at the new owner's feet. The animal was a rough-coated female, mostly black with white paws and band around the ribs, the white face marked with a clownish black mask. Davenport looked at the young dog in bemusement as she wagged her tail hopefully. "What kind of sheep dog wants to play fetch?"

Gabriel Mitford waved a disgusted hand at the animal. "A bad one. Been trying to train her. Only collie I ever had who wasn't born knowing how to herd. Couldn't even work ducks." He looked glumly at the dog, who rolled over and waved her white paws playfully in the air. "Going to have to put her down."

As if hearing that she was under sentence of death, the collie jumped to her feet and licked Reggie's hand. Automatically scratching the shaggy head, he received a lolling-tongued grin of pleasure in return. "Any chance someone might want her for a pet? She's a friendly creature."

"Hill folk don't want an animal that can't work," the shepherd said, gesturing the dog away. Ears drooping, the collie headed back to the milling group of herd dogs.

Alys raised her arm and signaled the men to their positions so work could begin. Reggie wore old, rugged clothing, and now he pulled off his coat and boots and tossed them aside before joining Gabriel Mitford and a shepherd named Simms in the icy thigh-deep water. Aided by two dogs, a lad drifted sheep out of the fold two or three at a time. Alys and an ancient, wizened shepherd did a quick check on heads, mouths, and ears, sending animals to a smaller fold if they needed medical attention.

Sheep that passed inspection were wrestled into the water by three muscular young fellows. It was a process the sheep much resented, and they protested long and loud as they kicked and fought their fate. Once forced into the water, they floated easily and Reggie pulled one over to him. In spite of their staggering stupidity, he'd always liked sheep, though it had been a grave disappointment when he first hugged one as a child and learned that the soft-looking fleece was dense and dirty.

There was a trick to flipping a sheep onto its back and scrubbing its belly without being kicked by a flailing hoof, and Reggie watched Gabriel before he tried it himself. The outraged ewe managed to catch him in the ribs with a kick; he'd have a ferocious bruise there later. Still, he managed to clean her underside without drowning either of them. Then he turned the animal upright and squeezed the thick wool in large handfuls, forcing out most of the dirt and grease.

Pointing his indignant victim toward the other side of the stream, he released her, and the fleece got a good rinse as the ewe swam across the pool. On the far bank she scrambled out of the water and was rewarded with a handful of hay and guided into another fold to dry in the late-spring sunshine. By the end of the day most of the lambs would be weaned by the simple fact that they could no longer identify their mothers' scents.

A good washer could clean a hundred sheep an hour, and clearly Gabriel and Simms were two of the best. It took time for Reggie to pick up the technique, but soon he was working at a creditable rate. Within ten minutes of beginning, he was as wet as any of the sheep, and with an inward chuckle he wondered if any of his London acquaintance would recognize him. The work was satisfyingly physical, and the result—a clean sheep—was something that could be immediately appreciated.

The workers settled into a steady rhythm with little conversation. Every half-hour or so a pewter tankard of hot water liberally mixed with whiskey was passed to the washers to help them keep warm in the bone-chilling water, and all three of them partook liberally. When the whiskey came around for the third time, Reggie accepted it from Simms and took a deep pull, clasping the tankard for a moment with both hands so it could warm his numb fingers before he handed it over to Gabriel. "What do you think of Miss Weston as a steward?"

"Does well enough." The burly shepherd tilted his head back, draining the last of the tankard, then tossed it up on the bank. "Likes sheep."

As he grasped the next bleating ewe, Reggie realized that his steward had just been paid an enormous compliment. But then, if they hadn't trusted her judgment, the shepherds would never have let her work with their flocks. He glanced up at the bank, seeing her intent expression as she expertly checked over a well-grown lamb, then urged it on. Amazing that she could be doing such thoroughly masculine work, yet manage to look so fetchingly female. Those pantaloons really did the most remarkable job of outlining her shapely backside. . . . With a grin, he realized that it was just as well that he was standing in cold water.

It was a long, hard afternoon for all concerned, but Alys still found time to be impressed at how well her employer took to sheep washing. Even when an ornery ewe reared up, planted both hooves on his chest, and shoved him backward into the water, he had emerged smiling as the rest of the work crew roared with laughter. His willingness to do a hard job on the same terms as his employees had won him instant respect and acceptance. Had Davenport planned that, or was he genuinely indulging a childhood ambition? Either way, the results were worthwhile.

Toward the end of the afternoon, Simms, who was smaller than the other two washers and could absorb less alcohol, subsided into the water with a peaceful smile. Davenport and Mitford fished the drunken shepherd out and laid him by the small fire, where he snored contentedly, and one of the sheep wrestlers joined them in the water to finish the last of the flock.

Traditionally the washing ended with a meal for the workers, and Alys had arranged for a small mountain of hearty fare to be brought to the site. They shared ham, boiled new potatoes, and warm bread, washed down by ale, and by the time they finished eating, all the men were very merry. Even Alys drank enough ale to feel a warm glow of satisfaction at a job well done. She always enjoyed the communal activities of farming, like sheep washing and harvesting, and today there was a particularly friendly spirit in the air; doubtless the new owner was responsible for that. By this time, he had made the acquaintance of every worker present, and they were relaxed in his presence.

She and Davenport were the only ones who had ridden to the site, and as dusk fell they headed to their horses so they could ride back to the manor together. Reggie must have been freezing in his wet clothes, but he showed no signs of discomfort, perhaps because of the amazing quantity of alcohol he had put away. As he swung lightly into the saddle, Alys was impressed at how well he carried his drink.

The long ride back began in companionable silence, but halfway home Alys glanced back and saw the playful, incompetent sheep dog following behind, her black tail waving. "Don't look now, but I think you've made a conquest."

Davenport glanced back and chuckled. "More likely Gabe sent the worthless beast after us to get rid of her."

Having been spotted, the dog came closer, loping along next to Davenport's horse as if sure of her welcome, a canine smile on the clownish face. Alys barely restrained herself from commenting that Davenport was irresistible to almost any female creature; such a remark would have been most unsuitable. But true, alas, too true. Hastily attempting to rein in her ale-lightened spirits before she embarrassed both of them, she said, "I gather you and Mitford knew each other as boys?"

"Yes, we used to swim and wrestle and stalk through the hills. He was never much of a talker, but he knew the downs and the woods like the back of his hand. I'm not surprised to find him chief shepherd."

"It's a good life for a man with a contemplative nature," she agreed. Being a shepherd was a responsible position, better paid than most farmwork, and Mitford did his job very well. One reward for his skill was the privilege of running some sheep of his own with the Strickland flock.

They were both weary, with the satisfied fatigue of accomplishment, and they finished the ride in silence. At the stables they dismounted and led their horses inside, accompanied by the dog, which kept as close to Davenport as possible and seemed determined to prove how well-behaved she could be.

This late in the evening the stables were empty, the scents of hay and leather and healthy horses soft in the air, the only sounds the shuffle of hooves and an occasional equine whicker. Alys observed again how her clothes affected the way her employer treated her; when she dressed like a lady, he treated her as one. Now that she was in coat and pantaloons, he let her unsaddle and groom her own mount. She enjoyed his assumption that she was competent to do what any man took for granted.

As Alys emerged from the box stall, the collie, which had been exploring the stable, made a sudden dash in front of her to rear up and plant its paws on Davenport, who was standing a few feet away. The dog's sudden weight jarred him backward, almost tipping him into a pile of loose hay that would be transferred to racks the next day.

"Down!" he ordered. The dog obeyed instantly, settling on her haunches and wagging her tail across the well-swept stable floor. Glancing up, Davenport said ruefully, "Why do I get the feeling that this beast wants to move in with me?"

Alys chuckled. "Because she undoubtedly does. Are you hard-hearted enough to turn your back on those brown eyes?" She was fond of dogs, and leaned forward to scratch behind the collie's ears. As the dog wiggled happily under her hand, she briefly considered taking it home, but discarded the notion. Attila would not like sharing the house with a canine.

Straightening, Alys was very close to Davenport, only a yard away, and she was struck once more by how tall he was, and how intensely masculine. She was also close enough to realize that he was much drunker than she had thought. There was a kind of haziness about him, a rakish, unsteady air that she had not seen before. Surely he must be drunk indeed to look at her like that, with such warmth in his light blue eyes, as if she was utterly desirable. He was near enough to touch, and she yearned to close the distance between them, to discover if that was really desire she saw on his face.

But Alys had been exercising self-control for years, and nothing would have happened if fate hadn't taken a hand. She started to step back from her employer, determined to put distance between them. Then the collie, which had been sniffing curiously at the pile of hay, struck an unexpected quarry and a furry lightning bolt exploded out of the hay, yowling like seven demons from hell.

An enraged Attila attacked the collie, venting his fury at having his rest disturbed. The startled dog sprang into the air with a terrified yelp, paws flailing frantically. As Attila lunged forward, claws extended, the collie whirled and made a mad dash for escape. The dog had been standing between the humans, and its frenzied retreat knocked Alys into her employer.

If Davenport had been sober, he could have caught her easily enough. But his balance was not at its best, and as the collie bolted from the stable, pursued by an infuriated, hissing Attila, Alys and her employer went crashing down into the hay, with her landing hard on top of him.

Even though the hay softened their landing, Alys had the wind knocked out of her by the fall. Or perhaps she was breathless because she was lying full length on top of Davenport, his lean, muscular body under hers and his tanned face mere inches away. Light blue eyes twinkled at her from under lazy lids, and the expressive lips curved into a mesmerizing smile.

Alys was momentarily paralyzed by proximity. She struggled to catch her breath, knowing that she should scramble up and apologize, but before she could make any progress toward that virtuous goal, Davenport said in a pleased voice, "What a splendid idea."

Putting one hand behind her head, he pulled her face down for a kiss. All thought of escape or apology fled. Alys had been kissed by Randolph when they were betrothed, but her fiancé had acted with gentlemanly restraint, not wishing to offend her delicate sensibilities. Lacking the temerity to tell him that passion would not offend her, she had been left with the frustrated feeling that there was a great deal more to kissing than she was being taught.

Now Reggie was filling in the gap in her education. She might be an aging spinster, but he allowed no quarter for her inexperience. His kiss was deep, intense, and utterly enthralling as he explored her mouth with slow, rich sensuality. His clothes were still damp, and she could feel the fabric warming between their bodies as his long-fingered hands slid under her coat to knead her back and buttocks.

Though she might lack skill, Alys did her best to compensate with enthusiasm, molding herself against Reggie, kissing him back with all the abandon she had never dared show Randolph. She made no protest when he wrapped his arms around her and rolled over so that his long powerful frame covered her. The sweet green scent of crushed hay surrounded them, the dry, rustling sprigs a yielding cushion beneath her.

Transferring his attention to her ear and neck, he found every sensitive nerve ending, his expert touch sending shock waves of warmth into her most secret depths. One large hand moved down to cup her breast, his thumb teasing the nipple to taut response, and she gasped with pleasure, feeling as if she was dissolving into liquid fire.

"You've a rare talent for this, Allie," he whispered, his voice husky and intimate.

In a distant part of her mind Alys knew that she was about to abandon a dozen years of blameless respectability, and she didn't care. Nothing mattered but this, the passion that promised to fulfill the dreams of her restless nights. She felt unmistakable evidence that he did indeed desire her, and she was acutely aware of how well their bodies fitted together.

The sound of a throat being cleared was like a blast of icy water. Alys froze, torn between pure horror at being caught writhing in the hay like a dairy maid, and a raging fury that they had been interrupted too soon. She felt every muscle in Reggie's body tense. Then, with a sigh of

regret, he got to his feet. She felt cold and bereft, and
even the warm hand he offered to help her up was poor
compensation for what she had lost.

As she stood, wavering from the force of what she had
just experienced, Alys saw that the intruder was a stranger
to her, a wiry fellow dressed in London style. Though his
expression was carefully blank, she sensed the disapproval radiating from him, and felt her face burning with
shame.

Totally unabashed, Reggie steadied her with a light
grip on her elbow. "Lady Alys, this is Mac Cooper, who
came down from town yesterday. Mac, this is Miss Weston, more familiarly known as Lady Alys." After a quick,
perceptive glance at her face, he added, "Don't worry,
Mac never sees anything he shouldn't."

Releasing her arm, he brushed the hay from her back
and legs, his hands impersonal where they had been so
intimate. Alys supposed that his words were meant as
reassurance that everyone at Strickland would not have
learned she was a wanton before breakfast the next day.
But she would know, and so would Davenport and his
servant. That was two people too many.

Barely managing a nod at Cooper, she turned and fled
the stable, into the safety of the night. She was halfway
back to Rose Hall before her pace slowed. The night air
was cool on her flushed skin, and she stopped, not yet
ready to face her household, sure that the marks of her
employer's hands and kisses were blazoned across her in
streaks of scarlet.

Within sight of Rose Hall, she folded down under a
tree in the dark and buried her face in her hands, shud-
dering with embarrassment. Yes, Davenport had briefly
desired her, but drunks were notoriously undiscriminating. She knew from hard experience that only a drunk
would find her attractive; any female would have suited
him equally well. He and his servant were probably laughing over how susceptible she had been, amused that she
was so desperate for any man's attention.

Though in fairness, she reminded herself that Reginald
Davenport was not just any man. The blasted fellow was
so diabolically attractive that all he had to do was stand

around and wait for females to hurl themselves into his arms. The fact that she had been driven into his embrace by an incompetent sheep dog added a note of humiliating farce to what had happened.

For a handful of astounding moments she had forgotten propriety, reputation, and obligations. Now, alone in the night, Alys wondered with despair how she was going to face Davenport in the morning.

As Reggie brushed sprigs of hay from himself, Mac said, "Miss Weston is an unusual female, to be sure," in a voice frosted with disapproval.

A pleased smile still lingering on his lips, Reggie said, "She most certainly is."

"I see you're proud of yourself," Mac said sharply.

"Not exactly that, but certainly in charity with the world. What are you so Friday-faced about?"

Mac scowled. "Miss Weston is highly regarded here. Pity to see her ruined because you have nothing better to do."

"I doubt that she would consider it ruination," Reggie snapped. "If you were spying for any length of time, you'll have noticed that she was entirely willing."

Mac spat on the floor. "Did you see her face when she left? She may have succumbed to a moment's temptation, but she's probably thanking her lucky stars that you were interrupted."

Reggie reddened with anger. "I sincerely doubt that. If I have ever met a woman eager for ruination, it's Alys Weston."

"Why don't you just discharge her and get it over with quickly?" Mac asked caustically. "She'd still be out of work, but at least she'd have her reputation."

"As long as she does her job, I have no intention of discharging her, and she does her job superlatively well." Reggie's temper was rising dangerously near the explosion point.

"How long do you think she would be able to do her work if the locals found out she was your mistress?" Mac, grimaced. "She'd be forced out in a fortnight. Besides, since when have you taken to seducing respectable virgins? You've always said that they were nothing but trouble."

His temper well and truly lost, Reggie roared, "Bloody hell, Mac, who are you to tell me what to do?" before turning to storm out of the stable.

Mac's quiet voice followed him. "Your conscience."

Reggie swung to face him, an ugly glint in his pale blue eyes. "You should know that I haven't got a conscience."

"You will in the morning, when you're sober "

Mac's words pursued Reggie as he spun away into the night. Knowing that he would be dangerous to anyone whose path he crossed, he turned away from the house, needing to work his anger off. Bloody-minded little cockney prig. How dare he lecture his employer who had taken him from the gutter. Reggie was a trifle flown, but hardly roaring drunk. And if there was any seduction going on with Lady Alys, it had been entirely mutual.

Entirely mutual, and entirely pleasurable. Reggie had suspected that his steward had an ardent nature under her controlled exterior, but hadn't realized how dangerously close to the surface it lay. Though her response might have lacked polish, he would lay any odds that her capacity for passion equaled that of any woman he had ever known. Swearing softly for any number of reasons, he made his way through the thicket by the lake to his private clearing, making a mental note to have the old path cleared as branches slapped him in the face.

The moon was nearly full, and sheets of light silvered the water in front of him. Half of his problem was anger at Mac's officiousness, but the other half was pure frustration, he decided. His hands tingled with the remembered feel of Allie's lovely supple body, and just thinking of her fiery, uninhibited responsiveness made his temperature begin to rise again.

It was on this very spot that he had learned to swim as a child, and on impulse he stripped off his damp clothing; perhaps a swim now would cool him off. He dived into the lake, his body cleaving the chill water and bringing a measure of reason back to his brain. As he surfaced, sputtering, he admitted that Mac, damn him, had a point; he usually did. Alys Weston might be willing, even eager, to experience what she had been missing, but Reggie would do her no favor by taking advantage of that fact.

Any affair posed the risk of physical, social, and emotional damage. Remembering the dazed, shaken look in Allie's wide eyes when they had been interrupted, he bestowed a particularly scathing curse on himself. During his lengthy career as a rake, Reggie had learned that few females could enjoy an affair without having their emotions become involved, and Allie wasn't in that small number. Besides passion, she had a great capacity for selfless love; look at the family she had created for herself; look at what she had done for everyone on the estate. She was a giver by nature, and would be unable to prevent herself from giving away more than she could afford to lose.

His deep, powerful strokes had carried him the full width of the lake, and now he turned to swim back. Alys Weston might be physically ripe for an affair, but she was the sort of female who needed a man she could respect, while he represented everything that worthy, God-fearing folk despised. If she indulged her perfectly natural physical desire with him, she would hate herself, and him as well. The latter was a curiously unappealing thought.

He rolled onto his back and floated lazily in the moon-kissed water, stroking just enough to stay afloat. With Allie's looks and passionate nature, it was amazing that she had gotten to her present age unwed, but doubtless her height, forceful intelligence, and independence intimidated most men. A waste; such a very great waste.

While he certainly lusted after that lovely body, he also liked and respected the woman inside and had no desire to see her hurt. Which meant that he had damn well better stay sober around her, because he didn't trust himself an inch when he had been drinking. Reggie had resolved to behave himself in Dorset, yet he had been as lost to propriety as Alys Weston. When that stupid dog knocked her into his arms, her warm, willing body had caused him to instantly forget his good intentions.

With wry humor Reggie realized that the water wasn't cold enough to cool his simmering ardor. He had better find a topic other than Alys Weston to think about.

Distraction was provided when something splashed into the water at the edge of the lake. Automatically watchful, he floated and listened, though there shouldn't be any animals in the area that could threaten a human.

It took only a moment to identify the creature valiantly paddling toward him. The collie was ecstatic to find him, almost sinking in her attempts to wag her tail while staying afloat.

Raising one hand from the water to scratch her head, he asked, "Haven't you caused enough trouble for one night?"

A raspy tongue across his face was the only reply. "Aren't you ashamed of yourself, having been routed by a mangy cat?"

Shame was apparently as foreign to the collie as the herding instinct; the dog just tried to climb into Reggie's arms, not easily done when both man and beast were in the water. Side by side, they swam back to the shore, where the collie managed to shake an amazing amount of water out of its shaggy fur while Reggie pulled on his clammy, uncomfortable clothes and shivered in the chilly night air.

As he walked back to the house, collie at his heels, he decided to go up to London for a few days. He had hared off so quickly that he had left some business untended. Besides that, a brief absence would give Alys Weston some time to recover from her embarrassment. And if he was being strictly truthful, which he preferred to be in the privacy of his own head, he wasn't looking forward to the next time he saw her. She probably despised him just now, and with justice.

Back in his room to change, he found Mac unpacking and brushing out his master's wardrobe, unperturbed by the row that had occurred in the stable. Reggie felt a stab of guilt, remembering his uncharitable thoughts earlier. While he had helped the cockney out in the beginning, Mac had more than repaid Reggie's casual generosity. Hard to imagine anyone else putting up with Reggie's drinking, mood swings, and ups-and-downs of fortune. There had been times when Mac's pay had been months in arrears, and never once a complaint from him.

As Reggie entered the bedroom, his valet glanced up, his eyes widening slightly at the sight of the collie. "In case you haven't noticed, there's a dog following you."

Taking off his coat and beginning to unbutton his shirt, Reggie glanced back with a great show of surprise. "So there is. Fancy that."

Mac snorted, then asked with foreboding, "What kind of dog is it? Are you going to keep it?"

"It's a boarder collie, b-o-a-r-d-e-r collie," Reggie spelled out as he stripped off his wet pantaloons and drawers. "She's a hopelessly incompetent sheep dog. The shepherd was going to have her put down, so I decided to see if someone would take her as a pet." No point in mentioning to Mac that the dog was the one who had decided to abandon the working life.

Unaware of the plans for her future, the collie sat on her haunches, tail wagging, black fur matted with water, and an expression of imbecilic happiness on her face. Mac looked at her dubiously. He didn't know much about dogs, but this one seemed to think she had already found a home. "What's her name?"

"She doesn't have a name. Once you've named an animal, it's yours for life." Reggie toweled himself off vigorously, then pulled on the dry clothing Mac handed him. "I'm going up to London for a few days. Anything you'd like me to get for you?"

"See if you can find some sanity," Mac suggested. "I think you'll be needing it."

Reggie just laughed. In spite of everything, he felt better than he had for years. Snapping his fingers at the collie, he said, "Come on down to the library and I'll let you watch Mac and me test the quality of the local whiskey."

With a clicking of toenails, the dog trotted after him. The collie might be a hopeless herder and not very bright by some standards, but she knew a good offer when she heard it.

10

Having spent a restless, frustrated night mustering her courage to meet her employer without blushing, Alys found the note waiting in her office distinctly anticlimactic. In a few brisk words Davenport informed her that he would be in London for several days. In his absence, he hoped that she would think further about possible improvements to the property. Also, please see that a path was cleared through the brush to the little clearing by the lake. Yours, etc, R. Davenport.

It was as if the previous night's incident in the stable had never happened. Perhaps he had already forgotten it. As she stared at his bold, slashing handwriting, Alys wished vehemently that she could forget as easily.

Since he had been gone from London only a week, it was unlikely that the metropolis was any more crowded and noisome than when Reggie had left. Nonetheless, it seemed so, as drays and peddlers and pedestrians fought for space while expressing themselves at the top of their lungs.

It was early evening, and after stopping by his flat to change out of his traveling clothes, he went off to take care of his most awkward business first. Reggie had won five hundred pounds from George Blakeford the night before leaving London, but his opponent hadn't had the cash and had given a vowel instead. With all that he wanted to do at Strickland, Reggie could use the money, and Blakeford would probably be at White's at this hour.

There was also the matter of Blakeford's mistress, whom Reggie had mowed that same night. If he had been attracted to the very available Stella, Reggie would have pursued her openly; he didn't doubt his ability to take her away from Blakeford if he chose. But he hadn't been interested, and felt an odd kind of guilt for having casually succumbed to the doxy's lures. Blakeford was damned possessive about the woman, and Reggie preferred not to stir up trouble without a good reason; he had enough enemies without creating more unnecessarily.

Blakeford was in his usual spot at White's, making inroads on a bottle of port, so Reggie went over. "Mind if I join you?"

Blakeford nodded without enthusiasm, but did not look overly distressed at the company; presumably Stella had had the sense not to taunt her protector with her infidelities. Reggie sat down opposite and signaled for more wine. He and the other man were not really friends, though they moved in the same circles. Blakeford was tall and burly, a good boxer and a heavy gambler, with a face whose color showed his homage to port. He seemed a typical man-about-town, but Reggie had always sensed a dark, unpleasant side to Blakeford and preferred to keep his distance. Unfortunately, a certain amount of socializing could not be avoided under the circumstances. Crossing his long legs casually, Reggie said, "I've been out of town for a few days and just got back. Would it be convenient . . . ?"

Before he finished speaking, Blakeford nodded. "Had a good day at whist and the dibs are in tune. Have the vowel on you?"

Reggie produced the note and exchanged it for a handful of bills. His companion's mood was improved when he challenged Reggie to flip a coin for fifty pounds and Blakeford won. Reggie didn't mind; while flipping coins was a fool's way to gamble, fifty pounds was not a bad tithe to pay for goodwill.

Since cheer was abounding, they ordered another bottle of port while Blakeford recounted the news of the last week. Reggie carefully suppressed any indications of boredom; after he downed another bottle of port, perhaps knowing who had won or lost would sound more interesting.

As Blakeford broached the third bottle, he said abruptly, "I never had a chance to mention it before, but I was sorry when you were cut out of inheriting Wargrave. It must be hell seeing some upstart enjoying what should have been yours."

Reggie shrugged. That was old news by now. "It was never mine. I was only a nephew and always knew that a direct heir might claim the title and fortune."

"You're more philosophical than I would be." Blakeford grimaced, his heavy face sour. "I've been heir presumptive to Durweston for the last dozen years, and I wouldn't wish the uncertainty on anyone."

Reggie's lips formed a silent whistle. "You're heir to the Duke of Durweston? I never knew that. That's a prize indeed." He searched his memory for information about the duke, but with little success. Durweston was an elderly widower who lived in northern England, seldom coming to London. And when he did, he didn't move in the same circles as Reggie. "Are you concerned about Durweston marrying and getting a son, or is this another case of a missing heir?"

"The Duke of Durweston's only child ran away from home at eighteen and hasn't been heard from since." Blakeford shook his head in disgust. "Undoubtedly dead by now, though Durweston refuses to admit it."

After consideration, Reggie remarked, "Never met Durweston myself, but I've heard him called a stiff-rumped old Croesus."

Blakeford's laughter was bitter. "That's a fair description." He took a deep swig of port, his face brooding. "The old duke hates knowing everything will come to me. I'm only a second cousin, but there's no one closer, so he'll damn well have to make the best of it."

It sounded like Blakeford's situation was very similar to the one Reggie had been in, and he felt a surge of unexpected sympathy for the man. "It's a bad business, waiting for some old autocrat to die, not knowing what you'll have when he's gone." It was more than a bad business; it was a postponement of real life, as Reggie knew better than anyone else.

He sipped his own port, then offered what consolation he could. "Granted, being superseded was a shock at first, but I didn't come out badly. My cousin Wargrave just signed over an estate to me as a sort of compensation. If the missing Durweston heir turns up, perhaps he'll be as reasonable as Wargrave."

Blakeford grimaced. "No joy there—my cousin and I never got on. Besides, what is one paltry estate compared to Durweston?" He scowled blackly, then said with determined civility, "Hadn't heard that you had come into property. Tell me about it."

"The estate is called Strickland and it's between Shaftesbury and Dorchester. About three thousand acres, and it's been very well-managed."

Blakeford's eyebrows rose. "Unusual for an estate that hasn't had an owner in residence."

"Strickland has been blessed with a first-class steward." Reggie found himself smiling. "A female, and a most redoubtable one. An odd-eyed reformer who's nearly as tall as I am."

"You don't say!" Blakeford had been about to pour more port, but his hand stopped in mid-gesture and his face showed shock when he glanced up. "What do you mean by odd-eyed?"

"One eye is brown, the other gray," Reggie elaborated.

"I knew a woman with eyes like that once. What's her name?"

"Alys Weston."

Blakeford was very still for a moment, then resumed pouring, his hand not quite steady. "The one I knew was called Annie. Actually, I can't imagine her as a land steward. Though she had other talents," he added with a broad wink.

Something was not quite right about his manner, but after a moment Reggie shrugged the thought off. Probably Blakeford had been as obsessed with his Annie as he now was with his Stella. Some men were weak that way. His thoughts were interrupted by a familiar voice.

"Reggie! When did you get back to town?" Julian Markham's handsome young face shone with pleasure as he came up to them. As Reggie stood and offered a handshake and a smile, Julian continued, "Have you dined yet? No? Then join me and explain what took you out of London so quickly." Turning, he added, "Care to join us, Blakeford?"

Blakeford shook his head and rose to his feet. "No, I'm expected elsewhere. Good evening to you." As he stared sightlessly at the other men's departing backs, Blakeford's mind was dominated by one horrific thought. The bitch was alive; there couldn't be another woman in England who fit that description. Who would have believed it possible, after so many years?

Spurning the dining room at White's, Reggie and Julian Markham went to a nearby tavern renowned for its roast beef. As they settled down at a corner table, Julian commented, "I'm glad Blakeford couldn't come. He always seems angry about something. Makes it dashed difficult to relax."

After an appreciative eye at the round backside of the barmaid who had taken their dinner order, Reggie turned to his friend. "I know what you mean, but now I understand why he acts like a bear with a sore ear. It must be a confounded nuisance wondering if the missing heir to the Duke of Durweston is going to reappear."

"That's bad enough," Julian agreed, "but I suspect that what makes it worse is that the heir is a female."

"Good God, surely you're joking. Since when can a female become a duchess in her own right? Even with baronies, that's rare." Reggie was startled but intrigued; no question that Blakeford would feel particularly insulted at being superseded by a mere female.

Julian wrinkled his brow in thought. "I had a great-aunt who loved prosing on about such things. As I recall, the case was similar to that of Marlborough. The title was originally granted to a military hero who had no surviving sons but several daughters, so the patent of nobility specified that the title could pass to the eldest daughter if there was no son."

He grinned. "Just to make it more complicated, an incumbent duke has the option of willing the title to the nearest male heir if he doesn't want his daughter to inherit. Even if the missing heir is alive, I'm sure Durweston would pass over her, so Blakeford is worrying needlessly."

"How bizarre. There can't be another patent of nobility in England written that way." Reggie shook his head in amazement. "Why do you say that Durweston would consider his daughter unworthy even if she is still alive?"

Julian's grin broadened. "My great-aunt loved scandals even more than genealogy. Apparently Durweston's daughter was betrothed to some thoroughly appropriate fellow— the Marquess of Kinross's younger son, I believe. Instead, she up and ran off with her groom. If Durweston wasn't such a tough old devil, the shock would have killed him. He publicly disowned her, and not a word has ever been heard of the wench from that day to this." He shrugged. "My aunt's theory was that she died in childbirth, and the servant she married was afraid to inform his noble father-in-law. That is, assuming that the groom did marry her."

· Their dinners arrived then, and both men spent some time tucking into the beef and boiled potatoes. After they had finished and begun on their port, Reggie told his interested friend about Strickland, but the earlier discussion stayed in his mind. When the conversation slowed, he said thoughtfully, "Primogeniture really is an iniquitous system. I suppose in feudal times it made sense to pass the entire property to a single heir, because concentrating the power helped everyone survive. But now it means younger sons being raised in a luxury they will never be able to afford when they're grown, so they go into the church or the army or the government and spend the rest of their days resenting being poor relations."

"And heirs kick their heels, powerless to do anything but drink, gamble, and wait for their fathers to die."

There was rare bitterness in Julian's voice, and Reggie gave him a sympathetic glance. "Does that mean your father turned down your proposal for managing Moreton Park?"

Julian nodded bleakly. "I was so sure that he would agree. I had it all worked out, the crop plan, the prices of cattle to improve the herd, income forecasts." He broke off with a sheepish smile. "Of course, you know that, since you were the one who spent weeks helping me put the proposal together."

He shook his head in exasperation, a lock of brown

hair falling loose across his brow. "It just doesn't make any sense. I could double his profits, and he would save on the cost of keeping me here in London as well."

Ever since coming down from Oxford, Julian had been trying to persuade his father to let his heir assume some responsibility for the family fortunes, but Lord Markham had steadfastly refused to yield a single shred of power. At the same time, Markham complained that Julian was an extravagant wastrel, intent on destroying the family fortunes. If it would have helped, Reggie would have given his lordship a sharp lecture on how he was mishandling his only son. Unfortunately, Lord Markham would never listen to a man who he thought was corrupting his heir.

Julian was very fond of his father in spite of their differences, but if the older man continued so pigheaded, it would end with the son praying for the father's death. Having lost his own father so early, Reggie hated to see that, but could think of no way to help. Keeping his gloomy thoughts to himself, he topped up both goblets with port, saying pensively, "It isn't easy for a man who is aging to see himself supplanted by a young one in the prime of life, even when the younger one is his son. Perhaps especially when it is his son."

"But I don't want to supplant my father. I just want him to treat me like an adult, not a schoolboy."Julian sighed and leaned back against the oak settle. "Do you suppose if I married, he would decide that I was ready for responsibility?"

"Possibly, though I wouldn't stake serious money on it." Moving to a more profitable topic, Reggie suggested, "Why not come down to Strickland for a visit? If you are in the market for a leg-shackle, Dorset has its share of pretty girls."

Julian laughed. "I'd be delighted to see Strickland, and I never mind looking at pretty girls. Besides," he added with a mischievous smile, "I'm short of funds until next quarter day, and a spot of rustication would be in order. I wouldn't be able to get down there for a fortnight, though."

"Good. I'm going to Leicestershire to buy some mares,

but I'll certainly be back at Strickland by then." It would be good to have some company, and Reggie was also looking forward to his young friend's first sight of the delectable Meredith Spenser.

The evening was yet young when Reggie parted company with Julian and went to take care of another piece of business. This one, however, should be more of a pleasure.

The muscular ex-pugilist who opened the door of the discreet house on the edge of Mayfair welcomed him with a broad smile. "Good to see you, Mr. Davenport. It's been some time."

"It has," Reggie agreed, surrendering his hat. "Will you find out if Mrs. Chester will see me?"

"No need to ask, sir. Just go on up. You know the way."

Yes, he certainly knew the way. As he headed toward the stairs, he passed the open salon door and glanced in. This early, there were more females available than males to admire them, and in their bright, revealing gowns the girls looked like the inhabitants of some exotic aviary. Several waved and beckoned to him, while the men glanced up jealously to see who was causing such a flutter. A saucy redhead came to the door and draped herself against the frame, saying with exaggerated seductiveness, "I knew this would be a good night. You came to see me, didn't you, Reg?"

Reggie chuckled and patted her bouncy derrière. "Sorry, Nan, I'm here to see Chessie."

Sighing wistfully, she said, "Some women have all the luck," her voice floating after him as he climbed the curving stairs.

When he knocked on the paneled door, Chessie's husky voice invited him in. She had had a nearly unintelligible East End accent when they had met, but now she spoke the king's English as correctly as any lady born, and her chamber was decorated with all the flamboyant richness that one of London's most successful madams deserved. The lady of the house was at her dressing table, surrounded by an elegant clutter of expensive perfumes and cosmetics, but when she recognized her visitor in the mirror, she immediately rose and crossed the room to give him an affectionate hug. "Where have you been, you rascal? It's been an age."

Chessie had been a real dasher in her youth, and even though her blond hair now required assistance and she had put on a good few pounds over the years, she was a fine figure of a woman. The extra pounds were soft and pleasant in a hug, and Reggie released her with some reluctance. "In the country. I'm in town for only a few days, then I'll be off again."

Chessie went to a cabinet and took out a bottle of the special brandy that she kept for him and poured them two glasses. After they were seated, he regaled her with a brief account of Strickland.

"So you're turning respectable. A magistrate, no less!" she said, studying him thoughtfully with her gray-blue eyes. Glancing down at her brandy, she absently traced the rim of the glass with one finger. "I suppose we won't be seeing much of you now. I'll be sorry in a way, but I'm relieved in another."

"Oh? Glad to get rid of me?" Reggie asked with amusement.

"You know it's not that." Chessie tilted her head sideways as if debating whether to say more, her golden hair softly touched by the candlelight. "I've been worried about you," she said slowly. "You've changed in the last few years. You used to raise hell because you enjoyed it, but now it seems more like a bad habit that's making you miserable. You carry on like a man condemned to die in the morning. If you don't change your course, sooner or later that's exactly what will happen."

"You think I can't take care of myself?" he asked in a silky voice that masked his stab of irritation.

"Not that you can't, but that you won't bother to try," she answered bluntly. "I know men as well as any woman alive, and I know when one is sending himself to perdition." Visibly gathering her courage, she continued, "Blast it, Reggie, you're drinking far too much. If you don't stop, it will kill you soon, either directly or because you'll break your neck riding, or because you'll get into a fight and not be quick enough for once."

He finished his brandy and set the glass on the delicate end table with an audible clink. "Of course I drink too much. It's part of being an English gentleman. A really serious politician, for example, needs to be able to put away at least three bottles of bad port a night, and five or six is better."

"Yes, and it's killing a lot of them too. But it isn't just a matter of how much you drink, but how it affects you." She gave him a very level look. "And it affects you very badly."

His temper rising, Reggie snapped, "You think I can't hold my liquor?"

"It used to be that you could drink anyone under the table and be as good as new the next day," she admitted, "but over the last couple of years I think the booze has gotten the upper hand." She looked at him earnestly, willing him to really hear what she was saying. "Like I said, I've known a lot of men—"

He cut in sharply, "Several regiments' worth, at the least."

Chessie flushed, but she refused to back down. "Do you remember the first time we met?"

"Of course I do. A group of drunken bucks intent on gang rape is memorable." It had been at Ranelagh, shortly before the pleasure garden closed. Chessie had been very young and very new at Venus's trade. She had also been terrified and screaming for help, and he was the only man around who had seen fit to help a prostitute. That was the night his nose had been broken, but he had been less damaged than any of the men who had been attacking Chessie. One of his better fights, if he did say so himself; it helped that he had been sober and they had not. Uneasily he shoved the last thought aside and added belligerently, "What has that got to do with anything?"

"Reggie, I think you saved my life that night. Now I want to return the favor." She spread her hands expressively. "Yes, almost everyone drinks too much, but sometimes it goes beyond a bad habit and becomes . . . almost like a disease, or an addiction, like with opium eaters. Once that happens, a man can't control his drinking anymore. He's a drunkard, and booze becomes more important than anything else in his life. It ruins his health, rots his guts, turns him nasty. Eventually it kills him.''

"What a pretty picture you're painting," he said, his self-control etched with acid. "However, I assure you that I am not addicted to any form of spirits. I can stop whenever I choose."

"Have you ever tried?" she asked softly, her eyes grave.

Defiantly he reached for the bottle of brandy and poured himself three fingers' worth. "I've never seen any reason to."

Chessie sighed. She hadn't thought he would be receptive to the idea that he was a drunkard; she had never known a man—or a woman, for that matter—who was. But she had had to try. She and Reggie had lived together for several years after the night he had rescued her, and there had always been more between them than just business. It had hurt, these last years, to see him change. He had always had a quick temper, but in the past the clouds passed quickly and his usual good nature would reappear.

These days he seemed to be depressed or angry most of the time, more prone to use his quick tongue in caustic, hurtful ways. His remark about her having known regiments of men was an example; the old Reggie had never been unkind to his friends. Well, Chessie did indeed know men; well enough to know that there was no point in saying any more. "Did you have some other reason for stopping by, besides for a scold?"

He smiled faintly at that and reached inside his jacket for a folded paper, which he handed to her. She opened it, then drew her brows in question. "Why are you handing me our original business agreement?"

Reggie lounged back in the sofa, sipping his brandy. "It's time the business was all yours. You do most of the work, and Martin does the rest. It isn't right that I keep taking part of the profits."

Chessie studied the contract with bemused affection. Eight years before, she had been left in dire straits when her current protector abandoned her. No longer young, and tired by the precariousness of being a kept woman, she had turned to Reggie for temporary shelter. Not only had he rescued her once more, he had suggested that she go into business for herself, and lent her the money to get started. Yes, she had built the business up with plenty of hard work and fair treatment for both the girls and the customers, but she never could have done it without him. Crossing to the sofa, she gave him an energetic kiss. "You're a real gent, Reg. A quarter of this business is worth a lot. There aren't many who would give it away for nothing."

He shrugged negligently. "I don't need the income anymore and I've made back my initial investment many times over."

"Are you sure there isn't anything I can do to . . . show my appreciation?" Mischievously she ran a practiced hand down his lean body. There was a flare of response in his light blue eyes before he shook his head regretfully.

"I don't think Martin would like that."

"No, I don't suppose he would," she agreed with equal regret. Martin was the former pugilist who greeted guests, kept order, supervised the kitchen and wine cellar, and generally helped run the house. He was a fine fellow, her partner in more ways than one, but a bit possessive about his woman; stirring up old embers could cause trouble. As Reggie stood to leave, Chessie asked wistfully, "Will you still stop by now and again to say hello? Even if you are respectable?"

He grinned, his former irritation forgotten. "Of course I will. Since most of your male guests are respectable, I shan't look out of place." He gave her a quick kiss before leaving.

As he disappeared, Chessie shook her head. She and Martin had a very good arrangement, but still, there had never been anyone quite like Reggie. With a sigh, she went downstairs to take care of business.

The sun had reached its zenith and begun its downward path when Reggie woke the next morning. He lay very still, knowing that if he moved quickly he would probably be sick. Even the daylight glowing through his closed eyelids was a strain on his shattered nerves. His thoughts moving with painful slowness, he tried to piece together what had happened the night before. White's and Blakeford, then dinner with Julian, but they had parted early. He started to roll onto his side, then subsided as a stab of pain lanced his eyeballs.

After dinner he had gone to Chessie's, to return their business agreement. That visit he remembered all too clearly; she'd made a lot of damn-fool remarks about his drinking. *And you didn't believe her?* The inner voice that had given him bleak warning before echoed in his mind. He groaned, not wanting to think about the topic anymore. He should have brought Mac with him; some of his valet's magic elixir would have been a godsend just now.

After dozing for a while, he was able to move, albeit slowly, the next time he woke up. Luckily there was water in the pitcher, and splashing his face helped clear his bleary eyes. Wondering how he had gotten home the night before, he was starting to strip off his crumpled clothing when he spotted an unfamiliar chamber pot on a table by the door. Even in his present state, he had enough curiosity to investigate, and to his shock he discovered that the china vessel was stuffed with banknotes. Good Lord, what had he been doing the previous night? He must have ended up in a gaming hell.

Lifting a handful of notes, he tried to guess how much money might be there, but it was too much effort. At the moment, he needed to concentrate on the other reasons he had come to London. He must visit his bank, and there were other tasks as well, though he couldn't remember what they were just now.

Later, when a shot of Irish whiskey and fresh clothing had restored him to a semblance of life, he counted the money in the chamber pot. There was over a thousand pounds, and he glared at it in frustration. He would give the whole lot to know just what he had done last night. In a way, exact knowledge was unimportant; it had undoubtedly been a night of gaming and drinking like a thousand others, but he would never be sure unless he ran into someone who had been a witness to whatever had happened. Though Reggie had always taken risks, he had done so knowing the odds and feeling himself to be master of the situation; to lose his memory was to lose control of himself in a deeply disturbing way.

As he bundled banknotes into a leather bag to take to his bank, Reggie remembered what Chessie had said the night before, and his lips tightened. Perhaps—just perhaps—she had a point. At Strickland, he had drunk less and felt better. Now, after less than a day in London, he felt like death would be a welcome release, and for reasons stronger than just the physical results of carousing. Well, he would be out of London tomorrow. He would go to Leicestershire to look at some mares, but after that he could go home.

It was such a natural thought that he wasn't even surprised at how quickly Strickland had become home.

11

It has been almost a week since Davenport had left Strickland, and Alys had progressed from relief to a cautious hope that he would see fit to return soon, in spite of the inevitable awkwardness. The man was certainly a disgraceful reprobate and a complication in her orderly life, but it was . . . interesting to have him around.

She was hard at work in her office, checking accounts and thinking, for the thousandth time, that Britain ought to change to a decimal money system, when Davenport reappeared. A light knock sounded at the door of the steward's office and she bade the visitor come in without raising her head. Cat-footed, her employer crossed the room and was scarcely three feet away when he said, "Good afternoon."

Alys almost jumped out of her skin in surprise, her head whipping up and her pen spattering ink across the page. So much for dignity, she thought with an inward sigh. At least shock repressed the embarrassment she might have felt otherwise.

Davenport was his usual collected self, though amusement glinted in his light blue eyes. "Sorry to startle you," he said mildly as he lounged against the edge of her desk, "but you did say to come in. Anything noteworthy happen in my absence?"

"Everyone on the estate has now been vaccinated against smallpox, as you wished."

His eyebrows shot up. "That was quick work. Did any of the tenants or laborers resist?"

"Not for very long," Alys said with satisfaction. Backed by the landlord's authority, she had brooked no opposition and it had been a pleasure to accomplish so worthwhile a task.

"Congratulations on a job well done. Anything else?"

"Well, I've been putting together my proposal for improvements," she said hesitantly.

"Oh? What do you recommend?"

"To begin with, I think we should increase the livestock herds. Grain prices have been depressed since the war ended, and I don't see them getting better anytime soon. Some of the grain acreage can be converted to growing mangel-wurzels." Seeing a peculiar expression on Davenport's face, she explained, "Mangel-wurzels are a kind of beet root that makes excellent cattle fodder."

"I've heard of them," he said, the corners of his mouth quirking up, "but I've never actually conversed about them." His smile broadened. "Come, Lady Alys, forget about their nutritional excellence and try to say 'mangel-wurzel' with a straight face."

She stared at him a moment, then found that she had to smile. "You're right. It is an absurd name, isn't it?"

"Even a poet devoted to nature would have difficulty writing a decent sonnet to a mangel-wurzel." He chuckled. "Perhaps 'Some of nature's major puzzles/Are the mystic mangel-wurzels'?"

That was too much, even for a woman of habitual

seriousness, and Alys gave way to laughter. "I doubt that Wordsworth could do better," she said when her mirth had subsided. Reggie's gaze on her face was very warm and amused; remarkable how intimate shared laughter could be. Suddenly self-conscious, she rustled through the piles of papers in front of her, extracting several sheets and handing them to her employer. "Here is a list of new equipment we could use, in order of usefulness, with estimated prices and notes on the advantages."

As his gaze ran down the column of neat printing, she saw that he was impressed. "I'll study this in more detail later, but it looks plausible, though it won't be possible to buy everything at once. Anything more?"

She nodded. "We need to build more cottages for the laborers. The older ones are a disgrace, damp and unfit for human habitation, and all of them are overcrowded." She produced another set of papers. "Here are the cost estimates."

He scanned the pages until he reached the last, where his lips pursed in a silent whistle that was definitely not approving. "This would be very expensive, and there is no direct financial benefit to the estate."

"But there are many *indirect* benefits." She leaned across her desk earnestly. "Healthy, happy people are better workers."

His gaze was sardonic. "Possibly true, but unprovable. You used a similar argument in support of your school."

"Yes, and it's as true here as it was there." Alys rose, feeling that if there was going to be a battle, she would do better standing. "Those prices are extremely reasonable. Much of the work can be done by estate workers during the quiet season, and virtually all of the materials are local."

She was just getting her wind up for a more detailed presentation when Davenport raised a hand. "I didn't say that we wouldn't do it, though again, it would have to be in stages." Then, with a half-smile, "I am not wholly wedded to practical return. To prove it, I'll show you what I've brought back."

Intrigued, Alys followed him outside and across the yard to the stables. There, in stalls that had been empty, were three new mares. "Do you want to breed hunters?" she asked in surprise.

"You've a good eye for horseflesh," he said approvingly.

She reached out a hand to the nearest mare, a lop-eared chestnut with powerful hindquarters and a deep chest. "Well, these obviously aren't showy enough to be Rotten Row hacks, but they look like they would do very well in the field." The chestnut gave Alys a friendly nudge in the shoulder.

"That mare may have lop-ears, but she's very clever over fences and has the endurance to stay all day." Then, without a shift in his tone, Davenport continued, "I was going to apologize for what happened here last week."

Alys gave him a quick shy glance that contained all of the discomfiture she had anticipated from this meeting. Davenport was regarding her with a thoughtful expression on his dark, almost handsome face, the light eyes inscrutable.

"I'll be damned if I can honestly say I'm sorry it happened," he continued, "but I am sorry if I embarrassed or distressed you in any way."

Alys's gaze whipped back to the mare, and she concentrated on stroking the velvety muzzle. "I can't really say I'm sorry either," she said awkwardly, "but it would be better if it didn't happen again."

"Agreed. Subject closed?"

"Subject closed," she agreed. It had been a disgraceful episode, and she had behaved in a way quite unbefitting a lady of mature years and practiced dignity. So why did she feel so regretful that it would not be repeated?

The day after his return to Strickland, Reggie visited the Stantons for the dinner that had been postponed when he went away. The evening was an enjoyable one, as a round and smiling Aunt Elizabeth hugged him with almost as much enthusiasm as the collie had shown on his return from London. Several other members of the local gentry were present, and they greeted him with cautious approval. Over port, the men had discussed local issues on the assumption that he would soon be joining the ranks of magistrates. There were no single ladies present, though the matrons eyed the newcomer speculatively, as if trying to decide which of the available fillies they should throw in his path.

Mindful of his resolve to drink less in general, and not to disgrace himself in front of the Stantons in particular, Reggie had been moderate in his consumption of wine. Perhaps that was why he was so restless when he returned to Strickland. In the library he poured a very large whiskey, enjoying the familiar soothing glow that spread through his body, but it was not enough to relax him. Glancing around the room, he decided to have some redecorating done; after thirty or forty years it was hardly surprising that the place was drab. Perhaps fresh wallpaper and draperies would make the house seem less tomblike. . . .

Exasperated, he finished his whiskey in a gulp and decided to go outside. The collie, still unnamed and ownerless but ever eager for a walk, frisked along beside him. He was growing accustomed to the silly beast in spite of its penchant for tripping people. The night was warm and fresh with the scents of early summer, and as Reggie lit a cigar and wandered toward the lake, he felt more at peace with the world. The land was like a seductive mistress, beckoning him to partake of its charms. It was lovely indeed, but as small creatures rustled in the bushes and the hoot of an owl haunted the night, he felt very alone, not with the frantic loneliness of London, but with a kind of sad melancholy, a sense of years wasted and paths not taken.

Without thought, his feet had taken him past the lake and around to Rose Hall, the rambling outline of the house acquiring a certain elegance in the light of the crescent moon. The hour was late, well past midnight, and no lights showed in the steward's residence. As he leaned against a tall elm that stood on the edge of the grounds, he wondered if Alys Weston was ever lonely. She had her surrogate family, and every person on the estate needed and respected her; was that enough? She seemed a self-sufficient woman, so perhaps it was.

As he drew on the cigar, the tip flared with momentary brightness, then subsided to a dull glow again. A faint

sound came from the far side of the house, and he
thought he saw a shape moving away from Rose Hall, a
darker black in the night. Frowning, Reggie tried to
make out more detail, but without success. Perhaps one
of the children slipping away on some unsanctified expe-
dition? That would probably be harmless in the case of
the boys, less so if it was their nubile sister. Or perhaps it
was a servant, or someone who had been calling on one
of the house's residents, or perhaps nothing at all.

Dropping the butt of his cigar and grinding it under his
heel, he quietly circled around the building to investigate. Less quietly, the collie pattered along beside him.
Whatever Reggie had seen was gone by the time he
reached the far edge of the grounds. He whispered softly,
"Well, dog, are you any good at tracking?"

With typical acuity, the beast immediately turned away
from the trail to face the house and lift her clownish
head, ears pricked alertly and shaggy tail still. "Remind
me not to offer you to the local hunt," Reggie murmured.

Then the collie growled, a deep, throaty sound, and
began moving forward. "For heaven's sake, quiet down,"
Reggie hissed. "You'll wake everyone in the house."

He caught up with the dog and grabbed her collar, but
she still strained toward the building. As the collie began
barking in agitation, Reggie prepared to wrench her away
by sheer force, when he detected a scent that the collie's
sensitive nose had already recognized as different and
wrong. The still night air carried a whiff of smoke, not
the vegetal scent of his cigar but a sharp, acrid smell.

Suddenly tense, Reggie scanned the house. A faint
glow showed through the windows on the ground floor,
and as he watched, he saw the first tentative lick of fire,
followed with horrifying speed by a multitude of hungry
flames. Swearing, he released the dog's collar and sprinted
toward the front door.

Haunted by memories and by vague longings, Alys had
trouble falling asleep, and when she did, she was seized
by the familiar nightmare of rejection. *Why marry a
bossy Long Meg like her? Why, for money, of course.*
Once again she fled, running away to self-destruction and

dishonor, but tonight there was a change in events. For the first time, she dreamed that her father sent pursuers after her, hoarsely shouting hunters on horseback and baying hounds that closed in, panting for her blood as she sought frantically for a hiding place.

Her mind slowly fought free of the depths to recognize that the barking was real, not the baying of a nightmare pack. Instead, a single dog barked and a man was shouting and pounding on the door. For a moment more, she lay suspended in confusion. Then she smelled the smoke.

Instantly alert, she uttered an oath under her breath as she scrambled from the bed, feeling the floorboards hot beneath her bare feet. Without slowing, she grabbed her robe and pulled it around her as she ran down the hall, calling the children.

"Merry, Peter, William, get up!" Throwing open Meredith's door, she saw the girl sit up sleepily. "Quick, the house is on fire. Get out immediately."

Merry gasped, and in the dim light Alys could see her slim figure stiffen before she jumped from bed, pulled on slippers and robe, and followed her guardian into the hall. The boys were emerging, William rubbing his eyes drowsily but Peter alert and aware of the danger. "Peter and Merry, get outside and take William with you. I'll get the servants up."

Peter opened his mouth to protest, and she cut him off sharply. "Just do it!" He nodded and took his little brother's hand. This end of the hall was still cool, but smoke was spreading along the ceiling, swirling ever lower in thick, eye-stinging clouds.

Alys waited long enough to see her charges start down the center stairs, then headed to the attic. The narrow steps were at the far end of the house from the fire, and she shouted a warning as she ran up. As she reached the top, the cook, Mrs. Haver, emerged from her room, clutching a dark shawl around her plump shoulders.

"The stairs are safe, just go down quickly and get outside." The smoke had followed her up, and drawing in breath to speak made Alys start coughing.

Mrs. Haver darted back into her room and Alys chased

her, swearing. "For God's sake, whatever you have here isn't worth the risk."

"Easy for you to say." Mrs. Haver's voice trembled on the edge of hysteria as she lifted one end of the mattress and pulled out whatever treasure she had hidden.

As the cook turned, Alys grabbed her arm and propelled her out the door and toward the stairs. "Move!"

Without waiting to see if she was obeyed, Alys sped down the narrow, dark passage. The only other servant was Janie Herald, the young housemaid, and her bedroom was at the opposite end of the attic. In the dark Alys couldn't find the right door at first, mistakenly entering two storage rooms before finding the correct one. The little slant-ceilinged chamber smelled faintly of the inexpensive perfume Janie used, but there was no response to Alys's call. Fumbling her way across the room, she tripped over a piece of furniture, stubbing her toes painfully and falling across the narrow bed.

The bed was empty, the blankets unwrinkled. Momentarily breathless, Alys considered the possibilities. Janie had been walking out with a boy from the village; perhaps she had slipped out to meet him? Praying that was the case, Alys pushed herself upright and ran out of the room, her long legs carrying her rapidly down the length of the attic hall.

Smoke was heavy on the steps, but much worse on the lower floor, where ravenous flames were devouring what had been her own bedroom. A handkerchief was in the pocket of her robe, and with some vague memory tickling her, Alys made a quick detour into Peter's room to dip the fabric square into his water pitcher. Holding the wet fabric across her nose and mouth and bending low into clearer air, Alys forced herself to run toward the inferno.

The stairs to the ground floor were still clear, but only just, and her left side scorched as she made her way down. Above her there was a hideous grinding noise, then a deafening crash as timbers fell through to the ground floor. A blast of hellish heat hit her and the stairsteps trembled beneath her feet. As she reached ground level, a cloud of sparks surrounded her, burning tiny black holes in the robe and stinging exposed flesh. The lung-choking clouds of smoke were so thick that she could see almost nothing in spite of the fiery glare.

As she started toward the front of the house, she heard a wail of animal terror and saw Attila flying toward her, his tail singed and smoking. She stooped to catch the frantic, clawing cat in her arms and turned the corner toward the front door. Then she stopped in horror. The main hall in front of her was blocked by smoke and flame, an impenetrable barrier of vicious heat.

Alys whirled back the way she had come, but fire now engulfed the stairs. For a moment her fear erupted into a scream of pure terror. She was trapped in the inferno, and as the air was consumed by savage flame, she felt herself getting dizzy. There was no place left to run, so she crouched down on the floor, her suffocating lungs laboring vainly for breath.

Half-fainting, she tightened her arms around the cat's trembling body. The heat was unbearable, and there was no air left to breathe, no air at all. As she slid into unconsciousness, with a fragment of grim humor Alys wished she had seduced Reginald Davenport. Since she was going to burn in hell, it was a pity she didn't have any really enjoyable sins to suffer for.

When Reggie reached the front door of Rose Hall, he began pounding on the panels and shouting, hoping to wake up the sleeping inhabitants. The door was locked and too heavy to break down, so he pulled off his coat and wrapped it around one arm and smashed the nearest window, then scrambled into the drawing room. As he did, the three Spensers came running down the hall. From the noise and the heavy smoke, the fire was spreading swiftly. Reggie called out, "Merry, where is Lady Alys?"

Meredith, her hair a pale halo around her face, paused and glanced over at him, beyond being shocked at his sudden appearance. "She went up to the attic to wake the servants."

"Get outside with your brothers and stay there."

She nodded and left. Reggie had been caught in a

burning tavern once; no one who hadn't had such an experience ever realized the unbelievable speed with which fire could move. Praying that Allie and the servants were on their way out, he ran along the center hall that led to the stairs, colliding with a plump female as he turned the corner. She was heavy and middle-aged, and her exertions left her staggering and gasping for breath.

Slipping an arm around her waist, Reggie half-carried the woman to the front door. "Where is Lady Alys?" he asked sharply as he helped her outside.

"Lady Alys went for Janie." After an endless interval of coughing, she added, "Should be right behind me."

Behind Reggie, the flames had burst through the roof at one end of the house and the whole area was lit by garish, oscillating light. In the distance he saw people running toward the blaze from the direction of the tenants' cottages, pulling a fire engine behind them. He doubted that it would do much good, but at least someone was thinking. As Peter ran toward the group with the fire engine, Meredith stood a safe distance from the house, her little brother clinging to her, both of them watching the destruction of their home with mesmerized horror.

Allie should have been out by now with the missing servant, unless they had been overcome by smoke. Plunging back into the house, Reggie saw that flames had cut across the center hall a dozen feet in front of him, the incredible heat striking him like a weapon. As he halted uncertainly, trying to remember the house layout to find a way around the fire, he heard a scream from beyond the curtain of fire. It was Allie's voice. For just an instant he froze, knowing that she must be trapped on the other side.

The Oriental carpet in the drawing room. As soon as the thought occurred to him, Reggie darted into the room on his right, where a thick Persian rug held place of pride. Only a few light chairs weighed it down, and with a ferocious jerk on the nearest edge he tugged it free. The carpet was small enough for one man to handle, just barely, and he folded it in half, then in half again.

Out in the hall, he hurled the weight of the carpet

forward, gripping one fringed end in his left hand. The heavy wool smashed down across the flames, creating a temporary fire-free zone. He ran across it, keeping low so he wouldn't pass out from lack of air. There was fire on each side of him, and his eyes burned from the smoke. Beyond the carpet, the fierce blazing light revealed Allie's slender figure crumpled against the wall. Moving with all the speed and strength of an athletic life, Reggie lifted her in his arms and carried her back across the rapidly charring carpet.

As he made his escape through the front door, Reggie thought that it was absolutely typical of Alys Weston that she would be rescued clutching a scorched and yowling cat in her arms.

Blessed coolness surrounded her. Perhaps hell was ice and not fire. Her lungs were working again, drawing in air uncontaminated by smoke, and her head began to clear. Slowly Alys realized that she was being carried. A pair of familiar hind legs thumped against her stomach; from the feel she deduced that she had been holding Attila and he had just kicked away from her.

Her eyes stung as she forced them open. With some effort she brought Reggie Davenport into focus as he lowered her carefully to the ground. He stayed kneeling next to her, one powerful arm supporting her in a sitting position. His soot-smudged face was only inches away, the blue eyes very light.

"Are you all right?" he asked, his voice quiet against a background of crackling fire and smashing timbers. When she nodded, he continued, "Is the other servant still inside?"

Alys swallowed and attempted speech, her voice emerging as a charred croak. "I don't think so." She broke into a spasm of coughing.

Davenport's arm tightened around her as she struggled for breath. "I hope she isn't," he said grimly. He was coatless, and swathes of black marked his white shirt. "No one else will be coming out alive."

"I think Janie might have slipped out to see her young

man," Alys managed. "When I find her, I'm going to wring her neck."

He chuckled. "I don't blame you. You damned near died in there."

"I noticed." Alys lifted a trembling hand to her face. Her thick braid had come undone, and long strands of hair trailed across her cheek. Brushing them back, she looked up to see the children's concerned faces around her. Smiling with as much reassurance as she could muster, she tried to stand, but Reggie held her firmly against him.

"Stay still until you get your strength back. There isn't anything you can do."

Alys raised her head to look at the house she had lived in for four years, just in time to see the roof crash inward with thunderous force. Flames shot high into the dark night air, illuminating the men pumping water onto the blaze. It was a futile effort.

Her friend Jamie Palmer crossed the yard and squatted beside her, his face grave. "Are you all right, Lady Alys?"

She reached out to pat his arm, knowing that he was feeling guilty for not having been there to stop the fire before it could get going. "I've been better, Jamie, but there's nothing seriously wrong."

He nodded, then went back to the fire engine. Beside her, William's voice quavered, "Where will we live?"

Alys reached out to him and he came and burrowed under her arm, seeking reassurance. Before she could speak, Davenport said, "You'll come back to the main house. There's plenty of room there, for you and your servants both."

Alys had not yet thought that far ahead, and she was intensely grateful to let her employer take charge. They might have only the clothes they stood up in, but at least they would have a roof over their heads. As she struggled to her feet, she saw Janie Herald hastening across the yard, her young face frightened in the uneven light. "Oh, Miss Weston, it's dreadful! Did everyone get out?"

Reggie answered astringently, "Miss Weston almost

died in the fire because she was looking for you. Remember that the next time you go sneaking off."

The maid's expression was crushed and guilty, and she began to cry as she turned to the young man behind her. Alys quietly told Reggie, "You shouldn't have been so hard on her."

His dark brows rose sardonically. "Am I correct that the extra time you spent looking for her was the difference between getting out easily and being roasted like a Christmas goose?"

"Yes, you're quite right." Alys was too drained to argue; she had also just realized that his arm was still around her, and it was too pleasant a sensation to interrupt. Reggie glanced at the young Spensers. "There's no point in lingering. Peter, collect the older woman—the cook, I think?—and help her to the house. Janie can come too, unless she wants to go back to her family or to her young man. Miss Spenser, you keep an eye on William." Turning to Alys, he asked, "Can you walk on your own?"

She nodded and took a step forward, almost falling when she did. Even though her head was clear, her knees were remarkably weak.

With a muttered oath, Reggie grabbed her. "Good God, woman, you don't even have shoes on."

Then, without so much as asking permission, he scooped her up in his arms and started back toward the manor house. Though she was not a small woman, he carried her easily. When he had brought her out of the burning house, Alys had not been conscious enough to appreciate the experience, but now she was very aware of the strength and warmth of his arms. Settling her head against his shoulder, she prepared to enjoy the ride, but could not resist a faint chuckle.

"If something amusing has happened, perhaps you can share it with me?" Davenport suggested.

"I was just thinking that I've never been swept off my feet before," Alys said without stopping to censor her words.

He laughed. "You probably never gave a man a chance to do any sweeping."

She was still trying to decide if there were any deeper meanings to his words when they arrived back at the manor house. The housekeeper had been wakened by the commotion associated with the fire, and with a few quick words Reggie had arranged for rooms to be readied, milk to be heated for William, and brandy poured for the others. Alys also received milk because of the smoke she had inhaled. Then he carried her upstairs to a room that was already made up. Alys was exhausted and three-quarters asleep, but she struggled to sit up after he deposited her on the four-poster bed. "The children . . ." she said hazily.

"They'll be all right," he said, pressing her back against the pillows with a firm, impersonal hand. Alys was used to being responsible for everything, and for a moment she resisted; she hadn't been tucked into bed since she was in the nursery. But oddly, it was easy to trust that Reggie would take care of everything, and in her present state of exhaustion she welcomed relinquishing her burdens.

Sleep claimed her almost immediately, but with the last threads of awareness she felt him sponging the soot off her face; surprising how gentle a large man could be.

This time when she slept, there were no nightmares.

12

When she opened her eyes and saw the light-drenched brocade canopy, for a moment Alys thought she was home in Carleon. Then memory snapped her back to the present. Carleon was irrevocably lost; now she was steward of Strickland, homeless and owning no more than a night rail and a robe with burned spots. Oh, yes, she also owned a mare and a cat.

From the angle of the sun, it was late in the morning,

and she sat up in bed quickly. As she did, a knock sounded, followed by Merry's golden head. "Oh, good, you're awake." The rest of Meredith followed into the room, along with a tray holding steaming coffee and a plate of fresh rolls. "Mr. Davenport said not to disturb you, but I knew that without your coffee you'd never wake up properly."

Alys accepted the hot drink gratefully, then leaned back against the headboard of the bed. "When you decide whom to marry, I will send references to whatever lucky man you have chosen. You always know exactly what a person needs."

Meredith laughed and subsided gracefully onto a chair. She was wearing a plain calico dress that didn't quite fit, doubtless borrowed from a maid, but apart from that she showed no effect from the night's disaster. Alys asked, "How are the boys?"

Merry nodded. "They're fine. Mr. Davenport found some clothes for them in the village, and packed them off to school for their lessons. This afternoon a seamstress is coming to take our measurements so proper things can be made up."

Alys felt a spurt of annoyance at his high-handedness, but had to give him credit for efficiency. As she spread marmalade on a roll, Merry continued, "He said he was sorry that there weren't any women's clothes available in your size, but he found some men's things that should fit." The girl gestured and Alys saw the garments in question. "He said that when it's convenient, he would like to talk to you in the library."

It was borne in on Alys that Davenport had made a strong impression on Meredith; her entire conversation seemed to revolve around his words and wishes. Well, doubtless it was natural under the circumstances.

At that moment, another concern was laid to rest. Merry had left the door ajar, and now Attila strolled through with all his usual lofty dignity, though the tail held straight over his back was much less plumelike than usual.

"Oh, I'm so glad Attila is all right," Alys exclaimed as

the long-haired cat jumped on the bed, then marched up to sniff at the roll in her right hand.

"It takes more than a fire to disconcert Attila," Merry said with amusement. "This morning he showed up at the kitchen door and demanded to be fed as if he hadn't a care in the world. Some of his hair had charred ends, so I trimmed it off, but he appears to have taken no real harm."

"Apparently not. It didn't take him long to find out where the food is." Alys agreed, putting aside roll and mug to cuddle the cat on her lap. He settled down, purring. As she scratched his chin, Alys noticed that most of his magnificent long whiskers were gone, leaving only short stubs.

"Look at the poor fellow's whiskers," she said. Those whiskers that were left were curled into tight little corkscrews. She tentatively touched one and, made brittle by heat, it snapped off, leaving another stub. "He'll have to be careful going into narrow places until these grow back."

"Attila got off very lightly," Meredith pointed out. "If you hadn't been clutching him when Mr. Davenport brought you out of the house, he'd be in feline heaven now."

"I got off very lightly too," Alys said with feeling. "I thought my time had come last night."

Merry's face instantly sobered. "We all did," she said quietly, unable to suppress the remembered fear in her face. "We were sure you were gone. And Mr. Davenport too, when he went back into the house . . ." She shuddered, her brightness dimmed; she had already lost too many people in her young life.

"It takes more than a little fire to get rid of me," Alys said cheerfully, moving Attila to one side so she could swing her long legs out of the bed. "Ouch!"

"What's wrong?" Merry asked anxiously.

"Sore toes." Alys perched on the edge of the bed and examined her soot-stained feet. "I didn't pay much attention last night, but I banged my toes at least once, and the floor was very hot. Now, don't look so upset," she added quickly, "and don't you *dare* hover over me as if I were an aging relation."

She wriggled her toes experimentally. "There's no real damage, but I would dearly love a bath."

"The water should be here any moment," Meredith said serenely. Right on cue, a soft knock sounded on the door, and two maids carrying coppers of hot water entered.

"I'll write you *two* references, not one," Alys promised.

Once she was alone in her bath, she gave way to pure bliss as she soaked the soot and soreness away. Since her thick hair smelled strongly of smoke, she took the time to wash it too. It was an effort to get out of the water, knowing that the unavoidable world waited outside. She toweled her hair to remove most of the water, then combed and braided it into her usual coronet.

Her employer had done a good job choosing clothes; doubtless he was expert at judging a woman's measurements, she thought with a touch of acid. The trousers were inevitably a bit tight in the hip and much too loose in the waist; her own male work clothing was specially tailored to fit properly. The boots and socks were a little large, but would do. Reminding herself that beggars couldn't be choosers, she went downstairs.

Davenport was working in the library, but he stood as she entered. "You look well-recovered."

"I am," she said as she chose a chair. "Attila and I owe you a considerable debt of gratitude."

"You might, but Attila doesn't. I assure you, any rescuing of that worthless creature was purely accidental," he said with a smile as he sat down again.

The black-and-white collie trotted over from where it had been lying at Davenport's feet. Alys greeted the dog, adding, "Speaking of worthless creatures, I see you still haven't found a home for the dog."

"Last night the collie proved that she wasn't entirely worthless, so I think she's earned the right to stay here." At Alys's inquiring look, he explained, "We were taking a walk last night when she smelled smoke and insisted on investigating. If she hadn't, I might not have been on the scene at the right time."

Alys looked into the collie's limpid brown eyes. "Thank

you, dog." Looking up with a smile, she said, "If you're going to keep her, you'll have to give her a name."

"You mean I can't just call her Dog?"

"I suppose so," she said dubiously, "but it would be better for her self-respect if she had a name of her own."

His light blue eyes twinkled. "In addition to your other skills, you're also an expert on canine self-esteem?"

"No, but I have opinions on everything," she said with a straight face.

Reggie laughed. "Very well, if she must have a name, how about Nemesis?"

Alys grinned. "That seems appropriate, since she seems to be your fate." More seriously she asked, "I trust you are well? You were exposed to your share of smoke and fire last night. You could have been killed."

He looked faintly uncomfortable. "Don't paint me as a hero, Allie. It was in my own best interest to save you. With a less efficient steward, I might actually have to do some work myself."

Alys couldn't quite repress a sniff of disbelief. "You will do as much or as little as you please, either with me or without me." Then, curiously, "How did you manage to find me in that inferno?"

He shrugged dismissively. "I heard you cry out and knew you couldn't be too far down the hall, so I took the drawing-room carpet and threw it over the flames. It created a temporary barrier."

"That was quick thinking." There was silence for a moment. Deciding that it was time to start talking about the future, Alys said, "I also appreciate your letting us stay here last night. I'm afraid it will take a day or two to make long-term arrangements, but we can move to the Silent Woman this afternoon, and be out of your way."

He made a dismissive gesture of his hand. "Nonsense, there is ample room here. In fact"—he toyed with a letter opener for a moment, his beautiful long fingers graceful—"the simplest solution to finding you a home is for all of you to stay here."

Alys stared at him. For a moment she thought she detected a touch of diffidence in his suggestion, then dismissed the thought; diffidence was not a quality she could associate with Reggie Davenport. "Don't be absurd. It would be wholly inappropriate."

"Your contract states that I provide you with housing, and with Rose Hall gone, there is no suitable residence on the estate," he pointed out. "As you yourself said, the cottages are all full, and my housekeeper says there are no decent rental properties in the area."

Alys bit her lip, knowing he was right. As steward, she needed to be available, not miles away, quite apart from the fact that her wards' friends and the boys' school were all nearby. It would certainly be convenient not to have to move away, but she was uneasily aware that she had felt a treacherous tickle of pleasure at the thought of sharing a house with her employer; absurdly, she liked having the man around, liked talking to him . . . Distrusting the trend of her thoughts, she made herself consider Meredith. Would a responsible guardian let an innocent girl live under the same roof as a rake?

With his usual uncanny perception, Davenport guessed what she was thinking. "If you're worried about reputations, I should think that having the whole family here would rate as suitable chaperonage."

And a thirty-year-old, dyed-in-the-wool spinster certainly made a good chaperon. No rake could possibly be interested in her; at least, not when he was sober. Knowing that there was a grim look on her face, Alys said, "I'll consider it, and discuss it with the children."

"In the meantime, I hope you don't think that one more night here will compromise you?"

"I suppose not," she allowed ungraciously.

He appeared amused at her quandary, but he said merely, "Do you feel ready to look at what's left of Rose Hall?"

It had to be done sooner or later. She nodded and accompanied him outside for the short walk to her former home. It was nearly noon, a bright, early-summer day. Ordinarily she would have been up for hours. Fortunately, nothing urgent had been planned for today, and the routine work of the estate would carry on without her supervision.

A house looks much smaller when only stone walls

remain. Rose Hall was a desolate shell now, the windows
blank and empty, the roof and intermediate floors col-
lapsed all the way through to the cellar. Traces of smoke
still curled up from charred beams, and blackened fragments of wood and slate lay scattered across the lawn.
Incongruously, a few flowers still bloomed where the
beds hadn't been trampled the night before.

There would be nothing worth salvaging from the ruins;
the destruction was nearly total. Alys thought of how
close she had come to leaving her own burned bones
among the embers, and shuddered. She suspected that
for the rest of her life her dreams would relive the panic
of being encircled by fire. Perhaps, if she were lucky,
that would displace her other recurring nightmare.

"Did you lose much in the way of personal belong-
ings?" Davenport's voice pulled her back from her dark
thoughts.

"The usual things—books, clothes, mementos. The bits
and pieces that define a life." Alys shrugged, her face
determinedly composed. "There was nothing very valu-
able kept in the house. My savings and most of the
jewelry Meredith inherited from her mother are in the
bank at Shaftesbury. The only real loss for me . . ." She
stopped.

When she didn't continue, he prompted, "The only
real loss was . . . ?"

"I had a locket with my mother's picture in it."

"I'm sorry." His voice was very gentle, and his sympathy brought a quick sting of tears to her eyes. Perhaps
that was why her all-too-perceptive employer changed
the subject.

"Have you any idea what might have caused the fire?"

The practical question restored Alys's control. "To be
honest, I hadn't thought about it." She began circling the
remains of the house, her brow furrowed. "At this season, the fireplaces weren't lit. The only source of fire
would be the banked coals in the kitchen, or a lamp or
candle if someone was still awake."

"I doubt it was a lamp. When I walked by, I didn't see
any lights anywhere in the house; I remember thinking
that everyone must be long since asleep. As for the

kitchen, it was on that side of the house, wasn't it?" Davenport gestured. When Alys nodded, his eyes narrowed in thought. "From what I could see, the fire began at the opposite end. Certainly that part of the house was destroyed before the rest. Most likely, the fire started in the west end of the cellar. I came along about the time the flames had burned through to the ground floor and become visible."

Alys frowned. "I know that sometimes fires can start spontaneously in piles of rags or rubbish, but our cellar was quite orderly, and a little damp to boot. I can't think of anything there that might have started a fire."

Reggie absently rolled over a blackened piece of wood with the toe of his polished boot. "This may sound preposterous, but do you have any enemies?"

"Good God! Do you really think it could have been arson?" Alys stared at Reggie, wondering if his wits were wandering.

"I don't know what to think, except that a fire has to start somehow, and this one doesn't appear to have been an accident," he pointed out. "Besides, when I was wandering by, I thought I saw someone sneaking away from the house. It could have been your hot-blooded housemaid, but when she showed up at the fire, she was wearing a light-colored dress. The person I saw was dressed in dark clothing. If I really did see someone."

"What kind of madman would set fire to a house full of sleeping people?" Alys was appalled at the thought.

He shrugged. "Someone who likes fire. If that sort of madman is around, there might be other fires set in the area." He turned to face her. "But we must face the possibility that the blaze was deliberately set to threaten someone in the house. Does Miss Spenser have any heartbroken swains that might conceivably fire her house from pure frustration?"

Alys made herself seriously consider the idea before answering. "No. While she has any number of admirers, she is always charming to them. I can't imagine that any are lovelorn or unstable enough to do something so dreadful."

Relentless in his questions, he next asked, "Was any-

one angry enough about the smallpox vaccinations to
retaliate against you? Though I would have been a more
proper target, you were the one that carried out my
orders."

Alys considered it, then shook her head. "No. There
was some grumbling, but no one was really outraged."

"I hope you are right. I would hate to think that you
were endangered by my actions." His light blue eyes met
hers, and she was moved by the concern she saw there.
"Perhaps I'm just naturally suspicious. I'm not even sure
I saw anyone last night. But—just in case—be careful.
And talk to your wards."

"I will," she said soberly. "I surely will."

Alys had her discussion with her charges over tea that
afternoon. Though each had lost cherished personal possessions in the fire, their gratitude that no one had been
injured or killed kept their losses in perspective. After
some consideration, Alys decided to mention the possibility of arson, but not that it might have been deliberately aimed at someone in the house. Davenport's
overheated imagination must be a result of his own colorful past; murder by arson wasn't something that would
happen in peaceful Dorset.

She half-hoped that her wards would be reluctant to
live in the manor house, but they received the idea with
enthusiasm.

"By Jove, Mr. Davenport really wouldn't mind having
us here? He's a great gun." Peter gave his approval
quickly, then subsided into silence, probably plotting the
best time to ask Davenport for driving lessons.

William liked the idea of being so close to the stables,
while Meredith got a speculative expression on her lovely
face. "We would actually be living here, not just guests?"
When Alys nodded, Merry said dreamily, "This house is
so much better for entertaining than Rose Hall, don't
you think?"

"It is a good house for entertaining," Alys admitted,
"and Mr. Davenport has insisted that we treat it as
home. He has been very generous." He had even tried to
pay for replacing their wardrobes, and a brisk argument

had ensued, resolved only when Alys agreed to let him pay half of the costs.

She continued, "He doesn't really know what he is letting himself in for. If you plague the poor man to death, or it's obvious that matters aren't working out, we'll have to make different arrangements. But since you all like the idea, we'll try it."

Her decision was greeted with whoops of joy. Of course, the pleasure Alys herself felt was just because her wards were happy.

After the boys left, Alys had a private talk with Meredith. Her eyes dancing, Merry assured her guardian that she had no intention of succumbing to Mr. Davenport's elderly charms, adding that he had acted in a most respectable—indeed, positively avuncular—fashion. Not entirely convinced of her employer's respectability, Alys resigned herself to trusting in Meredith's considerable good sense.

The only real objections came from Junius Harper, who arrived shortly after tea, bubbling with solicitude and indignation. Alys received him in the small salon, grateful that Davenport was away from the house.

Junius clasped her hand fervently, saying, "I spent last night with the bishop in Salisbury, and have only just returned. You can imagine the perturbation I felt on hearing the dreadful news! Sweet, fragile Miss Spenser . . . such danger must have been a great strain on her delicate nerves."

While Merry certainly had cause to be distressed, it was Alys who had come closest to meeting her maker prematurely. But as everyone knew, she didn't have delicate nerves. Disengaging her hand, she said, "It was a frightening experience, but none of us took any injury."

As they seated themselves, the vicar's expression changed to one of dire foreboding. "As distressing as the news of the fire was, that was nothing to the agitation I felt on learning that you had spent the night in this . . . this house of infamy!"

Amused by his priorities, Alys said, "Calling Strickland a house of infamy is a bit strong, Junius. Besides, would death really be preferable to a 'fate worse than death'?"

Ignoring her digression, he intoned, "I do not hesitate
to tell you that I was shocked. Nay, more than shocked,
appalled."

Wishing he *had* hesitated to say it, Alys said with
asperity, "Brave of you to risk your immortal soul by
calling here."

Blind to sarcasm, Junius said, "I hope I know where
my duty lies. But I must insist that you remove yourself
and the children immediately. I am surprised that you
did not think to go to the vicarage last night. Even
though I was not there to receive you, you know you
would have been made welcome, and Miss Spenser would
not have been exposed to that rake's wiles."

The vicar's generosity was not quite enough to balance
the surge of temper Alys felt at his peremptory words. "I
was in no condition to consider alternative residences,
and Mr. Davenport's offer was most welcome. And need
I remind you that you have no right to insist that I do
anything?"

"Surely I have some right as your spiritual adviser, if
not as your friend," Junius said stiffly.

Feeling ashamed of herself, Alys took a more concilia-
tory tone. "I know that you have taken Mr. Davenport
in dislike, but I assure you he has been most gentlemanly. He also showed great presence of mind and courage last night. Did your informant mention that he saved
my life, at great risk to his own?"

The vicar dismissed that with a quick flick of his hand.
"Physical courage comes easily to his type. It is his
morals—or rather, his lack of them—that concern me. I
will have no peace of mind until you and your charges
are away from here."

"Then resign yourself to having your peace cut up,"
she said, her eyes glinting with exasperation. "Mr. Davenport has invited us to live here, and we have accepted."

Horror showed on the vicar's face. "You cannot mean
it! It is bad enough to have stayed one night in the
aftermath of a disaster, but to *live* here? It is wholly
unacceptable. Miss Spenser's reputation will be ruined
forever."

"Between her brothers and me, she will be adequately

chaperoned." Alys was quite willing to use Davenport's own arguments. "Besides, we must live somewhere, and there are no other houses available in the area."

"You could live at the vicarage."

She sighed. While Junius was not a stupid man, he could be quite maddeningly obstinate. "If it is propriety that concerns you, the vicarage would be no improvement, since both your household and this are bachelor establishments."

"Surely the differences between the homes of a man of the cloth and a libertine should be obvious!" Junius said hotly.

"Of course there are differences. For one thing, Strickland is considerably more spacious," Alys snapped, struggling with the desire to give Junius a really crushing set-down. "While your offer is magnanimous, it would look very odd indeed for us to move in with you. Mr. Davenport's legal obligation to provide his steward with housing is at least a legitimate reason for our living here."

Junius's face reflected a tumult of passing emotions. Finally he said, "If you need a reason, you can marry me. Besides providing a proper home for the children, you would also be able to give up an unladylike employment that must surely be distasteful to you."

Not only was she not the sort of woman men desired, she couldn't even inspire a decent proposal! Provoked beyond tact, Alys exclaimed, "That is the most bird-witted reason for marriage I have ever heard. Believe me, there is no need to sacrifice yourself in such a way. All three of my wards are pleased at the prospect of living at Strickland, and I think it will work out very well.

"As for my employment, I don't find it in the least distasteful; indeed, I enjoy it." While she knew that Junius approved of her good sense and charitable endeavors, Alys had never dreamed he would actually make her an offer. His mind might approve of her, but it was quite obvious that the less godly parts of his person fancied Meredith.

A little wildly, the vicar said, "If you won't marry me, then let me pay my addresses to Miss Spenser. It is unthinkable that such sweet goodness be corrupted by a man such as Davenport."

Two proposals within a minute! The vicar must be setting some sort of record. "I assure you, Junius, such draconian measures as marriage are not necessary. Meredith will come to no harm here. Your lack of faith in her virtue is most unflattering, I might add." Offering a sop to the cleric's anxiety, Alys went on, "Besides, it is quite possible that Mr. Davenport shall soon tire of rusticating, and we won't see him again for months, if ever." She didn't believe that, but the possibility might reconcile the vicar to the situation.

He stood, his movements agitated. "I see that your mind is quite made up. I will pray that you come to your senses before it is too late."

As Junius was taking his leave, Davenport entered the small salon, with Nemesis faithfully shadowing his heels. His eyes took on a glint of unholy amusement when he saw Alys's visitor, but he greeted the vicar with civility, as if they hadn't come close to blows on their first meeting.

"No doubt you are surprised to see me here, Davenport," the vicar said belligerently.

"Not at all. Since you are a friend of Miss Weston and her charges, I would expect you to call," Davenport said with perfect affability.

"I shall be calling again." Junius's tone made it a challenge.

"But of course." Davenport raised his brows. "You don't strike me as the sort of man to flinch at entering the lion's den if his cause is just."

While Alys suppressed a choke of laughter, the vicar gave his host a suspicious glare, unable to decide if he was being mocked. Deeming discretion to be the better part of valor, he stiffly took his leave. After he left, Alys said, "It was good of you not to forbid him the house, when he behaved so badly the first time you met."

Davenport gave his teasing half-smile. "If this is your home, I hardly have the right to forbid your guests. I'll admit I would rather the good vicar didn't run tame here, but I daresay my godless presence will reduce the number of his visits."

Alys was sure that he was right, and took a certain guilty pleasure in the thought; Junius could be rather a trial. "Were you looking for me?"

Reggie nodded. "I thought it might be useful to talk about sharing the same establishment. The house is large enough that we needn't live in each other's pockets, but we should know what to expect of each other."

"An excellent idea," Alys agreed, sitting down again. Over the next hour they discussed a variety of issues. Davenport felt no need to eat in solitary quiet, so meals would be taken together, at country hours; Alys tentatively suggested that William could eat in the nursery, but was glad Davenport thought it unfair that the child be condemned to eat alone merely because he was the youngest.

The bedrooms assigned to the guests the night before would become permanent; the young people were in a cluster in the east wing, Davenport was at the far west end of the house, and Alys's spacious chamber was in the center, flanked by empty bedrooms on each side so she would have more privacy. Although it wasn't said aloud, the location was a good guardian position, since, at least in theory, Alys would hear any surreptitious night traffic. Propriety was such a silly business; any two people wishing to misbehave together could surely find a way.

They had discussed the duties of Alys's servants and reached an amiable accord when Alys saw Attila enter the door of the salon. The cat immediately went into his hunter mode, belly tight to the carpet, hindquarters and tail quivering, golden eyes narrow and feral. Then, moving with panther swiftness, Attila darted across the carpet and pounced on the collie, which was peacefully sleeping with her muzzle on her master's foot. Nemesis jumped up yelping and whirled madly, looking for the attacker.

As Alys scooped the cat up in her arms, Davenport concentrated on calming his beleaguered dog, his face alight with amusement. "Your cat, Lady Alys, is a bully."

"I'm afraid you're right," she said ruefully, struggling to keep Attila from going after Nemesis again. "I hadn't realized just how much of one. I know cats don't much like other cats unless they are raised together, but I'm surprised that Attila will tackle a dog so much larger than he."

As the trembling collie pressed against Davenport's leg, he ruffled her ears comfortingly. "You're going to have to get used to him, Nemesis." He chuckled. "I have a feeling that the humans of our households will get on better than the pets."

As they laughed together, it was easy to believe that was true.

13

In the event, adjusting to life in the manor house proved painless. Even effervescent William recognized that the owner of the house was unused to the vagaries of children and didn't press his attentions unless invited to. Dinner was the only meal they all took together, and it proved a comfortable occasion. Davenport tended to speak little, but watched the young people with obvious amusement. Very quickly everyone was relaxed and volunteering information on his respective activities. Peter screwed up his courage to ask for instruction in driving, and with dazed delight he found himself the eager student of a veritable top-sawyer.

William's heart was won when a lively pony, just the right size for him, appeared in the stables, and Merry quickly fell into a teasing, amiable way with Davenport. It was only to be expected; all of the children had missed having a father, and, if not precisely paternal, Davenport certainly made an excellent honorary uncle. Only with Alys did he maintain a certain reserve, friendly but not entirely relaxed. Perhaps he feared she would pursue him ruthlessly if he gave her any encouragement.

If that was true, it was odd that her employer subverted the seamstress. When the last lot of clothing was delivered, it included several gowns Alys had not ordered, all in brighter colors and more daringly cut than she usually wore. Meredith admitted with a smile that she and Davenport had planned it between them; when Alys confronted him directly, he pointed out that she was no longer a governess, so why did she dress like one? Surely there could be no need to restrict herself to navy blue and brown when she was dining with her family.

Once again, his high-handed ways annoyed her, but she didn't send the gowns back. In her fashionable youth she had been restricted to demure white muslins that did nothing for her coloring, and now it was a pleasure to wear rich green or rust or teal. She thought she looked rather well; certainly the children agreed, and the admiring warmth in Davenport's eyes sent a glow through her entire body.

The days quickly returned to the normal pattern of work and family; it was nights that were difficult. Alys told herself the problem was a strange bed, but she was all too aware that she was sleeping under the same roof with a man of quite overpowering attractiveness; a man, moreover, who had showed occasional signs of interest in the fact that she was a female.

As she lay in her fourth night of insomnia, she finally asked herself what she wanted from Reggie Davenport. An affair? While it was just barely conceivable that in the heat of passion she might throw caution to the winds, it was quite impossible for sober, unglamorous Alys Weston to cold-bloodedly embark on such a wanton course. If she were absolutely candid, she must admit that the idea of being his mistress was enormously appealing. Yet how could she set such an example to the children? An affair could not be kept a secret for long, and would surely jeopardize her position as steward.

So an affair was out of the question, and there was no other possibility. Her employer appeared to enjoy her company, had even found her not wholly lacking in appeal, but he was certainly not going to marry her. If Davenport wanted to set up a nursery, there were any number of more eligible females in the area, or he could go to

London and have the pick of the crop. The very respectable fortune he had acquired would offset his rakish past,
and with his personal magnetism he would have his choice
of ladies who were far younger, prettier, and wealthier
than she.

Alys reminded herself that if he ever did marry, he
would doubtless make the very devil of a husband, though
she feared that her thoughts had a faint whiff of the fox
complaining about unobtainable grapes.

As she rolled over in her bed, she faced her worst fear
with brutal honesty: that in a moment of drunken indis-
crimination, Davenport would take her to his bed and
find the experience too uninteresting to repeat. Even the
thought brought a sick knot to her stomach. The least
pain and humiliation lay in accepting that her present
friendly, limited relationship was the most that she could
ever have with him.

Her logic was faultless, and there was a certain relief in
having worked the matter through. Unfortunately, her
stomach was still knotted with anxiety; perhaps some
brandy would help. With a sigh, she sat up and fumbled
for her new summer-weight dressing gown, an attractive
garment in gold velveteen with braid trim.

The most convenient brandy supply was down in Davenport's library. It was his particular retreat, but she
expected it to be empty at this hour and was startled to
find him lounging in his favorite wing chair, coat and
cravat off and his feet on a brocade stool. Candlelight
touched the tooled-leather backs of the books and cast a
warm glow across the room. Her employer had a book
open in his lap and a half-empty goblet in his hand. A
decanter was within easy reach, and Nemesis snored
peacefully by his feet.

It was a perfect picture of a man at his leisure, and
Alys halted uncertainly in the door, admiring the play of
light on the planes of his lean face. She was about to end
the brief moment of self-indulgence and go away when
he glanced up and saw her. Smiling lazily, he said, "Come
and join me."

"Are you sure I'm not disturbing you?" Her earlier
thoughts caused her to hang back, even though she yearned

to accept his invitation. "I didn't realize that anyone was still awake."

"You're not disturbing me. It's no bad thing to have company in the dark watches of the night." He raised his goblet in a wry toast, then drank deeply.

As Alys entered the library, he waved a casual hand at the decanter and urged her to help herself. As she did, a quick glance revealed that the book on his lap was in Greek, a fact which shouldn't have surprised her, but did. While he must have had the usual education of his class, he radiated such physical force that it was easy to forget just how intelligent he was. She, who had worked with him, should know better.

Usually her employer was impeccable, well-dressed in an unobtrusive way, but when he had been indulging he became faintly disheveled. Tonight he looked distinctly rakish, and she guessed that he had been drinking through the hours since she and the children had gone to bed. His speech was clear and unslurred, though slower than usual, so perhaps his manner of dress was a better gauge of his sobriety.

Alys curled up in the wing chair opposite, legs tucked under her, and sipped the brandy, feeling the slow burn of it on her tongue and down her throat, enjoying a sense of contentment. After several minutes had passed, she spoke to his earlier remark. "You're right about the dark watches of the night. They can be very lonely indeed."

"Sometimes. Often." His voice was very low. "Always."

The disconnected words were a confession of sorts, and she was disconcerted when he raised his head and his clear light eyes met hers with no trace of the reserve he wore like armor. She could not decipher the complex blend of emotions in his gaze—surely vulnerability could not be among them—but she was sharply aware that it was very late and that they were alone. The tautness in her midriff changed to a more pleasurable kind as tension coiled deep within her.

"What keeps you awake late at night, Allie?" he asked, his voice soft and intimate. "Don't hard work and a clear conscience count for anything?"

His openness called for a like response, and there was

deep regret in her reply. "Who among us has a really clear conscience?"

"Lord knows I don't." He tilted his head back and finished the brandy in his goblet, then leaned over to pour more. "Though in all modesty, I'm sure my sins utterly surpass yours."

She smiled faintly. "If even half the stories about you are true, you're probably correct."

"I should think that about half is the correct proportion. The question for you is . . ." He paused, an amused glint in his eyes. "Which half?"

"Would you tell me what was true if I asked?" she inquired, her head tilted and her heavy braid falling over her shoulder.

"Probably. I generally answer direct questions. Most people are too well-bred or too afraid of the answers to ask." His amusement became more pronounced. "It would be interesting to see if you are as unshockable as you claim."

Perhaps it was the brandy, or her own intense curiosity about him, but she recklessly decided to take Reggie up on his willingness to be forthright. And she might as well start with the worst. "Did you really have a pregnant mistress run away to you, kill her husband in a duel, and then abandon her?"

There was an odd expression on his face, and for a moment she thought he wouldn't answer. "A good place to start," he said finally, "since that story is exactly half-true."

"Which half?"

"The lady in question did indeed seek my protection, I did kill her husband in a duel, and we did not marry." His words were cool and precise.

Alys's hands felt chilly, and she wondered that he could admit to such monstrous behavior so calmly. She learned that she was not as unshockable as she pretended, and it was an effort to comment without a tremor. "In what way is the rest false?"

He leaned his head against the chair back and watched her through half-closed eyes. "She wasn't my mistress, and I didn't abandon her."

Feeling irrationally relieved, she settled more deeply in her chair. "It sounds like an interesting story. May I hear more?"

She saw him subtly relax. Had he thought she would not believe him? "The lady in question was the sister of a school friend of mine, Theo. Since my guardian and I shared a profound mutual dislike, I spent most of my school holidays with Theo's family. Those were some of the better memories of my youth. His sister was a pretty little thing who tagged around after us."

He took another sip of brandy, his gaze distant. "After Eton, Theo's father bought him a pair of colors. He and I continued to correspond, but over the years I lost touch with the rest of his family. In the interim, his sister Sarah married, his parents died.

"Then one day Sarah showed up on my doorstep, bloody and beaten within an inch of her life." His voice had a hard, angry edge. "Her husband was a vicious bastard who regularly bounced her off the walls when he was in a jealous fit, which was often. When she became pregnant, he was sure she had been unfaithful to him, and damn near killed her. Her brother was fighting in the Peninsula, too far away to know how bad the situation had become. But he had told her once that if she needed help, she could come to me."

He shrugged, his powerful shoulders flexing under his white shirt. "Since her brother couldn't protect her, I did."

Amazing how different his version of the story was from that of Junius Harper. Alys released the breath she had been holding. "By eliminating her husband?"

"Exactly." His expressive mouth quirked sardonically. "If her husband had assaulted another woman as he did her, he could have been convicted and jailed. But since she was his wife, beating her was perfectly acceptable. There was no possibility of divorce; violence isn't enough to free a wife of her husband."

"After Sarah took refuge with you, did her husband challenge you to a duel?"

"Not precisely." Reggie smiled unpleasantly. "He hired a couple of bully boys to murder me in an alley. When I escaped more or less unscathed, I challenged him."

Alys's goblet was forgotten in her lap, her fingers locked around the stem. "And then you killed him."

"I executed him," he corrected. "Since the law didn't offer justice, I took it into my own hands."

"And Sarah?"

"I offered to marry her if it would make things easier, but she said the last thing she wanted just then was another husband." He grinned suddenly. "I'll admit I was grateful that she didn't accept, though I think we would have dealt tolerably well together.

"Anyhow, after her son was born, even her late husband's vengeful relatives admitted that the boy looked very much like his father. To the outrage of the entire county of Lincoln, she went back to her husband's estate and took control of the property on her son's behalf. Last year, she scandalized everyone all over again by marrying a local physician, a man quite beneath her in fortune and birth. From her letters, she's quite pleased with her life, though the high sticklers won't receive her." Reggie gave a teasing smile. "She's rather like you—a strong-minded woman."

Ignoring his last sentence, Alys said thoughtfully, "So you let the world think what it wished, and of course it preferred the most scandalous interpretation."

"Of course," he agreed.

Next question. "Is it hard to kill someone?"

He was surprised at first, then thoughtful. "If you want to know if I enjoy killing, the answer is no. However, on the occasions when I have found it appropriate, I have felt little compunction and no remorse. The world was not a better place for having Sarah's husband in it, and my conscience would have troubled me infinitely more if I had attended her funeral, knowing I had done nothing to help her while she was alive."

"Have you fought many duels?" Fascinated by this glimpse of the masculine world, Alys intended to take full advantage of Reggie's willingness to talk.

He considered a moment. "Between fifteen and twenty, I suppose. I've never actually counted."

"Was Junius accurate about the number that . . . were fatal?"

"The estimable Mr. Harper is quite well-informed," he answered obliquely.

"Tell me the circumstances of the other fatal ones," she prompted.

"What a bloodthirsty wench you are," he said, his tone cool and ironic.

"Not really." Alys colored. "I'm just curious. Men make such a commotion about honor, but I've never quite understood what is worth killing for."

He sighed. "Well, I said I'd answer direct questions. Once I killed a Captain Sharp fond of fleecing green boys from the country. Everyone agreed he was a disgrace, but no one did anything. A lad I knew slightly lost his fortune to the man and shot himself the next morning. So I did something."

"What about the duel in Paris last year?"

"The French had trouble accepting defeat, even after Waterloo. Some retaliated by forcing quarrels on Allied officers. They would then choose to fight with swords, with which most French officers are extremely skilled. A number of Allied officers were killed." He gave a bored shrug. "I didn't like that."

"I have the feeling you are very good with a sword," Alys murmured.

"Tolerably so," he agreed, volunteering no more.

"Were your other duels also mercy missions?"

He made a face. "Don't think me heroic. On several occasions I felt impelled to administer rude justice, but more often than not my duels were the result of too much drink, too much temper, or quarrels forced on me which I could not easily avoid. When one has developed a reputation, a certain kind of man feels compelled to challenge it."

"What of the other time you killed someone in a duel? Was that another occasion when you acted as Justice?"

For the first time Reggie shifted restlessly, recrossing his legs and slouching further into his chair. "Bacchus was the deity in that case. I never meant to kill the fellow. It was just a stupid quarrel over a woman, but . . . I'd had far too much to drink. My aim was off." His voice was very flat.

"The other deaths you can live with very easily, but not that one," she said softly.

"Exactly so." He gave her a satirical smile. "Are you satisfied in your pursuit of knowledge about rakes?"

"Not in the least," Alys said, widening her eyes. "Surely duels are only a small part of being a rake. On another occasion you explained about gaming, but there must be a multitude of other vices to explore."

His face eased. "There are, but to be honest, I haven't tried every single one."

"No?" she said in disappointment. "How about orgies? Have you ever participated in any of them?"

Caught in the middle of a swallow of brandy, he choked and began coughing. In a sputter of amusement he asked, "What do you know about orgies?"

"Very little," she admitted. "I was hoping that you would explain them to me."

He eyed her suspiciously. "You may be unshockable, but I find that I'm not. Explaining what might be called an orgy would bring a blush to my manly cheek."

She shook her head sorrowfully. "And here I thought the first requirement for aspiring rakes was an utter lack of embarrassment."

He gave a wry smile. "No, the first requirement is not to give a damn about what other people think."

"I expect that you were born that way," she said with a sunny smile.

His amusement vanished as quickly as it had come. "Not born that way, but I learned it early."

Wanting to erase his dark expression, she asked, "What are some of the other requirements for being a rake?"

He gave the matter serious consideration. "The one thing that is utterly indispensable is overindulgence in the fair sex."

"Discreetly put," she said with approval. "Exactly how many women must one indulge with in order for it to become *over*indulgence?"

"Ten," he said promptly.

She burst out laughing. Really, this was the most extraordinary conversation. Her behavior was every bit as outlandish as his. "That's it? Slake your wicked lust with ten different women and you are automatically a rake?"

"Ten is the minimum requirement, but more would be better," he allowed.

Prompted by an inner demon, Alys asked, "How many have you . . . ?" Her voice trailed off as she realized that this question was one she really did not want to know the answer to.

"Once again, I did not keep count." He sighed, his face suddenly weary. "Too many. Too damned many."

He stood and went to reshelve his book, his movements betraying him as his speech had not. Reggie still had the grace of the born athlete, but now there was a precise, slightly exaggerated quality to his actions, as if moving normally required conscious effort. Alys disliked seeing him like this, being less than he should be, but if he were not drunk, they would not be having this remarkable conversation. To cover the thought, she asked randomly, "What were you reading?"

He slid the book into its slot, part of a matched set of volumes bound in blue leather. "The *Odyssey*." He ran his long fingers lightly over the gold-tooled titles. "When I was six years old, my father began teaching me Greek in this room."

"Was he a scholar?"

Davenport turned and faced her, leaning his shoulders against the oak bookshelves. "Not really, but like many men of his education and generation, he loved the classics. He spent over a year in Italy and Greece on his Grand Tour." After a moment's reflection he added, "He was a good teacher."

She had a sudden poignant image of the father and son bending over the old volumes as sunlight slanted through the library windows, the man reminiscing of his travels, the boy listening eagerly, wanting to learn and to please his sire. She herself had learned mathematics and accounts that way. Did he miss his father as much as she missed hers? His father had died; she had lost hers to anger and implacable pride, a combination as final as death.

Her throat tight, she mused, "I'm not surprised that you enjoy the *Odyssey*. I rather fancy you as Odysseus."

His mouth quirked up. "The villainous hero who spent twenty years getting into trouble while he tried to find his way home again? Perhaps."

"Exactly." Alys chuckled. "I always thought the fellow sounded rather rakish. Why, just look at that business with Circe." After consideration she added, "Though it took you longer than twenty years to find your way home."

A flicker in his eyes showed that her words had struck some chord, and he shifted his lean frame to a new position. Dryly he pointed out, "Don't forget, he had a faithful Penelope waiting."

"Well, Odysseus wasn't eight years old when he left for Troy," she said reasonably. "You may have been precocious, but not *that* precocious."

When he smiled, she decided to take a risk and probe still further. "Among all those women you've overindulged with, surely there must have been a Penelope who wanted to wait for you?"

His laughter was sardonic. "God God, Allie, while I have known many women, I doubt that any of them were fool enough to want to marry me. Females are practical creatures, after all. Even the ones that pursued me rather than vice versa were interested in one thing only, and it wasn't marriage."

Alys hoped the candlelight covered her blush. From the first moment he had come swaggering into her life, she had understood perfectly why a woman would pursue him. But there was so much more to Reggie than physical magnetism, and she certainly could not have been the first female to perceive that. "Perhaps some of them were interested, and you didn't notice since you didn't share their interest," she murmured.

She swirled the brandy in her goblet reflectively. "I would have thought that at least once in your life you considered giving up raking and settling down with one woman."

His expression hardened. "Oh, everyone is a fool for love at least once, and I was no exception. It's part of being young."

She, too, had been such a fool; the pain of first love was not one that ever quite went away. "What happened?"

"Nothing much. I met a girl and became absolutely mad for her for reasons I can't begin to remember. For a few weeks she appeared to feel the same way."

"And then?"

His expression became a self-mocking sneer. "I made an impassioned declaration, and she informed me that while I was all very well as a flirt, she certainly had no intention of marrying a man with no expectations to speak of."

Alys winced. The curtness of his tone indicated how deeply wounding that rebuff had been.

Recognizing her fellow feeling, he said harshly, "Don't waste any sympathy on me. She was quite right—I was wholly ineligible. Besides," he added with a bitter twist to his mouth, "I had my revenge."

She cocked her head. "Not, I trust, by challenging her to a duel. I suppose it would have been easy to ruin her reputation."

He gave a short, humorless laugh. "I could have done that, but I didn't."

The silence stretched until Alys said, "You can't leave me in suspense after such a provocative statement."

He smiled reluctantly. "I suppose not. Very well, I'll tell you, but don't blame me if this time you *are* shocked." He shifted from one foot to another, brushing his dark hair back impatiently. "The female in question—I won't call her a lady—captured an aging gentleman of substantial wealth. Then, after she was safely married, she indicated to me that she was available for . . . illicit sport."

Alys watched in fascination. "And you turned her down?"

"On the contrary." His eyes were ice pale. "I accepted, then exerted myself to the fullest to ensure her satisfaction."

He fell silent again, until Alys asked in exasperation, "How was that revenge?"

"You are sure you really want to know?" When she nodded, he continued, "Our little . . . encounter was quite unlike anything she had experienced before. She positively panted for an encore."

Suddenly Alys knew what was coming. "And you refused her."

"Exactly so. With a few choice comments on how unrewarding I had found her." His voice was dry in the extreme.

Alys gasped at the sheer ruthlessness of using physical intimacy to enslave a woman, then callously rejecting her. His revenge was an eerie reflection of her own worst nightmares. It was also a measure of how deeply hurt he had been by a heartless girl's casual cruelty. "That is quite wickedly clever," she said slowly. "It was also absolutely appropriate."

"You mean I still haven't shocked you?" His dark brows arched with surprise and a certain respect.

"A little, perhaps," she admitted. "But there is a rough justice to what you did. In comparable circumstances I would do something similar, if I were sharp-witted enough."

He laughed with real amusement. "More and more I have the feeling that your proper appearance is no more than a facade. Underneath, you have the soul of a marauder."

She considered, then nodded. "Very likely you are right."

His eyes were intent on hers, pale and clear as aquamarine, and she could feel the energy change between them, becoming taut and sensual. His deep voice husky, he said, "Come here."

Alys sat stone still for a moment. Earlier she had decided she could never embark on an affair in cold blood, but her blood was not cold now; it sang warm and urgent in her veins.

She rose and walked over to him, halting an arm's length away, her eyes meeting his with question, doubt, and longing. This close, she felt his intense virility drawing her, as if they were opposite poles of a magnet, seeking their mates.

For a moment they stood that way, motionless and utterly intent on each other. Then he raised his hands.

She thought he would bring her close for a kiss, but instead he grasped her heavy braid and untied the piece of yarn at the end. Combing his fingers through the thick tresses, he released her hair from its maidenly restraint, loosening it, twining the shining strands through his long fingers until they spilled in a silken mantle over her shoulders, tumbling halfway to her waist.

"You have beautiful hair," he said softly, his fingertips drifting across her cheek and throat in a deeply erotic caress. His blue eyes held hers, and the desire she saw there was a potent aphrodisiac, releasing the hidden part of her nature as surely as he had unbound her hair. She caught her breath, and her lips parted, wanting more, not knowing how to ask.

Putting one finger under her chin, he lifted it. She had been uncomfortable with his height, but now she realized that he was exactly the right size, tall enough to make her feel fragile and feminine, not so tall that it took more than a slight inclination of his head to bring his lips to hers. It was a brandy-flavored kiss, rich and heady and intoxicating. All her senses were heightened and she was acutely aware of the pulse of blood in her veins, the subtle library scents of leather and oak, the strength of the arms that drew her to him.

As they came together, passion flamed between them, fierce and mindless, and tentative touch became crushing embrace. Ever since she had been an awkward, yearning girl, Alys had longed to learn love's mysteries. Now she had found her teacher in this improbable man, with his cynicism and mockery, his wry self-knowledge and dangerous sense of justice. She knew herself for a fool, and didn't care.

She was so sure of her desire, so totally immersed in the moment, that when he pulled back, the shock of deprivation was like a splash of frost-cold water. Dazed, she opened her eyes.

"Bloody, bloody hell!" he swore, his hands gripping her arms with bruising strength as he held her away from him.

"What's wrong?" she whispered, bereft by her aloneness, terrified that he was repulsed by her wanton behavior.

He shook his head, desire and fury warring on his face. "I said I wouldn't do this." He released her and stepped back, rubbing his temples as if trying to clear his mind. He repeated in a harsh undertone, "I said I wouldn't do this."

He lifted his eyes to her, his expression twisted with self-contempt. "Allie, I'm sorry. You deserve better."

Then he turned away. A set of French doors led outside, and he crossed the room to them. As he fumbled with the key in the lock, she cried out, "Where are you going?"

He glanced back at her, his face bleak. "Out. Anywhere until I sober up." Then he was gone.

Alys sank into one of the chairs, her knees too weak to support her. Her body cried out to continue what it had begun, and her mind was an ache of confusion. Was the statement that she deserved better a gentlemanly way of avoiding doing something he would regret in the morning? *How many? Too damned many.* The rake's lament.

She did not doubt that for a handful of drunken moments he had wanted her, but even in his present undiscriminating state he realized that by dawn's sober light he would regret it. It would take a great deal to titillate the jaded palate of a man who had known women beyond counting; there was no challenge or sport in bedding an unattractive, overeager spinster.

As the collie came over and whimpered sympathetically, Alys huddled in the chair, her face buried in her hands, her shoulders shaking with uncontrollable sobs. Though more kindly phrased, this was a rejection as painful as the one Randolph had given her. The only comfort she could find was the fervent hope that in the morning he would remember nothing of what had transpired between them.

14

Reggie rode all night, letting his horse have its head at every crossroads, not caring where he went as long as he kept moving. When he first left the stables, dizzy and on the edge of passing out, only the skill and habit of years kept him in the saddle. In recognition of that fact, he had saddled up a calm chestnut hunter instead of Bucephalus. The stallion was a lively handful under the best of circumstances, and in Reggie's present jug-bitten state Bucephalus would probably have broken his neck. Not that that would have been a bad idea. Through frustration and brandy-induced confusion, one thought loomed with brutal clarity: he was failing again.

The roads and lanes ran through fields of ripening summer grain that rippled pale in the moonlight, lined by dark hedges and shadowing trees. He and the chestnut wound their way up to Shaftesbury, across the barren, undulating downs, then south again through quiet lanes and occasional sleeping village greens. Light mists pooled where the road dipped lower. He had gone out without his coat, and as the alcohol wore off, the night's damp chill bit deep through his linen shirt.

As his mind cleared and a headache began pulsing in time to the horse's hooves, his thoughts were as cold as his body. It had been a mistake to invite Alys Weston and her foster family to move in with him. It had seemed an irresistibly good idea to fill the empty spaces of the manor house with youth and laughter, and Strickland was large enough to give him privacy as needed.

In one way, the idea had worked. The three young Spensers shared intelligence, enthusiasm, and good manners, and he enjoyed their company. The problem was with Lady Alys herself. He had found her attractive from the first time he saw her, and knew that having that lithe body under his own roof would be a constant temptation. However, contrary to popular opinion, he was quite capable of resisting temptation—when he was sober. All too aware of his weaknesses, he had known that he must be careful about his drinking, since self-control and judgment were the first things to go when booze went down the throat.

What he hadn't expected was how preoccupied he would become with the knowledge of Allie's nearness. Her nearness, and her willingness. It didn't help that he had yielded to the impulse to buy her something different from her governess gowns. He had known she had a good figure, but had not realized just how splendid it was until she had appeared for dinner in one of her new dresses. He had been tempted to turn her into the first course.

Strangely enough, Allie seemed quite unaware of how attractive she was, the result of too many years where work and propriety came first. Or perhaps she had been scorned when she was a growing, gawky girl, too tall and too unusual for mere prettiness, and had never learned to see herself as the striking woman she had become.

Nonetheless, he had not thought sharing the house with her would cause problems. Unless he was half-sprung, he knew how to keep his hands to himself, so all he had to do was restrict his serious drinking to late in the evening. Since he was nocturnal by preference, this was no hardship, and for the first several nights he had gotten quietly disguised with none the wiser. Except Mac, of course. Then his plan had broken down.

A vainer man might have thought Allie had sought him out deliberately, pretending surprise at finding him in the library, but Reggie did not number vanity among his faults. It had been chance that had brought her downstairs at such a late hour, a chance he should have guessed would occur sooner or later. Short of locking one or the other of them in a bedroom at night, it would surely happen again, and next time, whatever remnants of decency he had might not stop him in time.

He thought of the shock and hurt on her face when he

had pulled away, and winced. The blasted woman was such a mixture of intelligence, worldly wisdom, and vulnerability. He had enjoyed the outrageous discussion he had had with her, enjoyed her curiosity and open mind and lack of missishness. It was different from talking with Chessie; while he had never had to watch his tongue with his former mistress, she lacked the education and turn of mind to appreciate his more oblique mental flights.

Tonight he had realized that in many ways Allie was a kindred spirit, as isolated by circumstances, as intense and unconventional, as he himself. There were two major differences between them. First, as a woman, she had been raised to be proper and restrained, to deny her passionate nature. Second, and more important, she had chosen to use her gifts of talent and intelligence constructively, while he had thrown all his away. He was generally considered a rake, but "wastrel" was a more accurate term, for he had wasted so much over the years. So much money, so many choices. Most of all, so much time; time that could never be recaptured.

Eventually Reggie stopped and tethered his horse, stretching out under a tree on the dew-moistened grass. He was enormously tired and wished he could sleep, but when he closed his eyes everything began spinning and nausea threatened. Instead he lay wakeful, thinking darkly of his desire to change his life, and what a bad job he was making of achieving that.

The first chirping of birds began, multiplying to a chorus as dawn began tinting the eastern sky. There was a certain intellectual curiosity in feeling the aftereffects of drink slowly develop, bit by wretched bit; more often, one slept through the process.

When the sky was perceptibly lighter, he rose wearily, feeling the ache of fatigue and depression in his very bones. He let the horse amble until they came to an intersection with a collection of fingerposts pointing in different directions: Fifehead Neville, Okeford Fitzpaine, Sturminster Newton. He had read once that the absurd double names many English villages bore were a result of Norman designations being tacked onto the original Saxon. It was the sort of fact he loved, utterly useless. In a debate at Eton he had once successfully defended the proposition that a fact should be loved for itself alone.

Signaling his mount to the left, he headed toward Strickland, unsuccessfully trying to avoid thinking about Alys Weston. It would be so easy, so infernally easy, to fall into an affair with her. She was ripe for appreciation, eager for experience, and for a little while she would even welcome it; that had been clear last night. But the same quirky sense of honor that made him administer rough justice as required would not let him ruin an innocent. More than an innocent, a good woman, though that was a rather colorless description for someone so vibrantly, forcefully alive.

Then what was he going to do about her? For one thing, he could divert some of his funds into rebuilding Rose Hall. When the embers had cooled, he had checked over the walls thoroughly and found them sound. If construction began soon, perhaps by early autumn Alys and her brood would be back where they belonged.

And the manor house would be empty again.

The days were very long this near the solstice. Though the sun was well above the horizon, the hour was still early and even the farmers were barely stirring. Instinctively Reggie was heading toward home—as a Muslim bowed to Mecca, he always knew in which direction Strickland lay—and now the countryside looked familiar. It took his tired, sodden brain a moment to realize that he was now skirting the fields of Fenton Hall.

That being the case, it wasn't a surprise to turn a corner in the deep lane and come on Jeremy Stanton, out for an early ride. Certainly his godfather was startled, but then the leathery face creased in a smile. "Good morning, lad. You're out early." After a shrewd glance he added, "Care to join me for breakfast?"

Reggie flushed, wishing he could beat a retreat without being unbearably rude. He was unshaven, coatless, grass-stained, and generally must look like hell. "I'll pass, sir. I should be getting home."

Stanton's eyes twinkled. "I'm disappointed that you think I'm too old and respectable to deal with the aftereffects of a night's debauch." He calmed his restive mount. "If you're worried about Elizabeth seeing you, she won't be up for hours. I realize you might not be able to face food, but perhaps a cup of coffee?"

Reggie hesitated, on the edge of bolting, then smiled wryly. "That's an offer I can't turn down. It's been a long night."

Accepting that without comment, Stanton turned his horse and they trotted companionably along the lane, then up the tree-lined drive to the manor house. Little was said until both men were ensconced in the sunny breakfast parlor with steaming coffee and fresh warm rolls on the table between them. Between sips of his beverage, Reggie clasped the mug between his hands to warm them.

Breaking open a roll and spreading it with sweet butter, Stanton said reminiscently, "Do you realize how much you resemble your father just now?"

"Certainly there is a general resemblance," Reggie agreed, "but I don't recall him ever looking as if the sexton had just dug him up in the churchyard."

Stanton chuckled. "You're too young to remember, but many were the times he was here looking just like you. And for the same reason," he added. The words were casual, but the older man's gray eyes were shrewdly observant.

Coloring under the examination, Reggie growled, "Are you trying to insult me or my father?"

"Neither." Unoffended by the rudeness, Stanton went on pensively, "Drink is one of the curses of the Englishman, I think. We're told from the time we're mere lads that a hard head for liquor proves we're real men, so of course we drink ourselves to oblivion, with rowdiness and ill temper along the way.

"With maturity and increased responsibilities, most men decide that boozing interferes with the serious business of life and reduce their libations. Some, however, drink more and more." He added a spoonful of raspberry preserves to his roll, spreading it neatly over the entire surface. "Your father and I drank together often. He was one of the wittiest men I ever knew, though as a child you wouldn't have seen much of that. Oh, we were merry as grigs over our bottles."

Taking a bite of his bread, he chewed and swallowed it before going on. "It was all good sport, until drinking almost ruined both our marriages."

"How fortunate that I don't have a marriage to ruin," Reggie said caustically. "If you're trying to tell me something, just come out with it. You may call me a lad if you wish, but I'll be damned if I'll sit still for a lecture."

"I don't intend to give you one," his godfather said peaceably. "I just want to fill you in on a bit of history that you might be unfamiliar with."

"You're right, it is quite unfamiliar to me," Reggie said shortly. "I don't remember my father ever taking so much as a tankard of ale."

"That's because he gave up every form of alcohol when you were a child. About four, I think."

Reggie was about to pour more coffee, but he paused in mid-gesture and shot Stanton a suspicious glance. "I told you once I don't remember anything from when I was younger than four."

"With good reason, perhaps," his godfather said, still imperturbable. "Excellent preserves, these. Sure you wouldn't care to have some?"

Reggie had enough to digest without adding food. Scowling at his coffee, he forgot his host for a time. Abruptly he asked, "You said drink almost ruined your marriage. What happened?"

Stanton shrugged. "I woke up one morning, or afternoon actually, and Elizabeth and the children were gone. She'd packed them up and gone to her parents. She wouldn't even see me for a fortnight. In fact, her father's solicitor called on me to talk about a legal separation."

Reggie stared at him, aghast. "But you and Aunt Beth have always been as close as inkle weavers."

"Now we are. That wasn't always the case, I fear." Undimmed by time, remembered pain showed on his thin face. "When she would finally agree to talk to me, she told me that she was tired of sleeping alone while I drank myself into a stupor downstairs, she was tired of running the estate and the house both, and she was *damned* tired of seeing her children hide from their father because they never knew what mood he would be in."

The thought of plump, gentle Aunt Beth swearing was as incongruous as imagining her brandishing a sword. As incongruous as the thought that Jeremy Stanton's children might have been afraid of him. Reluctantly intrigued, Reggie asked, "What happened then?"

"I thought about it and decided that my wife was a much better companion at night than a half-dozen bottles of burgundy. So I told her I would stop drinking." He smiled ruefully. "I thought it would be easy. Elizabeth said she wouldn't come back until I had been sober for six months. It took me over a year to achieve that. But in the end, I did. I haven't had a single drop of alcohol since."

Reggie remembered how his godfather had refused a drink at Strickland, and how he had drunk only water the night Reggie had come for dinner. So that wasn't just caprice, but settled habit. "And my parents? What kind of problems did they have?"

Stanton shrugged his shoulders. "It was a similar situation. Since it occurred at the same time as my own problems, I'm not sure of the details. Since you were there, perhaps you might recall some of what happened if you tried."

"What would be the point of the exercise?" Reggie said, his voice hostile.

"There might be some relevance to your own life." Stanton was as immune to hostility as to rudeness.

"Are you implying that I can't hold my drink?"

"Since you are your father's son, perhaps not." Stanton regarded him gravely. "You would know that better than I."

Coldly furious, Reggie was about to curse Stanton for a meddlesome old fool and stamp out, but something stopped him. For the second time in a matter of days, someone was talking to him about his drinking, and both people were in the very small handful who had demonstrated a genuine concern for his welfare. As all the fatigue and depression of the past night closed in on him again, he set his elbows on the table and buried his face in his hands. Without looking up, he muttered, "Maybe I do drink too much, but I haven't a wife or family. Whom am I harming?"

"Yourself," Stanton said softly.

The silence stretched. Thinking of the depression that had been dogging him, for the first time Reggie wondered if it might be a result of drink. And while he did not have a wife or child to lose, there was Strickland. He remembered the last night in London, when he had gone out gambling and won a thousand pounds in some unknown way. He could as easily have lost. If he had been on a losing streak, would he have been fool enough to put up Strickland as a stake? Chillingly, he knew that it was possible.

His voice muffled by his hands, he said gruffly, "Perhaps you're right and I should drink less."

"Possibly that would work," was the noncommittal reply.

Lowering his hands, Reggie glanced up with narrowed eyes. "Would you care to elaborate on that statement?"

"Some men can reduce their drinking, and that eliminates the problem." Stanton grimaced. "I tried that. It didn't work. As soon as I had swallowed that first mouthful of booze, I would forget—or rather, no longer care—about my good resolutions. Then I would drink until I was unconscious. For me, the only answer was to stop altogether. There was no middle ground."

"I have a strong will."

"I don't doubt it." Stanton's shrewd old eyes studied him. "But I'm not sure that strength of will is enough in this case. It wasn't for me."

"How did you stop if will wasn't enough?" Reggie challenged.

Stanton's mouth quirked up. "You're going to laugh at this, but the only thing that helped was prayer." Seeing his godson's look of distaste, he continued, "This is something I've told no one else, but for me the turning point came seven months after Elizabeth left. First I'd tried moderating my drinking. That didn't work. Then I tried stopping altogether. That would last a few days or weeks.

Then, when I was sure I had my problem under control, I would have just one drink. Next thing I knew, it would be the morning after and I had the devil's own headache and no memory of the night before."

So those terrifying memory losses were not exclusive to Reggie. "What happened then?"

Lines showed around Stanton's mouth, and Reggie realized that this was no easier for him to say than for Reggie to listen to. "I woke up in the drawing room one morning, lying in my own vomit, and knew that I couldn't stop drinking. I had tried my damnedest, and I just couldn't do it. I was going to lose my wife and children forever, and without them there wasn't much point in going on." He grimaced. "So lying there, too sick and miserable to stand, I prayed. Nothing formal, mind you. Just a desperate lot of drivel asking Anyone Who might be out there to help me, because I couldn't help myself."

His eyes were very distant, and he absently crumbled a roll, pulling it into shreds with his thin parchment-colored fingers. "This is hard to describe. I don't know how long I lay there, mentally babbling, but suddenly a . . . a sense of peace came over me. There really aren't any words for it." He started to elaborate, then changed his mind. "After that, things were different. I didn't have the same need to drink. Oh, I won't say I wasn't tempted sometimes, but it was possible to say no."

The old man leaned back in his chair, at peace again. "Within a few months I felt better than I had in years, and didn't miss the drink at all. Then Elizabeth came home. It took time for her and the children to really believe I'd changed, but eventually it all worked out. You've seen the results."

Yes, he'd seen the results. Reggie stood and walked to the window, his thumbs hooked in the waistband of his buckskin breeches, his shoulders taut. Without looking at his godfather, he said stiffly, "I'm not sure any of that is relevant to me, but I appreciate your concern. I don't suppose it was easy to say."

"No, it wasn't," came the calm voice, "but it needed saying. Maybe, in time, it will even seem relevant."

After a long interval, Reggie turned to his host and

took his leave. As he rode back to Strickland, he thought long and hard about what his godfather had said, and decided there was some good sense there. Reggie's drinking hadn't gotten out of hand until the last couple of years. It had been one hell of a strain waiting for his uncle's absurd will to be resolved, and during that period he had drunk and gambled and gotten himself into the worst financial straits of his life.

Then, after his cousin Richard appeared to claim the estate, Reggie had deliberately thrown himself into every manner of what-the-hell-does-it-matter folly. During that period his gambling prospered and his finances were repaired, but he had been acting like a damned fool, no denying it. Had it not been for the uncertainty and frustration over Wargrave, his drinking would never have become an issue.

The solution was clear. All he need do was stop drinking for a while, both to prove that he could and to break the habit of overindulgence. Then he could return to normal social drinking. It was all quite simple; Stanton might not have had the strength of will to control his tippling, but Reggie did.

He thought of Stanton's talk of prayer tolerantly. No doubt when a man was of an age to see his end approaching, it was natural to take refuge in religious superstitions. Reggie had no need of such. By the time he reached Strickland, he was feeling in charity with the world, a state of mind immediately tested when he led his horse into the stable and encountered Lady Alys about to start her daily rounds. Wearing a new bronze-colored riding habit today, she was very tall, slim and elegant.

Allie stiffened fractionally when she saw him, then inclined her head politely. "Good morning. I was about to ride over to several of the tenant farms, but I can postpone that if you wish to discuss anything now."

He shook his head and began unsaddling the tired chestnut. "No, carry on with what you intended. I want to talk about the improvements, but that can wait until later."

She raised her brows. "I thought we had settled that."

Her glossy brown hair was once more in a neat coronet of braids. Remembering that beautiful hair loose around her face brought Reggie a quick pang of regret for what he had forgone. "I've decided Rose Hall should be rebuilt this summer, which reduces the funds available for machinery and rebuilding cottages. I'll want your opinion on what is most needful."

A pulse beat visibly in her throat. "I see."

She obviously thought he was trying to get rid of her. Well, he was, but his motives were pure, amazingly so. Quietly he said, "I think it would be for the best."

"You needn't feel guilty about last night," she said with cool control. "You weren't forcing me."

Remembering how deliciously she had responded made his voice brusque. "You don't have to remind me. I'm quite clear on what happened. It would have been better if it hadn't."

Her face paled under its unladylike tan. "Quite right," she said, her voice clipped, then turned and led her mare out of the stables.

Reggie watched her slender figure leave with a combination of regret and irritation. Since he was being noble, he should at least get credit for it.

Unrelieved sobriety proved much harder than Reggie had expected. By the second day, thoughts of drinking were becoming an obsession. He would imagine himself opening the library cabinet and pouring amber fluid into a glass, could almost feel the soothing warmth after he swallowed. Several times he caught himself about to act out that vision. Then, fiercely determined, he turned away. It was the haying season, so he spent the morning hours swinging a scythe with the laborers, finding respite in the mindless rhythms of farmwork.

When the lunches of bread and cheese and ale appeared, he left, removing himself from temptation. *It's only ale,* his longing mind would whisper, *not wine or spirits. Quite harmless.* So must the serpent have whispered in Eden, but Reggie had gotten drunk on beer and ale often enough to know they were not essentially dif-

ferent from spirits. If he was stopping, he must stop
entirely, without self-deception.

In his first afternoon of sobriety Reggie visited a horse
fair near Dorchester, and for a ridiculously low price he
bought four young horses with excellent potential as hunters. The next afternoon he began schooling them, a task
which required patience and concentration and focused
Reggie's mind on something other than his ever-increasing
need for a drink.

Though Dorset was not first-class hunting country, there
was enough variety of terrain around Strickland for training purposes. Some of the schooling was done over the
countryside, but some took place in the paddock, and
young William would come and watch when he could.
The boy had the makings of a real horseman, and Reggie
would tersely explain what he was doing and why. Twice
he took Peter out for driving lessons; while the older
Spenser lacked his brother's all-encompassing fascination
with horseflesh, he was eager to learn and was on his way
to becoming a very pretty whip.

No matter how hard he worked during the day, in the
evenings Reggie was intolerably restless, too tense to
read, too bad-tempered to talk. During the hours he
used to spend drinking, he took refuge in walking around
the estate, his long strides quick and impatient. The sun
set very late at this season, and in the cool hours of
waning light he became intimately acquainted with his
ancestral home, from the high, lonely downs dotted with
sheep to the rich water meadows with their ripening
grain.

Even walking until full dark could not subdue his tension. Eventually he would end at his private cove on the
lake, stripping off his clothes and swimming back and
forth across the water until exhaustion made it possible
that he might rest.

By the third day he was feeling so irascible that he
canceled a driving lesson with Peter Spenser, knowing
that he would have trouble being civil. Reggie considered
taking his meals apart from his new housemates, but
decided not to change the routine; after all, it was his
house. So he ate with the others, saying as little as

possible rather than risking wounding someone's feelings with his sharp-edged tonge. The young Spensers cast occasional puzzled glances in his direction; Alys did not look at him at all.

Even Mac seemed to be tiptoeing around him, as if he were a volcano that might go off at any moment. Only Nemesis seemed to perceive no difference, and, as Reggie thought with what humor he could summon, the dog was notably brainless. In spite of his slanderous thoughts, he was glad that the collie accompanied him on his expeditions and slept on the foot of his bed.

On the fifth day, he began wondering when it would become easier; each day was worse than the one before. Grimly he cut hay, worked the horses, prowled about the estate, and swam. As he returned to the manor house, he wished without hope that tonight he might sleep soundly.

It was after midnight when he reached his room, his body still thrumming with need in spite of his fatigue. *Just one little whiskey, to help him sleep. Just one. Hadn't he proved that he could go without?* No, he hadn't, not when the craving for drink was so powerful that it damn near blotted every other thought from his head. One thing Reggie had, perhaps in excess, was strength of will, though often it had been called stubbornness. Now that he had decided to stop drinking for a time, he would not deviate from his resolution until he no longer craved alcohol. Only then would it be safe to drink again.

Intent on his inward battle, he didn't notice that he was not alone until he was ready to climb into his bed. For a moment the sight of a rounded female form made his heart leap with anticipation; if Alys Weston was willing to go this far, not a man on earth could blame him for giving in to temptation. And making love to her was one thing that he was sure would distract him from his aching desire for alcohol.

The thought had hardly formed when he realized that it couldn't possibly be Allie; too short, too round. Pulling down the edge of the blanket, he exposed the soft brown curls of a dozing housemaid. As he stared at the girl, trying to remember her name, her wide eyes opened and an expression of fright appeared on her round, pretty face.

Caustic with disappointment, he said, "Don't you belong in the attic with the other maids?"

She gulped, then whispered, "I thought you might like a . . . a bit of company, sir."

Could Mac have thought a woman might improve his temper? The cockney had never turned to pandering before, but Reggie supposed it was possible. "Who put you up to this?"

The girl looked even more frightened. Stuttering, she said, "N-no one, sir. I've f-fancied you from the time you came here, and . . . and I thought you might not mind."

For a moment he was tempted; the chit was a pretty little thing, and if he were cupshot he would certainly have accepted her offer. But with that dying-kitten expression, she looked less like a lusty wench intent on pleasure than like Joan of Arc waiting for the torches. Perhaps she was here less from desire than from hope of material gain, which was an unflattering thought. "This is not the best way to earn a better position or a higher wage," he snapped. "Get back to your own bed and we'll pretend this didn't happen."

It was hardly the most graceful way of rejecting her, but even so, he had not expected her sudden tears. Exasperated, he pulled the blanket down as encouragement to leave and discovered that she was naked. At the sight of her rosy body his resolution wavered; it had been weeks since he had had a woman, and having Alys Weston constantly under his nose was keeping his rude male instincts at constant simmer. Then, as he examined her more closely, his eyes narrowed. "You're increasing," he said flatly.

She looked at him with horror, as if he were the devil incarnate for guessing. Admittedly the signs were not yet obvious, but Reggie was no green innocent. She yanked the blanket up around her shoulders, her helpless sobs worsening. Clearly he wasn't going to get rid of her until she recovered. After pulling on his own robe, he glanced about the room, finding her plain shift and dressing gown folded neatly over a chair.

Handing her the shift, he said, "Better put this on," then turned his back and took his time rifling through his chest of drawers for a handkerchief. By the time he gave one to the girl, she was standing by the bed in the hastily donned shift, tying her robe around her. Accepting the handkerchief gratefully, she buried her woebegone face in its snowy folds. Reggie sat on a chair and waited for her to emerge from the handkerchief, curious as to just why she had come. Gillie, that's what her name was.

When Gillie's sobs had subsided to hiccups, he said with as much gentleness as he could muster, "Did you think that if you . . . visited me, you could pass the child off as mine?"

From the stark look in her pansy eyes, he had guessed correctly. "Didn't you think I could count?" he asked, beginning to find some amusement in the scene. "Sit down and relax. I won't eat you."

She gave him a bewildered glance, then perched nervously on the edge of the bed. Probably the chit had only the vaguest understanding of procreation and gestation. Patiently he asked, "Won't the father marry you?"

She crumpled the handkerchief in her hands, not meeting his eyes. "N-no. We'd been walking out together for ever so long, and he s-said we'd marry someday, b-but when I told him wh-what had happened, he asked how he could be sure it was his."

Another sob escaped her. "The next day he told his pa he was going to Bristol to get a job as a sailor, and off he went. H-he didn't even say good-bye." She bent over, her face covered by her hands, her shoulders shaking.

Reggie's mouth tightened; at times like this, he wasn't very proud of the male sex. While he was no paragon of virtue, at least he hadn't left a string of bastards scattered across the countryside. He stood and sat next to Gillie on the bed, patting her shoulder comfortingly. Still sobbing, she turned and burrowed against his side, and he held her until she had cried herself out.

Finally she straightened up and wiped her eyes with the damp handkerchief. Her nose red and her face blotched, she still had a certain dignity as she said haltingly, "I'm very sorry, Mr. Davenport. It was bad of me to try to trick you, b-but I was that desperate. I . . . I don't know what to do." She swallowed hard, then said fiercely, "I won't go to the workhouse, I won't. I'll have my baby in a ditch first."

"Is the workhouse that bad?" Reggie asked.

She nodded and looked at her hands. He filed the thought away; magistrates administered the Poor Law, and perhaps he should look into local conditions. But that was for later. "Won't your parents help you?"

She shook her head, her curly brown hair falling over her forehead. "They're Methodists and ever so strict. My pa said that if I ever got myself in the family way, he'd never have me in the house again. Even my mam . . ." Her voice trailed off.

He thought a moment more. "Does Mrs. Herald know?"

"Oh, no, Cousin May would never have hired me if she had known," Gillie said bleakly. "When she finds out, she'll discharge me right away."

"Where would you go then?"

"I . . . I don't know, but not the workhouse. Maybe I can walk to London and find work there."

Reggie frowned. The only work she would be likely to find there would be on the streets, with all the dangers that entailed. He could send her to Chessie, but he doubted the girl had the temperament of a good prostitute. Making an abrupt decision, he said, "You can stay here. I'll tell Mrs. Herald not to let you go, and not to make you work too hard."

She looked up at him hopefully. "You would really let me stay until the baby is born? You don't even have to pay me. I'll work as hard as I can just to have a roof and food."

"Yes, and you can stay on after the baby is born. It shouldn't be difficult to work something out." He shrugged. "You'll be paid for what you do. Perhaps you can work part-time when the baby is small."

As desperation was replaced by hope, her eyes started to fill again. "God bless you, Mr. Davenport. I don't know how to thank you. You don't know what this means." She laid a shy hand on his forearm. "If . . . if there is anything I can do for you . . ."

Her meaning was obvious, and once again he was tempted; at least now she didn't look like she was offering herself to be sacrificed. But he knew enough of human nature to realize that in her present mood the girl was likely to fancy herself in love with the first man who was kind to her, and he didn't need any more complications in his life. "Just don't do it again," he said crisply. "Lust is a normal part of life, but if you want to indulge in it after the baby is born, take precautions. If you don't know an older woman who will explain, ask me and I'll tell you what to do."

Gillie blushed violently, but nodded. Besides being pretty, she seemed fairly intelligent. In time she would probably find a husband; illegitimate children were not all that uncommon.

Suddenly tired, he stood and offered her a hand up. "Off to bed now. I'll talk to Mrs. Herald in the morning." He scowled ferociously at her. "Make sure the other maids don't get ideas. I'm not sure if I'll be as tolerant another time."

Unintimidated by his expression, she gave him another shy smile, then slipped out the door. Pulling off his robe, he climbed into bed, then pinched the candles out. The girl's problems helped keep his in perspective.

Alys's bedroom had been chosen with an eye to her monitoring night traffic. Wakeful herself, she had heard Davenport come in late for the last several nights. Tonight, half an hour after hearing his light, booted steps, she heard a different sound and got up in time to open her door a fraction and see the girl leaving Reggie's room. She froze for a moment, feeling ill. The moonlight wasn't quite bright enough to distinguish details, but she was sure the girl was one of the housemaids, either Gillie or Janie by the size and shape.

Outside Davenport's door, the girl paused, wiping her eyes as if she had been crying, then pattered off toward the stairs that led to the attic. Alys eased the door shut, then pressed her forehead against the cool panels as her left hand clenched the brass knob convulsively. So he was carrying on with one of the maids. She wondered how long that had been going on; the girl was sniffling as if she were a virgin who had just been seduced.

Not that it was any of her business what Reggie Davenport did. Feeling wretched, she returned to her bed, drawing herself into a ball and tugging the covers close for warmth. She had thought there was a little understanding between her and Reggie—some laughter, a certain similarity of mind—but no doubt it had been her imagination.

If any connection did exist, it certainly did not include his interest in her as a woman, and she had been a fool to think otherwise, even briefly. Remembering how he had kissed her, she pressed a fist against her mouth, her teeth cutting into the knuckles as she fought against crying out with pain. She had been watching her irascible employer closely all week and guessed that he had stopped drinking. Now that he was sober, he clearly wasn't interested in her; he'd been drunk the times they'd kissed, and apparently the experience had been so dreadful that he was altering his entire way of life rather than run the risk of a recurrence. He had been quite definite that it shouldn't have happened, and wouldn't happen again.

Strong and confident in so many ways, in her sense of herself as a woman Alys was utterly vulnerable. And so she wept through the night, until she fell into the sleep of the utterly exhausted as dawn began tinting the eastern sky.

15

The next morning Reggie talked to his housekeeper about the pregnant housemaid. Mrs. Herald clucked her tongue disapprovingly, but she was a kindhearted woman and agreed that they couldn't just put the girl out when she had nowhere to go. Having had children of her own, she was also willing to assign Gillie's duties with an eye to the girl's condition.

The only other person Reggie told was Mac Cooper,

who raised his eyebrows in an unusual show of emotion. "That pretty brown-haired lass? Pity her lover isn't around to horsewhip."

"I agree," Reggie said. He was dressing for dinner, and now pulled a fresh white shirt on. "If it's any comfort, the young man will probably find that life as a common seaman is quite punishment enough."

Mac nodded, then said with a questioning note, "You've not been drinking the last few days."

"Very observant you are," Reggie said dryly as he tied his cravat.

Undeterred, the wiry valet said, "Sobriety is no bad thing."

"Glad you approve." Reggie pulled on his waistcoat and began buttoning it. His basic philosophy of clothing was to buy quality, let his valet care for the garments properly, then ignore how he looked. The resultant casual elegance was widely imitated among the younger bucks.

Mac put on his lofty upper-servant expression. "I'm sure that it is not for me to approve or disapprove."

Reggie made a rude noise. "Since when have you not had opinions, you old fraud?"

"Oh, I never said I didn't have opinions," Mac said with a hint of a smile. Then he said more seriously, and with the overtones of cockney that showed up when he was concerned, "It's that worried I was getting."

Shrugging into his beautifully tailored coat, Reggie gave his servant a hard look. "In other words, I was going to hell in a handbasket and everyone noticed except me?"

Mac considered for a moment. "Yes," he said simply.

Reggie smiled with reluctant amusement; Mac was never one for roundaboutation. Then he headed downstairs for dinner. He was glad Julian would be arriving the next day; the household would benefit from some of his friend's easy good nature.

After his master left, Mac automatically went through the motions of cleaning and straightening. So little Gillie had been given a slip on the shoulder. Perhaps he would ask her if she wanted to go for a walk this evening; she'd be in need of a bit of cheering up. A slight smile on his face, he completed his work and headed to the servants' quarters for his own dinner.

Much of a steward's job involves moving around and keeping a watchful eye on how work is progressing, and Alys spent her morning doing exactly that. After riding up to the pastures to consult with Gabriel Mitford about when the sheep would be ready for shearing, she stopped to check on the haying. Most of the grass meadows had been cut, the fragrant shocks piled into small stacks that dried the hay and kept it cool. She dismounted into the ankle-deep stubble to talk with the bailiff, who allowed that the work was going well, adding with a countryman's caution that if the weather continued sunny they would be finished the next day.

As Alys mounted to ride to her next task, she caught sight of her employer in the middle of the field, part of a line of laborers moving steadily forward against the tall grasses. She had been told that he was working on the haying, but had not chanced to see him. Now Davenport drew her attention, and not just because he was the tallest man there. His dark hair was tousled from the breeze, his sleeves casually rolled up, his open-throated shirt revealing his darkly tanned skin. Absorbed in work, he was unaware of her scrutiny. His lean body moved in a steady, graceful rhythm, his powerful arms and shoulders swinging the scythe from right to left, the mowed grass falling neatly to his left. For a moment she was struck by the beautiful image of a man and the land, and the sense that he belonged here.

As she watched, the knot of misery that had formed in her breast the night before dissolved. It is said that every man is the hero of his own play, and every woman too. Alys was the heroine in the story of her own life, and ever since Reginald Davenport had come to Strickland she had viewed him in terms of the role he played in her own personal drama. As her employer and a forceful, magnetic man, he had automatically become a leading player. He had absolute power over her livelihood, had saved her life, and, perhaps inevitably, had come to be a focus of her secret dreams and unadmitted desires.

Now, for the first time, Alys changed her perspective and tried to see how his world must look to him. Though he had not said so in words, she believed that the central drama that now absorbed him was an attempt to rebuild his life, to find some sense of connection and meaning. He had changed in small ways since he had come to Strickland, and by stopping his drinking he was trying to change on a much more fundamental level.

In her life she had seen many men who routinely drank themselves insensible. Most would have vigorously denied that they were drunkards, and only the barest handful ever attempted to stop, no matter how destructive their habits. Yet Reggie, a self-admitted rake, was making the effort, and the desperate, angry tension she had felt in him these last days was a measure of the difficulty of what he was attempting.

She was only a peripheral element in Reggie's world; his happiness or misery, his drinking or sobriety, had nothing to do with her. If she vanished from the earth, he would scarcely notice; it was quite obvious that he was capable of running his own estate. The silent battle that he was waging with his inner demons was far more important to him than she would ever be.

The thought was a curiously liberating one. Davenport was a complicated man; one who could act with both heroism and villainy, though he was neither hero nor villain; who, while not old, was certainly not young; who had had the foolishness to create problems for himself, but the honesty to admit when he had done so. From what she had seen, he was fair and compassionate in his dealings with those around him. He was also very much alone.

Regrettably, he needed neither her professional skills nor her femaleness, her wistful fantasies nor her regrets. What Reggie *might* need at this difficult time were friendship, acceptance, and understanding. Those things she could give freely because, quite simply, she liked him, even though he was far more important to her than she would ever be to him.

As she urged her mare forward and rode away, she resolved to work harder at being a friend, no matter how snappish his temper, and even though he did prefer house-maids as bed partners.

After eating a late lunch at the manor house, Alys was on her way to the stables when she saw Reggie working with a tall gray gelding in the paddock. Moved by her new resolution to be more friendly, she decided to stop and watch for a while before going out for the afternoon. William was ahead of her, his small, sturdy body balanced on the paddock fence while he watched, enthralled, barely turning his head to greet his guardian when she joined him.

Alys had to admit that Reggie was a sight worth watching as he put the gelding through its paces. She knew that he was a superb rider, and now she saw that he was a superb trainer. Rather than using his strength to dominate a horse, he worked *with* his mount, not against it, patiently guiding and correcting the gray with nearly imperceptible shifts of weight and touch. When he was done, the result would be a vastly superior hunter. It was an understatement when she commented, "Very light hands."

William nodded reverently. "I think he could ride Smokey without any reins at all."

When Reggie's circle-turning exercise brought her into his view, he hesitated a moment, then trotted the gelding over to where she and William sat. Though he appeared pleased to see her, his expression was a bit wary, lacking its customary glint of subversive humor, as if unsure how she would greet him. Well, she had been rather unforth-coming lately; they had exchanged scarcely a dozen words in the last five days. She smiled cheerfully. "From the looks of those hindquarters, I'd guess that Smokey is a good jumper."

She thought his face eased at her friendly greeting. He pulled the gray up close enough to the fence for William to pat it, which the boy promptly did. "You're right. A little wild, but very strong over fences, and with tremendous stamina. He'll do for the hardest hunting in the Shires."

"A high compliment," Alys agreed. "Are you training the new horses for sale or for your own use?"

"For sale," he said. "This one will be worth ten times his purchase price in another year, and two of the other three I bought in Dorchester will be as good."

"And the fourth?"

"She's too small for flying country like the Shires, but will do very well in rough, hilly counties like Devon, where long runs aren't possible and cleverness is more important than speed." He calmed the gelding when Nemesis slipped through the fence and caused the horse to edge away nervously. "A horse that's bred for racing but isn't fast enough is a sad creature that has failed in its purpose in life, while a horse bred for hunting is far more versatile. The fastest can be raced in steeplechases, and the rest are almost always suitable for some kind of hunting or riding."

"So hunters are philosophically more satisfying than racehorses?" she asked with amusement.

"Exactly, and better business as well."

Who would have thought that a rake would have a shrewd head for business? By this time, Alys was no longer surprised. She shifted on the fence, beginning to find the narrow board uncomfortable. "If you intend to expand the horse training, you'll be needing more men for the stables soon."

William chimed in, a hopeful gleam in his blue eyes, "I can work as a stable lad."

Reggie smiled. "I think Lady Alys would prefer that you keep to your schooling." He glanced at her. "You're right, though, more will be needed, and soon. Do you know anyone in the neighborhood with experience in horse training?"

Alys bit her lower lip, considering. "Well, Jamie Palmer, the supervisor at the pottery, used to be a groom, and was very good with young horses."

"Can the pottery spare him?" Reggie asked.

"He'll be missed," Alys admitted. "Still, his assistant is very capable, and I know Jamie would prefer to work with horses if he has the chance. Shall I ask him?"

Reggie shook his head. "I'll stop by the pottery myself. I'll want to know him better before offering the position." He gathered his reins, preparing to go. "By the way, did I mention that a friend of mine, Julian Markham, is coming for a visit? He will be here very soon."

"No, you didn't."

Alys must have looked doubtful, because Reggie said with a trace of humor, "Don't worry, he's one of my more respectable friends. He won't cause any trouble."

Before Alys could think of an appropriate response, they were interrupted by the sound of hooves and the jingle of harness, as a smart chaise drawn by four matched bays swept into the yard between the stables and the paddocks. Alys said, "At a guess, I'd say your friend has arrived."

His eyes popping at the sight of such a bang-up equipage, William scrambled down from the fence for a closer look. Alys followed at a slightly more dignified pace, while Reggie dismounted and tethered the gelding, then came through the gate.

The driver of the chaise handed his reins over to his groom, then jumped lightly to the ground while Reggie stepped forward to welcome him. Alys was glad to have a moment to collect her thoughts. She had vaguely assumed that a close friend of Reggie's would be about his age, but Julian Markham was considerably younger, and quite the handsomest man she had seen in the last dozen years; since Randolph, in fact. Even after hours of driving, he was elegant to a point just short of dandyism in a well-tailored burgundy coat and gleaming boots.

After shaking hands with his friend, Reggie turned and introduced him to her and William. Markham bowed gracefully over her hand when she offered it. When he straightened up, she saw his gray-blue eyes widen slightly when he realized that she was as tall as he. Or perhaps it was her mismatched eyes that surprised him, or her tan pantaloons. Whatever he thought, he was far too well-mannered to show disapproval. Smiling, he said, "Reg told me of you, Miss Weston, and of the superlative job you have done at Strickland."

For a moment she wondered if he was being sarcastic,

but Julian had a smile of singular sweetness and charm. On the whole, she thought he was quite adorable, and had a moment's trepidation about whether Peter or Meredith was going to be more impressed. Peter would see him as the perfect London gentleman, while Merry would be hard-pressed not to consider him as husband material. Well, perhaps he was.

As Alys made a suitable reply, Merry herself appeared on the scene. Smudges of dry clay marred the shapeless, ill-fitting gown that had been acquired from a maid after the fire, and her golden hair was tied with a plain blue ribbon, with tendrils escaping around her face. Clearly she had been at the pottery, working on her china designs.

Davenport said, "Meredith, I'd like you to meet a friend of mine who has come for a visit."

Merry turned to greet the newcomer, and for an instant horror flickered across her face. Alys almost laughed out loud; to meet the most beautiful and elegant young gentleman of one's life when one looked like an urchin was the stuff of nightmares. Actually, Merry could not look less than very pretty, but Alys fully sympathized with the girl's feelings.

Involuntarily Alys glanced at Reggie just as his eyes turned to hers, and they silently commiserated for a moment about the painful tribulations of youth. Then he stepped into the slight pause and performed the introductions.

The speed with which Meredith rallied and gave Julian her best smile was a credit to her remarkable aplomb, and in a moment the two young people were chatting easily. While William went to investigate the chaise and team, Alys gestured Reggie to one side and said in a low voice, "As a good guardian, I'd better find out if your friend is eligible."

"Extremely so." When Alys gazed at him inquiringly, he elaborated. "Heir to a viscountcy and a substantial fortune, no major vices, and a natural gentleman."

"Good heavens, a paragon," Alys murmured. "How on earth did the two of you become friends?"

Just as she realized how insulting that sounded, Reggie grinned at her, looking like his old self. "For the best of all possible reasons—because our friendship infuriates his father."

She laughed. "Now that I have been properly put in my place, tell me: when you asked him down, did you have matchmaking in mind?"

A slight smile quirked his mouth. "It had occurred to me that they might suit. It would solve your worries about finding a worthy husband for your ward, and he would be lucky to have her—Merry has far more to offer than most of the chits that come onto the London Marriage Mart."

Alys was oddly touched that he was sensitive to her wards' welfare. She glanced over at Merry and Julian as they started laughing about something. Clearly there was already mutual attraction, in spite of Meredith's deplorable gown. The two of them looked very well together, and not just because both were exceptionally good-looking. Perhaps it was the general air of intelligence and good nature that both had. But in a practical world, it took much more than looks, compatibility of mind, or even love, to make a marriage. "Would his family object to his marrying a girl whose birth and fortune are lackluster by society's standards?"

"They would not be enthralled," he admitted, "but I think they could be brought around."

"I hope so. I would hate to see Merry hurt." Alys smiled wryly. "This is absurd. In three minutes, we have planned both their futures."

He shook his head. "They'll do that on their own. We have simply considered some possibilities."

Merry and Julian turned back to them, and Alys and Reggie broke off their private conversation. Deciding that being a gracious hostess was momentarily more important than stewarding, Alys suggested, "Would you like some refreshment after your journey, Mr. Markham? It is almost time for afternoon tea."

"Thank you, Miss Weston, I'd like that very much."

Alys collected her wards—easily in the case of Merry, who was anxious to change, with some difficulty in the case of William—then carried them off to give the men a few minutes of privacy. As soon as they were out of earshot, Julian demanded, "Why didn't you tell me that there was a nonpareil down here, Reg? I would have chucked my other obligations and been here a fortnight ago." Then an alarmed expression crossed his face. "Unless . . . Is she your . . . ?" He stopped, embarrassed to go on.

"My *petite amie*?" Reggie suggested helpfully. "Not at all. As should be obvious, she is a young lady." Not having been introduced, Nemesis now approached Julian, tail wagging. As the collie started to rear up on Julian's immaculate pantaloons, Reggie said, "Nemesis!" sharply.

The dog settled back on her haunches, tail still hopefully sweeping back and forth on the ground. "As should be equally obvious, this is my dog, a brainless but amiable one. Don't let her climb all over you, she has enough bad habits."

Julian bent over to ruffle Nemesis's ears. "You certainly are getting bucolic. All you need now is the pack of foxhounds." He straightened up. "You had better explain how matters stand here before I commit some dreadful *faux pas*. Are Miss Spenser and her brother visiting Miss Weston, or do they live in the neighborhood, or what?"

Reggie turned and entered the paddock. "They all live here at Strickland, together with a middle brother. Come with me while I return this horse to its stall and I'll explain." As he untethered the gray gelding and led it inside, he briefly described how Alys had come to be steward and guardian of the Spensers, and how the fire had left them homeless.

Much intrigued, Julian said, "And I thought Dorset was supposed to be a quiet county. It sounds like you've no shortage of excitement. But then, excitement follows you around. You're the only man in England who would acquire an estate whose steward is not only a female but also a splendid Amazon." He chuckled. "You told me that there was no shortage of attractive females here, and you were right."

Reggie felt a flash of irritation. "Lady Alys is not your type," he said shortly as he uncinched the gelding's saddle.

"Is she yours?" Julian said with a gleam of speculation.

Reggie gave him a scathing glance as he turned the gelding over to a stable lad for grooming. "All women are my type. Or none. It comes to the same thing."

Properly chastened, Julian accompanied his friend into the manor house. He should have known Reggie would have no interest in a virtuous spinster, even a splendid Amazon.

Strickland became much livelier after Julian Markham's arrival, and within a day the visitor was on first-name terms with everyone in the household. While William continued to dog Reggie's heels, along with the real dog, Peter Spenser found in Julian a new idol, one more approachable and less alarming than Davenport. Within days Peter was starting to mimic Julian's manners, his neckcloth knot, even his turns of speech.

Alys suspected that Julian was a little amused, but he was young enough to remember the awkwardness of fifteen, and kind enough to be tolerant of the imitation. Altogether, he was a fine young man, exactly the sort she could wish for Merry.

Still, she was concerned that her ward would be unacceptable to the Markham family, and she had a brief word with Meredith about not developing expectations. Merry had laughed, assuring her that Julian was behaving with the utmost propriety and had given her no reason to build feather castles, but Alys still worried. Though Merry might not admit to having her feelings engaged, there was a suspicious glow about her. Worrying was part of being a parent, even a surrogate one.

Alys noted that Reggie still was not drinking, but his air of tension diminished slightly and he talked and smiled more easily, though he continued to spend much of his time working with his horses. Unoffended by being left to the devices of the younger members of the household, Julian and the Spensers went on excursions to local points of interest. The first time Alys went with them, but she disliked taking time from her steward's work during the estate's busiest season. Besides, she decided that her chaperonage was not required; a young man who showed no impatience at having a young lady's two young brothers along as chaperons must be trustworthy.

The subject of the assembly in Dorchester came up at dinner after Julian had been at Strickland for a week. With twinkling eyes Meredith suggested that they make up a party to go to the assembly so Julian could see what high style they kept in Dorset.

Julian laughed. "'Does that mean that the waltz has come to Shaftesbury?"

"There is a rumor that it will be introduced at this assembly," Merry said, "but some fear that even if one is played, no one will know how to dance it!"

"We can certainly prevent that from happening. If you like, I can teach you to waltz." He glanced across the table. "At least, if you permit, Lady Alys."

After a moment's consideration Alys said, "I must say, I would like to see how it is done. Any dance so thoroughly condemned by high sticklers should be worth learning."

In a spirit of general merriment they all adjourned to the drawing room, even William, who had nothing better to do and was not ready for bed. Alys was thumbing through the sheet music, looking for some waltzes Merry had ordered from London, when Reggie stopped her. "Peter is interested in learning to waltz, and you'll be needed as a partner. I'll play the accompaniment."

Alys was startled. "I didn't know you played the piano."

"Wait until you've heard me before you decide," he advised as he seated himself on the bench.

In fact, Reggie played quite well. As Alys watched his long, beautiful fingers stroke the keys, first tentatively in a series of rippling scales, then with more confidence, she wondered when a rake would have found time to learn and practice the piano. Between orgies, perhaps?

Shaking her head in bemusement, Alys joined the others and watched as Julian demonstrated the steps and technique of waltzing. Ever punctilious, he would dance first with Merry, then with Alys. Peter watched, then started practicing with whichever female wasn't benefiting from Julian's superior skill. Within half an hour there were two couples twirling about the drawing room, while William watched with uncomprehending boredom.

By the time the tea tray came, the dancers were all in a good mood, and Alys was positively exhilarated. She had much enjoyed dancing in her salad days and privately thought she was rather good at it, even if she was far too tall. It was great fun to dance again, though she would never do so in public.

On the day of the assembly, Alys's path intersected Reggie's in the stables at the end of the afternoon. The annual sheep shearing had begun, and with his usual interest in trying everything himself, Reggie had participated. Since Alys had been otherwise engaged most of the day, she now asked, "How did the sheep shearing go?"

Reggie removed the saddle and blanket from the mare he had been riding. "It certainly requires more skill than washing the foolish beasts. Did you know that to shear a sheep's foreleg, you have only to press a spot under the shoulder and the leg will shoot straight out for clipping? Quite extraordinary."

When Alys grinned, he continued, "Yes, of course you would know that. I knew it once, but had forgotten. Gabe Mitford spent some time teaching me the basics of shearing, but it was obvious from the pained expression on his face that I wasn't up to his standards. Every time I made a cut, he winced, as if convinced I had just ruined the entire fleece."

"Well, it is easy to do that, and wool is one of our most important products," Alys pointed out. "*Did* you ruin any?"

"One or two," he admitted. "However, Gabe allowed that I wasn't doing badly for a beginner."

Reggie was standing on the far side of the mare, and she watched as he took a handful of clean straw and began brushing sweat and foam from the brown hide. On impulse Alys asked, "How are you doing with sobriety?"

His light blue eyes were as cold as chipped ice when he glanced up. "I can't imagine what business that is of yours."

She felt a hot flush of color rise in her face. "None at

all. I am merely an employee who has no choice but to tolerate your bad temper." She pivoted on her heel and was heading toward the stable door when his low voice reached her.

"Allie, I'm sorry. I shouldn't have snapped at you."

She stopped, still fuming, then turned back to him. His hands lay quiet on the horse's back and his long dark face was rueful. "I know I've been difficult lately. I've tried to be as silent as possible to minimize the effects of my evil temper. Forgive me?"

Alys knew just how difficult it was to apologize; she wasn't very good at it herself. "Forgiven and forgotten. I've been known to be irritable a time or two myself. And I *was* impertinent."

"Then I'll cancel your remark out with an impertinence of my own." At her puzzled expression, he continued, "Wear that gold dress tonight instead of one of your dark chaperon dresses."

"How biblical, an impertinence for an impertinence," she murmured.

"Well, I'm much better at impertinence than I am at sheep shearing," he said reasonably.

She had to laugh. "A point well taken," she agreed as she exited the stables. She was not entirely displeased that he had an interest in her appearance.

16

Public assemblies were gatherings of the families of local gentry, professional men, and prosperous merchants, not the most exclusive of company. Furthermore, the low-ceilinged assembly room attached to the King's Head in Dorchester should have seemed paltry to a woman who had had a London Season, but to Alys the long room with its simple floral decorations was lovely. Though she had brought Merry here a number of times, there was something special about tonight. Perhaps it was because of Julian Markham, so handsome that every female eye in the room swiveled to look at him when their party entered. Or perhaps they watched Reggie, who looked very tall, dark, and devilishly attractive in immaculate black evening garb. And of course Merry was dazzling in a simple muslin gown trimmed in forget-me-not blue ribbons that matched her eyes.

If the truth be known, it was Alys herself who felt special. She wore the low-cut golden gown Reggie had requested, and it was the most dashing garment she had ever owned. Merry had pulled her guardian's thick glossy hair back into a loose twist, then let it tumble in curls down her back, with one lock falling forward over her bare shoulder. When Alys had come down from her bedchamber, Julian and Merry had complimented her looks extravagantly, while Reggie had studied her from crown to toe, a slow, approving smile on his face. Tonight she did not feel like a chaperon, though naturally she would behave like one.

Alys and Merry knew almost everyone present and the girl was immediately besieged by admirers. Alys herself was considered an Original, not at all what one would wish one's own daughter to become, but she was generally well-accepted. Tonight, however, she was wondrously popular, with mothers of nubile daughters coming over to press their greetings, offer sympathy about the fire, and, not coincidentally, be introduced to Julian and Reggie, who were the most attractive men present, as well as the most eligible.

Reggie had a sardonic gleam in his eye at the attention; during a pause in the rush, he murmured to Alys, "A few months ago, most of these good matrons would have had their husbands call me out if I so much as said hello to their darling daughters."

"Timing is so important in life," she returned sweetly, "and now is your time for being a desirable *parti*." She nodded to an approaching woman. "So nice to see you again, Mrs. Baird. Have you met Mr. Davenport yet?"

Mrs. Baird bore down on them. Besides examining

Reggie with scowling intensity, as if half-expecting him to ravish her on the spot, she tried to probe Alys about Julian Markham's background and expectations. Amused, Alys blandly turned the queries aside.

When Mrs. Baird withdrew in defeat, Reggie said *sotto voce,* "That woman resembles nothing so much as a ship of the line in full sail."

Alys chuckled. "She has three daughters who are more like frigates, but give them a few years and they will be in the same nautical class as their mother."

Reggie groaned at her bad joke, then escaped to talk with some of the men whom he had met in the last few weeks. Alys watched him for a moment. From the way the gentlemen welcomed him, he was well on his way to being established in the county. Then she returned to her duties, chattering with the other older women and keeping an eye on Meredith. After dancing with Merry once, Julian displayed a sterling example of *noblesse oblige* by dancing with the shyest, plainest girls in the room.

Having herself been plain and shy, Alys knew just how wonderful it was to have a young man like Julian claim a dance. Besides his handsome appearance and exquisite manners, he had the ability to make a female feel like she was the only woman in the world while he was with her, and tonight he was giving a dozen girls shining memories they could cherish their whole lives.

The dancing started promptly at eight and would end at midnight. At ten o'clock, after a portentous pause, the musicians struck up the first public waltz to be played in Dorchester. For a moment the dance floor was empty. Then Squire Richards and his wife, who often visited London, stepped onto the floor, followed by another couple. Julian had been saving his second dance with Merry in hopes of a waltz, and now he found her and led her out. They were both so beautiful that they drew the eye as they swirled into the waltz, Merry laughing up at her partner, her golden hair spilling back over her gauzy gown.

Alys was watching her ward fondly when Reggie materialized at her elbow. "Shall we show them how it is done?" Then, before she could refuse on the grounds of age, dignity, or propriety, he swept her onto the dance floor.

For a moment she tensed with the fear that she would disgrace herself, become an object of derision. When she had danced in public as a girl, she was always miserably aware of her height, but with Reggie that was not a problem; here was a man she could literally look up to. She relaxed, raising her eyes to meet his. He laid one hand on her waist and with the other clasped hers firmly. "Good girl," he said softly as they began dancing.

"I am hardly a girl," she said absently, far more aware of his closeness than of her words.

"No, for which heaven be thanked, but you are hardly in your dotage either." His eyes were very blue, his steps very sure, and a faint smile curved his lips. When she had first met him, she had thought him almost handsome; now she could not imagine why she had qualified her appraisal. He was more than handsome, he was devastating, and like the shy girls who had danced with Julian, she, too, savored her moment of magic.

Though they had shared passionate kisses, there was a different kind of eroticism in this waltz. With only a handful of couples on the floor, there was room to move freely, to yield oneself to the passion of the music. Secure in his arms, Alys understood why the waltz was considered so improper; certainly her thoughts were as she gave herself over to delight. She should have known that if Reggie chose to dance, he would do it well, and she made no attempt to talk. She simply enjoyed the experience, her body pliant, her golden dress belling out behind her; losing her usual self-consciousness in the rapid rhythms of the waltz, feeling the slow fire of his touch stealing through her body.

Far too soon the music ended. Breathless from exertion and his proximity, Alys laughed and swept into a deep, formal court curtsy before her partner, not even considering how odd it would appear that she knew how to do such a thing.

With a lurking smile Reggie bowed in reply, then led her from the floor. "Now that I have revealed that I

know how to dance, I suppose I must stand up for a few
more sets or be thought rude," he said with resignation.

Alys dimpled. "Very proper of you."

"That's what I was afraid of," he murmured before
going to ask Meredith for the quadrille that was forming.

Alys thought her moment's frivolity was over, but Julian came over and insisted she join him. "Leave it to
Reg to persuade you to dance," he said admiringly. "If I
had known you could be convinced, I would have tried
earlier."

Julian was a delightful partner and she enjoyed the
quadrille, though it was not the same as being with
Reggie. The musicians then struck up another waltz.
Wistfully Alys realized that Reggie really shouldn't ask
her again. Instead, he asked Mrs. Richards, and sturdy
Squire Richards himself led Alys out.

This time more couples were willing to reveal steps
that must have been practiced in secret, and the floor
was fuller. Though it was not like dancing with Reggie,
Alys enjoyed herself again, not even minding the fact
that the top of Squire Richards's head came only to her
nose. The squire was a skilled waltzer and complimented
her freely on her own mastery. "Been hiding your light
under a bushel, Miss Weston." It was the closest Alys
had ever come to being the belle of a ball. It was quite
close enough.

The party of well-dressed strangers arrived shortly after eleven o'clock, entering and standing in a cluster by
the door as they gazed around with bored condescension.
There were three women and two men, and their loud,
slurred voices indicated that they had been dipping rather
deeply. All were dressed in the height of fashion, the
women with a flamboyance that suggested the muslin
company. Alys guessed that they were Londoners who
happened to be in the neighborhood, coming to observe
the natives from lack of any better amusement.

The musicians were taking a short break and Alys had
been standing at the side of the room with Reggie, explaining how fleeces were stored and shipped, when one
of the newly arrived females caught sight of him and
crossed the room to his side, her face brightening. The

woman was red-headed and floridly attractive, and her dress was cut to a depth that made Alys's gown seem positively puritanical.

Completely ignoring Alys, the redhead laid one hand possessively on her companion's sleeve. "Reggie, darling, I had no idea that you were in the neighborhood. What are you doing so frightfully far from town?"

He said coolly, "I live here."

"Here?" she asked incredulously. "Amongst these rustics?" For the first time noticing Alys, she made a leisurely scan, tilting her head up as if the other woman was scraping clouds. "Good Lord, Reggie, where did you find such a strapping creature?" She giggled tipsily. "Her eyes are peculiar."

In the face of the redhead's petite, voluptuous prettiness, Alys's buoyant pleasure in the evening evaporated, leaving her feeling horribly gawky and deformed. And as she watched the woman's provocative behavior to Reggie, Alys also felt homicidal.

Reggie removed the redhead's clinging hand as if it were an unwanted thread. "What are you doing in Dorset if you mislike it so, Stella? It *is* Stella, isn't it?"

Stella's hazel eyes flared angrily. Then she smiled with dagger-edged sweetness. Slanting a glance at Alys, she cooed, "If you prefer, you can use some of the names you whispered when we were . . . together before."

Alys had no doubts about what "together" meant in this context. Perhaps she should feel flattered that this trollop seemed to consider Alys a rival, but fury at having to witness such a scene was her predominant emotion. She was tempted to stalk away, but morbid curiosity kept her rooted to the spot. Curiosity, plus the belief that Reggie was no more pleased at what was happening than Alys was.

When Reggie ignored her last remark, Stella said pettishly, "Believe me, I wouldn't be here if I had a choice, but George has taken a house nearby. Some dreary aunt of his is dying, and he visits her regularly so she won't forget him in her will. It's incredibly tedious, but he says we'll go to Brighton soon."

"Where is George now?" Reggie asked, his expression bored.

Stella shrugged carelessly, an action that almost un-moored her silk gown entirely. "Outside with the car-riage. He'll be along in a moment." Her companions had drifted after her, and one of the men came up and clapped Reggie on the shoulder. " 'Lo, Davenport," he said boskily. "Haven't seen you in town lately."

"That's because I haven't been there, Wildon," Reggie said with barely restrained impatience. Wildon was an acquaintance, not a friend, and Reggie disliked familiar-ity from a near-stranger. Was he himself equally oafish when in his cups? An unattractive thought; the sooner he got himself and Allie away, the better. Taking Alys's arm, he said, "Good to see you all. Give my regards to Blakeford. Sorry I missed him, but we were just leaving."

Under his fingers he felt Alys's muscles tense. He couldn't blame her for being upset; as if Stella's rudeness wasn't bad enough, by this time they were the objects of attention of a circle of curious Dorset gentry.

Before Reggie could move away, Stella made one last bid for attention. "Do settle a question for us, Reggie, darling. On our way over, we were talking about whether chivalry is dead. Charles here"—she waved at the near-est foxed gentleman—"says that defending a lady's honor is old-fashioned, utterly *passé*."

She fluttered her darkened lashes at him and undu-lated her bountiful curves. Her voice coaxing, she said huskily, "But you're a gentleman. Wouldn't you fight for my honor?"

"Why should I?" Reggie said in a clear, carrying voice. "*You* never did." His words were unthinking, a result of his anger at how this coarse little slut was distressing Alys. Hard to believe he had ever been willing to forni-cate with Stella, even drunk. It was time to get rid of her once and for all.

The horrified silence that greeted his words had a gelid quality. Except for one weak gasp, the circle of Dorset gentry might have been carved from stone. Stella herself seemed to have trouble absorbing what he said, her mouth going slack with shock. Then her face turned murderous, all her pouty prettiness gone.

Under his light clasp, Reggie felt a tremor in Allie's

arm and glanced quickly at her. Her face was rigid, as if she was trying her hardest to suppress either laughter or strong hysterics. Or, more likely, both.

Having delivered his lightning bolt, Reggie was momentarily nonplussed; while he had made his share of scenes in his life, he had usually been drunk enough not to care what happened next. Stone-cold sober was quite a different matter. Looking up, he saw George Blakeford approaching. Speaking easily, as if he hadn't just offered deadly insult to the man's mistress, Reggie said, "Here comes George now. I have a hunter he might be interested in. Do you know if he's going to be riding with the Cottesmere this season?"

As the drunken Wildon replied, the musicians began to play and the onlookers dissolved as if the interlude had never taken place, though Reggie was sure they would be discussing his comment for years to come. Under cover of the renewed activity, Allie jerked her arm free of his grip and slipped away without a backward glance, cutting through the crowd to a side door. As her tall, slender figure disappeared, Reggie turned to follow her, but then Blakeford arrived. He seemed more sober than his companions, and his eyes had sharpened with interest at the sight of Reggie. Fairly caught, Reggie spent a few interminable minutes exchanging commonplaces as Stella glared daggers.

Finally making his escape, Reggie worked his way over to the side door Allie had used, finding a passage that led to the garden behind the King's Head. Making his way along the flower-lined paths, he found her at the far end of the garden on a stone bench, spinning a pale rose nervously between her fingers.

She stiffened when he sat down beside her. It was too dark to see her features in detail, but moonlight gave a milky translucence to her fair skin and laid subtle highlights in her hair. In a stifled voice Allie said, "I was feeling a bit faint and wanted some fresh air."

At least she wasn't throwing things at him. Mildly Reggie said, "You? Faint? The woman who can work twelve hours straight in high summer and never tire?"

She eyed his dark outline warily, unsure why he had

followed her outside. "All right, I wasn't faint, I was furious."

"That's more like the Lady Alys I know," Reggie said with approval. "Are you going to favor me with a colorful description of my morals, manners, and ultimate fiery destination?"

"I considered it," she admitted, "but try as I might, I can't quite blame you for that . . . that bit of muslin's behavior."

"Well, you *could*, but I would prefer that you didn't."

The silence between them was comfortable. He was only inches away from her, and she could feel the radiant warmth from his body. Eventually Alys said reflectively, "She is quite attractive, in a vulgar sort of way. Since most men are at the mercy of their animal instincts, I can see why you would have been interested in . . . consorting with her, even if a bed was all you had in common."

Reggie made a choking sound and his voice trembled on the edge of laughter. "A bed never entered into it, actually." A thought-provoking statement, one she would prefer not to pursue. He continued, "Tell me, does anything shock you?"

Alys sighed. "Nowhere near enough. I should have been shocked at that appalling set-down you gave her, but instead I thought it quite possible that I would shatter into small pieces if I didn't laugh." She shook her head in amazement. "Honestly, Reggie, how could you say something like that, even though she was behaving badly?"

"It was easy; appalling insults are one of my specialties. Certainly they have gotten me into trouble often enough." She heard a faint rustling sound as he crossed his legs. "Stella isn't a particularly nice person, you'll have noticed. And I didn't insult her until she had insulted you."

Allie bent her head. "I don't understand women like that." As she played with the rose, its sweet, fragile fragrance scented the night air.

"I don't either." After a long pause he said in a low voice, "I'm sorry that my evil past intruded on tonight, Allie. I know quite a lot of rackety folk, but I didn't expect any of them to turn up here."

It was a perfect opening. She asked, "I gather that the man you two were discussing, George Blakeford, is her protector?"

"Yes, Blakeford is quite besotted with the woman."

"Is he a friend of yours?"

She felt him shrug. "Not really. We've been acquainted for years, but not friends." He chuckled ruefully. "And if we had been, we wouldn't be after Stella tells him what I said."

"Might he call you out?" Alys asked with alarm.

"I doubt it. The man is no fool. He might spread a little slander about me, but what's another drop in an ocean?"

He was amazingly calm about it. Alys considered asking more about Blakeford, but knew that it would look odd. Besides, it was just coincidence that George was in the area; the miracle was that no one else from her past had ever appeared to haunt her.

When the silence had stretched too long, Reggie asked, "Are you ready to go back in?" Music and humming voices from the assembly sounded clearly in the night air.

"No!" Alys spoke more abruptly than she had intended. Well, he could ascribe her unwillingness to lingering cowardice, which was better than if he knew the truth. "I'm sorry, but I have had quite enough of crowds for one night. Do you think Merry and Julian could be persuaded to leave a little early? The dancing will be over soon anyhow."

"As you wish. I'll go collect them."

Reggie stood and offered his hand to help Alys to her feet. Not that she needed assistance, but it restored the sense of being delicately female that had been shattered by Stella. She appreciated that he had come out to soothe her injured feelings. "While you extricate our companions, I'll get the coach," she offered.

Amused, he said, "I can manage both. Since you're dressed very much like a lady tonight, you must accept being treated like one." Alys looked up at him, trying to read his expression in the dim light. Reggie still held her hand from helping her rise, and the air between them had weight and substance, a legacy of the melting sensuality of the waltz.

With odd intensity he raised his other hand and gently touched her face with gossamer lightness, his fingertips skimming her brow and cheek and throat, then circling under her heavy hair to brush her sensitive nape. She caught her breath, vividly conscious of his nearness, of his irresistible masculinity, and had a sudden fierce hope that he would kiss her again.

But he was sober tonight, so of course he didn't. He would have to be drunk to consider her worth the effort. She tried not to let the bitterness of that thought destroy memories of the simpler pleasures of the evening.

His hand dropped and he stepped back. "Come along now, and I'll put you in the carriage before I collect the others."

Silently she accompanied him toward the garden gate. Since he didn't want her, there was nothing else to do.

On the ride back to the rented house, the other two couples were noisily engaged in preliminaries to the night's final entertainment, but George Blakeford was driving the carriage, so Stella was left alone to seethe in her fury. She had actually been glad to see Reggie Davenport, thinking that he might help alleviate her boredom when George was off toadying to his aunt. She had not forgotten their prior encounter, and the thought of further explorations at greater length had been delightful.

She tugged her shawl closer, as if she could shut out the memory of how he had publicly humiliated her. Davenport must be interested in that oversized rural creature with whom he had been talking, or he would never have insulted Stella the way he had. One way or another, she would make him pay for that; Blakeford was a dangerous man, and properly directed, he would avenge her. All she need do was decide the best way to inflame her protector against Davenport.

George was unusually abstracted tonight, not falling on her as soon as they were alone in their chamber as he usually did. As he untied his cravat, he asked abruptly, "When I came into the assembly room, I saw a very tall female in a gold dress with Davenport, but she was gone by the time I joined you.''

Stella turned so that he could unfasten her gown; it was too expensive to let him rip it off. "Surely you didn't think the creature was attractive?" she said crossly. "Davenport never introduced me to her. She was most peculiar, far too tall and with mismatched eyes. Lord only knows where Davenport found her; perhaps he likes women with wooden legs as well.''

At her words George's impatient hands stopped for a moment. Then he resumed. "There is no accounting for tastes," he said in a husky voice. "For myself, I find redheads irresistible.'' Pushing the dress from her shoulders, he slid his hands around to cup her breasts.

Now to put her plan into effect, while her lover was lustful and irrational. As she rubbed back against him, Stella said in a quavering voice, "It was dreadful finding Davenport there tonight. I was hoping never to see him again, after what . . . after what he did the last time.''

With startling speed Blakeford spun her around and seized her shoulders, his lips a hard, narrow line. "What do you mean?"

She widened her eyes, trying to look innocent and vulnerable. If she didn't play this exactly right, George would be furious with her, dangerously so. "Remember that night you had the card party at your house and you lost five hundred pounds to Davenport?"

"I remember.'' Blakeford's expression was ugly. "I also remember you wagging your tail at him.''

"Georgie, darling, not at all!" she protested. "I was just being hospitable since he was your guest. But . . . but he misunderstood. You remember how drunk he was. And . . . and when I chanced to meet him in the hallway . . .'' She bowed her head and gave a convincing shudder, as if unable to continue.

Blakeford's hands tightened bruisingly on her upper arms. "What happened?" he hissed.

Under his painful grip, Stella was able to produce genuine tears. "He . . . he *forced* me, George. It was just awful. I tried to scream, but he had his hand over my mouth.''

"Why didn't you tell me about it then?" he snarled.

Stella said huskily, "I was afraid of what might happen. You know his reputation, how dangerous he is. I couldn't bear to think that something might happen to you."

She began unbuttoning her lover's shirt with expert hands. "I thought it best to forget the incident, but when I saw him tonight, I was frightened. He insulted me horribly, for no reason. And the way he looked at me!" Trembling, she went on, "What if he comes after me again? He is so *large*. So *strong*."

Each of her words had been chosen to subtly imply that Davenport was more of a man than Blakeford, stronger, more virile, more dangerous. She understood her lover's pride and possessiveness well enough to be sure he would not let anything foolish like honor constrain him in pursuit of his goals. If he wanted revenge, it was quite possible that Davenport would be found with a lead ball in his back, and no one would ever know who did it. Stella savored the thought.

As her hands roved further, Blakeford's groan was more than just fury. "I'll make him pay, Stella, for what he did to you, and to me."

His mouth crushed down on hers. He was not entirely convinced that Stella had been unwilling when Davenport made his advance; in spite of Blakeford's obsession with his mistress, he knew that she was a slut. But she was *his* slut, and, by God, Davenport would pay for having trespassed.

Damn Davenport to hell anyhow; first the man had taken Stella, and then he had saved "Alys Weston's" life. If he hadn't been around that night, she would be dead and none would be the wiser. Blakeford had been disappointed when he learned that the bitch had survived the fire, though at the time he had had no particular interest in whether Davenport lived or died. Now, after Stella's revelation, it was doubly infuriating to think how close the fire had come to removing both problems. Vengeance must wait a few days or weeks, until the time was right, but it would surely come.

Under Stella's expert ministrations, Blakeford ceased

thinking of revenge and murder. As he pulled his mistress to their bed, his fiercest desire was to make love to her with such force that he would completely obliterate her memories of being touched by another man—especially by a man who was large and strong and dangerous.

17

The first time that Julian Markham had seen Meredith Spenser in her clay-smudged dress, he had thought that she was a remarkably pretty girl. A few hours later when he had seen her gowned for dinner, he had known she was a dazzler, and by the time he had spent a dozen hours in her company he knew that he had fallen quite hopelessly in love. It wasn't just Merry's considerable beauty, but also her intelligence, her buoyant good nature, and a wisdom remarkable in a girl of nineteen. Love was a novel and delicious sensation and he kept it to himself, biding his time and saying nothing to Merry that might give offense.

In the fortnight since Julian had come to Strickland, he and Merry had spent nearly every daylight hour together, riding and driving, sometimes lunching *al fresco,* often with one or both of her brothers. The degree of privacy they had could never have occurred in London, and was a tribute to the confidence that Lady Alys had in her ward, and in Julian himself.

The confidence was not misplaced; nothing untoward or improper had been said between Julian and Merry, but as they laughed together, and talked of everything and nothing, the conviction grew in Julian that she returned his feelings. He decided to talk to her the day before he would have to depart for a family engagement that could not be avoided. While he was sure that Merry cared for him, he was not quite so confident that he wished to leave without assuring himself of her affections.

This afternoon Meredith had taken Julian to the potbank. Julian would cheerfully go anywhere with Merry, but found it surprisingly interesting to see how clay was prepared and pottery was made. "It used to be that there were little local potteries all over Britain," she explained as she showed him the room where slipware was cast, "but now that roads are so much improved, pottery can be shipped longer distances and the industry is getting centralized in places convenient to raw materials, like Staffordshire. A pity there are no canals near here, because they are ideal for shipping, but Dorset is too agricultural."

Julian studied her enchanting profile as she stood to lift a heavy plaster-of-paris mold from a shelf. "You know the most remarkable things," he said admiringly.

She chuckled. "Remarkable, unladylike things is what you mean." She opened the mold for him. "See? The liquefied clay, which is called slip, is poured into the mold. The plaster pulls the water out, and we have a molded vase or cup or whatever. Very elaborate pieces can be made this way."

"Merry," Julian said, laying one hand on hers where it held the mold, "one reason you are so special is precisely that you are unmissish."

She gave him a swift, uncertain glance, then pulled away to return the mold to the shelf. "Neither my aunt nor Lady Alys would ever permit me to be missish. Shall we go and look at the bottle oven so you can see how the pottery is fired?"

He obligingly followed her outside to the oven, which was large enough for two dozen people to stand inside when it was empty. At the moment, it was half-filled with earthenware waiting to be fired a second time. Merry explained the different items of interest, including several small, dainty teacups in their own protective firing container. "Those are some of my trial pieces. I'm working on designs for when we're ready to expand."

Keeping his eyes on Merry's face, Julian murmured, "Very pretty and very nice, indeed."

For a moment he thought he saw sadness in her deep blue eyes. Then she smiled mischievously. "An expert flirt can turn anything into a compliment." She led the way out of the oven, saying, "It should be full enough to fire tomorrow. After this second firing, I'll be able to decorate them. I'm pleased with how they are turning out—the shapes are rather good."

"So is yours," he agreed as he admired her silhouette in the door of the bottle oven.

A teasing laugh was his only answer. The works supervisor, Jamie Palmer, was outside, and she waved at him as she and Julian left. The day was lovely and they had walked over from Strickland. As they aimed their steps back toward the manor house, Julian said, "Merry, I want to talk to you."

They were walking along a hedgerow. Acting as if he hadn't spoken, she picked a sprig of pale pink flowers from a lanky plant growing among the hawthorn. "This is valerian. Did you know the roots make a tea that will help someone sleep?"

As she sniffed the cluster of pink blossoms, Julian asked, "Why are you trying to avoid talking to me?"

She stared down at the blossoms, not meeting his eyes. "I don't want our summer idyll to end," she said softly. "But I suppose it already has."

Gently lifting her chin with one finger, he looked into her sapphire eyes, and was shocked to see tears gathering. Suddenly frightened, he asked, "Merry, what's wrong? Is it that you don't want to hear me say that I love you because you don't feel the same?"

Her eyes shut as the tears spilled over, and she shook her head. "Oh, no, not that, not that at all."

It seemed the most natural thing in the world to take her in his arms and hold her. Julian knew that he loved her sweetness, beauty, and gaiety; now he discovered a tenderness beyond anything he had ever experienced. "Hush, love," he whispered. "If I love you and you love me, what cause is there for tears?"

Merry pulled away from him. "I never expected being in love to hurt so much." She gave a brittle smile. "Alys used to laugh at how well I had my life planned. I had decided that I would find a kind man of moderate fortune who would adore and cherish me, and in return I would make sure he never regretted his choice." She dug a fine muslin handkerchief from a concealed pocket and blew her nose in a futile attempt to recover her composure. Julian found even her pinkened nose endearing.

Realizing that some serious talk was needed, Julian sat down in the shadow of the hedgerow, sparing one pained thought for his fawn-colored inexpressibles as he took Merry's hand and tugged her down beside him. "Why are you finding love so uncomfortable? I've never been happier in my life."

She stared bleakly down at the crumpled muslin square in her hand. "It hurts because I can't believe that we will have a 'happily ever after.' We are too far apart in birth and fortune." She sighed. "Why couldn't your father have been something less lofty than a viscount?"

"I wouldn't have thought you would mind the idea of being a viscountess. You will make a very good one." As she looped her arms around her drawn-up knees, he added, "Since my father is quite hale and hearty, you should have years as the Honorable Mrs. Markham before you have to face becoming Lady Markham."

Her smile was rueful. "Julian, my mother was the daughter of a minor country squire, my father a city merchant who was reasonably successful, but nowhere near rich enough to overcome my deficiencies of birth. I will have a portion of five thousand pounds. That is quite decent by the standards of rural Dorsetshire, but I can't believe it is what Lord Markham wishes for his only son and heir."

Obviously she had been doing some clear thinking, and his respect for her increased. "I don't expect my father to like it, but he hasn't the authority to forbid my marriage or to disinherit me." Julian smiled reassuringly. "He should be delighted to hear my news, since he has suggested several times in the last couple of years that I marry. I think he wants to see the succession assured for another generation." He halted a moment. "I've gotten ahead of myself. *Will* you marry me?"

"I would like nothing better." As Julian began to

smile, she added, "But not at the expense of separating you from your family." She swallowed hard and looked away. "That is why love hurts. I find that I care more for your happiness than my own."

Her voice broke, her self-possession deserting her. "I know too well what it is to lose one's parents. I won't be the cause of cutting you off from those whom you are closest to."

The depth of Merry's generosity showed Julian that there were deeper levels to love than he had realized, and he had an insight that a lifetime with her would introduce him to kinds of loving that he could not even imagine now. Sunlight shafted through the hedge to touch her golden hair to a halo, and her lovely face was such a blend of sorrow and longing that Julian could restrain himself no longer.

Leaning forward, he touched his lips to hers, first as lightly as a butterfly wing, then with increasing pressure as she responded with such sweetness that he ached, longing to enfold and protect her forever. Like any young man in his position, he had had his experience with the physical side of loving, but now with Merry he discovered a whole new dimension of desire, as a simple kiss moved him more deeply than the most unrestrained passion in his past.

When he found himself wanting to pull her down full-length into the soft grasses, he knew that it was time to stop. He released her, his breath unsteady. "Lord, Merry, we had better get on our feet and moving, or I am going to betray Lady Alys's trust."

Her face shaken and vulnerable, Merry hastily rose and tucked her hand into Julian's elbow, clinging more tightly than she usually did. They strolled along the footpath by the hedge, in no hurry to get anywhere. When Julian got himself under control, he said, "Why are you so sure my family will object to you? It isn't as if you're an opera dancer."

She giggled, as he had hoped she would, but sobered rapidly. "I'm just being logical. I'm not the least bit romantical, you know. You could do far better for yourself."

Julian stopped and turned her to face him, his hands lightly resting on her shoulders. "No, I couldn't," he said seriously. "Remember that." Having lost parents, aunt, and several homes already in her life had made Merry pessimistic, he decided. What mattered was that she loved him. All he had to do was convince his father that there wasn't a better, sweeter girl in all of England. Uneasily he knew that he had his work cut out for him, but he had no doubts about his ultimate success.

Making an effort to hide her fears, Merry raised one hand and laid the back against his cheek for a moment. In some ways, Julian was far more innocent than she. But at least she had had her summer idyll. In an everyday voice she asked, "How did you meet Reggie? I've often wondered. You are so different, yet you are obviously the best of friends."

Accepting the change of subject, Julian let go of her shoulders and they resumed their stroll. "In a gambling hell. I was just down from Oxford, feeling very much the thing, and got into a game of whist with some deep players. Over the course of a very long evening, I lost every penny I had, including my allowance, a small inheritance I had just gotten from a great-aunt, and vowels drawn against my future expectations."

"Good heavens," she said, shocked to her practical soul. "How dreadful. Did you lose it to Reggie?"

"No, but he was in the game, playing casually and running about even, neither winning nor losing much." Julian grimaced. "As I floundered around, losing more and more, Reg watched me like an angry eagle, which didn't help me feel any less of a fool. Soon I was so far in debt that I would cheerfully have jumped in the Thames rather than confess to my father. It was the most wretched night of my life.

"I was quite drunk, of course, and must have looked desperate. I finally had the sense to drop out of the game and was going to leave, but he told me very harshly to sit down and watch how the game was supposed to be played." Julian smiled with self-mockery. "When Reggie says, 'Sit,' one sits." Merry nodded with understanding.

"I've never seen such an example of concentration in

my life," Julian continued. "Reggie was so absorbed it was frightening. Over the next four hours he won everything of mine back, and several hundred pounds besides. Then he took me home with him, saying that I was too drunk to walk the streets. I wasn't sure I wanted to go with him, but did since the alternative was Markham House and a lot of explanations I didn't want to make.

"The next morning, I woke up with the devil's own headache, and Reggie proceeded to give me the dressing-down of my life." Julian smiled reminiscently. "My father is a dab hand at that sort of thing, but Reg is in a class by himself. He called me a stupid young cawker and spelled out in excruciating detail the folly I had committed. Then he asked me to promise that I wouldn't gamble again until I learned how to do it properly, and after I agreed, he burned all my vowels."

Fascinated, Merry asked, "And he asked nothing in return?"

"He made me buy him breakfast that morning."

Merry started laughing. "That's an incredible story. Yet it sounds like Reggie. I've gotten the feeling that his reputation does him considerably less than justice."

"Too right," Julian agreed. "He undertook to give me lessons in intelligent gaming, and I have never gambled more than I can afford to lose since. London can be treacherous, and it has been a blessing to have a friend who is up to all the rigs. The irony is that my father is absolutely convinced that Reggie is leading me direct to perdition. Whenever I've tried to correct his misapprehensions, he just rants and raves."

"So your father isn't very reasonable?" Merry asked in a stifled voice.

Guessing her thoughts, Julian patted the small hand curled around his arm. "Not always, but he will be about you."

Merry wished she could share Julian's confidence. In her heart, she did not believe that she would ever see him again after he left tomorrow.

Julian asked for a private interview with Lady Alys later that day, after she had returned from the fields and bathed and dressed for dinner. She was delighted to grant his request for Merry's hand, with the proviso that there be no formal engagement before he had talked to his father. He saw that she had the same doubts as Merry about whether Lord Markham would approve.

The rest of the household had retired after an evening of music and charades when Julian broke his news to Reggie. His friend's dark face split in a grin. "Wonderful, though not unexpected. Anyone with half an eye in his head could see what was going on."

"And here I thought I had been a model of discretion." The two men were lounging in the library, Julian sipping a glass of port, Reggie smoking a long, slim cheroot, and Nemesis snoring by the open French door. With an infatuated gleam in his eyes, Julian said, "Isn't Merry the loveliest of creatures? And such a delightful disposition."

Patiently Reggie spent the next half-hour listening to similar encomiums on the young lady's myriad perfections, making agreement noises as required. Finally Julian broke off with a laugh. "I'm babbling like an idiot, aren't I?"

"Yes, but anything less would be inappropriate to the occasion," Reggie said genially, tapping ash off his cheroot.

Julian frowned at his port. "Both Merry and Lady Alys think that my father will oppose the marriage. What do you think?"

"I think it very likely," Reggie admitted, "but I imagine that with persistence and tact you can win him around. While it isn't a brilliant match, it is respectable. If you have trouble winning your father over, just take Meredith to meet him."

"Brilliant idea, Reg," Julian said enthusiastically. "Who could resist her?"

Before he could continue in that line, Reggie held up one hand. "You needn't repeat her splendid qualities—I don't think they've changed in the last five minutes."

With a sheepish expression Julian rose and went to the liquor cabinet, taking out a decanter of Reggie's best brandy. "Shall we have a toast to my success with my father, and to my future happiness?"

Reggie hesitated. "You must have noticed that I haven't been drinking."

"I have noticed," Julian said cheerfully, "but this is a special occasion." He poured a generous measure in two Venetian cut-glass goblets and brought one over to Reggie.

Reggie accepted the goblet and stared at the dark amber liquid, wary of the fierce longing that literally caused his mouth to water and his heart to beat faster. He had vowed to stop drinking until the craving went away, and while it had subsided in the last fortnight, there were still times when the desire for alcohol nearly overwhelmed him.

Then he mentally shrugged. Since he had always enjoyed drinking, it was unrealistic to wait for the craving to go away. It was like assuming that abstinence would end sexual desire. On the contrary, abstinence increased desire; he should have realized that sooner. He had proved he could stop; now it was time to resume his normal habits.

Reggie raised the goblet. "You're right, this is a very special occasion. May I be the first to wish you and Merry long life and every happiness?"

As Julian beamed, Reggie drank the entire glass of brandy in one long swallow, then hurled the empty goblet into the fireplace, as befitted a toast from the heart. As the crystal shattered and spun away in glittering fragments, he savored the marvelous feel of the brandy going down. The sweet burn of it tingled on his tongue, warmed his throat, then curled and soothed throughout his entire body, stilling the incessant longing that had been at the back of his mind since his last drink. Now he saw clearly that he had been torturing himself for the last few weeks unnecessarily. He could no longer remember why he had even thought it necessary to prove that he could stop.

Crossing to the liquor cabinet, he poured himself another glass of brandy, then turned to Julian with a smile. "Now, what else can we drink to?"

When Alys and Meredith had retired early for the evening, they had gone to Merry's room for a comfortable coze. Alys had expected her ward to be ecstatic at having won Julian's heart and hand. Instead, Merry had been deeply sad, convinced that when Julian left the next day his father would prevent him from ever returning. Nothing Alys said could change Merry's mind.

When Alys went to her own bed, she found herself unable to sleep even though she had had a long and tiring day. Julian was a kind and thoroughly honorable young man; she couldn't believe that he would have spoken to Meredith and her guardian if there were a serious likelihood that the match would be blocked. Nonetheless, Merry's conviction of disaster, coupled with Alys's own doubts, held sleep at bay.

Hours passed, and Alys ached with fatigue, but her anxious mind allowed her no rest. Being a surrogate parent was so stressful that she didn't know how a real, biological parent managed to survive the experience. Her bedroom allowed her to hear traffic on the stairs and in the halls, and eventually she heard Julian come upstairs and go to his room. She knew it wasn't Reggie; his step she always recognized.

Finally, after mauling her pillows and blanket with restlessness, she decided to go downstairs and see if Reggie was in the library. Her employer had considerable worldly experience, and doubtless was acquainted with Julian's father; perhaps he could give an informed opinion on the likelihood of Lord Markham's accepting Merry into the family.

Fumbling in the dark, she found her gold velveteen robe and slippers and pulled them on, then made her way downstairs to the library. As she had expected, light shone under the door. What she did not expect was the scene that greeted her eyes when she opened the door. Reggie was there, all right, sprawled casually in his favorite chair, his long legs crossed in front of him. And if she was right that his sobriety could be measured by his neatness, he must be roaring drunk.

Reggie glanced up at her entrance and smiled hazily. His coat and cravat lay where they had been tossed on the floor, his white shirt and tan pantaloons were blotched by spilled liquor, and a heavy miasma of brandy fumes hung in the air. One empty decanter lay on its side on top of the liquor cabinet, and another, nearly empty, sat on the table next to Reggie.

Because the night was a warm one, the French doors were open and a puzzled-looking Nemesis lay across the doorstep. The dog jumped to her feet and pattered over to Alys, making whimpering sounds, as if seeking aid for her master.

While Alys surveyed the scene with distaste, Reggie lurched to his feet. "Good . . . good to see you, sweet Alys. Julian had 'nough and retired. Good lad, but no 'ead f'r drink. Night's young 'n I could use a drinking companion. 'Ave . . . have some brandy." His speech was slurred and as he poured the remaining brandy into another glass, his hand shook, spilling half of the spirits over the tabletop.

She had seen him very well-to-go before, but his present state was far beyond that. The superbly conditioned, athletic body nearly fell over when he turned to bring the glass to her. "I didn't come here to drink," she said sharply. "I wanted to talk, but obviously you're in no state for that."

He drank the glass himself, a drop of brandy escaping down the side of his mouth. Comprehending only part of her statement, he said with pleased surprise, "Glad you didn't come to drink. C'n think of better things to do m'self."

For a drunk, he moved with amazing speed as he closed the distance between them in two swift strides, then enfolded her in a hungry embrace. Alys found herself supporting much of his weight and was carried back against a bookcase. For a moment she acquiesced, feeling the same fierce response his kisses always ignited in her. Then he shifted his grip, pulling her tighter and murmuring in her ear, " 'S been hard keeping my hands off you. Anyone ever tell you what a glorious body you have? 'S enough to drive a man mad."

His words shattered her temporary cooperation and she twisted away in exasperation. "Let go of me, you drunken rakehell! The only time you ever notice my 'glorious body' is when you're too disguised to care what female you fondle. If you're randy, go find your housemaid."

As she pulled away, he almost fell, but retained his grip on her left arm. Using her to regain his balance, he said with drunken reproach, "Coyness don't suit you, Allie, I know what you want, and be m-more than happy to give it to you." He slid one hand around her head in a travesty of the gentle gesture he had made in the garden of the King's Head.

Alys was not alarmed, not yet. As he drew her toward him for another kiss, she turned her head sharply away. "You're drunk, Reggie. Just go to bed."

But he had no intention of letting go. Since her lips were unavailable, he concentrated on kissing what was within his reach, nibbling across her cheek to her ear. Alcohol had not reduced his expertise, and Alys was horrified to realize that in another minute she would be willing to give herself to a man too drunk to know or care who she was. The horrid sense of *déjà vu* gave her the strength to push him away again, this time furiously. "Damn you, get away from me!"

Taken by surprise, he staggered back into a small table carrying a globe. The table pitched over, the globe frame smashing and the colorful sphere bouncing across the carpet. Reggie managed to avoid falling, but only just, and when he regained his balance again his expression was ugly. With the volatility of the drunkard, he had tilted from boozy goodwill to fury. "Don't play with me, y'r bloody ladyship. Don't you think I know why you're always twitching around me? Underneath that proper face you're as hot as they come, and we both know it."

The fact that he was right was unbearable. Alys felt as if he had spied on her soul, and was using what he had learned to torment her. She wanted to weep. She also wanted to murder him for seeing too much, for invading her heart and imagination so easily and uncaringly.

Torn by her roiled emotions, Alys was critically slow at realizing her peril. His blue eyes narrowed with menace, Reggie was moving toward her with dangerous delibera-tion. Gone was the amused, tolerant man she had worked and bantered with; this was a cold, angry stranger, and she feared his intentions. She was too far from the door to escape, and she backed up slowly, keeping her eyes on

Reggie as her heart accelerated toward panic. She was tall and strong for a woman, but she was no match for her employer if he wanted to ravish her. Her retreat ended in a corner of the room with bookshelves stretching away on both sides, and she tensed, ready to fight.

Into the angry breach came Nemesis. Sensing that something was wrong, the collie trotted between the humans, barking with short nervous yelps. Intent on his quarry, Reggie stumbled over the dog and almost fell. Swearing, he kicked at the collie, connecting with a glancing blow along the ribs. With a howl that was as much shock as pain, Nemesis raced across the room and bolted out the French doors.

The dog's intervention had given Alys a moment to think, and when Reggie closed in she was armed with a heavy volume of French dramatists. She hurled it into his stomach, followed by the largest book within reach, a massive leather-bound edition of the complete works of Shakespeare that caught him on the side of the head, then clipped his knee on its downward journey. The combination of the books and his own unsteady state sent him crashing breathless and choking to the floor. Alys whipped past him and was almost out the door when she collided with Mac Cooper as the valet came dashing into the library.

Coming on top of the battle she had just fought, the impact took her breath away, and Mac caught her to prevent her from falling. She had seen little of Reggie's valet, knowing him mostly as a rather dapper, distant figure, but now his face was alive with concern. "Are you all right, Lad Alys?"

No, blast it, she wasn't, but she damned well wouldn't admit it. "I'm fine, no thanks to your drunken master," she snapped.

Mac released her, then knelt by Reggie, who was being violently sick as a result of having caught a book in his gut. Alys started to leave, but the valet looked up and said, "Don't go. I'm going to need help getting him upstairs."

"Why not just leave him here?" she said waspishly. "It might do him some good."

"Not likely, not when he won't even remember what happened."

That at least was a blessing. As Alys hovered indecisively, Cooper waited until Reggie was through retching, then said calmly, "Time for bed, Reg. Let me help you up."

Groggy and green-faced, Reggie muttered, "Don't have to help me home, 'm already there."

Ignoring the comment, the valet started lifting one arm. Since he wasn't making much headway, an exasperated Alys went to help. Between them they managed to get an incoherently muttering Reggie up and moving, though it was a slow trip. Halfway up the staircase their unruly burden almost managed to knock all three of them down the steps, and Alys would have a bruise on her thigh where she was shoved into the railing.

Within three feet of his bed Reggie suddenly went berserk, swearing and hurling a wild punch at his valet. If it had connected, Cooper would have been in trouble, but the valet deftly dodged, then gave his master a short, neat clip on the jaw, using just enough force to knock him out. By the light of the lamp burning on the bedside table, Alys saw that Reggie was dead to the world as they deposited him on the bed. "Is he like this often, Cooper?"

"Aye, though not husually so bad," the valet admitted as he rolled his master onto his back. " 'E'd been off the booze for ha while, and Hi'd 'oped . . ." His voice trailed off.

Alys was interested to note that Cooper now had a thick cockney accent, quite unlike his usual genteel tones. "Why do you put up with him?"

She didn't expect an answer, and was surprised when the valet glanced up at her. His accent more under control, Cooper said, "I stay with him because if it hadn't been for Reg, I'd have been transported or hanged a dozen years ago."

At Alys's startled face, he said, "S'truth, Lady Alys. I was the scrawny product of a flash house, stealing whatever I could to survive. I'd been caught and put in Newgate twice already, and if I was up before a magistrate again, they wouldn't be making any more allowances for my youth."

"So . . . how did you meet Reggie?"

"My specialty was robbing well-breeched swells who were too jug-bitten to defend themselves. I made the mistake of trying it with Reg, and he broke my arm. I started howling and begging him not to turn me over to the watch, and he said that since I was such a poor excuse for a thief, I should find an honest job. I said I wanted one, but who would hire a footpad? He was quite amused by that, then said he needed a valet and if I was willing to learn, he'd take me on. And if I tried to rob him again, he'd break my neck, not my arm."

Cooper's mouth quirked. "The first few months were right lively. There have been times I've wondered if I would have been better off on the streets, but it's never been dull. Reg has gotten us into some rare trouble, but always gets us out again."

Alys gave the little cockney a hard stare. "Why did you tell me that?"

"Thought you might need reminding that Reg has some good qualities."

"You're right, mate," she said sourly. "I'd forgotten."

"But no harm was done, was it?" Cooper said soothingly. "You get some rest, Lady Alys. I'll clean up the library."

For a long moment she studied the limp, powerful figure sprawled across the wide bed, then sighed and left. Why couldn't Reggie be a simple hero or villain?

18

Reggie was finally ready to concede that there was a hell. The prospect of fire hadn't seemed so bad, but this poisonous swirl of nausea, pain, and black, soul-deep depression was a worse torment than any medieval theologian could have concocted.

He shifted slightly, then stilled as his head threatened to split. Reluctantly Reggie accepted that he was alive; the only virtue to that state was knowing that in the natural course of events he should eventually feel better. He had read once that drinking was the perfect puritan vice, since it had its own built-in punishment. It seemed unfair that even the resolutely non-puritanical had to suffer as well.

The mists closed in again, and when they had rolled over and away once more he tried opening his eyelids, which felt as if they had been sewed shut. The glare of light sent a spike of agony through his head and scalded eyeballs, and his empty stomach heaved. *This way of life is killing you.* He must have made some sound, because Mac's calm voice penetrated his frozen brain. "Can you drink this? It will make you feel better."

With Mac's arm supporting him, Reggie managed to drink. Mac's elixir was mostly apple juice this time, with other ingredients, including a generous dose of spirits. His nervous stomach began to settle down. Burning eyes still closed, he asked in a grating voice, "What time is it, and has anything happened that I should know about?"

"Almost noon. Mr. Markham left early this morning, with regrets that he couldn't wait late enough to say good-bye." A hint of irony underlay the valet's voice. "Master William inquired after you, saying that you had an engagement to ride with him this morning, but I said you were indisposed."

Reggie groaned, remembering that he had promised to take the boy onto the downs. Well, it would have to be another time. "Anything happen last night?"

"You might ask Lady Alys about that," Mac said, bland as an egg. "I'm sure that I can't say."

Reggie's stomach lurched again as he dug into his brain, trying to remember if something had happened with Allie. Search as he might, he drew a blank; the last thing he remembered was Julian yawning and bidding him good night. Had Allie come downstairs? Or, God forbid, had he gone into her bedroom? *What the hell had happened?* With foreboding, Reggie asked, "Where is Lady Alys?"

"Working somewhere on the estate. Took bread and cheese with her and said she would be out all day."

Making a supreme effort, Reggie pushed himself to a sitting position, then hung his head forward until the world steadied. "Bring me some whiskey."

"Wouldn't coffee be better?" Mac suggested. "I've a pot right here."

"Then pour a cup, and put some whiskey in it."

"I don't think that's a good idea," Mac said.

"Goddammit, just do as I tell you!"

It was very rare for Reggie to take that tone, and Mac knew better than to disagree. Within two minutes a huge mug of coffee liberally spiked with whiskey was in Reggie's hand, and he gulped it down, ignoring how his mouth and tongue burned. Within ten minutes he started to feel better, and pushed himself up and over to the washbasin. Water in his face helped, though his hand was too unsteady to risk shaving; he let Mac do that.

After three more mugs of doctored coffee, a floating feeling had eradicated the worst of his misery. Ignoring Mac's worried face, Reggie changed into riding clothes and headed toward the stables, trying to guess where Allie might be today. Would the sheep shearing still be going on? He couldn't remember. But he had a very bad feeling about the night before, and Mac's suggestion that he ask Lady Alys what happened boded ill. Surely he wouldn't have hurt her, no matter how cupshot he was? She wouldn't be out riding today if she had been hurt. *Physical injury is not the only, or even the worst, kind of damage.*

He shook his head to chase the inner voice away, then immediately regretted the action as a wave of dizziness surged through him. He should have had more whiskey to steady himself. *What was it that got you into this condition in the first place?* Swearing under his breath, he entered the stable door.

As his eyes gratefully responded to the lower light level, his ears were struck by the sudden ear-splitting neigh of an enraged horse. For a moment he stopped dead. It sounded like his stallion, Bucephalus, but what would have set the horse off like that? Then, as the enraged whinnying continued, the high-pitched scream of a child began.

William. Oh, God, William, who had always been fascinated by the stallion. Reggie had warned him more than once to keep clear of the horse's unpredictable temper. His own physical ills forgotten, he raced the length of the stables to the large box stall at the far end that held the stallion. It was lunchtime and no one was around. As he ran, the ominous boom of hooves smashing against the stall was added to the screaming of horse and child.

Reggie grabbed a pitchfork that was leaning against the wall, then spent a moment reconnoitering over the half-door. Inside the stall, William cowered in a corner, his small body drawn into a ball, his arms up in a futile attempt to protect his head. On the floor, half-buried by straw, lay a carrot the boy had brought as a present, while above him Bucephalus reared in the air, a thousand pounds of lethal horseflesh with flailing iron-shod hooves. One hoof struck the wall by William's head and gouged a deep gash as the other hoof grazed the child's arm. Viciously the horse rose to strike again.

Shouting to distract the stallion, Reggie charged into the stall, brandishing the pitchfork. Too furious to recognize the one human for whom he had any affection, Bucephalus wheeled and struck at him. With agonized regret Reggie stabbed with the fork, drawing blood from the stallion's shoulder, trying to do as little damage as possible while knowing that he risked ruining the animal forever. "William, get out!" he yelled.

Behind him he heard scuttling sounds as the boy escaped through the door. Backing away quickly, Reggie was able to get out of the stall without using the pitchfork again. The crazed animal continued screaming and kicking as Reggie dived out to safety and latched the door behind him. It was quite possible that Bucephalus would lethally injure himself even if the stab wounds were minor.

Reggie dropped the pitchfork against the wall and turned to William. The boy appeared uninjured, though he was badly shaken and dragged one sleeve across his

eyes to wipe incipient tears. The terror Reggie had felt
for the boy's safety combined with the aftereffects of
drink and the fear that his favorite horse might have to
be destroyed. Completely out of control, he grabbed
William's shoulders and shook him. "You damned little
idiot! Do you know what you've done with your disobedience? That horse may have to be destroyed. I should
have let him kick your head in!"

Then, as Reggie's hand curled into a fist, time and
space seemed to shatter into a kaleidoscope of fragments. There was blond, blue-eyed William, white-faced
and trembling in his grip, more frightened of Reggie than
he had been of the horse . . . but he was also a dark-
haired boy, smaller, equally terrified, and somehow that
child was Reggie. The endless equine screaming was also
that of a woman, and the man was not Reggie, but
another man of similar height and coloring and drunken
fury.

A wave of dizziness and panicky, hysterical fear engulfed Reggie, sweeping him away and shattering him on
the knife-edged rocks of memory. With horror, he realized how close he had come to striking William with his
full, dangerous adult strength. Releasing the boy, he
stood up, dazed and unseeing.

The scene in front of his eyes was not the stables, but
his mother's morning room, a room he had avoided
without knowing why. It was a lifetime ago and his
parents were fighting about his father's drinking, one of
an endless series of conflicts. His mother was crying and
saying that her husband must leave Strickland and never
come back, that she would not let him hurt her sons.
Drunk and enraged, his father had railed at his wife,
then turned violent.

Reggie had been drawn by the sounds of fighting.
Indelibly etched in his mind was an image in silhouette,
both his parents standing in front of a window, his father's powerful arm frozen at the moment of impact as
he struck his wife on the side of the head. How could
Reggie have forgotten an image so sharply edged, limned
in agony? How could he bear to remember?

He had been small, three or four, but he hadn't hesitated. As he heard his mother cry out, heard the sickening thud of flesh and bone colliding, he had hurled himself at his father, shrieking his own childish fury, his fists flailing, wrapping himself around his father's leg, kicking and biting, doing everything he could to protect his mother. Drunkenly, mindlessly enraged, his father had grabbed him by the shoulders, lifting and hurling him through the air.

That short flight had seemed very slow, almost languid. There was no pain when he hit the wall, though he could feel the snap and stab of breaking bones before his body crumpled and tumbled to the floor. His eyes had been open but he could neither move nor feel, and his spirit seemed to detach from his body, floating painlessly above the turmoil. From above he had seen his mother scream, then fall to her knees and sweep the broken body of her son into her arms. He had believed her as she wept hysterically that her husband had murdered their son; surely he must be dead to see and hear, yet be powerless to act.

Then he was back in his own body, feeling his mother's arms tight around him, her desperately beating heart beneath her soft breasts, comforted by the rose scent she wore. He remembered his mother's frantic tears, his father's anguished expression as he cried out that he hadn't meant it, Annie, that it was an accident, that she must believe he had meant no harm.

And cruel as a blade, he remembered the fury and revulsion between his parents. As he faded into unconsciousness, he carried with him the horror-etched images of their faces, and he remembered quite clearly telling himself that he mustn't die. Though he had been too young to define it in words, he had known instinctively that death would separate his parents forever, isolating his father in an endless hell beyond forgiveness.

As awareness cleared, Reggie found himself blindly staring at the stable wall, his hands knotted in front of him on the splintery surface, kneading and clawing as if release lay somewhere within the wood. In an agony of despair he knotted his right hand into a fist and smashed it into the wall with all his trained strength, striking again

and again in a futile attempt to destroy the memories and
the anguish and the knowledge.

The fierce pain of the blows engulfed his hand and
stabbed up through his wrist and arm, and it was welcome. He looked down to see the skin gashed on his
knuckles and rivulets of crimson trickling between his
fingers. Staring mutely at the blood, he attempted to
establish a fragile control on himself.

Finally recalling that he was not alone, he turned to
William. There were tear tracks on the round face beneath the bright blond hair, and the boy was staring at
Reggie as if he had never seen him before, bewildered
and frightened by such incomprehensible adult behavior.

Reggie inhaled deeply, trying to find some sanity in his
whirling, disoriented brain. He knelt to bring himself to
the boy's level and said unsteadily, "Come here."

After a long moment's hesitation, William approached,
and Reggie placed one hand on his shoulder. "Are you
all right?"

William nodded warily.

Holding the boy's gaze with his own, Reggie said, "I'm
sorry I was so angry. I was afraid you would be killed.
Then, when I knew you were safe, I went a little crazy.
Stupid of me, but adults are often stupid." That elicited a
more vigorous nod, and William began to relax. "Now do
you understand why I said to keep away from Bucephalus?"

"Yes." The boy swallowed, then said in a faltering
voice, "I'm sorry I caused trouble—I . . . I just wanted to
make friends. W-will Bucephalus have to be destroyed?"

"I hope not." Reggie stood. "Go and get the head
groom. We'll see what can be done."

William went scampering off and Reggie looked into
the stall. The neighing and kicking had stopped, but the
stallion was still agitated, prancing nervously, patches of
sweat and foam marring the sleek black coat. Reggie
began talking softly, concentrating on soothing the animal's fear, and the process helped bring his own agitation
down to a manageable level.

By the time the head groom arrived, Reggie was in the
stall stroking Bucephalus's neck and checking the extent
of the horse's injuries. The puncture wounds weren't

deep, though there would be scars to mar the glossy hide. A hock was also sprained, but the horse seemed to have escaped serious injury. Eventually Reggie left the stallion in the groom's capable hands and went back to the house, finding his way to the library and folding wearily into the old leather-upholstered wing chair, knowing that he could not hold thought at bay any longer.

This had been his father's room, his father's chair, and as Reggie slumped back, legs outstretched and eyes closed, the missing pieces of his childhood fell into place. No wonder he had forgotten everything before the age of four, and no wonder Jeremy Stanton had been unsurprised to hear that. His godfather had made some cryptic comment that doubtless Reggie would remember if there was anything he needed to know.

What had been blocked out was the ceaseless fear and fighting caused by his father's drinking. His mother had swung between hope and anger and despair, and with a child's sensitivity Reggie had known that something was horribly wrong. Though he had adored his father, he had also feared the unpredictability of the man's moods. Sometimes his father was a great gun; other times he must be avoided at all costs. Reggie's habit of endlessly watching and analyzing other people's behavior, of looking for weaknesses that could be used if defense was needed, had originated then, when he was scarcely old enough to walk.

A few months after the birth of Reggie's younger brother, Julius, matters culminated in that last fearsome brawl. Horrified by what he had done, his father had stopped drinking. Reggie had been in bed for some time with his injuries—concussion, broken ribs and shoulder—and he had been frightened at first when his father visited. With a stricken expression in his eyes, his father had patiently worked to regain his son's trust, playing games and teaching lessons and reading aloud. By the time Reggie was up and about, his father was truly sober. Anne Davenport had not insisted that her husband leave Strickland once he stopped drinking, and in time, the family had healed.

Then had come what Reggie thought of as the Golden

Age. His parents had been happy with themselves, their marriage, their family. The days seemed endlessly full of light and laughter. Another child was born, a red-haired sprite named Amy. Reggie had basked in that time, tagging after his father all around Strickland, playing with his younger brother and sister. And he had buried every memory of the Dark Age that had gone before.

Until today, when the demon of drunkenness had driven him to the edge of injuring another child. His throat and chest ached at the thought, both for William and for the child he himself had been. He ran his hands through his hair, trying to distract himself with restless activity. As he did, his eye fell on a paper pamphlet on the table next to him, placed as if it had been left for him to read.

Lifting it, he read the title, "The Effects of Ardent Spirits upon Man." Underneath was printed, "Benjamin Rush, Physician, Philadelphia, 1784." He stared for a long time, wondering who had left it for him, before opening the pamphlet.

A dark chill curled around his heart. Inside was the name "Reginald Davenport," written in a bold masculine hand. For a moment he wondered if this was something he had bought, then forgotten; could his memory lapses have gotten that bad? Then, as he studied the signature, he released the breath he had been holding. The hand-writing was similar to his, but not identical. Since he was named for his father, it was logical to assume that the tract had belonged to his father and had been here in the library for all the intervening years. He began to read.

Time passed as he read and reread, with long spells of sightless staring. The monograph was short, only a few thousand words, yet in it Benjamin Rush had described in great and ominous detail the effects of drunkenness, from *Unusual garrulity* to *Captiousness and a disposition to quarrel*, to *Immodest actions* and *A temporary fit of madness*. And everything in between.

The physician had gone on to call drunkenness an *odious disease*, described the physical effects, both immediate and long-term, and had said, *It is further remarkable that drunkenness resembles certain hereditary, family, and contagious diseases*. In other words, like father, like son.

Ardent spirits . . . impair the memory, debilitate the understanding, and pervert the moral faculties. Everything that was happening to Reggie.

He glanced once more at the last pages, where Rush made dire predictions and mournful commentary on the many ways drunkenness destroyed lives. The physician classed death as among the consequences of hard drinking: *But it is not death from the immediate hand of the Deity: it is death from suicide.*

Reggie closed his eyes, remembering that internal voice of warning: *This way of life is killing you.* With the veils ripped from the past, he identified that voice as that of his father, the first Reginald Davenport, who had come perilously close to destroying his life, his family, and his firstborn son with drinking. In an odd burst of fancy, Reggie wondered if his father was keeping an eye on his only surviving child, trying to prevent his namesake from repeating the pattern of self-destruction. Unlikely though it was, the thought was a warming one, the only positive reflection he had had all day.

What was dark and inescapable was the knowledge that Reggie was coursing down the same merciless path that his father had followed. Jeremy Stanton had been skeptical of whether it would be possible to cut back on drinking; he had implied that only quitting entirely would work, and the older man's hard-won experience was proving accurate. As soon as Reggie had swallowed the first glass of brandy the night before, judgment and good sense had gone out the window, resulting in the worst drunkenness—and the worst aftereffects—of his life. The weeks of sobriety had done nothing to control his drinking; indeed, he had been worse. If the physician Rush was right that alcoholism was a disease, it must be a progressive one. And the only cure that Reggie could imagine was absolute abstinence.

Massaging his temples, he leaned back in his chair, wishing that the ache and the dank, choking depression would go away. Even now, the desire to drink was a hot siren call, with every fiber of his body longing, pleading, and cajoling to have just a single glass, a single mouthful. In a bottle lay surcease from pain. It would be so easy to

blot out the intolerable memories, the guilt, the hope-
lessness. . . .

If he was going to kill himself, a pistol would be
quicker and cleaner.

Alys had worked with grim determination all day, trying
to blot out the recollection of her employer's drunken
advances and angry attack. His drinking was getting worse,
and for the sake of the children's and her own safety, it
would be necessary to move out of the manor house.
Next time, Merry might be the target. It sickened her to
remember how he had behaved; what was worse was
knowing how much she cared for him, flaws and all.

She stayed out past dinnertime, preferring her own
company, and by the time she returned, dusty and weary,
shadows were lengthening. She walked into the house to
find a delegation meeting her: Merry, her sapphire eyes
showing the strain of parting from Julian; William, looking unnaturally abashed; and Mac Cooper, looking inscrutable. Only Peter, who was on a holiday with a
schoolfriend's family, was missing.

Alys glanced at the concerned faces. "Is something
wrong?"

"Not a disaster, exactly," Merry assured her, "but
we're worried about Reggie."

"Has he gone off again? He makes something of a
habit of that," Alys said with studied neutrality.

Cooper spoke up. "No, he's been in the library all day,
since an accident with that black devil's horse of his."

Beginning to be alarmed, Alys listened to William
explain how Reggie had turned rescuer again and had
nearly succumbed to an urge to wring William's neck.
Alys could understand that impulse, since she had occasionally shared it, but she frowned as the boy described
how Reggie had smashed his fist into the wall over and
over. Was the man going mad? Perhaps he had been
drinking steadily all night and all day.

She glanced at Cooper. "If you're all so concerned,
why doesn't someone just go into the library?"

The valet replied, "I was about to, but then you came

in. Might be better if you checked on him, Lady Alys."
His aitches were firmly in place.

"Why me?" she asked in exasperation, but Cooper
just met her eyes with an opaque expression. Wearily she
accepted that since she had been running everything and
everyone at Strickland for years, she should be the one
to ensure that the owner was alive and as well as could
be expected.

Ironic though the thought was, it produced a small stab
of anxiety. Surely he would not have done anything
foolish? "Has he eaten anything today?" she asked.

Cooper and Merry looked at each other. "Not that I
know of," the valet said.

"Then have the cook get a tray together with enough
food for two people and a large pot of hot tea. I'll go
wash up, then take it in to him," she ordered.

She didn't take the time to bathe and change, but she
did wash her hands and face and let her hair down, since
long hours in tight braids sometimes gave her a headache. After tying her hair back carelessly in a scarf, she
went downstairs. The tray was waiting, and she chased
the concerned watchers away, saying the man would
never come out if he had an audience.

Then she entered the library, setting the tray quietly
on a table to the left of the door. Reggie was a lean,
silent shape slouched in his favorite chair, half-turned
away from her, the room too shadowed to see his face.
But his clothing appeared neat, so perhaps he had not
availed himself of the liquor cabinet. "Are you still among
the living?" she asked softly.

His head turned in her direction. After a lengthy silence
he said, "I've read of penguins that jump around on an ice
floe, trying to decide if there are any sharks in the water.
Eventually they push one of their number into the sea. If
the sacrifice isn't eaten, they all dive in." His voice was slow
and rusty. "You, I assume, are the sacrificial penguin."

It was not what she had expected; obviously there was
some life in the old boy yet. She chuckled. "I have been
called many things in my life, but never a sacrificial
penguin. How did you know that there was a committee
out there, trying to decide what to do about you?"

"Occasionally the door would open, very carefully, then close after a few moments."

"After they had determined that the shark was still lurking here." Without asking if he wanted any, she poured two cups of tea, with heavy dollops of milk and sugar in Reggie's cup, then went and put it in his hand. Close up, he looked dreadful, with haunted eyes and a gray tinge to his dark skin. As he stared at the dainty cup, she said helpfully, "It's called tea. People drink it. It's the English cure for whatever ails you."

He smiled faintly, then raised the cup and swallowed deeply. "In that case, you had better order a larger pot."

Still without consulting his wishes, she moved the tray to the table next to him. Taking the chair on the other side, she proceeded to select a substantial supper for herself. "I'm told the roast chicken and the pickled mushrooms are particularly good tonight," she said. "Rumor also has it that you haven't eaten in twenty-four hours. Food might help."

Slowly he reached out and took a plate and began to eat. He put away less than Alys, but then, he hadn't been outside working all day. Alys periodically topped off the teacups. She was just finishing a portion of Ripon pudding when Reggie said abruptly, "How much do I have to apologize for?"

Alys swallowed her pudding. "You don't remember what happened last night?"

"No, but Mac implied rather strongly that I have a lot to answer for where you are concerned."

Alys sipped her tea and considered. Her lingering anger had largely dissipated at the sight of Reggie's strained face. Combining her intuition and guesswork with what William had said, she was willing to lay odds that he had crossed some kind of significant mental frontier. "You were drunk and amorous," she said at last, deciding on honesty tempered with discretion.

"*In vino veritas*," he muttered. "That's what I was afraid of. Did . . . did I hurt you?"

"It was a near-run thing for a moment," she admitted. "When you refused to take no for an answer, you cornered me, and I threw a few books at you."

"Bloody hell." His face sank behind one hand. "Thank God you are a most redoubtable female—I've got enough to live with." He sighed heavily. "I seem to spend a lot of my time apologizing to you, Allie. For what it's worth, I regret most deeply what happened."

"I think we're about even," she said cheerfully. "The volume of French drama that I threw into your stomach didn't do you much good."

He raised his head at that, and in the dusk she could see a faint smile. "Too many French plays could give anyone a bellyache." She was glad to hear more life in his voice; Reggie without a sense of humor was an alarming prospect.

He lifted a pamphlet. "Did you find this and leave it out for me as a not-so-subtle hint?"

Peering through the dusk, she could just make out the words "The Effects of Ardent Spirits upon Man." It looked familiar. She frowned a moment. "I think it might have tumbled out when I was grabbing books off the shelves. Mac Cooper probably found it when he was cleaning up. It does seem to the point."

"Doesn't it, just." He fingered it absently, then laid it down. "It was written by an American physician. He talks about drunkenness as if it is a disease."

It was an interesting thought; Alys made a mental note to find the pamphlet and read it later.

"As you had noticed, I stopped drinking for several weeks, thinking that would solve the problem." The silence stretched. Eventually he went on, "The results last night make it clear that that approach didn't work. I've reached the conclusion that I must stop entirely."

"I don't suppose that will be easy." She knew her words were inadequate, but was unsure what else to say.

"No, I don't expect it will. However, I see no alternative." From the levelness of Reggie's voice, he could be commenting on the weather rather than announcing what must have been a fiercely difficult decision.

"If there is anything I can do to help . . ." she offered tentatively.

"Thank you," he said in a very low voice. "I don't

think this is the sort of thing anyone else can help with, but I do appreciate the offer."

On impulse Alys stood. "Why not come outside for some fresh air? It's a lovely evening." Being holed up here like a badger in his set couldn't be helping his state of mind.

After a pause he said, "Very well."

She led the way out the French doors into the fresh summer evening. The lawn had been cut today and the sweet green scent enticed the nostrils. Above their heads a spectacular sunset flared, with towers of clouds gilded in gold and orange and indigo. It was lighter outside than in the library, and she could see Reggie's face clearly. His blue eyes held a stark expression in their depths, and he moved slowly, without his usual lithe grace, but he looked composed.

They wandered down to the lake, by unspoken consent settling on a bench and watching the colors fade in the sky overhead. Neither talked, but Alys thought her presence was affording Reggie some silent comfort. She hoped so.

When only a golden rim on the horizon remained of the sunset, Reggie said, "It's getting late and you've had a very long day. I should let you get some rest."

"It's good to take the time to be silent now and then. I don't do so often enough." Alys rose. "I want to show you something on the way back. One of life's very small wonders."

He followed her passively to the wool room. It was a large, clean chamber in one of the more distant barns, and tonight it was nearly full of fresh-cut fleeces. Alys opened the door and picked up one of the rolled fleeces to show Reggie. There was just enough light left to see a faint mist, like the bloom on a fruit, clouding the ivory-white wool. "See? The fleeces are still warm and alive. As the sun goes down, they cool."

With some interest he took the fleece from her, squeezing its springy bulk in his hands. "Interesting. Who would have guessed that fleeces have their own local dew?"

"That's not all. Listen."

They were both very still. Inside the wool room was a

gentle stirring, almost like breathing. At Reggie's questioning glance, Alys explained, a little shy at what a simple thing it was, "The fleeces will rustle softly like that all night long. The fibers are interlocked and tense, and they shift to be comfortable, like people."

He smiled, the most relaxed he had been tonight. "Life is full of small wonders. Thank you for showing me this one." His somber gaze held hers, and she thought his words were for more than just the rustling fleeces. It was one of those moments of inexplicable intimacy that sometimes occurred between them, and in that moment she determined not to move her charges away from Strickland, at least not if he stayed sober. He was going to need people who cared about him.

Reggie laid the fleece back in place and they started back toward the manor house. They were almost there when Nemesis came galloping up, her clownish white face vivid in the dark. Wagging her tail happily, she reared up and planted her front paws against Reggie, demanding to be caressed.

He caught the collie's head in his hands and tousled her ears, a process that sent her into raptures. "Where have you been, you worthless creature?" Alys saw him pause before he glanced at her. "Did anything happen with Nemesis last night?"

"Well, you kicked her, but she wasn't really injured."

He grimaced and returned the collie's forepaws to earth. "It's a poor sort of man that will kick his own dog."

"Don't worry about it," she said with a downward glance. "It's pretty clear that you're forgiven."

"Would that all one's crimes could so easily be set aside." Then, harsh, "I don't know if I can do it, Allie. It was hard to stop drinking when it was temporary. Now, to face a lifetime . . ." A thread of despair, of being defeated before he even began, sounded in his deep voice.

Alys tried to imagine herself in his position. What if she had to deny herself her cherished morning cup of coffee? The mere thought of a lifetime of that denial gave her a shiver of empathy. Yet that was only coffee, something she enjoyed but did not crave. How much worse it must be for Reggie, who had drunk heavily for perhaps twenty years, who suffered from the disease called drunkenness. . . .

Her exercise in empathy gave her an idea. "A lifetime is too long a time. Can you refrain from drinking for the rest of tonight?"

He exhaled wearily. "That I think I can manage."

"Then think only of that. Tomorrow morning, think only of the morning. What is forever but a collection of minutes or hours? Surely you can always refrain for the next five minutes. Or if that is too much, then the next minute."

It was full dark now, and Reggie's face was a pale blur as he turned to her. After a long interval he said, "Perhaps . . . perhaps I can do it after all." He raised one hand and touched her cheek. "Thank you, Allie, for everything."

It was a measure of what a low mind she had, Alys decided, that even as she rejoiced to hear that Reggie was determined to stop drinking, that even as she pledged to do whatever she could to help, she felt a stab of deep sorrow at knowing that when he was sober he would never kiss her again.

19

The three men lingered over their port to give their wives ample time to chat about babies, since the Ladies Wargrave and Radford were increasing, and Lady Presteyne was the proud mother of a six-month-old son. The host was abstracted, and eventually Lord Presteyne remarked, "You're unusually silent even by your standards, Richard. Is impending fatherhood weighing that heavily?" David Lancaster spoke with the freedom of a friend who had known the earl since both men were officers on the Peninsula, with no thought of peerages in their futures.

The Earl of Wargrave smiled apologetically. "Sorry, David. Every now and then I wonder how my black-sheep cousin is faring."

The third man sharing the port raised a sardonic brow. "There are no reports that Dorsetshire has been destroyed or blown into the sea, so perhaps Reggie is behaving himself."

Richard grinned. "I'll admit that you know my cousin much better than I, Jason, but surely he isn't that bad?"

Lord Radford's dark eyes twinkled. "I'll admit bias, since Reggie and I have known each other nigh onto thirty years, and have rubbed each other wrong the whole time."

David looked curious. "You've mentioned this cousin in letters, Richard, but apart from the fact that he's your heir and you settled an estate on him, you've said very little. What makes him so black a sheep? Is he dishonest?"

When Richard cocked an inquiring eye at Jason, that gentleman said, "Reggie Davenport has always defied classification. He's not dishonest—quite the contrary, in his own perverse way he's belligerently honorable—but he's one of the most maddening men I've ever met."

"Why?" Richard's question was characteristically succinct.

While he considered his answer, Radford tilted his chair back from the heavy mahogany table that graced the dining room of Wargrave Park. "That's a good question. I suppose the problem with Davenport is that he always goes one step too far. We met when he had just come under his uncle's guardianship. Since the Wargrave and Radford estates adjoin and both of us were bound for Eton, someone had the brilliant idea of sending us off to school together. We had two endless days in a coach to become acquainted."

He sipped his port reflectively. "Later I understood better why Reggie behaved as he did. He was a child who had just lost his whole family and been pitched into one hostile environment and was now on his way to another. I was more than willing to make friends, but he was like . . .'' Jason searched for an appropriate metaphor. "Like a rabid dog, snarling and snapping at everyone. If I had been older, I might have made more allowances, but at that age I was just angry.

"Anyhow, at Eton he was a King's Scholar, what was called a Colleger by the other students." Radford made a face. "Both of you were lucky to escape the ravages of the English public-school system. To be a regular student is bad enough, but the Collegers lived in such appalling conditions that even the most neglectful of parents hesitated to subject their sons to that, in spite of the fact that Collegers received full scholarships at Eton, automatic admission to King's College at Cambridge, and, if they wanted it, an assured, comfortable lifetime as a fellow of King's. There were always vacant spaces for Scholars because many parents would let their sons spend the first few years at Eton as regular students—Oppidans we were called. Then at sixteen they would become Collegers and have to tolerate only a year of mistreatment before Cambridge."

"I see," Richard said slowly. "My grandfather must have put my cousin in for a scholarship as the simplest, cheapest way to get Reggie off his hands for life."

"Undoubtedly," Radford agreed. "It's exactly the sort of thing the old earl would have done. Anyhow, the Collegers were treated like animals in a zoo. They were fed only one meal a day and they shared one huge room in a drafty stone building over three hundred years old. Every evening they were locked in the Long Chamber at eight o'clock and not released until the next morning."

He shook his head in disbelief. "The whole lot of Collegers, all fifty or sixty of them, were left to their own devices without any masters or other adults to keep order."

"Good Lord, it sounds like the law of the jungle," Lord Presteyne said. "Hard to believe that parents allow it."

"Exactly. I'm sure that you've heard of the kind of sexual abuse that goes on under those conditions." Radford drank more port, his eyes flinty. "Reggie had the dubious distinction of being the youngest and smallest of the Collegers his first several years. And he was a good-looking lad, as well."

Richard's eyes narrowed and he looked very much the man of war he had been. "So he was victimized by the older boys?"

"No. That's where your cousin's legend began." Radford smiled. "If anyone tried anything with him, he fought like a bull terrier and would not stop fighting, no matter what was done to him. Anyone interested in bullying him had to beat the lad unconscious, and when he woke up, he would come up swinging. Reggie seldom started fights, but he always finished them, and even the worst bullies in the college didn't want to deal with that." He shook his head admiringly. "Damnedest thing you ever saw—sixteen-year-old boys wary of a lad half their age and size. It was the same thing with the masters—no matter how much they birched him, he would never break."

David said, "Pity he didn't go into the army. With that background, he'd have ended up a general." His light words did not disguise the compassion in his voice.

"I believe he wanted to, but his uncle wouldn't buy him a commission. A strange man, the old earl." Radford smiled sardonically. "I would have died rather than admit it at the time, but I admired Reg tremendously. Besides being tougher than an East End stevedore, he was one of the best scholars and best athletes in the school, both at Eton and later at Cambridge. But he and I got off to a bad beginning and never overcame it."

"I would have thought you and he had a lot in common," Richard observed. "Horsemen, sportsmen, men-about-town."

"Yes and no. It didn't help that he and I were frequently rivals, with the honors about even as to who won. But more to the point, Reggie always went one step too far. The fashionable world is surrounded by an invisible fence. I always knew exactly how far to go without exceeding the limits. That made me dashing." Radford's expression was self-mocking. "Your cousin always chose to be one step outside the barrier. That made him dangerous."

"I appreciate your explaining more of my cousin's history, Jason," Richard said, his hazel eyes abstracted. "I think I understand him a bit better now."

"I doubt if understanding will make him any easier to deal with," Radford said pessimistically. "I keep thanking my lucky stars that you appeared to inherit the Wargrave honors. If Reggie had become my neighbor, we would have been building earthworks and firing cannon at each other."

Lord Presteyne grinned. "I really hope I have the opportunity to meet this man sometime."

"Perhaps I'll pay a call at Strickland later in the summer," Richard said, his expression thoughtful. "I have some business in Hampshire, and Strickland is almost on the route."

Privately Lord Radford thought Richard took his position as head of the Davenport family too seriously; his cousin was unlikely to welcome the earl with common civility, much less open arms. But as the three men rose to join their wives, the part of Radford that had admired the young Reginald Davenport hoped that the blasted man would come about before it was too late.

Reggie knew that he was going to fail, could feel himself slipping inexorably toward disaster like a man on a steeply pitched roof. When he had stopped drinking earlier it had been very difficult, but at least he had known the deprivation was temporary. Now, no matter how desperately he followed Allie's suggestion to think in terms of a day, an hour, a minute, he could feel himself sliding toward the moment when his will would break. Such thoughts did not make him an easy companion.

He spent much of his time training his hunters, since he had discovered that mental engagement was a stronger defense than mere physical activity. In the evenings he stayed with the rest of the household, speaking little but listening to the young people's chatter as a way to keep the craving at bay.

At Allie's suggestion, Meredith and Peter were working on plans to redecorate the manor house. The project gave Merry something to think about besides Julian's absence, and offered Peter an outlet for his excellent taste in all things visual. The two young Spensers would discuss their ideas with Reggie, since he had the final say. Reggie had to admire the neatness with which Allie had involved all three of them.

He acquired a pipe, both for the smoking and the endless fidgeting it took to keep the damned thing going, and he continued with his furious late-night swimming. Only Allie and Mac understood what he was trying to do, and he could feel both of them watching him while trying to be unobtrusive about it.

When his nerves frayed and he was on the verge of defeat, Allie always seemed to be there, calmly ignoring his flashes of irritation, anchoring him to sanity. He supposed that to her he was another project, a piece of property of doubtful value that would benefit by improvement. Whatever her motives, he was grateful. When the young people had gone to bed, they would stay up late talking, their conversation ranging over farming, politics, literature, and a hundred other things. Two topics they never discussed were her past and his future.

As the endless days dragged by, few incidents were intense enough to pierce his inner ferment. An event that did occurred when he and Meredith and Peter went into Dorchester to look at some wallpaper and fabric that had just arrived from London. On the way in, Peter had taken the ribbons, proud of his growing skill at driving. Merry's lovely face was serene, but she was too quiet. Allie had privately told Reggie that Julian wrote often, saying how he missed her and declaring his intention of returning to Strickland within a month, but the fact that he didn't mention how his father had received news of his proposed marriage was ominous.

In Dorchester, Reggie had let Peter and Merry off at the shop, then taken the barouche around to a livery stable. He was just leaving after bestowing his horses when he came face-to-face with George Blakeford. With determined civility Reggie said, " 'Morning, Blakeford."

The other man stopped in his tracks and glared, his thick muscular body stiff with anger. "I should call you out for what you did to Stella."

"Oh? What did your ladybird say I did to her?" Reggie asked, not without some curiosity.

"She told me that you had ravished her the first eve-

ning you met her, and publicly insulted her at that
assembly."

"I plead innocent to the one charge and guilty to the
other," Reggie said, suddenly bored. Stella was obviously every bit as much a troublemaker as he had suspected. "Very bad of me, but not a dueling matter. Now,
if you'll excuse me . . ."

Blakeford's beefy hand shot out and clutched Reggie's
arm, his fingers digging deep. "Don't you brush me off,
you bastard. If you come near Stella again, you're a dead
man."

Reggie loathed being manhandled, and with shocking
suddenness their positions changed as Reggie broke the
other's grip, then grasped Blakeford's wrist and twisted
bone and tendon with a force just short of breaking the
joint. "Don't threaten me, Blakeford," he said in a quiet,
deadly voice. "Use that fire and vinegar to give Stella
what she needs so she doesn't go around putting her
hands in other men's breeches."

Blakeford turned almost purple with rage and tried to
wrench himself free. Reggie released him, saying, "Don't
be a fool by getting into a public brawl about a whore's
virtue. If you really believed that I had ravished her, you
would have come after me with a horsewhip weeks ago."

His words checked Blakeford's actions. His restraint a
visible effort, the man said hoarsely, "You'll regret this,
Davenport. For too many years you've done what you
wanted and not given a damn, but retribution is just
around the corner."

"I don't doubt it," Reggie said. "But in the meantime
I have an engagement." He circled around Blakeford
and headed toward the High Street with an itchy feeling
between his shoulder blades. He had no doubt that if
Blakeford had been carrying a pistol, he himself would
have been a dead man.

As he joined Merry and Peter and was drawn into a
debate on the relative merits of figured cream-colored
satin damask versus blue-and-dove-gray striped brocade,
he spared one last thought for George Blakeford. It had
been a mistake to lose his temper and talk about the
man's little trollop as he had. Where women were con-

cerned, men could be very irrational, and Reggie had an uneasy feeling that the encounter might have repercussions. He shrugged philosophically; his reputation was already so bad that it couldn't be blackened much further.

George Blakeford wanted to crush Davenport's throat with his bare hands; to beat that cool, contemptuous face to a bleeding pulp. Only the memory of his greater goal kept him from indulging his bloodlust. It was far more important that Alys Weston die, and in a manner that could not be traced to him. A thousand pities that the fire had failed; though he had racked his brain, he could think of nothing else that would appear so much like an accident. A second fire would be too suspicious; besides, fire had proved to be an inefficient manner of killing a specific person.

He was finding it surprisingly difficult to get at someone who spent virtually all her time on an estate where everyone knew her, and where strangers stood out like red flags. What made it even harder was Blakeford's new resolution that any "incident" must destroy both Alys Weston and Reggie Davenport. It would have to be an ambush, the sort of thing that could be attributed to a roving band of cutthroats; there were plenty of those since the war had ended and so many soldiers had been turned off to starve.

It was taking time to find men for the task. They couldn't be local, and they mustn't be connected to Blakeford. But he had already found two desperate men who would do anything for money, one of them a former army sharpshooter. When he had located two or three more, all he would need was an event that would lure his two victims away from the estate. It might take weeks or months, but he was prepared to wait as long as necessary to ensure that there would be no escape. And in the meantime he would contemplate the sweetness of his revenge, and his victory.

Alys usually did not involve herself with the internal affairs of the manor house, but it was not easy to overlook a housemaid who turned green and dropped a china washbasin right in front of her. It was a hot, sultry day, and Alys had stopped by her bedchamber to change into a fresh shirt at the same time that the maid Gillie was cleaning the room.

Amidst fragments of one of the pottery's prettiest basins, Gillie swayed and threatened to faint. Alarmed, Alys had grabbed the girl and helped her to a chair, then pushed her head down to counteract the faintness. Luckily the water-filled pitcher was still intact, so Alys wet a towel and took it to Gillie after ringing for the housekeeper. After a few minutes of having cool water patted on her face and throat, the maid's color improved and she sat up. "Thank you, Lady Alys, I'm ever so sorry," she said feebly. "I'll clean up the mess right now."

"Sit a little longer," Alys ordered. "In this heat it's easy to overdo."

Gillie smiled crookedly. " 'Tis naught to do with the heat, miss."

Before the conversation could progress further, the housekeeper, May Herald, entered and took in the situation with one glance. "You go lie down for the rest of the afternoon, Gillie. You should take better care of yourself."

"I want to do as much as I can, ma'am," the maid said, her pretty chin lifting with a touch of stubbornness.

"I know, but don't be a fool, girl. Take advantage of how lucky you are," Mrs. Herald scolded. "Now, off with you."

With a shy bob of her head to Alys, Gillie stood and carefully made her way out. Frowning after the maid, Alys asked slowly, "Mrs. Herald, is that child increasing?"

The housekeeper nodded. "Yes, haven't you heard?" She bent over and picked up the largest fragments of the broken basin. "Mind you, I don't approve in the least, but it's to Mr. Davenport's credit that he didn't just turn her out. Most gentlemen couldn't care less what happens to foolish wenches like that one." Straightening, she added, "I'll send a girl up to finish the cleaning later this afternoon," then bustled out.

Left standing alone in her chamber, Alys felt as if she had been punched in the stomach. So Gillie was the maid she had seen sneaking away from Davenport's bedroom, and she was carrying her master's by-blow. Silly of Alys to be surprised; babies were one of the natural consequences of sex. Anyone who worked on a farm knew that. There was no reason on earth that Alys should feel betrayed.

But what did reason have to do with it? Her mind and fingers numb, she found a fresh shirt and changed into it. She must compose herself before she went out, or anyone looking at her would know something was wrong. She sat on the edge of the bed, staring sightlessly ahead and trying to understand why she felt such hurt. And then she knew.

Feeling too fragile to sit upright, she lay back on the bed, her body limp, her eyes still blindly open. She was in love with Reggie, with all his careless charm and indisputable weaknesses. Amazing how long she had been able to conceal that fact from herself. It had been less humiliating to pretend he was merely a convenient object of her fantasies. Yes, he had aroused her senses as no other man had, but he had also treated her as an equal, respecting her judgment, listening to her ideas, teasing and stimulating her until long-buried parts of her personality had come to life. He had paid her the rare compliment of treating her as a friend.

What a pathetic picture she presented, the aging spinster, a simple-minded female who had not let friendship be enough. Her most profound wish was to see a flawed, cynical man magically transformed into a perfect mate. She wanted him to swear love eternal, beg for her hand and heart, and never look at another woman. Instead, he had a pregnant mistress under his roof, and had only ever noticed that Alys was female when he was drunk.

She sat upright, trying to break the despairing circle of her thoughts. Pride came to her rescue. She could accept being thought mannish and eccentric, but she'd be damned if she would let anyone think she was pathetic—least of all Reggie. He needed a friend far more than he needed another mistress, and because she loved him, she would continue to offer friendship.

Friendship was better than nothing. It was also far more difficult.

*   *   *

The servants' grapevine being what it was, it didn't take long for Mac Cooper to hear that Gillie was feeling poorly. Not being busy just then, he went to the garden and picked a handful of flowers, then carried them up to the attic in a vase.

He had never seen Gillie's little room before, and he was glad to find that it had a window that opened and let a bit of breeze in. She was lying on her narrow bed with her eyes closed and her soft brown hair in limp curls. Mac studied her for a moment, glad to see that she appeared recovered, then put the vase on the dresser and turned to go. Before he could leave the room, Gillie's eyes fluttered open. She tensed at the sight of her visitor, so Mac said soothingly, "Don't worry, I just brought some flowers. You go back to sleep."

"I wasn't really sleeping." She glanced at the flowers and a look of pleased surprise came into her brown eyes. "Thanks ever so, Mr. Cooper. No one ever brought me flowers before."

Her gaze shifted to his face, and she asked shyly, "Mr. Cooper, why do you do things like that?" She gestured at the vase. "At first when you asked me to go walking and gave me little presents, I thought you wanted to tumble me, but you've never even tried." Then, bleakly, "Half of the other men on the estate have tried. After all, they all know what kind of girl I am."

He had been waiting for something like this. Taking the one wooden chair that the room boasted, he turned it and straddled the seat, crossing his arms on the back. "You're wrong. They don't know the kind of girl you are. I do, which is why I haven't tried anything."

Her pretty face was puzzled, and Mac ached to smooth away the tired lines. but it was still too soon. In her soft Dorset accent she said, "I don't understand what you mean."

"Making one mistake about a man doesn't mean you're a short-heeled wench," he said. "I expect you were in love with the fellow. A pity he was too much of a fool to appreciate it."

Her eyes closed suddenly and tears seeped from under the lids. She said apologetically, "I'm sorry, I seem to cry all the time now." She opened her eyes again, the thick lashes clumped from her tears. "Why are you so nice to me?"

He hesitated, not sure of how much to say. "I like you," he said simply. "And"—this was much harder to say—"I've been thinking it might be time I found me a wife."

The brown pansy eyes widened. "You . . . you want to marry me?"

That much surprise was a little insulting. He said stiffly, "Is it such a ridiculous idea? I'm not so bad a bargain."

Seeing his reaction, she said quickly, "Oh, no, that's not what I meant. 'Tis that, well, you're a London gent, and I'm just a country girl. And you're the master's man, and I'm only a housemaid. A *pregnant* housemaid. Why would you want to marry me? You can do ever so much better."

He hadn't analyzed even to himself the complex mixture of tenderness, desire, and protectiveness she roused in him. Choosing his words carefully, he said, "You're a pretty lass, with a good heart and a good mind, for all your lack of education. I noticed you right from the beginning. And . . . well, you need a man, I think." As her grave eyes regarded him, he added clumsily, "But I wouldn't want you to marry me only because you needed a husband."

His vulnerability touched her. Until now Gillie had seen him as a rather grand London gentleman, far above her touch, who had singled her out for reasons she hadn't understood. Now she looked at him simply as a man, and liked what she saw. He really wasn't old, maybe not even thirty. Wiry rather than muscular, but she didn't mind that. And he liked her. Smiling shyly, she said, "I wouldn't marry just for a husband."

No more was said on the topic, but when Mac took his leave, he thought they understood each other tolerably well. And when he brushed a very light kiss on her lips, she kissed him back.

20

That night Reggie went through the motions of dinner with his surrogate family, played backgammon with William, who had an unnatural talent for the game, and admired the watercolors Merry had made to show how the drawing room would look after redecoration. But he felt as if he were behind a wall of glass, removed from what the others were saying and doing. Reality was the demon on his shoulder, whispering that sobriety was a dubious goal, hardly worth the effort it was costing him. All men drank, and Reggie had always held his liquor better than most. What, after all, had he done that was so serious, except be tempted to thrash a brat who had seriously misbehaved?

He fought that demon, and the other one that whispered that he was doomed to fail, so why stretch his failure out even longer? What made him think that he could ever succeed at anything? What had he ever achieved except ephemeral successes at trivial things like horseracing and hazard? And even if he did succeed at sobriety, what would be the point?

He had been fighting the demons for days, but they grew stronger by the hour. In his heart he knew that it was only a matter of time until he slid off the edge of the slanting roof and fell into infinite darkness. But he wasn't ready to let go yet.

The tea tray had come and gone and his companions were about to retire for the night. His voice amazingly nonchalant to his own ears, he asked, "Allie, would you care for a game of chess? It's early still."

He had assumed she would accept; she always had in the past. But tonight she hesitated, then said, "Not tonight, Reggie. I've a touch of the headache."

As her tall, slim figure left the room, he knew that he had reached the edge of the roof, and the precipice lay beneath him. With suppressed violence he went into the library and read the pamphlet on ardent spirits again. So must his father have read and reread it; the edges of the pages were frayed from handling. His father had stopped drinking, as had Jeremy Stanton. If they could, so could he. He had proved his will over and over, in his schooldays, whenever he had set out to master a new skill, in his endless subterranean struggles with his uncle.

As he crossed to the French doors to go outside, he could feel the bottles in the liquor cabinet as vividly as if they were a bonfire. White heat, calling him to be consumed in the flames. One hand on the doorknob, he stopped, his body refusing to obey his will and leave, beads of sweat forming on his forehead. He had deliberately left the cabinet stocked, knowing that for the rest of his life he would be surrounded by drinkers and drinking. Perhaps he had been asking too much of himself.

He had to get out now, before it was too late, before the insatiable hunger within him won. *Can't you stop for the next hour? If that is too long, then for the next minute?* His hand tightened on the knob, his knuckles whitening, the force of his grip numbing his fingers. *Why bother? What are you trying to prove? And to whom?*

His will broke.

In a few swift moves he crossed the room, opened the door of the liquor cabinet, grabbed the first bottle that came to hand, and removed the cork. And as a chorus of internal voices deafened him with their cries of triumph or condemnation, he took the drink he had sworn he would not take.

Alys was slow in her preparations for bed, her fingers abstracted as she unbraided her hair and brushed it. She should have stayed downstairs and played chess with Reggie. For all his cool air of control, she knew how difficult the last fortnight had been for him. Earlier today she had vowed to be a friend, yet the memory of Gillie, his pregnant mistress, was too fresh. As they had played chess, she would have been wondering if he was still sleeping with the girl, and how many other bastards he had fathered. Tomorrow she would be able to deal with such thoughts, but tonight her irrational hurt was still too raw.

Her thoughts troubled, she plaited her hair into a single braid. She shouldn't be here; she should be downstairs. With an intuition too strong to be denied, she abandoned reason and left her chamber, her steps swift and light on the steps as she made her way through the softly lit house to the library.

The words that she had been about to utter died in her throat as she opened the library door and saw Reggie. Across the width of the room, he stood by the liquor cabinet, a half-empty bottle in his hand, an expression of pain and anger and defeat on his face. He looked up as she entered, and their gazes locked, his bleak beyond words, hers horrified. There was nothing to say, nothing that could be said.

Alys wanted to cry, or to scream with rage, to encourage him not to give up, or to rail at him that drinking would kill him, and she could not bear to think of him dead. She did none of those things. After an anguished moment that stretched to near-infinity, she whirled and fled the library, unable to watch what he was doing to himself.

Reggie watched her go, stricken to the heart by the expression on Allie's face. She had believed in him, had helped him in every way possible, and now she saw him for what he was. There was not yet enough booze in his system to blot out the image of her face, so he raised the bottle in his hand and drank as deeply as he could. He was a craven, a weakling, and a fool, and what could be more appropriate than proving it?

But the spirits he drank inflamed as well as soothed; in his hand was not surcease but madness. He stared at the bottle and whispered, "No."

Then, gripped by despairing fury, he hurled the bottle across the room into the empty fireplace. With bright tinkling sounds and glittering fragments, it shattered against the firebrick.

"No!" It was a scream of desperation, a repudiation of

the pain he had experienced and the pain he had given to others.

"*No!*" Blindly, hopelessly, beyond control, he seized another bottle and sent it crashing after the first with the full strength of his powerful body. He grabbed the next, a cut-glass decanter, and threw it after the others, the glass plug spinning away in midair before the decanter's fractured shards joined the others on the hearth and sprayed across the carpet.

The library was redolent with the mingled scents of brandy, Madeira, and port, sweet-sharp aromas that had beguiled him over the decades even as the liquors had stolen his mind and broken his will. There were a dozen more bottles in the cabinet, and one after another he hurled them away, rejoicing in their destruction. When he was finished with bottles, he threw goblets, uncaring that the antique glass had survived a century before this ignominious end.

Breaking every bottle of spirits on earth would not be enough to cure what ailed him, for his soul was in thrall to a deeper destruction than this. For a moment he wanted to throw himself into the mound of broken glass, to roll and thrash until he bled in a thousand places, until there would be an end to the grief and loss of living.

The desire for that easy pain of slash and bleed beckoned him, but he was not ready for that, not yet. After teetering on the brink for long moments, he fled through the French doors into the dark velvet night. It was the night of the new moon, the night of the hunted, when small frail creatures might elude the predators that sought to rend their flesh.

Fueled by despair and lit only by the stars, he ran with all the strength and endurance at his command. His strides long and heedless, he headed toward the downs in all their wild solitude. When a vicious pain in his side slowed his pace, he walked until he had recovered enough to run again, knowing in his fractured, desperate heart that it was Death itself he was trying to outrun.

Safe in her room, Alys cried as she hadn't in a dozen years, mourning Reggie as if he were dead, knowing in her bones that if he returned to drinking it was just a matter of time until an agonized, undignified death would claim him. She could not bear the thought.

She should have stayed with him. Friendship was for better and for worse every bit as much as marriage was. If she had been there earlier, he might not have begun drinking. If she had stayed, perhaps he would have stopped. If she could not even try to help, she was unworthy to be anyone's friend.

Her mind a jumble of arguments, pleas, and determination, she made her way back to the library, then halted in shock at the sight of the destruction. In the smashed glassware, puddling liquors, and alcoholic scents, she saw his desperation, but of Reggie himself there was no sign. The only movement was the soft rustle of curtains as a breeze curled lightly through the open French doors.

He might be losing the battle, but he wasn't defeated yet. Swiftly going up to her room, she changed to her practical masculine clothing, knowing that it would be a long, hard search. Then she plunged into the moonless night to find him.

In the thick darkness he fell more than once, but he ignored the bruises and tears. He pushed his endurance harder than he ever had in his whole active lifetime, quartering the estate from the high downs to the water meadows, following the hedgerows, groping blindly through the shadowed copses. His mind held nothing so clear as thought, only raw emotions, agony as acute as when his family had died, but less pure and honorable than that true grief had been.

Finally, when every fiber of his body trembled with exhaustion and his very bones ached, he found himself by the lake in his private watching and dreaming spot, and there he sank to the ground, dulled by weariness. The lake was so still that the stars reflected in the dark mirror of the water. Perhaps he could find a final peace there. It would be easy to walk in, feeling the calm waters welcome him. So easy . . .

He was too broken even for the simple act of willing his own destruction, so he lay back in the soft, short grass, hearing the silken rustle of the birch leaves. The soil of Strickland welcomed him, as it would receive him into his final resting place. It was then, in the bitter ashes of defeat, that he remembered what Jeremy Stanton had said. *I had tried my damnedest, and I just couldn't do it. So I prayed . . . a desperate lot of drivel asking anyone who might be out there to help me, because I couldn't help myself.*

Reggie had thought himself different from his godfather, tougher and stronger, yet he also had found that he couldn't do it alone. Will was not enough. In his heart he surrendered, and his mind jangled with inchoate phrases and broken prayers as he, too, sought for a strength beyond himself.

His despair had been a tidal wave, on the verge of smashing him beyond any hope of healing. Now, like a tide, there was a subtle shifting of the current. Not a great revelation, no soaring trumpets or flame-edged promises, just a simple knowledge that he was not alone. That he had never been alone, though he had been too blind and self-absorbed to realize it.

Like the tide, the turning point was drawn out, with no clear moment at which hope took over from defeat. He knew that the battle was not yet over, that struggle still lay ahead, but he knew also that whatever help he needed would be at hand.

It was when he had reached that understanding that Alys found him.

Even in near-total darkness he knew who came. His raw senses were unnaturally receptive, and he recognized not just her step and her scent, but the ineffable feel of her caring. Without speaking, she sat cross-legged beside him, not quite touching, her face a pale blur in the thick velvet dark.

He reached out a hand to her, and she took it, her fingers far warmer than his, her clasp light and sure. Linking his fingers with hers, he brought their joined hands to his chest, against the beat of his heart. The tide of hope was running stronger now.

Her voice gentle in the night, Allie asked, "How are you doing?"

"Better." His voice sounded harsh to his own ears. He swallowed. "Talk to me, Allie. Please."

And so she spoke of Strickland, of the children, of her plans for the pottery, of the promise shown by the students in her school. He listened to the healing flow of words passively, immersing himself in the details of normal life.

Finally Alys stopped. "I think I'm getting hoarse," she said in her rich voice. "And while I never thought the day would come, I seem to be running out of things to say."

His fingers tightened on hers and she had a faint impression of his amusement. "You've done well," he said. His voice was closer to normal now. "Now it's my turn." He began to talk, telling her of his childhood at Strickland, of how he had remembered his father's near-disastrous drinking, and how that had forced his realization that he must stop himself. He told her of the short idyllic period when he had been part of a happy home.

Not knowing if it was the right thing to do, she asked softly, "What happened to your family?"

"Smallpox." As the evil word fell between them, she shuddered, understanding why he had been so obdurate in his insistence on vaccination. Then he sighed. "That isn't quite the whole truth. My father was away when the outbreak hit. God only knew where the disease came from. There was a smattering of cases in the village, but the manor house was much harder hit. My little sister, Amy, died first, then my brother."

"Did you catch it too?"

She thought he must have escaped, and was surprised when he answered, "Yes. The only time I've ever been sick in my life. Ironic, isn't it? It killed everyone else, and left me without so much as a single scar. I think I must have some kind of magical immunity to disease, or I would have died of something ghastly years ago." His voice faltered. "The worst of the disease was over and I was recovering when I woke with the feeling that I must go to my mother. I could barely walk. It was nighttime, and there was no one around. The only servant in the house was an old woman who had survived smallpox as a girl, and she had fallen asleep from exhaustion.

"My mother was close to death then, but she opened her eyes when I came in. Then she smiled." Reggie's fingers tightened painfully around Alys's. "She said . . . that she was glad that one of her children would survive and grow up. She didn't speak again." His breathing was ragged. "My father was sent the message that his whole family was dead or dying. He was killed in a carriage accident hurrying to get back to Strickland. I've sometimes wondered if he would have driven more carefully if he had known that I was going to live."

Alys could have wept for the bleakness in his tone, and for the wretched uncertainty that lay behind his words. Before she could find a comment, he burst out, "A precious poor use I've made of the gift of life."

"Don't blame yourself for surviving," she said gently. "We are not in a position to understand such things."

"Do you believe in God, Allie?"

It was not a question she had expected from him, but he had always been unexpected. "Not in a way that Junius Harper would approve of," she said slowly. "I do believe there is a pattern, an order, to why things happen. I believe that my actions matter, even if only in a very small way." She thought a bit more. "If I have an ambition, it is to leave the world a little better than I found it."

"You're a wise and good woman, Allie." His voice was the softest of night sounds, scarcely louder than the soughing wind and the rippling trees. "I've spent my life fighting windmills, trying to change what couldn't be changed, wanting the approval of a selfish old man. I patterned my whole existence around a contest that didn't matter."

"Do you mean your uncle?"

"Yes. He sent his secretary to collect me from Strickland. I was frightened and alone, not fully recovered from my illness. When I reached Wargrave Park, for a moment I half-believed the earl was my father. There is a strong family resemblance among the Davenports—tall and dark and damn-your-eyes. I went up to him, and . . . he stepped back as if I was a plague carrier. Said that since I was my father's son, he couldn't expect much of me, but he hoped that I wouldn't disgrace the name any more than absolutely necessary."

Alys ached for the pain of that rejection on a boy so sensitive, who had already suffered so much. He had been scarcely older than William. "So that is where being the Despair of the Davenports began."

"Exactly." He shifted restlessly, and she flexed her fingers within his grip, not wanting them to go numb. "I learned very quickly that there was nothing I could do that would make him approve of me or turn him into a reasonable facsimile of my father. But I did learn that I could damn well make him notice me. The harder he and everyone else tried to make me behave, the wilder I got."

He gave a rusty chuckle. "It was at Eton that I made a really marvelous discovery. Most of the students who were King's Scholars had allowances from their parents to buy extra food, since a goat would starve on what we were fed. I didn't have any money, but from sheer desperation I bought food from an inn called the Christopher. It stood in the middle of the campus and kept many a lad from starvation. Anyhow, I found that while my uncle disliked giving me any money directly, he would pay bills that I incurred. From food, I expanded to the draper, the tailor, the bookseller, and so forth. By the time I went to Cambridge, I was living fairly comfortably, and the pattern was set; Wargrave would pay my debts for the sake of his own pride, even though he loathed me."

So Reggie had been a King's Scholar. Amazing. "Did you finish at King's College and become a fellow?"

"Yes, although very few people know or would believe it. After a couple of years I gave up the fellowship. Lacked the temperament for teaching." Another rusty chuckle. "I wanted to go into the army, but my uncle refused to buy me a pair of colors as long as I was the heir after his own sons. He insisted I stay in London, and gave me an allowance, though hardly a generous one. Since two of his sons wouldn't marry and the other had left the country, I was his hostage for the future. I got considerable satisfaction out of knowing that even though

he despised me, I was the Wargrave heir. The earl had
no choice."

"Ignoble, but understandable."

"More than ignoble. It was stupid. I should have said
to hell with him and bought my own commission at some
time when I was at high tide with gambling."

Hearing the bitterness in Reggie's voice, Alys asked,
"Why didn't you?"

He moved restlessly again. "Because, as a member of
his family and his ward, I felt that my uncle owed me the
commission. Certainly I would have cost him much less
in the army, but he preferred thwarting my ambitions.
He was a man who had to control everyone around him.
In return I tried to punish him by being as difficult and
disgraceful as possible. It was like a covert war between
us. In the long run, I thought I would win, if only by
outliving the old bandit." Then, flatly, "But in the end,
the victory was his. He set his lawyer to looking for heirs
of his youngest son, and my cousin Richard was located."

"That must have been very hard to accept," she said
sympathetically.

"Yes, but not for the reason you might think." With a
ghost of humor he added, "I had every intention of
shocking everyone senseless by running the Wargrave
estates profitably and well."

"Which you could have done, based on what I've seen
of you here at Strickland," she interpolated.

He squeezed her hand. "Perhaps. I'll admit that after
growing up on the fringes of society, never quite belong-
ing, I wanted the title and position of an earl. But far
more than that, I wanted . . ."—he searched for a word—
"the validation that I mattered. I wanted proof that
spending my life locked in a battle of wills with my uncle
had some meaning. But it didn't. I could have made a
thousand other choices that would have been better for
me, but in my pride and stubbornness, I stayed locked in
a pointless struggle with an evil old man. Without even
consciously choosing it, I spent my life on a fool's throw."

She stretched out beside him, lying on her side with
her head on his shoulder and her arm across his chest.
His arm curved around her as if she belonged there. "I

know a great deal about pride and stubbornness, Reggie. I bungled my own life for the same reasons. But I decided that something could be salvaged from the wreckage, and that's what I'm doing now."

He brushed his cheek against the top of her head. "But you're wiser than I, Allie." He laughed suddenly. "Not that that's a decent reason. I'm going to be thirty-eight on All Hallow's Eve, and by my age, innocence and ignorance are not valid excuses. When one bungles, one is either stupid or guilty."

She laughed with him, knowing that if laughter had returned, he had survived this crisis, then pressed more closely against his lean body. There was nothing the least erotic about this embrace, but it felt wonderfully right. "You were really born on Halloween?" she asked.

"Yes, and you needn't comment on how some demon must have been substituted for me as a child," he said dryly. "The possibility has been mentioned before."

"That is not in the least what I had in mind," she said with dignity. "Halloween is a perfectly respectable time to be born. I know because it happens to be *my* birthday."

"Honestly?" he asked. "You mean we actually have something in common besides Strickland?" She chuckled and cuddled closer.

As Allie lie quietly in his arms, Reggie felt closer to her than he ever had to any other woman, even in the most passionate sexual intimacy. In spite of his teasing words, he knew they had a great deal in common. The significant difference was that Allie used her intensity and will more productively than he ever had. In a way, they were opposite sides of the same coin: the rake and the reformer, both stubborn and proud; one a destroyer, one a builder; one a cynic, one a dreamer. And of course, one a man, the other a woman.

As he inhaled the fresh herbal scent of her hair, Reggie realized that his feelings for Allie had gone far beyond respect, liking, and even the sheer rampaging lust she inspired in him. He might have made it through this night without her, but her presence and generous spirit had joined with the tide of hope to heal him, to make it possible to face the rest of his life with more wisdom and grace than he had shown in the past. He was not ready yet to put a name to how he felt, but someday, when he was whole, when he was sure and sober, he would. Then, perhaps, if Allie was willing . . .

They dozed together, sharing their warmth as the night cooled and dew dampened their clothes. The sky was beginning to lighten when Reggie came awake. Allie stirred as he did, and they both sat up. "I'm definitely too old to be sleeping on the ground," he said ruefully.

He got to his feet, feeling the aches from last night's frantic running and falls as well as the cold earth. Allie came to her feet easily as he helped her, and they walked in silence back to the manor house, his arm circling her shoulders. They entered through the library doors, and found that all trace of last night's orgy of destruction had vanished. Only a lingering scent of liquor remained as proof of what had happened. Reggie paused a moment.

"I guess Mac has been here. He's always made it easy for me to keep on doing what I've been doing. It's a mixed blessing." If Mac hadn't been there to put the pieces back together after every debauch, might Reggie have hit the breaking point sooner? Hard to say, but it was possible that Mac's unswerving loyalty had had the negative consequence of helping Reggie avoid the fruits of his folly.

Too tired to consider abstractions, Reggie followed Allie upstairs. Outside her door, he drew her into a hug, feeling her slim body along the length of his. Desire was no longer dormant, but this was not the place, and certainly not the time, to travel that road. He stroked her back, feeling the heavy silk of her hair against his face. "Thank you, Allie," he whispered. "I think the tide has turned now."

"I know," she replied, her voice equally soft. "I knew something was different when I found you."

Perceptive as well as kind, generous, and beddable. He wanted to kiss her, but refrained. Instead, he let her go, then turned and went to his own bed. Tomorrow he must begin the business of living wisely.

21

The summer of 1817 was proving the happiest time of Alys's life. After his dark night of the soul, Reggie had become a different man, laughing and talking easily, his desperation and dark-edged humor a thing of the past, drink no longer an irresistible craving. He and Alys would often sit up late and talk, but she thought that it was not because he needed her as a distraction; now they were simply friends. Alas, as she had feared, there was nothing the least loverlike about him, but as a companion he was superlative, his wide-ranging mind and quirky opinions meshing with hers as no one else's ever had.

Reggie was still working very long hours, both with the farmwork and his horse training, but now he seemed to do it as enjoyment. The unhealthy color that had underlain his skin was gone, replaced by a deep tan that made his eyes shine like light, bright aquamarine. Altogether he was a delectable sight; Alys's dreams did not get any less restless. But in spite of her repressed longings, she was happy.

The crown of the summer had passed and the harvest was nearing when Reggie casually mentioned over one of their late-night chess games, "My cousin Wargrave will be visiting in a couple of days."

"Really?" Alys paused with her queen's rook in midair. "Did you invite him?"

"He said he would be near and asked for permission to call." Reggie grinned. "Of course Richard is really interested in checking up on the prodigal, for which one can hardly blame him."

"Are you looking forward to seeing him?" She set the rook down, capturing one of Reggie's pawns in the process.

"Yes, I am. Richard has been amazingly tolerant and

fair-minded toward me. When we first met, we shared the same roof for some weeks and he didn't see me sober the whole time. I was in a rather evil mood then as well." He stopped to tamp fresh tobacco into his meerschaum. "After a lifetime of burning bridges, it's time I built a few."

Propping her elbow on the table, Alys rested her chin on her palm. "I'm looking forward to his reaction to finding out that I'm the A. E. Weston he offered to find a situation for if matters didn't work out with you."

Reggie laughed, a devilish twinkle in his eyes. "So am I, Allie, so am I."

In the event, the Earl of Wargrave was not at all what Alys expected. With Reggie's remark that the Davenports were all tall, dark, and damn-your-eyes, it was a distinct shock to come home to the manor house in late afternoon at the same time that a dusty rider cantered up to the main entrance. As he swung from his mount, Alys asked, "May I help you?"

The new arrival was a pleasant-faced young man of Alys's height or a little below, and she gave him credit for not looking startled by the sight of her booted, breeched, and too-tall self. "I'm looking for my cousin, Reginald Davenport," he said in a soft, mellow baritone. "He's expecting me."

It took a moment for her to make the connection. Then she blurted out, "Good Lord, you must be Wargrave."

His face perfectly straight, he replied, "I'm not sure if I'm a good lord, but I do try."

As she burst out laughing, Alys decided that she approved of Reggie's cousin. Now, her eyes gleaming with anticipation, she offered her hand, saying, "And I am A. E. Weston, steward of Strickland." When Alys was dressed as she was, men were unsure whether to bow or shake her hand, so she took the lead to let them know.

The hazel eyes were startled for just a moment. Then they filled with amusement. "So you are the financial and agricultural wizard who put the estate back on its feet," the earl said, returning her firm handshake. "Is it a safe guess that the sick relative that took you away

from Strickland on my first visit was considerably less ill
than you thought?"

"A very safe guess," she agreed. "Tell me, my lord, if
I had taken you up on your offer of the stewardship of
Wargrave Park, would you have withdrawn it when you
found I was female?"

"Believe me, with your record I would have felt privi-
leged to have you." He looked hopeful. "Are you
interested?"

"No, just curious."

"Pity," he sighed.

By this time, Alys had decided that she liked the earl a
great deal. Perhaps he could stay longer than the overnight visit originally intended. "I believe Reggie's working back by the stables," she said. "Shall we see if we can
find him?"

Wargrave agreed, and they chatted as he led his horse
back to the stables. Noticing his limp, Alys correctly
guessed that it was a legacy of his military career. After
leaving the earl's horse with a groom, they continued to
the paddock, and for a few moments, before he became
aware of their presence, they were treated to one of
Reggie's superb exercises in horsemanship. Wargrave gave
a soft whistle. "He's every bit as good as I've heard."

"And then some," Alys agreed.

Reggie noticed the watchers and rode over, swinging
off his mount when he reached them. Alys sensed tension in the earl, and remembered that Reggie had said
that relations between the two men had been strained.
Having met the earl, she suspected that Reggie had been
the source of the problem.

As if there had never been a disagreement, much less a
fight to near-death, Reggie smiled and offered his hand.
"Welcome to Strickland, Cousin." Wargrave returned
the smile and handshake with genuine pleasure, and Alys
could see that everything was all right.

Blakeford felt an exultation so fierce that he wanted to
crow it to the hilltops. Finally, after a whole summer of
waiting, conditions were exactly right. He had found his
men, carefully cultivated his informants, and now the

results were at hand. In two days there was going to be an agricultural show in Dorchester, and Alys Weston and Reginald Davenport were going together. It was harmless information, or so the Strickland servant who had let it slip over a pint of porter had thought.

Blakeford had already chosen his ambush spot, a place where the road sank below the verges and trees clustered on both sides. There were ample places for his men to conceal themselves, and their victims would be trapped in the sunken road from both ends. Blakeford would be there himself to ensure that the job was done right; with luck, he would perform at least one of the killings. Trying to decide which of the two he would prefer to kill was a pleasing mental exercise.

The Earl of Wargrave proved an ideal guest, not raising so much as an eyebrow at the unusual household, not even to sitting down at dinner with a group that included a seven-year-old. Nor did he flinch when the younger members of the party smothered him in a combination of awe and questions, though Alys had the impression that he had to work hard to suppress a smile on several occasions. Peter was cast down on learning that the earl had managed to escape his valet and was traveling very light; Wargrave would not displace Julian Markham as Peter's ideal of a fashionable gentleman.

Though anxious to get back to his wife, the earl had agreed to extend his visit to include the agricultural show. He spent part of the intervening day accompanying Alys on her rounds, mostly watching but occasionally asking penetrating questions. At midafternoon, as they rode toward the dairy pastures, Alys said, "For a man who knew nothing about farming a year ago, you've made amazing progress."

"I've been doing my best." He gestured around him. "There isn't a single one of the Wargrave properties as well-run as Strickland. And if I don't learn to ask the right questions and hire the right people, there never will be."

"You'll manage, my lord," Alys said. "I've no doubt of it."

As they crested a hill, his hazel eyes slanted over to her. "Is it my imagination," he asked tentatively, "or is my cousin a new man?"

"It's not your imagination."

"I suspect you've had a hand in his rehabilitation," the earl observed.

Alys felt her cheeks coloring. "Any part I played was strictly incidental."

"Oh?" He invested the syllable with disbelief.

Could Wargrave have guessed her feelings for her employer? Acute perception might run in the Davenport family. Her voice brisk, Alys pointed toward the herd they were approaching. "Most of the dairy cows are Guernseys. Their milk is richer than that of other breeds, and we've been pleased with the results. If you have a milking herd at Wargrave Park, you may wish to buy some Guernseys yourself."

Cows were always a safe topic.

It was a crystal-clear morning, and going to an agricultural show was a holiday, though not one that everybody would appreciate. But three farmers would, and as Alys rode between Reggie and the Earl of Wargrave, her spirits were high. In deference to the fact that she was going off the estate, she wore a russet habit and rode sidesaddle, but even that nuisance wasn't enough to dim her spirits.

They were about five miles from Strickland when the road dipped into a shallow defile that ran through a clump of trees. Wargrave pulled back his horse a little, murmuring, "By the pricking of my thumbs . . .'

Reggie glanced over at him. "Is something wrong?"

Wargrave hesitated, then shrugged. "Not really. It's just that the road ahead reminds me of the kind of ambush spot I learned to be wary of in Spain. Even after three years, it makes my neck prickle." Signaling his horse back up to speed, he added, his voice casual but his eyes scanning the woods, "Is there a problem with highwaymen in this area?"

"Not that I've heard of." Reggie was equally casual, but Alys saw that he was also watchful. The roads were never entirely safe, and caution was routine. She herself had had a holster built into her sidesaddle and never rode out without a loaded pistol in it. But as she absently touched the unobtrusive pistol butt, she did not seriously think that the weapon might be needed.

From his vantage point in the trees, Blakeford watched the approaching figures with a frown. He hadn't counted on Alys Weston and Reggie Davenport having a companion. However, the second man was unprepossessing and shouldn't present much of a threat. Whoever the fellow was, he would have to be killed too; he should have picked his friends better.

Excitement keen inside of him, Blakeford adjusted the narrow black satin mask he wore to conceal his identity, then lifted his light, accurate sporting carbine, checking again that it was ready to fire. He and four of his cohorts were mounted and armed, ready to close in on the quarry from both ends of the defile.

The sixth attacker, a former army rifleman, lay on his stomach with the Baker rifle Blakeford had supplied pointed at the road, his arms holding it steady and his eye at the sight. The rifleman was a real prize, a trained sharpshooter, and with luck, Alys Weston would be eliminated by the first shot. Blakeford would take Davenport himself, and he assumed that one of the rogues he'd hired would have the sense to go for the other man. The quicker this was over, the better.

As the riders neared the center of the defile, Blakeford whispered to the rifleman, "Shoot the one in the middle."

The barrel of the rifle swung to the target and stopped. Then the man jerked his head up. "I won't kill no woman."

Blakeford stared in shock for a moment, then hissed, "You didn't mention any such scruples when I hired you. She's the main target of this attack."

The man shook his head stubbornly. "Won't shoot a woman," he repeated.

Blakeford was furious, but there was no time for argument. "Then shoot the tall man and I'll take the woman."

The rifleman shifted the rifle, starting to track the taller of the two men, then froze as his scan drew his line

of sight over the shorter rider. The rifleman swore and
jumped to his feet. "It's Captain Dalton!" Then, the rifle
in his hand, he yelled down at the three travelers, " 'Ware
ambush!"

Aghast, Blakeford saw his whole scheme teeter on the
brink of disaster. He chopped viciously down with the
butt of his carbine, cracking the sharpshooter's head and
stopping him before the man could say any more. The
rifleman went limp and pitched forward, his body and
rifle rolling down the embankment to the edge of the
road. Knowing that there was no time to waste, Blakeford
yelled, "Now!" to his other men, and aimed his gun at
Alys Weston's head.

Wargrave's comment about the dangerous look of the
road had been offhand, but all three riders had an extra
degree of alertness when the warning shout sounded
from the trees. Reacting instantly, Reggie yelled at Alys,
"Lie low and ride!"

Everything seemed to happen at once. All three of the
travelers bent over their saddles and kicked their mounts
forward at full speed. At the same time, a man's body
came crashing down the embankment and several shots
blasted in a ragged volley.

The warning had saved them all; the bullets passed
through the empty space where the riders had been a
moment before. As the three drove forward, rough-looking
horsemen thundered down into the road both ahead and
behind them. With the deadly firearms discharged, the
attackers must rely on hand-to-hand combat.

The world was full of shouts and shots and crashing
hooves, the acrid smell of gunpowder harsh in the nostrils. On each side of Alys, Reggie and Wargrave were
both being set upon by two men at once. This didn't look
like robbery; it was clear that murder was intended.
Even as he knocked aside the knife of an attacker, Reggie
yelled, "Allie, get clear!"

Alys tried to take advantage of the confusion to break
free so she would have a chance to use her pistol, but a
fifth man, his upper face disguised by a narrow black
mask, cut her off. As she tried to avoid him, he yanked

his mount to a standstill, raised the carbine he carried, and aimed it at her from less than a dozen feet. The deadly black mouth of the gun seemed enormous; he would never miss at this range. There was no time for thought, only reflex. Alys jerked back on her reins, causing her mare to rear and wheel, at the same time pulling out her own pistol.

The man in the black mask fired and Alys was sure she felt the spatter of burning cordite, but the shot missed. His carbine empty, he was temporarily harmless, so Alys pulled away from him and whirled her horse to see what was happening behind her, hoping her single pistol shot might help her companions.

Behind her a battle was raging, incoherent and cacophonous. In spite of their superior numbers and weapons, the attackers were having a hard time destroying two unarmed men who were trained and deadly fighters. As Alys watched, Wargrave ducked a saber slash, then wrested the sword away, unhorsing his antagonist in the process. Reggie was involved in a tussle with another attacker that ended when he knocked the man from the saddle with a savage blow of his fist.

As a third man raised a pistol on Reggie's back, Alys screamed his name and fired her own weapon at the attacker. An accurate shot was impossible, but by sheer luck her bullet winged the man, forcing him to drop his gun and bellow with pain.

Then the masked man came at Alys again, leveling a pistol as he drove his horse at her. Impossible for her to reload under these conditions; even as she wondered wildly why he was so intent on murdering her, she drew her arm back, then hurled her own useless weapon at him as hard as she could. The empty pistol gashed the man's cheek, causing him to jerk and sending his shot off harmlessly.

"You miserable bitch!" he swore. Grabbing at her bridle, he used his burly strength to immobilize her horse, then reached into his boot to pull out a long, viciously edged knife.

Having temporarily discouraged his own adversaries, Reggie looked around in time to see the attack on Alys.

With horror he saw that she was trapped in the side-saddle, unable to slide off and escape her attacker. Knowing he was too far away to reach her before the knife could strike, Reggie leapt from his horse and grabbed up the Baker rifle that lay by the edge of the road only two feet from him.

Alys was struggling fiercely with the masked man, trying to prevent him from getting a clear stab at her, but he was large and strong and she was unable to fight free. To Reggie, the movement seemed ghoulishly slow as her attacker raised his knife high, the thin blade flashing in the morning sun. Too frightened for prayer, Reggie dropped into approved firing position, one knee on the ground, the other raised to support the arm that held the rifle. As the knife stabbed downward, he cocked and aimed the weapon, praying that it was accurate and would not misfire.

His bullet struck home in the middle of the masked man's chest, knocking him backward off his horse as the knife spun glittering through the air. As the flat crack of the rifle echoed between the trees, a shout went up and the four attackers, now considerably the worse for wear, abandoned the fight. The two thugs that had been un-horsed scrambled onto their mounts and followed their fellows away as quickly as possible.

The entire skirmish had taken less than two minutes. As the hoofbeats faded in the distance, the little stretch of road was silent, even the birds shocked out of their songs by the gunfire. The masked man lay motionless on the ground, his clothing saturated with blood, while the man who had fallen down the hill and lain unconscious through the fight moaned and stirred.

Wordlessly Reggie crossed to Alys's mount and held his arms up, and she slid into his embrace. Though she had fought like a tigress and quite possibly saved his own worthless life, now that the danger was over her slim body trembled violently. He held her with rib-bruising pressure as he offered a passionate mental prayer of thanksgiving that she had been spared.

Wargrave trotted his horse over. "Are you both all right?" He looked as calm as a man riding in Rotten

Row, but his rust-brown coat had a black hole scorched along one shoulder.

"I think so. Allie?" Easy for Wargrave to be composed; it wasn't his woman who had almost been killed. If Reggie had had any doubts that he wanted Alys Weston to be his woman, they were resolved now.

She nodded, then determinedly stepped away from his embrace. "Sorry to be quaking like a blancmange," she said, lifting her chin.

Wargrave swung down from his horse. "Nerves are permitted," he said, his voice amused. "For someone experiencing her first taste of combat, you acquitted yourself very well indeed."

"If you hadn't been here, Richard, the odds would have been hopeless. I'm glad you decided to accompany us today." Reggie's voice was detached, but his emotions were not. While he rated his own fighting skills highly, the chances of their escaping this deadly ambush would have been nil if his cousin hadn't been with them, and a trained warrior. Even as it was, things could easily have gone the other way.

Wargrave said obliquely, "It was the army's loss when you couldn't join."

It was a typically elliptical exchange of masculine compliments, but entirely satisfactory to both men. Their gazes met and held for a moment, and Reggie knew that from now on he and his cousin were friends. Building bridges was a great improvement over burning them.

As Reggie kept one arm firmly around Alys, the earl knelt and removed the man's mask, revealing a heavy face set in angry lines even in death. Alys's gasp was drowned out by Reggie's shocked, "Blakeford!"

Wargrave glanced up. "You know him?"

Alys felt Reggie's rigidity in the arm that circled her. "I know him," he said grimly. "There had been some trouble between us recently, but . . ." He shook his head in disbelief. "It was a minor matter. Not important enough for him to want to kill me."

"It might not have been important to you, but obviously it was to him." The earl stood. "Don't waste too much time with regrets. They would be wasted on a man who hires a gang of cutthroats to ambush his enemies and anyone else unlucky enough to be in the way.''

In spite of Wargrave's pragmatic words, Alys felt a chill spreading throughout her body. Reggie might think Blakeford had been out to kill him, but Alys knew better. She was Blakeford's intended victim, and she knew why. Who would have dreamed that her past would reach out with such violence? A man had died today trying to murder her, and two other men might have died simply for being with her. Grimly she fought the wave of nausea that threatened.

On the other side of the road, the man who had been unconscious groaned, then struggled to a sitting position. He wore a jacket of military cut that was so grimy and faded that it was hard to discern the original dark green color. As he raised one hand to his head, his eyes darted nervously around the three watchers and strain showed on his thin face. Before he could speak, the earl crossed the road and dropped to one knee beside him. "You're the one that shouted the warning at us?"

The man nodded. "Aye. I wouldn't shoot the lady, and when I was targeting the tall gent, I recognized you, Captain Dalton.''

"I used to be Captain Dalton. A year ago I learned that my true family name is Davenport. I'm the Earl of Wargrave now." He looked hard at the man's dark green jacket. "Your face is familiar, but I don't think we ever spoke. You were in the Ninety-fifth Rifles, Johnny Kincaid's company?''

"Yes, sir. Corporal Willit, sir. Everyone in the regiment knew you and what kind of officer you were. I figured that if you was with these other folk, I was on the wrong side.''

The earl asked, his voice level but edged, "What was a former rifleman doing with a gang of murderers?''

"Trying to feed his family," Willit said sullenly. "After years of getting our arses . . ." His eyes shifted to Alys and he muttered, "Begging your pardon, ma'am. After years of getting our backsides shot off by Johnny Crapaud, we come home to no jobs and no back pay. I and my wife and our babe had been sleeping in the hedgerows for months when that fellow over there heard I was a sharpshooter and offered me a job."

Willit waved a hand at Blakeford. "He was a mean cove, but he was willing to pay us fifty pounds each for doing what King George paid us pennies for."

"The cases are not comparable, but I can understand why you accepted." The earl stood. "If you're willing to move your family to Gloucestershire, I'll find work for you."

The rifleman climbed unsteadily to his feet, desperate hope dawning on his face. It was the expression of a man who had learned not to expect justice. "You're not going to turn me over to the constables?"

"You've earned better than that. If you hadn't warned us, we might have all been killed." The earl fixed him with a steely glance. "Just remember to act like a rifleman in the future."

Willit straightened and executed a smart salute. "Yes, *sir!*"

When Julian Markham drove his curricle into the stable-yard at Strickland, he felt like he was coming home. The groom who took his horse greeted him like a prodigal son before saying apologetically that Mr. Davenport and Lady Alys had gone to Dorchester for a fair, adding with a broad wink that he believed Miss Spenser was at home.

There was no doubt that everyone in the place knew what was between him and Merry; Julian wondered if the servants had been laying bets on whether he would return. If only they knew how much he had been longing for this moment!

He took the front steps two at a time, knocking impatiently on the door and being admitted by one of the housemaids. Before he could even ask for Miss Spenser, Merry herself appeared in the entryway from the back of the house, a basket of fresh-cut flowers on her arm. In the moment before she recognized him, he saw the grave sadness in her wide blue eyes. Then her expression turned to shock, her lips parting as she shook her head, unable to believe that it was really Julian.

Julian's confidence had taken a beating in the last

weeks, and it was with a note of uncertainty that he asked, "Are you glad to see me?"

His voice convinced her that she wasn't seeing a ghost. With a wordless cry of happiness she sped across the foyer into his waiting arms, her flowers going flying in a shower of bright colors. While the housemaid watched with sentimental approval, Julian and Merry lost themselves in the sweetness of reunion, their voices mingling incoherently, their joy palpable as they tried to hug every bit of each other at once.

When Julian returned to awareness of the outer world, he led Merry into the drawing room, preferring not to have an audience, even an approving one. In the brighter light, he saw tears and he drew out his handkerchief, blotting them tenderly. "Merry, what's wrong? Has something happened here?"

She shook her head energetically, giving him a crooked smile. "I'm sorry to be such a watering pot. It's just that I didn't think I would ever see you again."

He did not reproach her for lack of faith. Instead, he settled them on the sofa and put an arm around her. As she pulled her legs up and tucked herself under his arm, he said gravely, "I'm back, but not so good a bargain as I was at the beginning of the summer."

At her questioning glance he continued, "You were right about how the world would see this match. I spent weeks arguing with my father, trying unsuccessfully to talk him around, but he was absolutely adamant." Julian's lips tightened as he recalled his father's remarks. Lord Markham had serious financial objections to the match, but much of his obduracy stemmed from the fact that Merry was living under Reginald Davenport's roof. Julian had offered to bring her for a visit so his father could see her suitability for himself, but the viscount had flatly refused to receive a female that he characterized as "a fortune-hunting hussy."

Merry sat upright, her golden hair haloing her distressed face. "Julian, I can't let you become estranged from your family."

He laid a gentle finger on her lips. "Isn't that a decision I should make? Believe me, Merry, I know what I'm doing. My father can cut off my allowance, but he can't forbid my marriage. He can't even disinherit me from the title. And he certainly can't change my heart."

Julian took a deep breath, then plunged into his most important news. "One reason I was away so long was that I was looking for a government position. A cousin who never got on with my father helped me find a post in Whitehall. With that and a small legacy I inherited several years ago, I can support you. We won't be rich, but we'll be comfortable. That is"—his voice hardened slightly—"if you still want me."

That was the moment that Merry realized that Julian, the confident, handsome man of the world, needed her as much as she needed him. Taking his face between her small hands, she kissed him on the lips, tasting his warmth and tenderness and desire, and matching them with her own. Her voice husky, she whispered, "How can you doubt it?"

As Julian pulled her slim body into his arms, he knew that Merry was more than worth what he was giving up.

Whoever said that it never rained but it poured was correct, Alys decided, though coming home to find Julian and Merry cuddled blissfully on the sofa was considerably more pleasant than being attacked by a gang of assassins. She and her companions had spent hours in Dorchester giving depositions and dealing with the aftermath of the attack. Reggie had been grim, Wargrave philosophical as he commented that it always took longer to clean up after a battle than to fight it.

The earl had also arranged transport to Gloucestershire for his newly acquired employee and the man's ragged little family. When last seen, the Willits had been sitting down to a substantial meal at one of the best inns in Dorchester, still not quite believing their change of fortune. Since his own and Alys's life had been saved by the man's warning. Reggie had tried to pay the Willits' expenses, but the earl had said crisply that riflemen always took care of their own, and that was that. With amusement, Alys had decided that in his quiet way, the earl was every bit as stubborn as his cousin.

In her official capacity as guardian, Alys sat down with
Julian and they discussed his changed circumstances. In
the long run, Merry would still be a wealthy viscountess;
in the short run, she would be comfortably situated.
More than that, she would be loved.

In the midst of her happiness on her ward's behalf,
Alys felt a pang that there would be no such happily-ever-
after for her, but she suppressed it ruthlessly. She knew
that she was not the stuff romantic heroines were made of.

22

Dinner that night was a joyous affair, celebrating both
Merry and Julian's official engagement and the mi-
raculous outcome of that morning's ambush. Champagne
had been ordered from the cellars and the happy couple
toasted, even William being allowed to drink to his sister's happiness. Reggie's glass was filled with water, and
Alys wondered how he felt, knowing there would be a
lifetime of not quite sharing such moments. If the thought
distressed him, it was not apparent. He appeared entirely
relaxed and at ease, a genial host surrounded by friends.

Over so much chatter, the arrival of a visitor at the
front door was not heard. Only when he had brushed
aside the maid and stomped into the dining room was he
noticed. Alys had a clear view of the intruder, a solid
middle-aged man with a handsome, forceful face, clad in
a caped greatcoat glistening with raindrops. Julian was
seated next to her, and she did not need to hear him
jump to his feet and exclaim, "Father!" to know that
Lord Markham had arrived in pursuit of his errant son.

Everyone at the table turned to the newcomer and
several servants' eyes rapidly took station along barely
cracked doors. A ferocious scowl on his face, Lord Mark-

ham barked, "I've come to put a stop to this marriage nonsense once and for all."

His face pale but determined, Julian said, "We have discussed this *ad nauseam* for weeks, and there is nothing more to be said. I would prefer to be married with your blessing, but the lack of it will not stop me."

"My God, boy, have you no more pride than to marry the cast-off mistress of a drunken rake like Reggie Davenport?" The viscount shot a venomous glance at Reggie, who was sitting at the head of the table, watching with narrow-eyed concentration.

There was a moment of paralyzed silence. Before an infuriated Julian could reply, Peter leapt to his feet. "My lord, you insult my sister. If I thought you would accept a challenge from someone my age, it would be pistols at dawn!"

While Peter's phrasing might have been melodramatic, there was no denying his sincerity or his anger. The viscount stared in astonishment at the upstart stripling as Reggie drawled, "Really, Markham, do you think I keep my mistresses under my own roof with their younger brothers in attendance? Credit me with some *savoir faire.*"

Suddenly remembering William's presence, Alys turned her best governess glare at the boy, coupling it with a quick jerk of her head at the door to order that he leave. William looked rebellious, but knew better than to disobey that particular expression. Reluctantly he withdrew, and promptly joined the servants in their discreet spying.

Since the males present seemed to have reached an impasse, Alys said frostily, "You also insult my guardianship, my lord. I assure you, Miss Spenser has been raised to the most *rigorous* standards of propriety. Only the sad destruction of our own home necessitated our temporary acceptance of Mr. Davenport's kind hospitality."

Markham swung to face her. "And who might you be?"

"I am called Lady Alys Weston," she stated in a voice reeking of grandeur. Though it was seldom necessary, Alys could act the toplofty *grande dame* to perfection. She did so now, giving her chin a haughty tilt and drawing herself up to her full height, though being seated diminished the effect.

More than a little daunted by Alys's chilly dignity, Lord Markham turned to Reggie's cousin and snapped, "If she's a lady, who are you, the Duke of Wellington?"

Richard stood. "Of course not, I haven't the nose for it. I'm the Earl of Wargrave," he said calmly, then executed a polite half-bow. "I understand you've been doing some interesting breeding experiments at Markhamstead."

The viscount was almost distracted by the reference to his beloved pig breeding, but duty held him to his purpose. "What are you doing here? They say that you cut your wastrel cousin off without a penny and told him to get out of London before he disgraced the Davenports any further."

Richard raised his brows. "I can't imagine how such vulgar and inaccurate rumors start," he said in a voice that would turn water to ice. "As you can see, my cousin and I are on the best of terms."

Alys choked down a laugh; the earl had mastered the lordly manner quite thoroughly, though this was the first time she had seen him use it.

Beleaguered on all sides, Lord Markham paused uncertainly. Deciding that it was time to take a hand in her own fate, Merry rose and went over to him. Casting a mildly disapproving glance at the diners, she said, "You're all being rather hard on Lord Markham. He's had a difficult journey in the rain, and of course he's concerned with his son's future. What father wouldn't be?"

Turning to the viscount, she said in her sweet voice, "You must be tired and cold. Would you like something to eat? And perhaps a glass of wine?"

The viscount wavered. The offer of food and drink was immensely appealing. Also, this beguiling golden-haired girl certainly didn't look like a tart, and she was the only person present who had the least sympathy with what he was doing to try to save his son and heir from a disastrous marriage. "Are you the chit Julian wants to marry?" he asked stiffly.

She nodded, her lovely face grave. "Yes. Truly, I don't wish to cause a rift between Julian and his family. I know how dreadfully difficult it must be for both of you." Her voice broke. "But Julian and I do love each other so."

Nonplussed, Lord Markham stared down into the great sapphire eyes, where tears trembled. He had come posting down to Dorsetshire immediately after learning that Julian had defied his explicit orders to end his foolish involvement with an ineligible female. The viscount had expected a confrontation, but not one quite like this, in which he was feeling like a brute for making this beautiful young creature cry. For just a moment Markham wavered. Then his resolve firmed; of course she would be beautiful; young men seldom lost their heads over antidotes.

Alys cast a glance at Reggie, wondering how he was taking this invasion of his home and the insults to his household. Seeing the glint in his eye, she was not wholly unprepared when he threw down the gauntlet in his own particular way. His voice pitched for clarity, he drawled, "For heaven's sake, don't you lose your head over a pair of pretty blue eyes too, Markham. With Julian's prospects, he can wed one of England's greatest heiresses. You'd be a fool to settle for a chit whose face is her major dowry."

Everyone turned to stare at him. While Lord Markham bristled like an angry tomcat, Peter and Merry looked wounded, Wargrave thoughtful, and Julian utterly shocked and betrayed.

Having seen Reggie's diabolical expression, Alys had just the faintest glimmer of what he might be doing, and under the table she kicked Julian before he could rip up at his erstwhile friend. When the young man turned to her, she shook her head in quick warning.

As Julian tried to interpret Alys's message, Lord Markham exploded at Reggie. "I would think that even a vulgar care-for-nobody like you would realize that money is not the only, or even the most important, criterion for marriage."

Reggie's dark brows arched superciliously. "Of course not. There are also land, title, and influence."

"That's exactly what a gazetted fortune-hunter like you would think," the viscount said scathingly. "People of quality know that a base of mutual affection and respect is vital to a successful marriage."

He glanced at Merry, his face softening. "It is far more important that a young woman have good sense and an amiable disposition than that she be rich. In fact, girls of modest fortune are much less likely to be extravagant with their husbands' money."

Reggie shrugged negligently. "It's as easy to fall in love with a rich girl as a poor one, and young men's affections are notoriously volatile. In a few months the boy will have forgotten what Merry looks like."

At that, Merry frowned in puzzlement. Then her brow cleared and the hint of a smile began dancing in her eyes.

"A man of twenty-five years is not a boy," Markham snapped. "Nor is my son a fickle, womanizing rake like you, Davenport. He is a gentleman of principle, the kind of son any man would be proud to have. Julian would never have offered for Miss Spenser unless his affections were seriously engaged."

"You would know your own son best," Reggie said, boredom written on his dark face. "I've always assumed that the reason you've kept him on a short leash in London is that he can't be trusted to run even a small estate properly."

Now Julian's expression also changed, the rigidity fading and a gleam of unholy amusement showing in his eyes.

"You are as ignorant as you are immoral, Davenport. In fact, Julian had prepared a brilliant plan for the running and development of my estate, Moreton Park. I have every intention of settling it on him on the occasion of his marriage."

As Julian's eyes widened, his father glanced at him a little sheepishly. "I didn't want it to go to your head, my boy, but I was most impressed with your plans, most impressed. I think it good for a young man to have a few years of sowing his wild oats before taking on the responsibilities of marriage and family, but you've had your fling now." He shot a venomous glance at Reggie. "And the more I think on it, the wiser it seems for you to move away from London, where there is so much bad company."

"I suppose he can't do too much damage to a single estate, but you'd be a fool to let him get leg-shackled to an unsuitable bride," Reggie said with his best supercilious air, which was very supercilious indeed.

Vibrating with fury, Markham took two steps toward Reggie before stopping, his hands curling into fists. "By God, if there weren't ladies present . . ." he snarled. "Don't you tell me how to treat my own son, and don't tell me what kind of female is suitable. What would a rake know about decent women?"

He glanced at Merry again. "Miss Spenser seems every inch a lady. Her birth and fortune are respectable and she is my son's choice. The sooner they are married and away from your wicked influence, the better!"

He turned to Julian. "I refuse to stay one moment more under this scoundrel's roof. I've already bespoken a room at the Silent Woman. I shall expect you and your fiancée to call on me at ten o'clock tomorrow morning. We have much to discuss." He gave Merry a last warm look. "And I wish to become better acquainted with my future daughter-in-law."

Then the viscount turned in a whirl of capes and marched out of the dining room, slamming the door as he went.

Behind him, he left profound silence, until the Earl of Wargrave leaned back in his chair and went off into gales of laughter. "Cousin," he gasped, "I wouldn't have missed that for all the sheep in Ireland."

As if his words were a signal, everyone else dissolved into a hilarity that was part relief from tension. Julian came around the table to give Merry a hug, and Alys was tempted to do the same to Reggie, who was leaning back in his chair with a smile lurking in his aquamarine eyes. In five minutes of applied obnoxiousness he had gotten a result that Julian had been unable to obtain in weeks of impassioned arguments. Who said that devilry didn't pay?

News of Lord Markham's visit spread through all levels of the household, producing much merriment and pride in the master's resourcefulness. The housemaid Gillie, who had been one of those to secretly watch the drama in person, was quick to seek out Mac Cooper and regale him with the facts as soon as her duties were done. It had become natural to look for Mac when she had something to share; telling him made a good story better.

Since a cold rain was falling and Gillie tired easily these days, they walked only as far as the barn, then reclined cozily side by side in a pile of hay while she did her best to remember word for word what Mr. Davenport had said to the Viscount Markham. Mac had gone off into whoops, admitting that it was one of Reggie's finest moments, then regaled Gillie with several more carefully expurgated stories of his master's outrageousness.

After they were both weak from laughter, the valet rolled over and placed a kiss on the maid's pert nose. "It seems like marriage is in the air. What do you say, Gillie girl, shall we do the deed also?"

Suddenly sober, Gillie searched his face. While their friendship had been quietly growing and deepening, he had not mentioned marriage since that time in her attic room, and she found herself shy again. Unconsciously putting her hand on her burgeoning belly, she said, "I'd like to marry you, Mac, more than I ever wanted to marry Billy. But . . ." She faltered a little, trying for words to express her anxiety. "I worry about whether you might resent the babe for not being yours."

Mac laid his hand over hers. Though it was intended as a friendly gesture, he felt pleased surprise when the baby kicked. "Lively little devil, ain't he?"

Then his thoughts turned inward, and by the light of the single lantern Gillie saw his expression change. "My ma was a housemaid like you." He grimaced, his face hard. "My father was a fine London gentleman, she told me, a lord, no less. Some gentleman!" His laughter was bitter. "After he got her in the family way, he turned her out of the house with ten quid. It might have been nice if there had been a man around willing to take care of her and me. A child needs a father."

He was silent for half a dozen heartbeats. "She did her best to raise me right, but she died, worn out working the streets, when I was six years old."

Gillie's heart ached for the terrified, abandoned boy he had been, and any fears she had had that he might resent her baby dissolved. She might be just a country girl, but she could see how much he wanted a family of his own to love and care for, and how much he needed to be loved in return. She didn't doubt that he cared deeply for her, and understood that his marrying her was also a way of mending the past.

Trusting him now, she reached out one hand and laid it on his cheek. "If you really want to marry me, Mac," she said softly, "I'll be proud and honored and happy to accept."

He leaned over and kissed her very gently, but the embrace rapidly developed into something far more exciting. Gillie was delighted to learn that a London man of the world knew a lot more about kissing than country Billy ever had.

As events progressed toward their natural conclusion, Mac suddenly pulled away from Gillie, his breath coming hard. "I'm sorry, Gillie girl, I don't want you to think that I'm one of those men who tell lies to get a tumble. I'm willing to wait until we're properly wed."

"But I'm not!" she exclaimed, her face flushed and hay in her hair. "Besides"—her lips curved in a smile—"we might as well, since there's no danger I'll catch a babe out of doing it."

Mac laughed, looking like the young man he was rather than the toughened cockney who had escaped one of London's worst stews. Then, very carefully, he proceeded to pleasure his lady in the sweet green warmth of the hay.

Life returned to normal. The Earl of Wargrave had left that morning. Julian and Merry also left for the Markham family seat for a fortnight's visit; his lordship had already succumbed to the girl's charm and was well on his way to forgetting that he had ever opposed the match. An autumn wedding was planned so that Alys would be finished with the harvest and free to play the role of mother of the bride.

News spread through the household that the master's fine London valet was going to marry the maid Gillie; tight-lipped, Alys told herself that it was absurd to think the business so distasteful. Such arrangements were the way of the world; Reggie was freed of a nuisance, and Mac Cooper doubtless was being compensated handsomely for taking a pregnant mistress off his master's hands.

But now it was late in the evening, the boys were in bed, and Alys and Reggie were enjoying one of their lazy late-evening visits. For Alys, these were the best times of the day; all her mental reservations about her employer's scandalous conduct always melted in his presence. They were in the library, the only place in the house where Reggie smoked, and he was blowing a cloud with one of his vile cheroots as Nemesis and Attila snoozed near their respective owners. Even the pets had declared a truce, largely because the cat found the dog too easily intimidated to be a challenge.

"Why not have some brandy?" Reggie suggested after exhaling a wisp of smoke. "I restocked the liquor cabinet while Richard was visiting."

After a moment's hesitation Alys went to the cabinet and poured herself a small brandy. "It doesn't bother you to have liquor here?"

"Believe it or not, it doesn't. I missed the drink for the first three or four weeks, but not now." He shrugged. "Looking back, I realized that I hadn't really enjoyed drinking in years. I drank because I didn't know how not to. Now that I'm sober, I haven't the least desire to go back to what I was, with my life ruled by a damned bottle." His blue eyes very intent on Alys, he added softly, "Life is infinitely more enjoyable now."

The warmth of his gaze very nearly made Alys blush as she curled up in the wing chair again, her legs tucked under her. She wore an informal green robe and her hair was tied back with a matching ribbon. There was a cozy domesticity to the evening, and at times like this it was hard to recognize Reggie as the abrupt, sarcastic rake who had first come to Strickland. Even then he had had humor, intelligence, and a basic integrity, but such positive traits were not the most visible part of him. Now, as his cousin had noted, Reggie was a different man: relaxed, mentally and physically healthy, and irresistibly attractive.

Diverting her thoughts, Alys commented, "I was amazed

that Lord Markham didn't realize how you were manipulating him. Is there some kind of history there?"

His intensity vanishing, Reggie grinned. "Some years back, we had a little *contretemps* over a woman. The lady in question preferred me, and Markham has neither forgiven nor forgotten. It was a good bet that his loathing was so profound that he would feel absolutely compelled to do the exact opposite of what I suggested."

"It's always a woman, isn't it?" Alys's voice was sharper than she had intended.

Reggie's face closed. "Unfortunately, yes." His voice brooding, he said half to himself, "If I had had the sense to keep clear of Blakeford's mistress, the man would be alive now."

"A simple squabble over a female doesn't turn most men into murderers." Alys clenched her fingers around the stem of her goblet, uncomfortable with her private knowledge. "You can't blame yourself for how Blakeford reacted."

"Oh, can't I?" Reggie asked, raising his dark brows sardonically. "Blakeford was always a little odd, but the fact remains that it was my actions that pushed him over the edge."

"Maybe his mistress wasn't the reason he arranged that ambush," she said, hoping she could persuade him without telling the truth.

"Can you think of another reason?" His long face twisted with self-mockery. "I can't imagine anyone wanting to kill you or Richard, but there are any number of people who would be happy to dance on my grave, and Blakeford was certainly one of them."

She hated to see his guilt, especially now when he had reformed his way of life; especially since he was wrong. Alys thought quickly, and came up with a reason that was plausible without giving away the truth. "I know you're wrong, because I was the one Blakeford wanted to kill. Granted, he may have looked on killing you as a pleasant bonus, but I guarantee that you were not the prime target."

Before she could tell the story she had devised, Reggie interrupted her, his face incredulous and his harsh tone an insult. "You really think that he was interested in you?"

His unexpected words struck Alys with the force of a physical blow. She had wanted to make Reggie feel better; instead she had provoked a reaction that shattered her defenses. For months she had lived in the closest proximity with a man whom she desired and had come to love, bleeding inside every time he casually referred to an old mistress, or got into trouble over a woman, or impregnated a maid. And Reggie, damn him, sat there looking astounded at the mere suggestion that a man could want her. She was overwhelmed with the agonizing knowledge of her undesirability, and a physical chill spread through her body, paling her face and numbing her fingers.

"Of course you're surprised." Trembling violently, Alys set aside her glass and stood. "How could I have forgotten that no man will touch me unless he's drunk or going to receive a fortune in return for the sacrifice of taking me to wive?"

Her voice broke. "Considerate of you to remind me what a pathetic excuse for a woman I am. Even you, who have bedded half the females in England, could bear to kiss me only when you were drunk." She could feel herself crumbling inside as the old unhealed grief about Randolph erupted and fed the anguish of her hopeless passion for her employer.

She was horror-struck by her own words; exposing herself so thoroughly to Reggie was the ultimate humiliation. Her eyes blind with tears, Alys fled for the door, needing to escape, knowing that his pity would be more than she could bear.

She was halfway to the door when Nemesis, true to her name, padded amiably into Alys's path. Tripping over the collie sent Alys stumbling clumsily to the floor, the skirts of her loose robe tangling around her ankles, her palms and knees bruising on the Oriental carpet.

As Alys reacted violently to his words, Reggie saw that she had misinterpreted the jealous edge in his voice. As he had looked back on what had happened, it had been easy to believe that there was a connection between her and Blakeford, and the mere thought of Allie being involved with the other man had produced a blast of jealousy as intense as it was irrational.

Now, as she disintegrated before him, Reggie saw that he had unwittingly opened a wound that ran to the very roots of Allie's being. She had always been so strong, so balanced, even when Reggie was teetering on the edge of self-destruction, that it had been easy to forget that she must have her vulnerabilities. And from the agony on Allie's face, her Achilles' heel was a belief that no man could desire her as a woman.

For someone of passionate nature to feel undesirable was tragic. That he, who was usually so acute at understanding others, should be so insensitive to her was unforgivable.

Like a kaleidoscope, the insight transformed his perception of Alys even as he hastened to kneel beside her. She was momentarily stunned by the fall, her arms supporting her upper body above the floor, her head bowed. Guessing how much she needed reassurance, he laid a hand on her shoulder and said gently, "Allie, it wasn't surprise I felt at the idea that Blakeford could want you. God knows I've desired you from the first moment I saw you."

She jerked away from his grasp and tried to scramble to her feet, but he caught her shoulders and rolled her over to face him. Her long hair had come loose and fell about her face in a mass of brown tresses shining with gold and auburn highlights. He chose his words carefully. "You are a lovely, desirable woman, and it has been an unbelievable strain on my self-control to behave like a gentleman around you."

Turning her head sharply and closing her eyes against him, she said flatly, "Very polite of you to apologize for giving offense, but don't bother to lie to me. Just let me go."

She could not quite conceal the tremor in her voice and she tried again to tug away. He tightened his grip on her shoulders, urgent to convince her of his sincerity. "You seem to think I only wanted to kiss you when I was drunk. In fact, the opposite was true. I wanted to all the time, but only when I was drunk did I forget my manners and act on my desires."

" *In vino veritas* ?" Her laughter was bitter. "Rather

than 'In wine is truth,' where men are concerned the correct phrase is 'In liquor is lust.' To a man who is jug-bitten, any available female will do." Tears in her eyes, she struck wildly at him, trying to break his grip. "Though even dead drunk, you never cared to proceed much beyond a kiss. Apparently even drunken rakes have some standards. Now, let go of me!"

Feeling Allie shudder under his hands, Reggie knew that she was too distraught to believe him. This emotional storm had been a long time building. Now a lifetime of pain had broken loose, splintering the calm face she usually showed to the world. Reggie's well-intentioned attempts to behave honorably had kindled her deepest self-doubts, and he wondered helplessly how trying to do the right thing could have gone so far awry.

So much for honorable intentions. Words would not be enough; he must prove by actions just how utterly desirable she was. Pulling her toward him so that she lay across his knees, he kissed her at the corner of one closed eye, tasting the salt of her tears. She gasped and her struggles slowed. Then her dark-lashed eyes opened, both brown and gray focused on him, her pupils wide and black with the intensity of her emotions.

Having gotten her attention, he kissed her slightly parted lips and was rewarded by instant fierce response. As her arms circled and clung, he embraced her and bore her down until they lay full-length together on the floor. The feel of her long, lithe body intoxicated him more than brandy ever had, and he loosened her robe. When he touched her full breast, she gasped, her whole body yearning to his touch, and the sound reminded him of where they were.

When he lifted himself away, Alys opened her eyes. "Don't stop, not this time," she whispered.

"I don't intend to." His breath was as ragged as hers as he scooped her into his arms and stood. "It's just that you deserve better than the library floor."

He could have taken her anywhere and she would not have minded. She had wanted to be swept off her feet, and now she was, blind to all consequence, deaf to all reason. She was barely aware that it was her room that he took her to, and she murmured a protest when he laid her on the bed and stepped away.

"I'm not going far." He struck a light and ignited the candles by the bed. "But I intend to see every beautiful inch of you. You and I have waited a long time for this—there will be no hurrying or hiding in the dark."

And true to his word, he did not hurry. Under his expert lips and hands, she felt like a flower unfurling into bloom as he discovered every secret of her body. Her long-buried fears and doubts could not survive in the light, and they melted away as her haunting dreams of passion came to life.

Hesitantly at first, then with his guidance, she explored him as well, running her fingers through the thick dark hair of his chest, feeling the hard ripple of muscle, discovering that his desire was as powerful and hungry as her own. Such passion could not be an illusion, and knowing how much he wanted her heightened and deepened her own desire.

When she could bear no more and was on the verge of shattering with longing, he covered her with his body, kissing her deeply and surrounding her with touch as he prepared her for the final intimacy. His hesitation inflamed her, but of course he thought she was a virgin and was moving with the care such a state deserved. Impatient of waiting and beyond explanation, she thrust her hips against his, whispering, "Now, love, please," and they were joined in an ecstasy of closeness beyond her most fevered dreams.

After the briefest moment of surprise, he was in command again, using his experience to deepen and prolong the pleasure for both of them. Until finally, at the end, he was no more in control than she, and they found boundless joy in each other.

23

Shared passion had more then fulfilled Alys's expectations; what she had not expected was the sweet languor of lying woven together afterward. Reggie shifted and for a moment she feared that he intended to leave. Instead he settled on his side, his arm and leg lightly enfolding her in a way that would not cause discomfort. In this as in every other aspect of making love, she thought rather sadly, he was an expert.

One hand resting on her breast, he said, "I want to dismiss once and for all your belief that you are undesirable." She turned her head and her gaze met his from mere inches away. He smiled. "I could spend a lifetime making demonstrations of this nature, but my guess is that something specific first gave you the absurd idea that men wouldn't want you."

She shifted restlessly, uncomfortable with how well he could read her. "Isn't it enough that I'm too tall, too masculine, too bossy, and odd-eyed?" She tried to make her tone light, but it came out brittle and defensive.

"Let's take those one at a time. Yes, you are very tall, but you look like a queen. In fact, they say Mary, Queen of Scots, was a couple of inches taller than you." He stroked the length of her thigh lingeringly. "If you were not as tall, your legs would not be quite as gloriously, maddeningly beautiful. You are perfectly and exquisitely proportioned, exactly the best height for kissing, and even an inch less would be regrettable."

He gave a wicked chuckle. "Sometimes I thought the sight of you in those pantaloons was more than I could bear."

"Really?" She turned her head to look at him, not at

all displeased at his words. "I just dress that way because it is practical."

"Of course," he agreed. "The fact that you look ravishing is strictly secondary. Have you really never noticed the way every man on the estate watches you?"

"Well, I'm their supervisor. Of course they notice me."

"And I own Strickland, but believe me, they do not look at me the same way." There was laughter in his voice. "As for your belief that you are too masculine, whatever that means"—he leaned over and kissed her breast with a thoroughness that sent tingles through her entire body—"no one who has ever looked at you could possibly think you masculine." Raising his head, he continued, "Every gorgeous inch of you is pure woman."

"As for being too bossy"—he appeared to consider the thought—"undoubtedly true, but that doesn't make you any less desirable." He dodged the playful swat she aimed at him. "And finally, your eyes are beautiful."

Now sure that she was being offered Spanish coin, she tried to glare at him, though her sense of well-being was too great to manage much of a glare. "You're being ridiculous," she scolded. "Now I can't believe anything else you said."

"You should—it's all gospel truth." He raised himself on one elbow and kissed the corner of one eye, then the other. "Besides having lashes a yard long, you have one beautiful brown eye and one beautiful gray eye. Where is it written that eyes must match?"

She dissolved into laughter at his absurdity; humor was another thing she had not expected to find with a lover. He added triumphantly, "And your dimples drive me absolutely wild," before proceeding to kiss them as well.

After several breathless minutes he rolled away. "I keep getting distracted, but there's still a great deal more to be said." He propped his head on one hand, his gaze intent and his dark face serious. "Allie, sex is a very basic part of the human animal, and it's a great tragedy that men and women almost never talk freely about it. Respectable women are taught that ignorance and distaste are signs of refinement. Heaven knows how you survived that kind of upbringing with your passion intact, but don't ever be ashamed of what you are and what you feel."

He toyed absently with her hair, twining a thick strand around his forefinger. "Sex is an area in which everyone is vulnerable in some way. A fundamental difference between the genders is that women worry about their desirability, while men worry about their performance."

"Is that really true?" She had thought herself alone in her fears, uniquely undesirable.

He nodded. "Your anxiety runs far deeper than most women's, and I intend to find out why, but I have never known a woman, even the most acclaimed of beauties, who did not worry about her attractiveness to men. In fact, the beauties worry the most because so much of their confidence is bound up in their appearance, and time will inevitably rob them. Even women who dislike the actual experience of intercourse usually want to be desired, because it gives them power over men."

Alys stared pensively at the shadowed ceiling as she thought about his words. There was so much that she didn't understand about men and women. Eventually she glanced at Reggie. "I have trouble believing that you worry much about your performance."

He grinned. "Less than most men, perhaps, but believe me, it is something all men are very sensitive about." Serious again, he said, "Allie, what happened that made you incapable of looking in a mirror and seeing what you are?"

She shrugged and looked away, still trying to evade his probing. "Meredith is my ideal of perfect female beauty, and obviously I fall far short of that."

"Merry is graceful and golden and very pretty indeed, and I have no doubt that to Julian she is the most beautiful woman in the world. But beauty comes in many forms that have nothing to do with mere prettiness." Lightly he traced the lines of her cheekbones and jaw. "You have beauty in the bones, and that will never fade." Then, implacable, "What happened, Allie? I am going to keep asking until you answer."

Even as happy as she was now, remembering caused a

sting of tears. "It would be impossible to explain that without telling you most of my life story," she whispered.

"Then you might as well start now, because I'm staying here until I hear it." His deep voice was warm and encouraging.

How many men knew or cared how a woman's mind worked? Suddenly she wanted most desperately to tell him her story, not the identifying details, but the essence that had brought her to where she was today. "I was the only child and heir of a rather prosperous family. My mother died when I was young and my father never remarried, so I was treated much like a son. That is how I learned so much about farming. My father and I were . . . very close. He was a ferocious, domineering autocrat, and we would have battles that threatened to blow the roof off Car . . . the house, but . . . we understood each other very well.

"When I was eighteen, I became betrothed. It was a perfect match. I adored Randolph, my father approved of him, and Randolph pretended to be in love with me." Her voice choked off.

"Pretended?"

Reggie's even question helped her to go on. "As it turned out, his words of love were all lies. Just a few weeks before the wedding, he and a friend called. I was out riding, but I saw them drive up to the house and came rushing back." Counting the days until her marriage, she had been overjoyed at the unexpected visit. "I knew he and his friend would be in the morning room, which had French doors, so I went directly there. I was just outside and the doors were open."

Even now she could see the softly fluttering blue damask draperies that concealed her from the men inside. She could hear the cool, contemptuous voices. "They couldn't see me. The friend asked how Randolph could consider marrying a . . . a bossy Long Meg like me. Ten feet tall and all bones, not the sort to warm a man at night, and with managing ways that would keep him under the cat's paw. That was bad enough."

She shuddered, her whole body shaking. "Far worse was being such a fool that I expected Randolph to defend

me. He had said often enough that he loved me. Instead
he said . . . he said that he was marrying me for money,
of course, and that once he had control of my fortune
he'd rule the roost.''

The hurt was like a knife twisting in her midriff. Then,
miraculously, Reggie laid his large hand on her solar
plexus, right where the pain was centered. "Steady, Allie,"
he said quietly. Warmth radiated from his palm, soothing
her turbulent emotions. He said nothing more, just lay
close to her, sharing his warmth and quietness.

Finally Alys opened her eyes and said with more calm
than she would have believed possible an hour earlier, "I
daresay it sounds trivial, doesn't it? You have survived
far worse."

"Don't discount your own pain," Reggie said, his voice
rough. "No matter how large or small the cause may
appear, the only true measure of an injury is how deeply
it hurts you. To be betrayed by the man you had trusted
with your love, to have your very femininity disparaged—
wounds don't come much deeper than that."

She rolled over, burying her head against his shoulder.
As she felt the knot of old pain slowly unwind and
dissipate, she knew in her bones that while there would
always be a scar, this part of her past no longer had
power over her. Reggie simply held her, his hand slowly
stroking her back, and she wondered how he could understand so much about pain and healing. A foolish question;
she knew enough of his past to know what a hard school
he had learned in.

Feeling lighter and freer than she had since her girl-
hood, Alys rolled onto her back and managed a creditable smile. "Feel better now?" he asked gently, his eyes
very warm. When she nodded, he asked, "What happened then?"

She sighed, some of her well-being ebbing away. "I
retrieved my horse and rode to the farthest end of the
estate and didn't come back until long after dark. Randolph and his friend had left when I couldn't be found.
When I came home, I marched into my father and told
him I wouldn't marry Randolph if he was Adam and the
only other choice was the serpent."

She could feel her body tightening again, and Reggie pulled the covers up, tucking them around her. "We had a battle royal. When I wouldn't give him a reason for changing my mind, he thought I was being foolish and missish. But I couldn't talk about what had happened, I *couldn't*."

"Understandable."

Once more his comprehension relaxed her. "Anyhow, he got very medieval and swore that I was no daughter of his and that he would disinherit me if I didn't go through with the marriage. Then he locked me in my room."

"Bread and water?"

She smiled faintly. "I didn't stay around long enough to find out. I put on my breeches, packed what money I had and what clothes could be carried easily, and at midnight climbed down a rope of knotted sheets in the approved romantic fashion. Except that I wasn't running to a man, but from one."

"Not one, but two. If your father had been more understanding, would you have left?"

"No." Her voice was deeply sad. "Other women have had broken hearts and survived. Being betrayed by my father was far worse because he had been the center and foundation of my life." She would not think of it, because that wound would never heal. Alys forced herself to continue her narrative. "After I ran away, matters became rather sordid," she said, her voice expressionless. "You know that I wasn't a virgin."

He moved his hand and laid it over her heart. "Allie, you don't have to explain anything to me. The woman you have become is a result of all the choices and mistakes you have made through the years. Don't apologize for your past."

"But I want to tell you. I don't understand myself why I did what I did then. Perhaps you will." She closed her eyes. "Three nights later I was staying at an inn, dressed like a female again. And . . . it was late in the evening. I was in the hall going to my room when I met a merchant who was staying in the inn. He was drunk as a wheelbarrow, and he . . . he made an advance at me. And I accepted."

The merchant's breath had been sour, his hands clumsy, and he neither knew nor cared that she was a virgin. Alys swallowed hard, her mouth bitter with the taste of self-loathing. "I must have been insane. It was over quickly. He was too drunk to know or remember what had happened, I think."

"Shall I find him and kill him for you?" Reggie's voice was deceptively gentle.

"No!" Alys felt a bubble of semihysterical laughter. Perhaps that was what Reggie had intended. "He didn't force me. The fault was mine alone."

He pulled her closer. Her skin was like silk, but softer and warmer. "That must have been a very poor introduction to the delights of the flesh."

"It was. What was worse was that I hated myself for doing it." She looked at him, her eyes wide and pleading. "Can you tell me why I did such a revolting thing?"

His gaze was thoughtful and unshocked. "I think so. Having suffered a devastating blow to your womanhood, you wanted to prove to yourself in the most basic way that a man could want you. At the same time, it was one in the eye to your father and the repellent Randolph, the kind of action that would have outraged them the most had they known." His face darkened. "Unfortunately, it left you with the idea that only a drunkard could want you."

Even in the midst of this discussion, she could not believe that she was actually telling someone about that night. "Reggie, how do you know so much about people?"

"I started studying the human species when I was very young. Besides, I'm something of an expert in the theory and practice of self-destruction." His smile was very wry. "My guess is that after the episode with the drunk, you renounced men and lovemaking in favor of penitence and good works, but you could not make your natural passion vanish."

"You're right again. I've always adored men and wanted so much to love and be loved by one, yet after that it seemed that I had doomed myself to spinsterhood. The man I loved had already rejected me, and after what happened at that inn, I knew no other man could ever want me. I was frantic with self-hatred. I even chopped off my hair and burned it."

She shivered and looked away, then laid a hand on his chest, taking comfort in the feel of lean muscles and hard bone beneath the softly textured mat of hair. Reggie might not love her, but he had undeniably desired her. "For a few hours I came close to destroying myself, no matter what the cost to my immortal soul."

"And then?" he prompted.

"The next day my groom found me. He saw me after I had overheard Randolph, and early the next morning he was the one who discovered that my horse was gone. Knowing something was wrong, he came after me without telling anyone. When I refused to go back, he said he wouldn't force me, but he wouldn't leave me unprotected either."

Reggie inhaled, enlightenment dawning. "Don't tell me—Jamie Palmer."

"Exactly. We had always been friends. He had no family and no real reason to return, so he stayed. I was grateful that there was someone nearby who cared what became of me." She smiled fondly. "My first position was as history and Latin mistress at a small school near here, and Jamie found work in the stables. Later I became a governess with Mrs. Spenser and he moved along and found another position. When I started the pottery and needed someone I could trust to supervise, he took it on, even though he prefers horses. He has been a good friend."

"Is he in love with you?"

She shook her head, not without some regret. "No, he never saw me that way. I was on some kind of pedestal as the young mistress, and he thought me far above his touch, even when I became just another working woman. He married one of the Herald girls, who is much more his style." She turned her hand palm-up. "And that is my total history. The rest you know."

His gaze was very intent on her face. "Have you ever thought of going back to your father?"

"Never." The single word was flat and uncompromising.

"It would be one thing if you hate him, but from what

you said, that isn't the case. Don't you want to make peace with him? He won't live forever—he might have died already."

"He isn't dead."

"How can you be sure?"

"I would have heard."

Alys in this mood could give lessons to an oyster on staying mum, but Reggie persisted. It was one of the things he did best. "Allie, take it from someone who knows—quite apart from the fact that you say a fortune is involved, living with anger is bad for the soul."

"Which interests you more, my soul or my fortune?" she snapped.

He refused to be drawn. "Give me some credit. Lord Markham might have called me a fortune-hunter, but if I had ever wished to marry an heiress, I assure you I would have been successful in my quest."

She smiled apologetically. "I'm sorry. I shouldn't have said what I did. But I can't go back, not ever."

"Because your father will never forgive you?"

She looked up at the ceiling. "That's half the reason. The other is that *I* can't forgive *him*. The one time above all others that I needed him to be understanding, that I needed him to show that he cared, he failed me." Her voice quavered. "Call it pride or stubbornness or sheer bloody-mindedness, but I will never return and ask for his forgiveness. Not now, not even if I knew he would restore me as his heir. Even when he dies, I won't go back."

Sheer bloody-mindedness was another thing that Reggie was an expert on, but he wasn't quite ready to drop the topic. "Would you go back if he asked you to?"

Her tone was sad and tired. "You don't know him. He has never admitted a mistake or made an apology in his life. He would never ask me back." There was another kind of pain in her voice now. A pity that she hadn't hated her father; it would have made their estrangement much easier. Then she marshaled her reserves and looked at Reggie again. "I don't need my father or his money. I haven't done badly on my own."

"No, you haven't," Reggie agreed, tenderly brushing

the hair from her face. Beautiful, stubborn, honorable Lady Alys. He wondered if it was the right time to ask her to marry him. The idea had been growing in the back of his mind for weeks. He had intended to wait longer, to prove to her that he was sober and would remain that way, but events tonight had changed everything. Allie was not indifferent to him; she loved Strickland and wanted children of her own. And he loved her. Strange that he hadn't realized that before. At some point in the last weeks lust and respect and companionship and gratitude had fused, and the result far transcended the sum of the parts. In an utterly conventional way he wanted her to be his woman, forsaking all others, until death did them part.

He had never made such a declaration, but he opened his mouth, hoping that sincerity would compensate for lack of style. Then, before he could speak, the part of his mind that never stopped began assembling random pieces of information into a new and stunning picture. His hand stilled, coming to rest on one of her lovely breasts.

Julian had told him of the missing heir to the Duke of Durweston, a female who had been betrothed to the younger son of the Marquess of Kinross. The marquess's younger son was Lord Randolph Lennox. Reggie knew him slightly, a handsome man a few years Reggie's junior, a paragon of gentlemanly virtues, an ideal mate for a girl who would one day be a duchess in her own right. The story went that the wench had run off with her groom a dozen years earlier, when she was eighteen.

Reggie felt a chill that began deep inside of him, curling icy tendrils around his heart. There was no doubt in his mind that his Allie was the missing heiress; the two stories fitted together too well. She might believe that her father would never welcome back a prodigal daughter, but Reggie didn't.

Blakeford was Durweston's heir after the missing daughter. Alys had said Blakeford had reason to kill her, and she was right; the duchy and fortune of Durweston would have tempted a better man than George Blakeford. And it was Reggie's own careless words that had brought Blakeford to Dorsetshire, intent on murder. Though it was impossible to prove, Reggie would wager a thousand pounds that the fire that destroyed Rose Hall had been set by Alys's cousin.

Allie's husky voice interrupted his thought. "Why are you looking so serious?"

He focused his attention on her. The Despair of the Davenports was sharing a bed with the greatest heiress in England. No wonder command came naturally to her—she had been raised to be ruler of the kingdom of Durweston. She had said the Lady Alys was an ironic nickname, but he would wager that it had caught on because Jamie Palmer had absently used her title.

When she had made her come-out Season in London, he would not have been allowed under the same roof with her. *If only she hated her father.* In sixty seconds, everything had changed, and with a sickening sense of inevitability he knew what he must do. After some effort he found a smile. "I was trying to calculate how many more times tonight I can make love to you before I must leave so your reputation won't be in shreds."

She gave him a slow, devilish smile. "You'll never find out by just thinking about it."

"You're right. There have been enough words." He bent over and kissed her, his sense of doom increasing his urgency. How could he have believed that there would be a happy ending for him? But for tonight, at least, she was his. And he would ensure that it was a night neither of them ever forgot.

The night spun past with a thousand small discoveries, with passion and laughter and the mingling of quiet breath. The more he gave her, the more she was able to give back, and Alys knew that if she died tomorrow, she would be content that she had been well and truly loved. Surely such fulfillment could not be only a fortunate conjunction of bodies. She wanted to say aloud that she loved him, that no other man had ever touched her heart or spirit or body as he did, that none ever could, but she kept silent, not wanting to destroy this perfect night.

Besides the mysteries of the senses, the night held another revelation. As Alys lay across Reggie's chest in a calm between tempests, she asked a question that had been in her mind, not realizing at first that she spoke aloud. "Besides Gillie's baby, how many other children do you have?" She felt him stiffen and was frightened of what she had asked.

"What are you talking about?"

Unable to withdraw her words, she stumbled forward. "About natural children, like the one Gillie is going to have in a few months. Surely over the years there must have been others."

"Why do you think I fathered her child?" he asked, more curious than angry.

Alys said awkwardly, "I saw her leave your room one night."

"Ahhh." After a long pause he said, "First of all, I don't know when her baby is due, but I guarantee it will be less than nine months after I came to Strickland." He chuckled, then explained Gillie's desperate attempt to involve him.

Alys was startled, and overwhelmingly relieved. "You didn't pay Mac Cooper to take her off your hands?" she blurted out.

"Don't suggest that to Mac, or he might forget that you are a lady," Reggie warned. "Believe me, getting married was his own idea, and he's very pleased with himself about it."

"Oh." Alys felt clumsy and not very bright.

Abruptly he answered her earlier question. "Over the years I have been careful not to sow bastards. I would not want a child of mine growing up an outcast. But there may be one."

The candle was nearly burned down, and its dying flicker showed Alys his impassive profile. "You don't know for sure?" she asked softly.

"I had an affair with one of the aristocratic Whig ladies whose morals are as liberal as her politics. Her first two children were by her husband. After that, I think she took pride in making sure that each was fathered by another man." His words were clipped. "Years later, I saw her in the park driving with several of her children. There was a girl who . . . looked a little like me, poor wight. I made inquiries. The child is the right age."

"The lady won't tell you?"

"She may not know. And if the girl is mine, what could I do about it? She is being raised with more than I could ever give her. Her parents are good people, in their way."

His harshness told her how much he cared about that child who was lost to him. Would his ache be less if he had another child, one he could raise himself and guide through life's tribulations, as he had not been guided? Alys wanted to find out. She had always wanted children, but with a ferocity that astonished her, she wanted them to be his children. She had not dared dream for years, but now for a moment she contemplated the thought of a lifetime at Strickland, raising tall children with Reggie, with laughter and friendship and occasional explosions. And most of all, with thousands of nights like this one, when their spirits were as intimate as their bodies.

It was too soon to dream. But he liked and desired her, and perhaps in time he would come to care more deeply. At the moment, she would do her best to win him, and what better way to woo a rake than through passion? So as roseate dawn softened the darkness, Alys set out to demonstrate to her beloved what she had learned in one night, making love to him with as much intensity as he had made love to her. And as they reached new heights of joy, it was easy to believe that love bound them.

24

Reggie had left her with a kiss just before the household began stirring, and Alys luxuriated in happiness for the minutes before a maid appeared with her coffee. She had not known there was so much bliss in the world. Though she should be exhausted after such an energetic night, she felt that today she could move mountains single-handed.

As she dressed, it was a shock to glance in the mirror; for just a moment she saw the beautiful woman Reggie claimed that she was. Then reality set in and she was simply Alys, albeit a bright-eyed, glowing Alys. But for an instant she had been beautiful.

A pity she would be spending the whole day at the far end of the estate; she wouldn't see Reggie again until dinner. Habit got her through her duties, but Alys kept finding herself staring blankly into space, a smile tugging at her lips as she experienced the delicious sensation of melting.

Late in the afternoon she returned to her office, and felt a curdle of panic when she saw the letter that awaited her, addressed in Reggie's bold hand. Could last night's passion have resulted in a letter of dismissal? She stared at the creamy paper for long minutes before opening it, fearing that her idyll was over almost before it had begun. Her lips tight, she finally lifted the envelope and slashed it open.

It was almost a relief to see the terse but not unfriendly lines. Reggie had unexpectedly been called away and might be gone for as long as a fortnight, though probably less. Sorry to leave so abruptly. Fondly, R. She stared at the note. Fondly? Was that a mark of affection or indifference? She read and reread his words, trying to find deeper meanings, without success.

Alys carefully refolded the note, her eyes fixed sightlessly across the room. Every time there had been any intimacy between them in the past, he had run away, but he had always come back. She must remember that he always came back.

In London Reggie called on Julian's great-aunt, a redoubtable dowager with a passion for gossip and a weakness for rogues. Over several pots of tea he learned that the long-lost Durweston heir was named Lady Alyson Elizabeth Sophronia Weston Blakeford, more familiarly known as Lady Alys. She had had one London Season, was extremely tall, rather shy, but with a great deal of countenance. Her ladyship had been surrounded by fortune-hunters, and there had been general approval of

her engagement to her father's choice, Lord Randolph
Lennox, a handsome and honorable young man with no
need to marry for money.

Finally, and damningly, the dowager mentioned that
Lady Alyson Blakeford had mismatched eyes.

It took three days to reach Carleon Castle, the great seat
of the Durwestons. Carleon encompassed a large part of
the county of Cheshire and it took Reggie half an hour of
riding along an avenue of elms to cover the distance from
gatehouse to castle. The estate was vast and prosperous;
Strickland could be lost here a dozen times over. Carleon
had begun life as a castle, and over the centuries the
building had grown and changed to reflect the power and
wealth of its owners. The King of England would not be
shamed to live within these golden stone walls, and kings
and queens had visited here.

The closer he came to the heart of the estate, the
angrier Reggie became. That she had left this for a life of
uncertainty and poverty was a measure of how deeply
she had been wounded. If offered the chance, he would
have cheerfully cut out the heart of Lord Randolph Lennox
and of the Most Noble, the Duke of Durweston, and the
anonymous drunken merchant, and every other man who
had ever hurt Allie. He took some comfort in the fact
that he actually had killed George Blakeford.

The entry hall soared thirty feet high, its proportions
designed to put mortals in their place. A butler with
more dignity than the Archbishop of Canterbury greeted
Reggie with disdain, his chilly eyes flicking over the
visitor's travel-stained clothing. "The Duke of Durweston
is not receiving."

Reggie pulled out one of his cards, on which he had
written *I know where your daughter is.* "Give him this,"
he told the butler curtly. Durweston would not be far away;
it was said that the duke had not left his estate in a decade.

The butler glanced contemptuously at the card. Then
his face grew stiffer, if that was possible. Without a word
he turned and left the entry hall.

In less than five minutes the butler returned. "His
grace will see you." Without deigning to check if he was

being followed, he turned and led the way through a series of passages that made Reggie wish he had emulated Theseus and brought a ball of string. Eventually they reached the duke's private audience room, another lofty chamber decorated with a royal ransom in furniture and art.

Durweston himself was seated behind an ornate gilded desk, and any faint hope that Reggie had had that his Allie was not Lady Alyson Blakeford died at the sight of that handsome hawk face; this man had to be Allie's father. The duke looked to be in his late sixties, tall and lean and fierce, with a shock of white hair and the expression of a man who is never opposed.

The duke neither rose nor greeted his visitor, merely scanned him with gray-green orbs the exact shade of Allie's right eye. Refusing to be intimidated, Reggie stared back, conspicuously relaxed and with a faintly bored expression as he waited for the other to speak.

At length the duke's gaze fell to the card on the desk. "Reginald Davenport. I've heard of you. You're a rake, wastrel, and scoundrel, a disgrace to a fine old family. Somehow you heard the news that my heir, George Blakeford, died and decided that there was an opportunity for profit." The chilly eyes were raised again to Reggie. "Now you are here like a vulture with a trumped-up tale about my daughter. I am no lamb for the fleecing. My daughter is dead. Get out."

Reggie's anger tinged with compassion. Over the last dozen years there must have been others who had come with spurious tales of the missing daughter. Durweston's hopes must have been raised and dashed more than once, making him bitter and wary. But he could not entirely believe that his daughter was dead, or he would not have admitted a stranger. Cold though he seemed, the duke cared about what had happened to his only child; he wanted to be proved wrong.

Equally cool, Reggie said, "You're right that I am aware of George Blakeford's death. As it happens, I killed him myself, with a Baker rifle. One bullet through the heart."

"Good God, you're the one who killed him?" He had

managed to penetrate the duke's composure; Durweston
was now regarding him with amazement. "It came as no
surprise to hear that George was killed in a brawl over a
woman, but I have trouble believing that even a man like
you would come here to boast about it. You're either a
murderer or mad, Davenport." A strong bony hand
reached for the bell cord. "Probably both."

"I killed Blakeford because he was doing his level best
to put a knife in a woman called Alys Weston. He
seemed to think that Alys was your daughter."

The duke's hand halted in midair. Then, a tremor in
the long fingers, the hand returned to the desk. His voice
sharp, Durweston said, "Tell me about this Alys Weston."

"She's the steward of my estate, Strickland, which lies
between Dorchester and Shaftesbury," Reggie said crisply.
"She's a couple of inches under six feet tall and has
bright brown hair, improbable dimples, and a figure like
Diana the Huntress. She is thirty years old, was born on
All Hallow's Eve, and she has the stubborn pride of
Lucifer."

With clinical detachment Reggie watched the duke's
craggy face quiver, as if from an internal earthquake,
then added the clincher. "Her eyes are of two different
colors, the left one brown, the right gray-green."

"My daughter is dead." Blue veins stood out on the
backs of Durweston's hands as his grip tightened on the
tooled-leather surface of the desk. "Don't think you can
pass off an impostor of the same physical description,"
he said hoarsely. "I would know instantly."

"And Great Britain is overrun with six-foot-tall females with mismatched eyes," Reggie said ironically.
"Very well, if you don't want her, I'll keep her for
myself." He pivoted on his heel and headed toward the
massive door.

"Wait!"

Reggie turned. Durweston had risen to his feet, his
face working. "Alyson never would have stayed away so
long."

"Then you can't have known her very well." Impossible not to feel compassion for an old man who was afraid
to hope. Having decided to come here, Reggie must now

finish what he had begun. "When she wanted to end her betrothal, you refused to support her. You said that she was no daughter of yours and locked her in her room. Not surprisingly, she felt that you had betrayed her and that you wouldn't want her back."

Durweston's face was white and he sagged back in his chair. "Only she and I knew what happened that night," he whispered, then waved at a chair. "Sit down. Please."

The duke looked so stricken that Reggie wondered if he should ring for help, but after a minute the old man's color improved and he looked up. "Do you know why she refused to marry Lord Randolph?"

"Yes, but if you want to learn the reason, you'll have to ask her yourself." Reggie was powerfully ambivalent, torn between satisfaction that the breach between Allie and her father might be healed, and the knowledge that success would take her away from Strickland forever. The ambivalence expressed itself in the sharpness of his tone.

Durweston nodded, accepting his words. "You say she's your steward, of all the outlandish things. How did that come to happen? She ran off with her groom."

"No, she ran off alone," Reggie corrected. "Her groom, Jamie Palmer, followed her to make sure that she took no harm." Briefly he explained how Alys had taught, then become a governess, and finally chanced into the position of steward. He also mentioned the radical reforms that she had instituted on his estate, and that she was guardian of three young people.

As Reggie spoke, disbelief melted away in the duke's face. He must know his daughter well enough to believe that not another woman in England would have behaved quite the same way. Silence followed Reggie's recitation, until Durweston asked, "Is she a good steward?"

"The best."

The duke brooded, his face dark and questioning. "Why didn't she come home?" he asked in a low voice. Vulnerability sat oddly on that arrogant face. "She must have known that I don't mean half of what I say when I'm angry."

"She was badly hurt," Reggie said quietly. "After

that, pride took over. I daresay you can understand that."

Durweston gave an infinitesimal nod, then asked a question whose answer he feared. "Will she come home now?"

"I think so, but you must go to her. She will never come to you."

The duke's face hardened. "Does she expect me to crawl to her?"

Suddenly weary of a man whose pride stood in the way even now, Reggie snapped, "Allie expects nothing. She doesn't even know that I'm here." He stood. "She said that her father never apologized or admitted fault. Obviously she knew her man. It was a mistake to come."

"Davenport." Durweston spoke gruffly, hating the truth in his visitor's words. "You say that she's at your estate, Strickland, and that it's in Dorsetshire?"

When his visitor nodded, the duke said, "I'll be there in four days. How much do you want for your information?"

Davenport's cool blue eyes could have chipped flint. "Keep your money. Just treat Allie better in the future than you have in the past."

Durweston hated Davenport at that moment, hated him for being strong and virile, in the prime of life, hated him for having had Alyson's company when her own father had been alone in his luxurious mausoleum. More than any of that, the duke hated himself for having driven her away. Harshly he asked, "What is my daughter to you, Davenport? Your mistress, and now you've tired of her?"

No longer cool, Davenport's blue eyes blazed with fury, his body taut and dangerous. In a distant corner of his brain the Duke of Durweston knew that he stood closer to death than at any other time since his own wild, risk-filled youth; his visitor looked ready to cross the room and do murder with his bare hands.

Instead, after a herculean effort to control himself, Davenport said in a soft, steel-edged voice, "Your daughter is what she has always been. A lady."

Then he turned and walked out the door.

*   *   *

Hard at work in her office and not expecting Reggie back for days, Alys paid no attention to the sound of a single horse cantering into the yard. She was vaguely aware of the pounding hooves of a team pulling a vehicle several hours later, but dismissed it as a loaded dray, since a delivery of timber was expected for the cottage construction. Therefore it was a complete surprise when the door of her office opened and she looked up to see Reggie's unmistakable frame outlined against the early-afternoon sunlight. Her heart leapt with delight, then paused when there was no sign of welcome in his posture.

When he entered, her eyes were so intent on him that she did not even see the man at his heels, not until Reggie said flatly, "You have a visitor."

Alys glanced over to the tall old man, then froze. Her throat tight, she whispered, "Father?" not believing the message of her own eyes.

His hair had not been pure white, and there were new, harsh lines in his face, but his height and upright carriage had not changed. His eyes suspiciously bright, he said in a voice on the edge of breaking, "Isn't it about time you came home, girl?"

Then she believed that it was he, and she stumbled to her feet, not even noticing that she knocked her chair over. As she hurled herself into her father's arms, she barely noticed when Reggie faded out of the office, giving father and daughter privacy for their reunion.

Alys wept as her father held her and whispered, "I'm sorry, girl, so sorry." There was no need for more specific apology.

The next half-hour was a jumble of confused impressions and babble, where everything and nothing was said, until the duke said, "If we leave in the next hour, we can be in London tomorrow evening."

"London?" Alys repeated, not understanding.

"I assume you prefer to visit there before returning to Carleon." Her father's gaze touched the plain gown she wore for a day in the office. "You'll want a proper wardrobe, and I want to show my daughter off. Pity it's summer—company in town will be rather thin. But we can come back later for the Little Season if you like."

She stared at him. "But Strickland is my home. I have a position here, responsibilities."

"Good God, do you think work for hire is proper for the next Duchess of Durweston?" He waved his hand at her office. "If you want to run an estate, there's all of Carleon to manage. I'll not stand in your way or countermand your orders." A slight smile hovered. "At least, I'll try not to."

Alys would have laughed at his afterthought if her emotions were not in such turmoil. Leave Strickland and the life she had built for herself? Leave Reggie?

"But there are the boys . . ." She faltered. "And I have a contract with Strickland. I can't just walk away."

"That's all taken care of," the duke said impatiently. "Of course your wards come with us. I understand there are just two boys now, that you managed to catch Lord Markham's heir for the girl." He shook his head admiringly. "Quite a feat of generalship, girl. You're wasted here. You need a wider field of endeavor.

"As for your contract, Davenport has already released you from all obligations." Her father paused, then said grudgingly, "Hate to admit it, but I misjudged the man. When he came to Carleon I thought that he was running a rig, but he wouldn't take a penny. He's behaved just as he ought."

The duke stopped speaking abruptly. He had a lively suspicion that Davenport had *not* always behaved just as he ought to Lady Alyson Blakeford, but it was a topic better left alone. No matter what she had done in the last dozen years, no one in the *ton* would dare cut the heir to Durweston.

Alys was still trying to assimilate her father's words. "Reggie went to Carleon? That's how you found me?"

When her father nodded, she asked in bewilderment, "How did he discover who I was?"

"I have no idea." Durweston eyed her narrowly, then decided to hurry her along. Though Davenport had behaved like a gentleman so far, the duke had a lively distrust of the man's influence over his daughter.

Alys stood. "I must talk to Reggie myself."

"Davenport thought you'd say that. He's in the house."

Outside, Peter and William had been drawn by the sight of the magnificent Durweston traveling carriage, and they stared at her as she crossed the yard. "Are you really the daughter of the Duke of Durweston?" Peter asked uncertainly.

The news certainly was spreading quickly. "Yes." Correctly interpreting the boys' expressions, she said firmly, "I haven't changed, you know. I'm still your guardian, and you still have to do your lessons and"—a speaking glance at William—"wash behind your ears."

William grinned, reassured. He had less understanding of what it meant to be Lady Alyson Blakeford. But Peter knew. His face bleak, he asked, "Will you be leaving us?"

Her heart twisted. The boys had lost too many people in their life. Peter was looking at her as if she were gone already. She put a hand on his shoulder. "I don't know quite what is going to happen, but I promise you, if I go, you and William go with me." *If I go* . . . But she didn't want to go!

Swallowing hard, she continued, "You've always wanted to see London. Wouldn't you like that?"

Convinced that he was not going to be abandoned, Peter flashed a wide smile. "That would be smashing!"

William looked less convinced, but before he could say anything Alys said again, "I've got to talk to Reggie." Her father had come up behind her, and she quickly introduced the duke to the boys, then escaped to the manor house.

Mrs. Herald met her in the front hall, staring as if Alys had suddenly sprouted purple feathers. "Is it true, Lady Alys?" she asked, round-eyed. "That you really *are* Lady Alys, I mean?"

"Yes, it's true," she said impatiently. "Where is Mr. Davenport?"

"In the library, your ladyship." It would be inaccurate to say that May Herald was awed—she was not a female easily awed—but she was impressed. The daughter of a duke, and a female that would be a duchess in her own right! It was a story Strickland would never forget. To Mrs. Herald, Lady Alyson Blakeford was already history.

Of course he would be in the library, scene of so many high and low points in their relationship. Her face stiff, Alys entered to find Reggie sitting in his favorite chair, cleaning his pipe. He glanced up as Nemesis trotted over to greet Alys. The collie sniffed her cold hand, then gave it a sympathetic lick.

There was a long silence as they stared at each other. She searched his face for some sign that he wanted her, that he even remembered that night of shared loving, but his long face was expressionless.

Still standing, she asked, "How did you find out who I was?"

He shrugged. "When you told me about your past, it jogged some things I had heard about the missing heir of the Duke of Durweston. It wasn't hard to put the pieces together."

So it was her own confidences that had led to this. Passionately she wished that she had said nothing, no matter how much relief confession had given her. She tried to speak evenly, but her voice broke as she asked, "Do you want me to go?"

"You don't belong here." Neither his face nor his voice showed a shred of emotion.

She couldn't believe it, could not accept that what was between them had been purely physical; that since he had had her once, he did not want her around him. But what did she know of such things? As she watched blindly, he stood and crossed to the French doors.

With one hand on the knob, he turned to her, a tall, lean silhouette, his features invisible as he stood in front of the light. "Good-bye, Allie. Don't ever be ashamed of what you are."

"Reggie!" It was a cry from the heart, but he was already gone. She stared at the glass doors, then numbly crossed to look out. He stopped by the carriage and she saw him talk to the boys for a few moments, then shake Peter's hand. Less inhibited, William gave him a fierce hug. Then Reggie walked away and she could see no more.

You don't belong here. If Reggie didn't want her, there was no point in staying at Strickland, no way she *could* stay. But how could she leave when the very thought caused a knife-thrust of anguish that choked her breath and clawed inside her like a ravening beast? Alys gulped for breath, fighting the grief that threatened to break out into shattering sobs.

The pride that had kept her going through long, lonely years came to her rescue. She was Lady Alyson Blakeford and someday she would be the fifth Duchess of Durweston. She would not stay where she was not wanted, nor would she cry. *She would not cry.*

Outside the library she met Mrs. Herald and gave crisp orders to pack everything that belonged to her, Merry, and the boys immediately. Then she went outside and informed Peter and William that they were leaving for London.

It was frighteningly simple to pack up a whole life; in the weeks since the fire, there had been no time to accumulate many possessions. She briefly considered going to her office, where account books were still lying open on her desk, but dismissed the thought. Reggie had said he didn't need her, so he could jolly well sort everything out on his own. Depressingly, she knew that he would have no problems, apart from having less time for his horses. Her records were always ordered, and by this time he knew almost as much about Strickland as she did. The bailiff was reliable for the field work; even the pottery was running smoothly and beginning to show a profit.

She said only one good-bye, and that was to Jamie Palmer. She found him in the barn, repairing a piece of harness. Unsurprised, he glanced up. "So you're going home, Lady Alys. It's time."

She looked at him, so solid and kind, and wanted to climb in his lap and cry. He was the one friend she had always been able to count on. "You don't want to go back to Carleon, Jamie?"

He shook his head. "Annie wouldn't like it. Her family is here, and now it's my home too. You don't need me anymore."

She almost did cry then, but didn't, since it would have distressed Jamie no end. He had never seen her cry.

"Thank you, Jamie, from the bottom of my heart. For everything. I'll never have a better friend." She offered her hand. "You'll keep an eye on the pottery and let me know if there are any problems?"

"Aye." He bobbed his head gravely, then shook her hand. "You'll not be coming back for a visit?"

"I don't think so."

Half an hour later they left in a rumble of wheels and hooves as a hastily assembled crowd bid her good-bye. As they headed north toward the Shaftesbury road, she did not look back.

Reggie had chosen a post in a clump of beeches on a hill overlooking the road out, knowing that they would have to leave this way. In no time at all, the splendid carriage was coming down the road, leaving a cloud of dust in the dry afternoon, William's pony and Alys's mare tethered to the rear. Reggie stared at the carriage hungrily, wishing he could see her just for a moment, knowing what a stupid, futile wish it was.

He hadn't intended to, but when the carriage curved round the bend and out of sight, he found himself running down the hill, crashing through the underbrush, racing at full speed to a vantage point where he could see the next loop of road. Just barely in time he made it, his breath burning in his lungs, and saw the gleaming black carriage for one last instant before it finally disappeared. The sight brought her no closer.

She was gone. Numbly he turned and began walking in no particular direction, unready to return to the empty house. She was gone, and it was entirely his choice. If he had wanted to keep her here, all he would have had to do was stay silent, keeping her from her heritage, her father, and her fortune. He had no one to blame but himself.

It was after dark when he returned to the manor house, and the first creature he saw was Attila; the fluffy cat was prowling back and forth in agitation. Mrs. Herald had heard Reggie enter and came to greet him. "Attila was nowhere to be found when they left. Lady Alys asked that you take care of him until she can send for him."

"Of course," he said woodenly.

As he went upstairs to change, Attila darted past him, halting by the door of the room that had been Alys's. Reggie opened the door and the cat went in, whiskers and nose twitching as he sniffed about looking for some sign of his vanished mistress. Finally he jumped on the bare bed and yowled plaintively.

"I know exactly how you feel, old boy," Reggie muttered. Then he headed toward his own room. He would just have to learn to live without her. Surely there must be a way.

25

Lady Alyson Blakeford could do no wrong. Alys found a certain ironic amusement in her change in status. In Dorset she had been respected; in London she was very nearly worshiped. Town was quiet, with most of the *beau monde* in Brighton or other fashionable resorts, but the arrival of the long-secluded Duke of Durweston and his prodigal daughter certainly caught the attention of everyone who was left. In fact some members of the *ton*, scenting excitement, hastened back to London. Intimate little gatherings were held to reintroduce her ladyship to People Who Mattered.

A lavish new wardrobe was promptly ordered and delivered almost overnight, since the modiste wasn't busy at this season. Duty calls were paid on ancient Durweston connections, who greeted Alys and professed themselves delighted to see the gel again. She could almost hear the sounds of mental wheels spinning as they examined her and speculated on possible marriage partners. In spite of the fact that she was on the shelf, she was still—again— the greatest heiress in England.

The magnificent pile known as Durweston House was

opened for the first time in a decade, and looked exactly as it had a dozen years earlier when Alys had her Season; apparently nothing so plebeian as dust was allowed within those august precincts. But she had changed; oh, Lord, yes, she had changed. When she entered a room, the tallest woman present, splendidly gowned, she held every eye. Head high and all banners flying, Alys did not flinch from being noticed.

It was all monstrously dull.

The only real pleasure came in expeditions with the boys to the Tower, Astley's Circus, and other such vulgar amusements. To everyone's surprise, the duke accompanied them and gave every evidence of enjoyment. With a slight pang of unworthy jealousy, Alys watched her father's growing friendships with Peter and William; the duke had always wanted a son, and she had never been able to be that, though heaven knew she had tried. But there was no question that her father was overjoyed to be reunited with his daughter. They cautiously began to reestablish much of their old closeness, and as they did, an ache that had been part of Alys for so long that she no longer consciously noticed it finally went away.

Not even that was worth the loss of Reggie.

Strickland was staggeringly empty, ten times as empty as it had been when Reggie first returned. Amazing how quickly he had become used to having other people there. He missed the young Spensers and their laughter and occasional squabbles, but mostly he missed Allie. Fortunately the harvest had begun, and that kept him busy, even though the excellent bailiff supervised the more routine work. There were invitations from the local gentry, who wanted to hear firsthand of Alys's ascension to higher station.

Reggie accepted some invitations, mostly to fill up empty hours of the evenings, when he missed her most sharply. Once those hours would have been filled with liquor, but he was determined not to go back to that, no matter how desperately lonely he was. Often he played the pianoforte, improving his skills and using the concentration as a drug for forgetting.

Attila and Nemesis had taken to sleeping on Reggie's bed. He supposed that his acquiescence could be taken as a sign of his declining standards. Irritable at Alys's continuing absence, Attila would occasionally pick a fight with Nemesis by biting the collie's tail or sinking a pawful of claws into her tender nose, and then matters would be lively for a while.

Even when irritable, Attila knew better than to bite Reggie.

A week after their arrival in London, the duke took the boys to Tattersall's; since females were not welcome, Alys took the opportunity to write letters. When the butler entered her sitting room with a caller's card on a silver salver, she was puzzled; it was too early in the day for formal morning calls.

The engraved name on the card sent a wave of panic and insecurity sweeping over her. *Lord Randolph Lennox.* She should have known that sooner or later their paths would cross, and that it would probably be sooner, since Lord Randolph and her father were friends. For a moment Alys considered refusing to see him. Then she squared her shoulders; hadn't she thought that his rejection no longer had the power to hurt her? Suddenly she was no longer so sure, but she knew that she must find out.

Nervously she checked her appearance in a pier glass. She wore a rich terra-cotta-colored morning gown and it flattered her figure in a demurely provocative manner. The severe coronet was gone, replaced by a fashionable tumble of curls and waves. After a critical appraisal, Alys decided that she was quite creditably attractive. But not beautiful; only once, the morning after she had made love with Reggie, had she been beautiful.

Randolph was waiting in the gold parlor. When she entered the room she paused at the door as they studied each other, neither of them speaking. Her former fiancé stood an inch or so taller than Alys, with hair like dark burnished gold and the beautifully proportioned face and figure found in classical sculpture. He was impeccably dressed, and the years had only improved his looks, adding maturity to the handsomeness he had had a dozen years earlier. With a shock, Alys realized that he had been only twenty-one when they were betrothed, just a boy. She had never thought of him as young.

"Alyson?"

His soft voice had a questioning note, and it broke Alys's abstraction. "Hello, Randolph." She smiled and offered her hand, determined to carry this off in a civilized fashion, as if a dozen years of anguish didn't lie between them. "Am I so changed that you can't recognize me?"

Randolph returned her smile with relief, and she realized that he was as nervous as she. How strange. He crossed the room and kissed her hand, then continued to hold it as he straightened up. His dark gray-blue eyes were intent on her. "You look marvelous, Alyson. It's wonderful to see you again."

"What, a Long Meg like me, ten feet tall, all bones and bossy? Of course, there is still the fortune." Alys was aghast; so much for being civilized. She had not meant to say those brittle, angry words, and now they hung in the air like the stench of burned flesh.

Randolph shut his eyes, a spasm of emotion crossing his face, and his fingers convulsed on hers. More to himself than her, he whispered, "God help me, that was the reason."

He drew in a deep breath and opened his eyes again. "For the last dozen years I've racked my brain, trying to think why you ran away. Since your father said that you had wanted to break our betrothal just before you left, I feared that the fault was mine. I wondered if you might have heard those words, but I prayed that I was wrong."

For years Lord Randolph had loomed in Alys's mind as a cynical, mocking betrayer, but that image crumbled at the sight of his stricken face. Disengaging her hand, she said, "Perhaps we should sit down. It seems that we have matters to discuss."

They chose facing chairs. Since Randolph seemed at a loss for words, Alys explained, "I was coming in from riding, just outside the French doors, and heard what your friend said. And I heard your answer." Once more

she saw the fluttering draperies and felt the twist of
shock in her solar plexus, but it was all very distant.
What she felt now was not pain, but the memory of pain.

Randolph stared at his linked hands for a long moment, then looked up. "Of course you thought I agreed
with what he said."

"How could I not?" she asked dryly. "I heard you with
my own ears. After your claims of love undying, it was
rather . . . unpleasant to learn that my fortune was my
principal attraction."

"It wasn't, you know," he said gravely. "The truth was
that I loved you, more than I had ever put into words."

"Ah, yes, who could not love all that beautiful money?"
she murmured, an edge of bitterness in her voice. Randolph had a very respectable fortune of his own, or he
would never have been acceptable to her father, but her
fortune was many times the size of his, and it was often
the rich who were the greediest.

His gaze was very level. "Alyson, I am a wealthy man
in my own right. Oh, no one objects to more money, and
I'm no exception, but I had no reason to marry a girl
unless I cared for her deeply. As I did for you."

Seeing Alys's skeptical expression, he turned one hand
palm-up helplessly. "You were unlike any other girl I
had ever met. Intelligent, enthusiastic, caring about those
less fortunate, amusing, sometimes imperious, more often oblivious of dignity. And you were so lovely I could
hardly keep my hands off you."

She flushed. "Don't mock me, Randolph. I prefer
honest insults to false compliments."

His slate-blue eyes met hers with patent sincerity.
"Alyson, I never lied to you. The only dishonest thing
you ever heard me say was my answer to Fogarty's stupid
question that day."

Strangely, she believed him. "If you really did care for
me, how could you say what you did?" Alys was discovering that remembered pain could still hurt.

He sighed. "I don't know if you can understand this,
but young men don't admit to having deep feelings. Lust
perhaps, but never love. Most of my friends were amazed
that I wanted to get married rather than immerse myself

in opera dancers. They could have understood better if you had been a conventional golden-haired china doll, but you were different.''

"So we're back to ten feet tall, all bones, and unable to keep a man warm at night," she said tightly.

Lord Randolph winced. Then, choosing his words very carefully, he said, "You were like a young foal, all legs and great eyes, not yet having found your balance, not at all in the common way. But to me you were beautiful, and I knew that as time passed you would only become more beautiful. As you have.''

Sudden tears stung Alys's eyes and she closed them sharply.

"Alyson, are you all right?" Randolph asked in worried accents. "I didn't mean to upset you.''

"I'm fine." She bit her lip, then opened her eyes and attempted to smile. "You're very convincing. But then" —her tone hardened—"you always were.''

His jaw tightened. "I suppose I deserve that.''

"Why, Randolph? Why did you tell your friend that you were marrying me for money when he asked why you were doing it?''

"Because it was a reason he could understand." His mouth twisted. "Fogarty would have laughed at me if I had tried to explain how I felt about you. Love makes one vulnerable. It was hard enough to tell you how I felt—to a romantically inclined twenty-one-year-old, confessing my feelings to a cloddish male friend was impossible.''

Alys regarded him with wonder. "It was as simple as that?''

He nodded. "As simple as that.''

Alys stared unseeing across the chamber. It was impossible to disbelieve Randolph; even a dozen years later, it couldn't have been easy for him to come here and expose himself in this way. "I don't know whether this is tragedy or farce," she said in a low voice, then glanced at Randolph, who was regarding her anxiously. "To think that my whole life changed through hearing an insult that wasn't even intended.''

Randolph's expression was bleak. "You spent a dozen years in exile because in a moment of weakness I denied my own heart. I'll never forgive myself for that. Nor do I expect you to forgive me. All of these years I feared that it was my words that sent you away, and it's almost a relief to know the worst."

He rose. "It was important to me that you know the truth. I can't imagine that you will want to see me again. I spend much of my time in the country, so I should be able to stay out of your path. I'm sorry, Alyson. I know that is inadequate for having ruined your life, but it is the best I can do."

Alys stood also. "Don't run away. Have some tea." Before he could object, she rang for refreshments, then waved him back to the chair. As she assimilated Randolph's words, her predominant emotions were relief and an upwelling of confidence. One man finding her lovely and desirable could be attributable to insanity or perverse taste, but two men had made such statements recently, and between them they were healing the crippling blow to her self-esteem that had occurred a dozen years earlier.

Seating herself, she said, "You were by no means solely responsible for sending me haring off the way I did—my father is at least as much to blame. And I see, looking back, that it was rather bird-witted of me to run away." She gave him a rueful grin. "Once I did, the pride of the Blakefords took over. I would have died rather than come back and admit that I was wrong. If a . . . friend hadn't interceded, I would not be here today."

The tea arrived, and she paused to pour them each a cup and offer a plate of delicate pastries to Randolph, who was looking much happier than he had earlier. After a blissful bite—her father kept the best chefs in Britain—she said, "You can disabuse yourself of the notion that you ruined my life. Mind you, I have no desire to go back to being a history mistress, but experiencing the world outside the golden bars of Carleon vastly improved me."

He looked at her uncertainly. "Are you saying that just to make me feel better?"

"Not in the least," Alys assured him as she reached for another pastry, then decided against it. She was going to have to be careful about such things now that she wasn't as active. She gave him a mischievous smile. "Do I look ruined?"

He laughed. "You look splendid, and you have grown into the remarkable woman I always knew you would be."

If Alys had been the sort of female who could toss her head coquettishly, she would have done so. Regretfully she decided that it just wasn't her style; she would have to learn how to accept compliments with dignity. She poured more tea into both cups. "Now that all that ancient history has been disposed of, tell me about yourself, Randolph. Surely you are married now, with a family."

"No. For years I kept hoping that you would return. I couldn't really look at another woman." A shadow crossed his face. "I finally gave up and married four years ago. She died in childbirth a year later."

"I'm so sorry." Alys said with compassion. Perhaps Randolph's momentary weakness had ruined his life more than hers. She changed the subject and they drifted into easy conversation, with Alys describing some of the more amusing aspects of her working career. Randolph made an appreciative and admiring audience. When he finally took his leave, he paused at the door, his handsome face intent. "I don't suppose that it is possible to begin again."

He had kind eyes. Alys studied him for a moment, then shook her head. "It would have worked then, but not now."

Randolph nodded, kissed her hand with regret, and left.

Alys was thoughtful and filled with gentle nostalgia as she went up to her chamber. Randolph was a thoroughly nice gentleman who had been born to make some lucky woman a good and loving husband, and she hoped that his luck would change in the future. One thing she was sure of: he would be wasted on a woman who had a regrettable preference for rakes.

The next day Meredith arrived at Durweston House, having received Alys's letter about her changed circum-

stances. Since home for the Spensers was where their
guardian was, Merry came to Alys at the end of her visit
to the Markham estate. A lively reunion followed, with
Merry's brothers vying with each other to tell their sister
of all they had seen in London.

Late that evening, just before bedtime, Merry found
her way to Alys's room for one of the chats they had so
often enjoyed in the past, a strictly girl-talk discussion.
There was no need to ask if Merry had reservations
about her engagement; the girl positively glowed. She
and Julian had visited Moreton Park where they would
be living, and Merry was bubbling with plans for what
she hoped would be her home for many years.

Filled with maternal delight that her foster daughter
was achieving her heart's desires, Alys was content to
listen and make appropriate remarks. It was a jolt when
Merry abruptly asked, "When are you returning to
Strickland?"

They were perching on the bed together, and Alys
drew her long legs up and wrapped her arms around her
knees in unconscious reaction to the question. "I'm not
going back."

"Of course you're going back," Merry said, her blue
eyes widening. "What will Reggie do without you?"

"He doesn't want me there." Alys tried to toss the
remark off casually, but her voice broke on the words.
"He made that quite clear."

Merry looked at her guardian in astonishment. "And
you *believed* him?"

"What else could I do?" Alys asked stiffly. "He never
wanted to have a female steward in the first place, and
he is quite capable of running the estate by himself."

Merry gave her a pitying look. "What has being steward to do with it? The man is mad about you. He may
not need you as a steward, but he certainly does as a
woman."

Alys's emotions were very raw these days, and to her
horror she found herself on the edge of tears. As she
bowed her head, Merry moved over and put a comfort-
ing arm around her guardian—something of a stretch—in
a reversal of their usual roles. "If he needs me that

much," Alys finally managed to say, "why did he tell me I didn't belong there?"

"Misplaced nobility," Merry said calmly. When Alys raised her head in surprise, the younger woman continued, "Alys, you are the cleverest, most capable woman I have ever met, but your instincts about men are lamentable. Because Reggie really cares about you, he is bending over backward to do the right thing. Given his lurid reputation and your exalted station, that translates into removing himself from the picture so you can find a mate more worthy of you."

Alys inhaled sharply as she considered what Merry had said. Her instinct had told her that she and Reggie shared something magical and that the caring was not only on her side. Then she had said enough for him to guess her identity, and everything changed. Given her terrible doubts about her desirability, she had dismissed her instincts as wrong.

Her brows drew together. Would he really think himself unworthy of her? She thought about how the world would view such a match, and decided that it was entirely possible. Perhaps she had been too easily persuaded to leave. Alys turned to her ward, eyes narrowed. "Are you really, really sure that Reggie cares about me as . . . as more than just a friend?"

Merry's eyes were pools of limpid blue. "I guarantee it. As you yourself said, I was born understanding men. The way he looked at you when you were absorbed in other things . . ." She shook her head. "It was like you were his last hope of heaven."

With a sudden chill Alys thought of his drinking. If he was lonely and miserable, might he return to it? It didn't bear thinking about, not after what he had suffered to stop. Jumping from the bed, she went to her clothes press and opened a drawer.

"What on earth are you doing?" Merry asked.

"Packing, of course. To go back to Strickland."

Laughing affectionately, Merry said, "You can't leave in the middle of the night."

Alys paused. "Well, I could, but I suppose I shouldn't. I must talk to my father, among other things. Tomorrow morning should be soon enough." She prayed that it would be.

Meredith rolled onto her stomach and rested her chin on her folded hands, now more the tomboy than the young lady. "Should I give you any hints on how to persuade Reggie to a proper acceptance of the inevitable?"

Alys gave a wicked chuckle. "No need. If you're sure he really wants me, I have a few methods of persuasion myself."

Meredith nodded with approval. Now that Alys had been put on the scent, Reggie hadn't a chance of escape. Not that he would want to.

Not surprisingly, the Duke of Durweston was not pleased by his daughter's announcement that she was returning to Strickland for a visit of indefinite length. "It's Davenport, isn't it?" he asked gruffly. They were meeting in his office, a chamber that the Sun King would have felt at home in.

"Yes, it is," Alys said. "I departed much too abruptly. There is business still to be settled." She wore a traveling dress, ready to leave as soon as this meeting ended.

"How can you throw yourself at a rake, Alyson, a man with the most sordid of reputations?" he asked with exasperation. "Have you no pride?"

She considered. "In general, yes. Where Reggie is concerned, not much."

"Will he marry you?"

'I hope so," she said, "but I wouldn't insist on it."

Perhaps that was too much candor; the ducal face turned the color of port wine. "I can disinherit you, you know," he growled. "The title and entail go to a daughter only if her father thinks her worthy of receiving it. I always thought George Blakeford's younger brother would make a decent duke, and he is next in line."

"Whom you choose as your heir is your affair." She met his gray-green eyes levelly. "I walked away from all this"—she waved her hand at the luxury around them— "once before. I have proved I am capable of supporting myself comfortably. Do you really think I am more likely to bow to your will at thirty than I was at eighteen?"

Her father's face was a study in conflicting emotions, and she took pity on him. Rising, she crossed and kissed him lightly on the forehead. "Father, don't let us become estranged over this. I have missed you too much."

He blinked rapidly. "I've missed you too, girl. But why can't you marry someone like Lord Randolph? He's a fine man, and he'd renew his proposal in a minute if you were willing."

"I know, but he's much too nice for me." She gave a teasing smile. "I'd keep him under the cat's paw for sure."

"He wouldn't mind."

"No, but I would." She looked at her father sternly. "You just don't like Reggie because he's too much like you. Don't think I haven't heard the stories about your wild youth. Honestly, except for the difference of a million pounds or so, you two are like peas in a pod."

"Don't try to turn me up sweet, girl." The duke snorted and tried with limited success to suppress a smile. "And a million pounds is a substantial difference."

"*Substantial,* yes," she admitted, "but not *significant.*" She gave her father a good-bye kiss, then sailed out. She wasn't going to let it be significant, and that was that.

26

Going without Allie was rather like stopping his drinking, only worse. The pleasures of the bottle had been limited, the punishment almost immediate. With Allie, the pleasures had been infinitely varied, from the rarefied to the earthily sensual, and if there was a negative aspect, he hadn't discovered it.

Reggie was dining alone, and even a hard day of physical labor didn't give him much appetite for the roast fowl. Pushing his plate aside, he absently began to eat a

dish of raspberry fool. He was going to have to do better
with his eating or the cook would be insulted; feeding
two boys who approached every meal like a biblical
plague of locusts had spoiled her. He sighed. Helping
Allie heal the breach with her father was one of the few
entirely unselfish things he had ever done. Reggie hoped
that virtue would prove to be its own reward, because
there weren't any others.

Abandoning his dinner, he headed for the music room.
Playing the piano was usually a good distraction. He
reminded himself that the first few weeks of sobriety had
been the worst, but after that things had become easier.
Surely in time Allie's loss would also become easier to
bear. He certainly hoped so.

After two days of carriage travel, Alys was tired and
rumpled, and she stopped at the Silent Woman and booked
a room where she could rest and freshen up. She had
flatly refused her father's offer of outriders and the crested
Durweston traveling carriage, but even so, her equipage
was the grandest ever seen at the modest inn. She was
recognized, of course, and time was wasted in greeting
people, since she didn't want to appear too high in the
instep for her old friends.

After a short nap and a light meal, she prepared to go
to Strickland, even though it was nearly dark and a
respectable female would have waited until morning. Well,
she was in the process of abandoning all claims to respectability; besides, her sense of urgency was too great.
She could never have rested knowing that Reggie was
just a few miles away.

Since she was acting like a scarlet woman, she had
decided to dress like one. She had brought a maid just to
style her hair, and her carefully chosen gown was bittersweet red, a rich, subtle color that made her skin and
hair glow. It was a creation of London's finest French
modiste, designed to make a female look like both a lady
and a strumpet at the same time. The silk was simply cut,
clinging and swirling over the curves of breast and hip
and thigh, it had an extremely low neckline, and she had
had the modiste put a knee-high slit in one side seam.

She had been thinking of Reggie when she ordered the dress; duke's daughter or not, she wasn't sure she would have the courage to wear the gown in public.

Looking in the mirror, Alys inhaled deeply and wriggled a bit, then nodded in satisfaction at the result. She looked her best, and if Reggie thought her half as attractive as he claimed, he would never be able to resist her in the red dress. And if he could, well, she would take stronger measures.

An hour of Mozart didn't quiet his restlessness, though at least his playing was getting quite competent. Impatient and irritable, Reggie closed the pianoforte and stalked off to the library, the part of the Strickland where he was most at home. The evening was unusually chilly and he knelt at the hearth and methodically built a fire. Most Britons would be aghast at having a fire before November, no matter what the temperature, but he could afford it, and small indulgences were a kind of compensation for what he didn't have. A very feeble compensation.

He tried to lose himself in the *Aeniad*—he had always rather identified with the roguish Aeneas—but tonight none of the usual distractions helped. The lonely, empty hours stretched endlessly in front of him, and tomorrow would be just the same, unless it was worse. What was the point? *What was the bloody point?* He ran his hands through his hair, then pulled his coat off and tossed it aside, edgy and uncomfortable in his own skin. A glass or two of brandy would help him through the night.

It wouldn't stop with a glass or two. So what if it didn't? So what if he did drink himself to death? Whom would he hurt? There was no Alys here to injure, or to look stricken at what he was doing to himself. And one of the housemaids, Daisy or some such, had been eyeing him with interest. She was rather tall, and if he was drunk enough, perhaps he could imagine, at least for a few moments, that she was Allie. . . .

He stood and went to the liquor cabinet, taking out the Venetian glass decanter that had replaced the one he had broken. Almost absently he poured a generous four fingers of brandy, then tilted the matching goblet and watched the firelight refracting amber through the liquid as he prolonged the anticipation. Sweet poison. Sweet surcease.

As he lifted the goblet, Nemesis raised her head and whimpered from her station by his chair. "What's the matter, don't you approve?" he asked, tilting the glass toward the collie in a mocking salute. "Here's to all well-intentioned females, and the men who aren't good enough for them." Then he raised the glass to his lips.

Having left her maid at the inn and her carriage and coachman in the stables, Alys quailed at the prospect of marching up to the front door. In spite of her boldness in coming here, she found that her new confidence was a fragile growth. Perhaps she should check and see what Reggie was doing; it was full dark now, and the best lit room in the house was the library. Perhaps he had company. Perhaps he had another woman there; Cousin George's Stella must be in need of a new protector. Maybe Reggie had imported a whole harem; even if he missed her, she doubted that monastic suffering was his style.

Walking softly around the house, she stood outside the French doors and looked in. Reggie was there, alone, and for a moment she simply admired the sight of him as he leaned against the mantel. He had removed coat and cravat and was in his shirtsleeves, all lithe power and dark male beauty. Then he raised his arm and with a chill she realized that his long fingers were wrapped around a goblet filled with a liquid the unmistakable color of brandy.

The cool touch of glass on his lips revived his common sense. Good God, what was he doing? Reggie lowered the goblet and stared at it. Anyone with the sense God gave a goose should know that getting drunk out of loneliness was a mistake of major proportions. He hadn't gotten sober for Allie's sake, or to live up to his parents' hopes, or for anyone else. He had done it for himself, for his own pride and dignity.

No, it hadn't been for pride. Pride was how one behaved when others were watching; honor was what one did when there was no one else to see. If he knew that he was going to die tomorrow, he would still not seek oblivion in drink. Whether it was life or death he faced, for the sake of honor he would do it sane and sober. And, hideously though he missed Allie, he was not truly alone, had not been since that night he had broken and been reborn.

With a quick twist of his wrist he tossed the brandy into the fire and watched as blue flames blazed up from the liquor. Then he carefully placed the empty goblet on the mantel. There would be no more smashed glassware; there had been enough high drama in his life. He was an honorable country gentleman, no more, and he intended to be no less.

As he watched the blue flames flicker and die, he heard a small sound from the direction of the French doors and glanced up, then stared in stunned disbelief as Lady Alyson Blakeford stepped into the room. She gave him a cheerful smile. "I'm so glad you threw that away. It's always much easier to talk to you when you're sober."

Attila streaked across the room and began banging against her ankles, making excited yowling noises. She bent over and scratched the tomcat's head affectionately, then straightened up. "I'm glad someone is pleased to see me," she remarked as she removed her dark velvet cloak and laid it over a chair.

Underneath she wore a shimmering dark red dress that showed an amazing amount of her splendid figure and lovingly caressed the rest. Reggie could feel himself tensing all over. "What are you doing here?" he said harshly.

Alys hesitated a moment, then strolled over to join him by the fireplace, leaning against the mantel with elaborate casualness. Her shining hair was pulled up loosely in a riot of curls that threatened to come tumbling down at a touch. She was like a grand and delectable confection suitable for a king. She looked like a duchess, not a steward. Things had been much easier when she had had hay in her hair.

Realizing that he was staring all too obviously at her luscious body, he raised his gaze to her face. Her wide, unique eyes sparkled with mischief, but underneath was uncertainty. "I have a contract with Strickland," she said. "It was very bad of me to go on holiday during the harvest." She reached out and drew a slim finger across the back of his hand where it lay on the mantelpiece.

Even that light touch almost destroyed his control. He snatched his hand away and backed along the mantel away from her. Building a fire had been a mistake; it was far too hot in the library. In fact, he was ready to go up in flames. "I released you from your contract. For God's sake, Allie, get back to London and live the life you were born to."

"To discharge me without my consent and without cause is illegal," Alys said blithely. She was wearing some subtle cosmetic that made her lips look particularly ripe and kissable, and he found that his breathing was heavy and irregular.

Then all pretense of lightness dropped away, leaving her face grave. "That's not the life I want, Reggie. I would much rather be here at Strickland." She drew a deep breath, which did dramatic things to the minimal bodice of her dress, and still more dramatic things to his loins. "And much more than Strickland, I want you."

He flung away from the fireplace, wishing she had had the grace to stay away rather than come here and make everything so much harder. When he had put a safe distance between them, he turned to face her. "Allie, you have a position and fortune that allow you more freedom than any other woman in England. You can do almost anything you want; you can have any man you want—or as *many* men as you want," he said bluntly. "You are just on the verge of taking wing and enjoying that freedom. The fact that I gave you your first real lesson on the delights of the flesh doesn't mean that you have to spend the rest of your life with me. There is so much more for you to discover."

She cocked her head to one side. "Do you mean that making love can be better than what we did?" she asked with disbelief.

Reggie felt his face tighten as vivid memories of that night eroded his will even further. "I can't speak for you, but from my point of view, it has never been better," he said quietly. "But it wasn't only sex I was talking about.

You can use your fortune and influence to help people on a scale impossible here at Strickland. You can rub elbows with the Prince Regent or the prime minister or the poet laureate if you choose."

"Much of that I can do no matter where I make my home. Are those the only reasons you went to my father and told him where to find me?" Alys shifted her stance by the mantel and her silk gown flowed across her willowy body, revealing an enticing length of long, shapely leg.

He had known she had a sensual nature, and now that she no longer believed herself hopelessly unattractive, she could teach Delilah a thing or two. Trying to steady his breathing, Reggie said, "When you spoke of your father, I heard echoes of myself in you. I wasted some of the best years of my life locked in a meaningless feud with a man I hated. I didn't like seeing you do the same with a man you loved."

Alys was deeply moved by his perception and generosity. She was also giddy with relief, realizing that Meredith was right; Reggie was being noble. Surely he could be cured of that. "You're right. I was letting my life be shaped by anger and pride, and I didn't know myself just how much it was hurting me until the breach with my father was healed. It is far better to live a life shaped by love." Brazen though she might be, it was almost impossible to say the next words. "That's why I'm here. Because I love you."

Reggie stood halfway across the room, tall and unyielding. "Don't confuse desire with love. You are a woman of rare passion, and for years that nature had been denied. Don't throw yourself away on me just because I was the one who helped you find yourself. How long would it be before you became curious about greener pastures? I won't bind you to promises that you won't want to keep."

He was thinking in terms of promises? This was definitely progress. She began walking across the room toward him, her steps slow and provocative. "I am no green girl, Reggie. I really don't have to sleep with half the rakes in England before I can properly appreciate what you and I have. Would you be talking this fustian if I was still Alys Weston?"

He was silent for a long moment. "No. I was on the verge of asking Alys Weston to marry me when I deduced who you really were. But there is an enormous difference between Mr. and Mrs. Davenport, and the Duchess of Durweston and her commoner husband, Reginald Davenport. You can't turn away from your heritage again, Lady Alyson. That cat's out of the bag and won't go back in."

In fact, the cat was still stropping her ankles, Alys realized absently. So Reggie had actually wanted to marry her. How could she get him back to that point? After some consideration she asked, "Is all this nobility because you have too much pride to take a wife who is wealthier than you?"

"That is one factor," he admitted, "but there are others. Good Lord, Allie, think of what everyone would say—that you were seduced by a fortune-hunter who took advantage of your isolation and inexperience to trap you into a bad marriage."

"That might be said," she agreed, "but in fact, you are the only man I can really trust, because you were interested in me when I wasn't an heiress." She chuckled. "Whose reputation are you most concerned about, yours or mine?"

"I'm concerned for both of us, blast it!"

She walked toward him, shaking her head sorrowfully. "I'm disappointed in you, Reggie. What kind of a rake cares what anyone else thinks?" She stopped close in front of him and looked up into his aquamarine eyes. "Will you be more agreeable if my father disinherits me? He half-threatened to when I said I was coming down here."

He stared down at her, raw emotion in his eyes. "Could you bear it if he does disinherit you?"

"Yes. Could you bear it if he doesn't?"

He let his breath out in an explosive sigh. "I don't know."

Too much money was a problem that could be solved; now it was time for a new tack. "Reggie, I am quite ridiculously in love with you." She slowly scanned him, admiring every lean, muscular inch. "And not just for your body, beautiful though it is. I love your honesty and your deplorable humor and the sense of honor you pretend not to have."

Raising her gaze to his, Alys asked the hardest question of all. "Do you love me?"

"Of course I do. That's why I don't want to see you make a decision you'll regret." His words were level, but his whole body radiated tension, and in his eyes she saw a love and craving as intense as her own. Reggie had always walked a lonely road, living by his own iron code, sustained by pride. Now that pride divided them. Also, perhaps, the small boy who had been shunted aside and taught that his wishes were of no account could not believe it possible that he was loved.

Her heart ached for him; for both of their sakes, she must convince him they belonged together. To overcome the barriers of pride and self-denial, she could return the humor and passion he had given her, as well as offering her own love. She reached out and deftly unbuttoned his waistcoat, then began on his shirt.

He grabbed her hands between his and held them away from him. "Good God, Allie, what are you doing?"

"Trying to compromise you," she said patiently. "Then you'll have to marry me, or not have a shred of reputation left."

For a moment he stared. Then his tension dissolved and he laughed, his eyes brimming with warmth. "You are the most impossible woman I've ever met, and far too much like me for my peace of mind."

Since he had released her, she neatly undid some more buttons, then laid her hand inside his shirt against his chest. His skin burned beneath her touch and he gasped, then caught her hand again. Deadly serious, he said, "Allie, if you don't leave here in the next ten seconds, I am never going to let you go again. The infinity of choices that you have now will be reduced to only those that include me."

"Splendid," she whispered, tugging his shirt loose with her free hand. "That is exactly what I want."

His blue eyes held her for one taut, endless moment more. Then Reggie surrendered, crushing her against him as his mouth met hers hungrily. No longer denied by logic or propriety, the desire that had bound them from the start blazed into an inferno that consumed all doubts and fears. His hands sought the hidden secrets of her body, sliding beneath the thin silk of her dress with fire and sweetness, gift and demand. There was none of the tentativeness of new lovers, and Alys pressed against him, glorying in the remembered feel of hard muscles and bone, and in the knowledge that they were beginning a journey that would last a lifetime.

They lay down before the fire, and Alys learned that lovemaking could indeed be better than what they had already shared. Now that they had given themselves to each other, there was an emotional resonance that took them to new heights and depths and widths of loving. And best of all, buried in the heart of passion, was the joyful knowledge that he had found his home in her, as she had in him.

Much later they lay drowsing together in front of the fire, covered by her velvet cloak. The first night they had made love, he had said that she deserved better than the library floor, but actually the library floor was an absolutely marvelous place. Attila was curled up against Alys's right side, and from the sound of canine breathing she guessed that Nemesis was lying by Reggie. Quite a cozy domestic scene. Her bittersweet red silk dress would never be the same, not after the way Reggie had torn it off. Well, if she was an heiress, she couldn't think of a better self-indulgence than buying gowns that the man she loved wanted to tear off.

She chuckled at the thought, then explained when Reggie asked what she found so amusing. He laughed, his hand moving in a lazy caress down her body. She pulsed against his touch, rubbing against him like a cat. "For a woman who was convinced that no man could want her a fortnight ago, you have come an incredible distance," he said softly.

She studied the relaxed expression on his face, the strong bones sculptured by firelight, and thought that she would dissolve with tenderness. "It's because you make me feel that I am the most beautiful, desirable woman in the world."

"You are." He leaned forward and kissed her very gently, his lips warm and firm against hers. "And, my beloved, you have performed the miracle of your reforming career in changing me from a care-for-nobody rakehell into a soon-to-be faithful and adoring husband." He kissed her again, on her throat, and she arched against him. "Just don't complain that I have become too boring and proper, because it is entirely your fault."

It was a freely given pledge of fidelity and she believed him absolutely. As his lips moved to her breast and his hand lightly feathered across her abdomen, she caught her breath at the wonder and excitement of him and gasped, "You, boring?"

He raised his head with a deliciously wicked smile and she pulled him to her for a proper kiss. As they went tumbling once more into delight, she whispered huskily, "Somehow, I don't think there is any danger of that."

News of the marriage of the greatest heiress in England and the Despair of the Davenports was received with mixed reactions. A red-haired tart named Stella shrieked and hurled a hairbrush across her bedroom, smashing a mirror. A dignified madam called Chessie whooped with delight when she read Reggie's letter, then drank a toast to the lady who had tamed him.

Junius Harper grieved. If he had known that Alys Weston was the heiress of Durweston, and that she was so desperate to marry that she would accept Davenport, he would have courted her more assiduously instead of secretly hankering after Miss Spenser. Gloomily he wrote letters to all his grand relations, asking them to find him a different living, and the sooner the better.

As Caroline, the Countess of Wargrave, told her husband, it proved that miracles did happen. Looking no further than his wife, the earl fondly agreed.

Jason Kincaid, nineteenth Baron Radford, smiled faintly and wondered if there was any chance that he and a sober Reginald Davenport might become friends. When Reggie visited his cousin Wargrave, Jason intended to find out.

Jeremy and Elizabeth Stanton rejoiced in the fact that Anne's son was now back where he belonged and behaving exactly as he ought. Happily they prepared themselves to become honorary grandparents when the time came.

Mac Cooper thought it perfectly reasonable that a future duchess had the discernment to appreciate his master. As he cuddled Gillie in their newly built attic apartment, Mac told her rather complacently that a man needed a wife. She couldn't have agreed more.

Peter and William had the best of both worlds; they were back among their friends at Strickland, but they now had holidays in London and Cheshire. As William said, the Duke of Durweston was quite a good old bird. It was as well, perhaps, that his grace never heard the compliment.

Merry agreed, regretfully, that it would not be politic to have Reggie give her away at her wedding, but the Blakeford-Davenports were the first guests invited to the Markhams' new home at Moreton Park.

The Duke of Durweston grumbled when his only daughter married by special license, though he knew it would have been ridiculous for Davenport to formally ask for the girl's hand when the rogue had already had the rest of her. Hot irons could not have persuaded him to admit it, but as he came to know his son-in-law better, the duke had to admit that he rather liked the impertinent rascal.

Evicted from the master's bed, Nemesis and Attila took to sleeping together in one entwined mass of fur. Occasionally the tomcat would bite the collie, but apart from a more-in-sorrow-than-in-anger yip, Nemesis never retaliated. Reggie's theory was that the collie was a born victim, but in her secret romantic heart Alys thought that they were seeing an unlikely love between two improbable creatures. She herself knew quite a bit about such things.

FLAMES OF PASSION